# AMERICAN
# APOCALYPSE
## WASTELANDS

# AMERICAN APOCALYPSE
## WASTELANDS

BY
NOVA

Ulysses Press

Published in the United States by
ULYSSES PRESS
P.O. Box 3440
Berkeley, CA 94703
www.ulyssespress.com

ISBN: 978-1-56975-977-6
Library of Congress Catalog Number 2011926015

Acquisitions Editor: Keith Riegert
Managing Editor: Claire Chun
Editor: RPC
Proofreader: Elyce Petker
Production: Judith Metzener
Cover design: what!design @ whatweb.com
Cover photos all from istockphoto.com: "Junker" © fullvalue; "Yellow cab in NYC 2" © Markanja; "Burnt out car" © eejay62; "Majestic sky" © Photodjo; "Golden rusty plate grunge" © isgaby; "Downtown Avenue" © buzbuzzer; "Chemical Drums" © magicinfoto

Printed in Canada by Transcontinental Printing

10 9 8 7 6 5 4 3 2 1

Distributed by Publishers Group West

*For Marilyn and Elizabeth*

Also by Nova
*American Apocalypse: The Collapse Begins*

# ACKNOWLEDGMENTS

I don't feel as if I wrote this book alone, as it was written live and online. The people who left comments and suggestions influenced the story line more than they will ever know. Many times the only thing that kept me writing was their kind words. For all of you—thanks!

I would also like to thank Bill McBride at the *Calculated Risk* blog. He was a significant factor in making this book happen. He graciously put up with my comments and snippets of book posts, for which I am ever grateful. Tanta Vive!

# CHAPTER ONE

I lay there. On my back in darkness. It wasn't very comfortable and I hurt. I am not fond of pain. But I'm no stranger to it. My ears were ringing and my thigh didn't feel right. I was tired. Very tired. The pain in my thigh almost had me worried. I wanted to check and see if I still had my balls; I just didn't have the energy to move my arm to do it. It was easier just to lie there.

I thought about opening my eyes. Instead I decided to keep them shut and live with the pain; the pain was the only thing keeping me tethered to my body. Once it began to ebb, and I knew it would, then I could float away. That would be fun. I imagined myself rising into the sky like a bird until I got enough altitude that I could practice soaring and swooping. The pain was beginning to recede and I knew it would be only a matter of minutes before I could let go.

Then I processed what I was hearing. Someone was yelling, "Max! Gardener! Night!" over and over. I recognized the voice. I recognized those names. I just wasn't able to connect them to the pain.

The voice though—that I knew. It was pulling me back from being able to fly. I so wanted to fly, but I wanted even more to respond to her. I always had, one way or another. I tried calling out to her. It was hard to form words. I did it anyway and with it came the memory of why I was laying here.

Night! Where was she? *Fucking assholes and their fucking flying machines*, I thought.

*Get pissed*, I told myself. Strength can be found in anger and I needed it. I had to get up. Hell, I had to start by opening my eyes. I didn't want to but what I wanted and what reality provided seldom matched.

Much closer now I heard Carol say, "Gardener!" Then she was next to me. Kneeling and leaning over, she told me, "It's going to be okay."

I felt her hand brush my cheek. I flared my nostrils and took a deep breath. I wanted to inhale her smell right into my soul. I heard her say, "Jake is going to take care of you." Then she was gone.

*Who the hell is Jake?* My eyes popped open. Some guy that looked vaguely familiar had taken her spot and was reaching into a bag next to him while telling me, "Whoa, buddy. You're hurt. Let me take a look at you and . . ."

*Fuck this*, I thought. I started to get up. Medic Man put his hand on my chest and pushed. I went back down, not that I had managed to move a lot. I was beginning to dislike this guy.

"Where's Night?" I asked him.

"Look. You're messed up. Stay put and let me look at you."

"Fuck you. Where's Night and where's Max?"

I looked over to where Carol had rolled someone over. Max. It looked as if he was breathing, but the right side of his face was a mess. I could see a wicked gash on his cheek, below the eye. I thought, *That is going to make a really cool scar.*

Carol knelt over him. For a second my heart hurt worse than anything I had felt so far today. I heard her tell the asshole next to me, "Take care of him first." I saw the plea in her eyes.

The guy grabbed his bag and told me to stay put. I watched him hustle over to Carol and listened as he said, "Okay, Max, I'm going to stop the bleeding. Then I'm going to see if you are hurt anywhere else."

*Well, fuck it*, I thought. I never had her anyway. But I did have Night, who, I realized to my surprise, owned as big a piece of my heart as Carol did, maybe bigger.

I sat up. Damn, my thigh hurt. I looked down and saw a chunk of wood sticking out from it. *Well, that sucks.* This wasn't going to be as easy as I thought. I rolled on my side, drew my legs in, and pushed myself up with my arms. I thought I was going to faint from the wave of pain that hit me. Oh yes, this feels familiar. I sucked some wind, moved my good leg, and used it to push myself upright. I almost made it.

I said earlier that I knew pain. Well, now I knew him even better. I waited until the light show inside my head stopped. I shook my head, hoping that would clear it, and looked around. I needed a Plan B.

Plan B turned out to be something long, black, and tubelike that Medic Man had left next to me. I grabbed it, pulled it close, and tried again to get up. This time it worked. Whatever the hell it was that I was using as an extra leg and cane was heavy. It also looked vaguely familiar. But the pain and the need to move overrode any ability I had to focus.

I started moving toward the motel, where I thought Night was. It had been hit and was really starting to burn. I was going to have to work my way around that. At least it produced a lot of light.

Behind me I heard Medic Man yell, "Hey!" I didn't stop. Damn, it hurt to walk. I heard Carol tell him something; she said it too low for me to hear. I did hear his reply. "He better not lose my fucking Barrett." That was interesting: a medic running around with a sniper rifle. The world never ceased to amaze me.

The Anchorage Motel was laid out like an L. The short side of the L held the main lobby and check-in. They sat inside a two-story great room built to resemble the prow of a ship. The back part of the second story contained living quarters for Night's parents.

The face of the motel nearest the road was almost all glass, and a large ship's wheel hung inside, suspended from the roof and filling the airspace of the great room. The wheel was what finally tipped me off that the motel was not named after Anchorage, Alaska. I'd been embarrassed by how long that had taken to click in my head. I wouldn't have to worry about it now, though; that part of the motel had taken a direct hit.

If I were a good person, I would have worried about Night's parents and whoever else might have been in there. I'm not, though, so I didn't. Instead I kept going.

Night lived near the far end of the L. Normally I could have walked to it in under a minute. Tonight it felt like an eternity just to make it around the main part of the structure. I was really hoping I wouldn't have to kick in any doors to find her, or move anything that weighed more than a few pounds.

I got lucky. I found her crumpled in a tiny heap. She was lying outside the door, off the sidewalk, in the grass. Not far from her room. It hurt me to see how small she looked lying there. Even worse was to see that she was hurt. Hurt badly.

The back of her head had been hit and burned by a chunk of debris. Her hair was still smoldering. I knelt down next to her and gathered what remained of her hair in the back and squeezed it in my fist. With the pain in my leg, it should have hurt to bend down but it didn't.

The skin on the back of her neck and one shoulder was burnt. It was not pretty. Plus, her back and both legs were bleeding in places. She moaned.

I told her, "Hey. It's okay." I tried to think of something calming and reassuring to say, but I didn't have anything stored away.

She rolled over, let out a moan, looked up at me, and said, "I knew you would come."

What could I say to that?

I smiled and told her, "We got to get out of here. I need you to stand up. Can you do that?"

She moaned, nodded, and began pushing herself up. I tried to help her. I wasn't much use. She gasped a bit when she saw Mr. Woodie sticking out of my thigh. "You're hurt."

"Yep."

"At first I thought you were happy to see me."

She smiled when I looked at her with surprise. Well, it may have been a wince, but that was close enough for me.

I was going to reply, probably with something lame that I would regret, when I got a really bad feeling about things.

"C'mon, Night, we got to move." I had my arm around her waist, partly to steady myself, mostly because I wanted to. I pulled away as we came around the corner. "Night, I need you to back up and go lie down on the other side of that hill. Now."

She didn't argue. She just went, which was good because the helo was back, looking like a black dragon out of *The Lord of the Rings*. It had come from behind us—fast and low, with no lights—and for a second I thought it was going to keep going. I didn't really believe it, though.

*Well, this is fucked*, I thought. It kept going, but not far enough. It went out about a half mile, made a U-turn, and came back toward us.

I knew Max and Carol were out front. I could see them huddled near some shrubbery that was not going to keep them safe from Sauron's minion. Shit, it wouldn't protect them from an angry crow.

I knew what I had to do. I wasn't sure if I could, but that had never stopped me before. I gritted my teeth and headed up the hill that Night was behind.

It really barely counted as a hill. It was more of a berm, added to stabilize the area where the motel had been built, after part of the original landscape had been cut away to build a Jiffy Lube. Hill or berm—I needed the extra height to get a clear shot.

The pain was back. "Use the pain. Use the pain," I muttered to myself. Use the fireball of pain that was exploding inside of me. Feed the fire.

One second I was ready to scream from pain. The next, I was ready to scream from rage. The pain was gone, replaced by a clear flame of burning rage. *C'mon, you fucker.*

I planted myself. My one good leg felt like it had grown roots and anchored itself in the Virginia clay. I swung the Barrett to my shoulder and steadied it. The sight was folded down but I didn't need it, not at this range. I found what I hoped was the safety, not the magazine eject, and thumbed it in the opposite direction.

The helicopter hovered there in front of me, maybe seven hundred yards out. Alive and evil in all of its arrogance, its muscles tensed for another lethal swipe. I pulled the trigger.

The gunship shook with the impact of the round. I grinned. Partially because I had hit it, partially because I had thought the recoil would be a bitch. It wasn't, so I pulled the trigger again. And again. Damn, it was loud. I liked that. It didn't make a popping sound; it boomed!

When the second round impacted, the dragon started shaking itself like a wet dog. The third time I hit it, I knew it was dying but I didn't care. I shot it again, just because I wanted to.

That's when it died for real. It skipped sideways, up, and then it just rolled over and went down. The engine or rotors screamed like the flying creatures in *The Lord of the Rings*. I watched it, waiting for the explosion, wanting to see the fireball. I didn't see it, though. Instead, the Barrett became impossibly heavy. I flipped the safety and set it down. The damn thing worked pretty well.

I called out Night's name and went to get her. Together we went back and found Max and Carol. Medic Man was still around. Good, we were going to need him. I was glad to see Max up and moving.

"Time to move," Max said. "Get off this hill now."

Medic Man tried to take Night from me. "Alright, Gardener, I'll take her."

*No*, I thought. *Who the fuck does he think he is?*

Max moved closer and quietly told me, "Hey, G, it's okay. We got to move. You can have her back when we get out of here."

It made sense. I just didn't want to admit it. I leaned down to her and whispered, "I'm not going anywhere. He's just going to help you walk."

Her only reply was a soft moan and quick increase in pressure from the arm that was around me. I let her go and watched as he took my place. I didn't like it and I almost fell over without her there to prop me up.

"Help him," Max told Carol, meaning me. I guess she was my consolation prize. Funny, all these years I had known her, and tonight I'd had more physical contact with her than in all the time previous.

Max took the Barrett from me and we started moving. As we did I looked out over the county spread out in front of us. There were more fires flaring up in the distance. The Burners were running amok. They were always the most active when what passed for our civil authority was busy putting out fires of their making.

"Carol," Max said over his shoulder, "when we get to the parking lot I want you to get in your car and get the hell out of here. We have maybe five minutes before what they have in reserve for when rapid response shows up. When they do, they won't be in a good mood."

She didn't answer him. He waited about ten seconds. Then he said, "Carol?"

"I know." She didn't sound too happy about it. "You have a plan, Max?"

"I always have a plan, Carol. I always have a plan. We'll be fine."

"You want to share it with me?" she asked. Max didn't say anything. I heard her mutter, "I thought so."

Medic Man spoke up, "I have an idea." He then proceeded to tell us about a truck he had nearby and his well-stocked basement. Apparently, Medic Man had some money and a plan of his own.

Max listened to him, thought about it for a second, and then said, "Sounds good. Let's do it."

He added, "See, Carol? I told you I had a plan." She laughed. Laughed isn't quite the right word. It was more a snort of amusement, affection, and sadness. We stopped in front of her car. Max told her, "Okay. Time to go, Carol."

She nodded and let go of me after giving me a quick squeeze. "See you, Gardener. Take care of Night."

I nodded, looked away, and scanned the horizon. I didn't want her to see my eyes right then.

She started toward her car, stopped, and looked at Max. He didn't say anything. He just reached out and laid his hand on her cheek, his thumb moving a strand of loose hair back in place. "See you later, Carol."

I reached over and steadied myself on Medic Man's shoulder. "Let's go," I told him. He didn't hesitate. It seemed that he was in as big a hurry to move on as I was, or at least to move away.

For me it was because I knew it was unlikely I would be seeing Carol again. For him? I didn't know. I did know that he and Carol had a history. That was obvious; when and where was not.

Behind us I heard her car start up and then pull away. We reached the edge of the parking lot and were just beginning to move into the trees when I realized something.

"Hold up," I told Medic Man. He stopped. "She didn't say goodbye to you." I could hear Max's boots crunching on the gravel as he hurried to catch up with us.

"No. We said our goodbyes a long time ago."

# CHAPTER TWO

We moved on and found Medic Man's truck. I was glad it wasn't far away. I would take one step. Then I would take another and lie to myself. *Just one more step.*

Max rode up front after helping Night and me into the back. I could tell just by looking at her that she wasn't doing well. Medic Man had Max elevate her feet and then he covered both of us with a blue tarp—a good thing, as I was starting to get really cold. It occurred to me that I might even die. That didn't bother me. I had been ready to die since I was born.

We made it to his house without a problem. I don't remember everything that happened, especially after Medic Man pulled Mr. Woodie out. Most of it was a series of disjointed clips, little one-minute movie scenes that I'm not even sure were real.

I remember Max convincing me to go with a shot of morphine. I didn't want to. But he convinced me that it was a good idea. He was right. Oh yes, that was a nice buzz—until Medic Man started working on me.

I remember Max telling me, "You know, we're going to have to get you chain mail underwear. You don't need a vest. The only place you ever get hit is in the ass."

I remember listening to him. It all sounded so far away. The last thing I heard him say was, "Damn, nice sized woodie you got there. I bet that's got to be at least six inches. You want him to save it for you? Kind of a keepsake for when you were actually well hung?"

Then I drifted away. Later I came to for a few minutes and was sure he was telling me, step by step, how to field strip an M-16. Every time I would pop back up to the surface I'd hear his voice and relax and go back under.

I had come to. I had been elsewhere and hadn't wanted to come back to the surface, but I knew something was wrong. Bad wrong.

I opened my eyes and saw Medic Man sitting at Night's head, holding her arms down. She was thrashing and moaning. He had bandaged the back of her head, neck, and part of her back. Watery stains outlined in red marked the whiteness of the gauze. The blanket that had covered her was off, and she was wearing nothing but the bandages on her back.

I knew what he was doing. She would tear the bandages off and open the wounds if she wasn't restrained. Yet I didn't like the way he looked and how he was positioned next to her, his crotch almost in her face.

He was getting ready to do something. I knew this. First though, he decided to look around, which only confirmed it. He saw me watching him and his face changed ever so slightly. He was good. His eyes didn't stay on me for more than a millisecond. He reached down, pulled the blanket up, and told her softly to be still. She already was. She had stopped moving a couple beats after I had opened my eyes.

He let go of her, got up, and went over to check on Max who was stretched out on the floor about eight feet away. His eyes were open and he was watching Medic Man too. For a second they glowed red.

I knew Medic Man had also seen it because he froze. Then Max closed his eyes, and the morphine pulled me back down. Just not as deep this time. It wanted to, and I wanted to go, but I could no longer accept its embrace.

Probably twenty-four hours later, maybe less, I started coming to for greater periods of time. Medic Man was always there. He brought me water without asking and gave me more pills.

When I asked him what they were for, he said, "Infection. It's what I am worried about the most. Then it will be muscle damage."

He was chewing gum like a fiend. I was conscious enough to overhear an exchange between him and Max during this period.

"I need your keys. I also need a gun—preferably a shotgun with a mix of slug and buckshot." This was from Max. It was good to know he was up and mobile already.

"Sure," Medic Man said. But he couldn't hide his surprise. "Let me give you the keys to the Lexus. I haven't unloaded the truck yet." *Interesting*, I thought, how casually and quickly Medic Man agreed to this. "So where you going?"

"Back to the motel." I didn't have to look to know Max was grinning. He continued, "You want to come?"

"Ah ... not really. I got to stay here. Look out for them. Just in case."

"No problem. Got any more speed?"

"Yeah, sure."

About ten minutes later, after hearing movement and the sound of a shotgun being racked, I heard Max say, "If I'm not back in twenty-four hours, tell Gardener it was real."

I laughed to myself when I heard that. I also decided to get up and take a leak. I had been through this before when I fell on a rake that was tines side up. This was worse, probably because the wound was deeper.

Night was awake also. Together we hobbled to the bathroom. I let her go first, and then I hobbled in. It was not fun. Thank God I didn't have to sit down. I made a mental note to avoid food high in fiber for the next four or five weeks. Maybe I could set a record for going the longest period of time without a bowel movement.

When I came out, Medic Man was standing there with Night, waiting for me. I asked him if he had a T-shirt I could have. He found one and gave it to me. I cut the back out of it and gave it to Night to wear. I think she was as touched by my doing that as she would have been if I had brought her a bouquet of flowers. I was never going to understand women, let alone the human race.

Medic Man wanted to take a look at us after that. Night was growing a lovely crop of blisters.

"How does it look?" Night asked Me.

I almost said, "Horrible," but managed to bite my tongue in time.

Medic Man answered for me. "It's not as bad as it looks. I don't see any gray or charred flesh. I think you got lucky. Just second-degree burns."

She was silent for a minute and then asked quietly, "Will I scar?"

"No, I don't think so. Maybe a few faint ones at the most," he said.

I could tell she was relieved. He hit me in the thigh with more antibiotics and gave me the pill version to wash down. Then he made us chicken soup from a can. He didn't even water it down very much. He was being remarkably generous with expensive supplies, for no reason that I could tell. I did not like that. Plus, I just did not like him.

We were sipping our soup out of coffee mugs when I asked him, "So, how do you know Carol?"

He paused, smiled into his cup of soup before looking up, and then said, "Well, I was married to her for a couple years."

Night was watching me. Why was she watching me? She should be watching him.

I replied, "Oh, that would probably do it." A totally lame answer that really made no sense. So this was the never-spoken-of first husband. Yeah, I didn't like him.

There was a bit of an awkward pause. Medic Man picked up the slack by telling me how he wanted to use maggots on my wound later. "It's an old remedy. They eat your dead flesh and leave the good flesh behind." He sounded excited about the idea. I wondered how excited he would be if it was his own flesh getting gnawed on by worms. I was getting tired again and let it go. Night helped me back to my mat and lay down next to me. I was asleep in less than a minute.

I woke up almost ten hours later when I heard Max's voice. He wasn't alone. Ninja had survived. That was it.

No one else. As soon as Ninja saw Night, he burst into tears. He just stood there, his head down, and sobbed. Night went up to him. She couldn't hug him and he had to settle for an awkward arm pat.

They were both crying. I didn't know what to do. I knew I was supposed to do something, so I went over, slapped him on the shoulder, and told him I was sorry. Then I left the room, but not before I noticed Medic Man's sneer.

That's when I remembered his name. It was Jake. "Jake the Snake"—that's what I decided I would call him, at least in my head.

Four days later, I woke up and stumbled out into the main area of the basement rubbing my eyes. Everyone was gathered around Jake's big flat-panel watching the Icelandic News Channel. Iceland was the cool country now, especially since it was almost impossible to emigrate there. It had become a combination of Switzerland and Israel. Its transformation from the first bankrupt nation to the only one with a growing economy had been amazing.

At first it had seemed like the people there were doomed. Following the financial ruin, the cod banks had disappeared. Climate change was a double-edged sword for them. The people who didn't flee for Scandinavia decided to make the best of what they had: unlimited geothermal power and the best-educated workforce left in the Western World. Greenhouses and what fish remained fed them.

Server farms were their version of Swiss gold. They were totally secure from the waves of government attempts to control the digital flow of information, that being the only truly valuable currency left in the world. Along with the ability to host, they had the tools and the desire—especially after being so thoroughly screwed—to broadcast. And what they broadcast was the truth—or at least what the U.S. government managed to suppress with the assistance of those who controlled the media.

"Damn, what time is it?" I asked.

Night answered. "Eight."

"Daytime or night?"

"Nighttime. Come on, sit down with us. The president is going to make a speech."

I groaned. "Who cares? Obama wore me out years ago when he was president."

"You might want to listen, buddy," Jake said. "I got a feeling it's going to determine what's next for a lot of people."

"Yeah, Jake. Whatever." Jake was, of course, sitting in his favorite chair. I thought of it as "the throne." It was a leather recliner and I decided that from then on I was going to sit in it whenever I had the chance.

As usual, Jake was armed. What was interesting was how he was armed. He was wearing a Colt, a Peacemaker it looked like, in a hand-tooled holster that was tied down. A lot like what I wore, but far more expensive. That was weird. Why that gun in that style? I had noticed it when I first saw him. He kept wearing it, too, which surprised me. I figured he would switch to something more modern. He seemed like the black plastic type, after all.

Iceland News cut to the White House and the president appeared on screen. She sat behind her desk dressed in military camo. No rank insignia that I could see. I wondered if she had a cute little beret to match. She wasn't as hot as Palin was a few years ago, but she wasn't as obviously ignorant either.

She dropped the bombshell right off the bat: martial law. Jake and Night responded with "Wow!" and "Damn." Max added, "She's going to lock us all down. For our own good, of course."

She wasn't done. It really was for our own good. As she put it:

In this sea of internal turmoil, where so many seek to profit by undermining the authority of the state, we have decided to increase everyone's personal and professional security by creating Zones all across the United States. Furthermore, we will stamp out the terrorist groups that have, through their wanton embrace of vandalism for the sake of vandalism, harmed so many of you, my fellow citizens.

She went on and on, of course. She was a politician, after all. Night wanted to watch the analysis of the speech afterward but Max overruled her. "You need to sleep and heal up, kiddo. We are going to need to move soon."

She went reluctantly. I joined her. I liked lying next to her. If we were both up to it, we talked in whispers. I liked feeling her breath in my ear. We had no privacy. Our bodies were willing, but with her burns and my thigh there was not a lot we could do even if we had privacy.

# CHAPTER THREE

One thing Jake had going for him was his inventory. The man had taken seriously the warnings of doom and The End of the World as We Know It. He had it all: ammo, weapons, and the high-end and hard-to-find pharmaceuticals that we were burning through.

He didn't say anything about it. He didn't have to. He pretended everything was just fine, but there was an edge to him that I didn't like, a hint of arrogance that came out only when he was dealing with me. I also caught his eyes lingering on Night's ass when he thought no one was looking.

After I was able to start moving around for more than fifteen minutes at a time without bleeding too badly I found out what he was after: He wanted to join our elite team of commandos.

I was standing on the deck outside holding on to the railing and trying to look like everything was just fine. The reality was that I was trying not to scream from the pain I felt. The sliding glass door opened behind me and I fervently hoped it wasn't Jake. I think he knew that Mr.

Pain and I were constant companions whenever I moved. He even offered me some painkillers, but I refused them.

He was almost successful in hiding his disappointment over that. It just confirmed what I already knew. I was going to have to kill him. The problem was that I was going to need to get a little stronger first, which meant he was going to get to live a little longer.

It wasn't him. It was Max. I knew it was Max as soon as he closed the door. I can't tell you how I knew; I just did. He came over to where I was standing and rested his hands on the railing, joining me in looking out over the overgrown lawn.

Jake wasn't really big into lawn care. It didn't look like he ever had been. I bet his neighbors loved that, especially as they were living in McMansions built after tearing down the houses that had once been there. Probably houses that had been a lot like Jake's: a three-bedroom, two-bath 1950s rambler with a basement.

"How are you feeling, G?"

I looked over at Max. He was staring straight ahead, his face expressionless. I was hurting too much to come up with something snappy. Instead I gave him what was running through my head.

"I'm not sure if I'm going to be able to walk right again." I paused and went to what was really bothering me, "I'm not as fast as I was. My stance is off and it's messing up my timing."

"Yeah, I imagine it would. What you going to do about it?"

"I don't know, Max. I really don't. Walk it back. Walk until it heals, and heals right."

"Yep. You're going to hate life for a while once you start."

"Shit, something to look forward to. God, I love having a goal-directed life."

Max laughed. "Yeah. There is that." He spat, and we both watched as it arced out into space and landed in the overgrown grass below us. "You know, he's practicing with that six-gun of his. He has a room upstairs with a timer and a mirror just for that."

I shook my head. "Doesn't make him less of an asshole, Max."

He didn't laugh. "In all seriousness, G, try not to shoot him until I think I know where everything is. He has a couple of safes I want to see opened first."

"You mean be a 'team player'?"

"I know it's hard for you to restrain yourself but give me this one. Okay?"

I grinned. "Sure, Max. No problem."

"We both know how it's going to end. Just don't let him get behind you until then."

I stood there and thought about that for about ten minutes after Max went inside. Then I found Night and told her we were going for a walk.

She was rather dubious about my idea. "You sure you're up to it?"

"Hell, Night. I think I might jog back. You think you're going to be able to keep up?"

Her eyes searched mine. She didn't say anything at first; she just shook her head. Then she took a deep breath, looked up at me, and said, "Hang on. I need to get ready." She came back carrying a daypack, really a kid's schoolbook bag, and told me, "Okay. Let's go walk."

That first walk was a bitch. Actually, all of them were for a while. The first was the worst because of how bad it hurt. The second was just as bad, but at least I knew what to expect.

The first time all I could do was fifteen minutes down the trail behind Jake's house. Once we were out of sight of his house I asked Night, "Anyone watching?"

She looked around. "Not that I can see."

I hobbled over to a tree, leaned against it, and screamed into my arm. Night came rushing up to me. I felt her hand on my back as she whispered, "You sure you want to do this?"

I growled at her, "Got no choice," and waved her back. Pain makes me snappish and I didn't want to let it spill over on her. I wiped the sweat off my face, looked at her, and asked, "You see that tree down there?" I pointed down the trail.

"There are a lot of trees down there, G."

"I know. That's where we are walking to."

I barely made it back to the house that day. Night ended up having to replace the dressing on my wound as soon as we got back.

Soon enough I would be showing her how much I enjoyed her help by "saluting" her when we returned from our walks. This was as much as I could do, with all the pain, to express how I really felt about her, what I intended to do when we were strong again. The first time I "saluted" her, she made my day by exclaiming, "Oh, my God! It's back and it's bigger!" I wished it could have happened that first day after that first walk, but the process took time.

Outside of the house, the world was getting stranger by the day. Jake had DSL, but he and Ninja both agreed that we had to be very careful about what blogs and web sites we visited. *Calculated Risk* had already been shut down, as had a number of others.

Their theory was that the Feds would be tracing IP numbers and making visits based on your viewing content. Iceland said it was cloaking traffic, but you had to get there first. Even getting bounced to them through Europe wasn't a good idea.

The price of gold continued to rise. That got Jake all excited but didn't do a lot for me. I didn't have any.

Martial law was not going very well apparently, based on reports that government troops had begun clashing with so-called domestic terrorists as soon as it was declared. The government was spinning this as a good thing. It saw the situation as justifying its actions. To me, it sounded like the state was losing control.

We saw smoke from fires almost every day. The Burners were still torching buildings they believed belonged to the "CorpState." The mainstream media hated, vilified, and generally made fun of Burners. Last week a special on the group had aired via every media format available. It included footage "never seen before" and was heavily promoted. I watched part of it. It looked like being a Burner was fun. They did attract seriously hot women.

Jake was pushing for a plan. Where were we going and how were we getting there? What was the plan once we got there? Did we have other people in mind? What was the organizational structure going to be? Would people be assigned ranks like in the military? I rolled my eyes and didn't bother to hide it as I heard that last item.

"What, you have a problem with that?" he asked.

"No. Just curious. What rank have you picked out, Jake?"

We were all sitting around the kitchen table and it got very quiet. He knew he was on the spot. I watched him as he reconsidered what he thought his rank really should be and dropped it a couple levels for modesty's sake.

"A major. After all, I'm pretty much bankrolling this operation." If he had looked around instead of trying to do the death stare at me, he would have seen how well that had gone over.

"So what do you see yourself as, Gardener?" He tried hard to make it sound like a casual question.

I let the silence hang for a bit and replied, "A contractor. That's where the money is."

The laughter following my answer almost broke the tension in the air. We stared at each other. I don't know about him, but I knew now it was just a matter of time.

My walks were getting longer. Max started going with me in place of Night. I pushed myself pretty hard but he took it to another level. He also had me do stretching exercises.

We were taking a breather—well, I was—when he told me, "It isn't about bulk where we're headed. It's about endurance. You want to be the wolf, not the buffalo. Bulk, even when it isn't chemical, is costly. It takes a lot of calories to keep it on. We are not going to have them."

"I should be good, then. I'm skinnier than I was when I was working, that's for sure."

Max laughed. "Yeah, a lot of that is going around."

Max had already told me the plan. We were headed to the farm where I had spent time healing from my fall on a rake and avoiding the people who didn't take it kindly that I had killed a few of their friends. People had a tendency to do that, I noticed.

Once I began to get in shape, we started to scout our route. This part of Virginia had a trail for every direction you wanted to go. Some of them had been county bike trails once, and the asphalt surfaces still remained in a lot of places. There was a lot of traffic on them now, most of it legit. All that bike riding was doing wonders for the asses of America's women. Work may have been disappearing, but women's bodies were coming back strong.

Max and I came back from one outing and found Jake had moved his fast-draw machine into the living room. It was a draw timer. You stood there and drew when the light flashed, and it gave you a readout of how fast you were. I'd been tempted to try it when I first saw it in his practice room, but then I would have had to ask Jake how to use it—and I did not want to do that.

I knew Jake had heard us come in, but he ignored us while he went through his routine. Ninja and Night were watching—Night reluctantly, and probably only out of boredom.

He was fast. Very fast. I had a feeling what was coming next.

"Hey, Gardener! Come on over here," he called out.

I looked at Max and shrugged. I walked over to where he stood. "Whatcha got, Jake?"

He was beaming. He even had his thumbs in his gun belt with his elbows sticking out like wings. He reminded me of a preening pigeon. "This is a timer for fast draws. You can set it for different times. As you know, the faster you are on target, the more likely you are to be the one who walks away."

He wasn't talking to me. He was talking to everyone else. Very casually he asked, "So, you want to give it a try? I have two. We can compete against the clock."

I just stared at him. I wasn't contemplating whether or not to go against the timer, I was deciding whether or not to kill him right now.

Ninja got excited and started chanting, "Do it, Gardener! Do it!"

Ignoring Ninja, I grinned at Jake. "Sure, why not?" Ninja cheered. I looked around. Max's face was impassive. Night was smiling.

Jake explained how it worked. We would each stand facing a timer set for two seconds, a light would flash, and we'd draw. Our times would be displayed on a digital readout. He asked, "You want to warm up?"

"No, I'm good."

"Not good enough." Then the asshole laughed. I didn't. I had a special surprise planned for him.

We went three times. He beat me by .02 seconds the first time; the second time, by .04 seconds. The third time I beat him by .01.

He loved it. He told me, "You're pretty good, Gardener. If you practiced, you could improve." I think he thought he was being gracious.

Everyone looked stunned, everyone except Max. His face hadn't changed, but when my eyes slid across his, he winked. If you didn't know him as well as I did, you would have missed it or thought it was a twitch. I knew better. Max didn't twitch.

I watched as Jake looked at Max. Waiting for the recognition, the approval. Max's face didn't register a change. He looked at him, nodded, said "Nice," and walked away.

I laughed, slapped him on the shoulder, and said, "I think we found our gunslinger."

Ninja looked stunned and then shrugged. I limped down the hall into the bedroom we were now using. Night followed me. Behind me I heard Ninja ask Jake, "Want to play *Halo*?"

We were lying in bed a couple days later. Since I was able to handle the stairs, Night and I had moved into one of Jake's spare bedrooms. He wasn't thrilled about it but it was obvious to everyone that we needed some privacy, especially since Night was also healing up rather nicely.

She was resting her head on my chest. She had cut her hair very short, using a pair of scissors and the bathroom mirror, and had begun wearing a bandanna to cover the back while it grew in. At first I was startled by the new look, but I was adjusting all right.

As her fingertip idly traced patterns only she could see on my chest and across my abs, she whispered, "Jake made a pass at me this morning."

"Really?"

"Yes."

"Tell me more."

She sighed. "I was in the kitchen washing dishes"— she paused and poked me in the ribs with a finger—"your dishes as a matter of fact."

"Ouch!"

"Anyway, he came in and started talking to me. I didn't think anything of it. Then he walked up next to me. I thought he needed a glass or was going to offer to help."

She sighed at the absurdity of what she had just said. I might be a little slack on doing the dishes but I still did chores. Jake didn't do shit. His attitude was, *It's my place, my food. You do the grunt work.*

"So I'm standing there and all of a sudden he has a handful of my ass and is squeezing it." She stopped.

I gave her about a minute. Damn, I hated having to drag stuff out of people. "Then what?"

"I slapped him and told him, 'Touch me again and I will kill you.' He just laughed. Then he drew on me. I told him, 'You think you're good. Wait until I tell Gardener.'"

I interrupted her, "Let me guess. He probably said something like 'Go ahead, baby, but I'm faster.'"

She pulled her head back enough so she could see my face. "That was pretty much it."

I laughed. "Did he do his Hollywood spin when he holstered them?"

"Yes." I could tell by her expression and the flatness in her reply that she wasn't getting the reaction she expected.

"Don't worry about it. I'll take care of it."

She gave me a hug. I thought that was it. In fact, I was drifting off to sleep when she said, "Gardener?"

"Hmm?"

"Can you take him?"

"I already have. He just doesn't know it yet."

# CHAPTER FOUR

I let a couple of days go by. When we crossed paths, I acted as if nothing had happened. Now I knew why Jake had seemed a little tense around me for the past few days.

On the third day we were sitting around the table talking about Max's plan to head for the farm. Max asked Jake if he wanted to go with him early the next morning and recon the route he had chosen. Jake agreed, of course. I knew he resented the fact that Max never asked him along when he went out. I thought it was sort of funny actually.

The next morning I was sitting at the kitchen table with Max, drinking coffee, when Jake came out of his bedroom.

"Hello, sleepyhead," I said.

He shot me the evil eye and pointedly looked at the clock to let me know he was on time. I grinned at him. He didn't bother to address me. Instead he asked Max, "He's going?" Meaning me, of course.

"Yep. We might as well practice how we are going to move cross-country."

Jake liked that. I knew about jock sniffers. That there were camo crotch sniffers was a revelation to me. Jake, I thought, definitely fell in that category.

"Great idea. I can walk point."

"Yeah. We'll all be doing some of that." Max said.

We headed south down the path behind the house. It was already warm for so early in the morning. It was going to be another hot, muggy summer. Max had a shotgun and his .45 while Jake and I just wore our gun belts. I was wearing a daypack with our lunches, a medic kit, and water inside.

We went down the path, single file, not talking. Max went through a couple of hand signs that we would use. They were basic stuff like STOP! and DOWN! and I SEE THE ENEMY! Jake loved it.

It was closing on midday when I took point from Jake. I kept us going for about twenty minutes, and then I flashed STOP! and went forward about fifteen feet. Here I shrugged off my daypack and tossed it underhand into a bush about five feet from me.

I stood there for a few beats and enjoyed having the weight gone. I wiggled my shoulders to loosen them up and stared at Jake, who was behind me. I started walking toward him. As I did, Max quietly slid to the side and off the trail.

"What's up, Gardener?"

I told him, "It's time for you to go."

He laughed. "Me? Why?"

"You think I was going to let you live after you touched Night?"

He started laughing. "Shit, Gardener, she ain't nothing. She's just a throwaway piece of Asian ass. We're better than—"

I drew. He drew.

My first round hit him in the chest and staggered him. He looked stunned, probably because he hadn't even cleared his holster. *Time this, prick*, I thought, and shot him again.

He went down to his knees. Then he went face-first into the hard-packed clay of the trail. I walked over to him. He was going, if not gone.

Max joined me, looked down at Jake, shook his head, and asked, "You hungry?"

"Yeah. Let's eat."

We found a downed tree off the trail to sit on after I retrieved my pack. Jake's body was cooling where he had fallen.

Max indicated the body. "We're going to have to do something about that."

"Yeah, I know, Max." I was looking inside the pack. I was hungry and curious what Night had packed us for lunch. "Alright!"

Max looked at me curiously.

"She packed the last of the Twinkies!"

"That's love, Gardener. I would have eaten them and left you with something healthy like a can of tuna fish instead."

I tossed him one. "She packed enough for two."

"Nice. Very nice."

We also had Tupperware containers with rice and beans, plus an apple for each of us.

"Hey, Max. Did you know what was going to happen here with me and the asshole?"

"No. I knew something wasn't right. Hell, I probably would have ended up getting around to it myself eventually."

"Hmm … you say anything to Night before we left?"

"Why do you ask?"

"She only packed two lunches."

He laughed and laughed. Max wasn't the kind of guy who spent a lot of time laughing. He was still chuckling as we stood over the body. We always looted our kills. It kept our cash flow positive a lot of the time.

I found a set of keys and held them up to look closer at them. Puzzled, I said, "He brought his car keys?"

"Habit. A lot of people are still running on old habits. That's what keeps getting them killed."

That made sense to me. I dug Jake's wallet out and did a quick check for cash. He had $549 in new dollars. Handy for the few places left that took it. Cash was on its way out. The new national ID was going to be upgraded to a debit card, and eventually it would tie into all your accounts. Max had pointed out the obvious to me: "Real-time spending data is also real-time GPS until they figure out how to tag all of us."

"You want his weapon, Max?"

"You don't want it?" Weapons and anything else always went to the winner of the encounter.

"No. Let someone else get lucky."

I grabbed his arms and Max took his feet. On a count of three, we tossed him into the bushes and vines that lined the trail.

"Damn, Max. There's a lot of poison ivy in there. Not going to be much fun for whoever decides he's worth pulling out."

"Yeah. We'll be gone by then."

We made sure we left nothing behind. I reloaded and pocketed the brass. A pocketful of spent brass was like having a pocketful of quarters now. Some places, you could spend them like change, too.

# CHAPTER FIVE

We pushed on after eating. Despite the interruption, we were actually out here to plan our exit strategy. We needed to move but the big question was how to do it. By road, bicycle, or foot?

It was starting to look as though our move would be on foot. The government had really clamped down hard around D.C. Iceland was reporting that government influence was waning in certain states. The federal government was, if you believed the Icelandic News, starting to have a serious problem projecting authority and collecting revenue.

The Icelanders aired an interesting program on it. It wasn't that our federal government was hated, although that sentiment was certainly rising. People still saw themselves as Americans and flew the flag. The abstract idea of America was still valid, but the reality wasn't.

The change was gradual at first and then picked up speed. But there wasn't a single tipping point. It depended on the state, where in that state you lived, and, often, how well established the area was. Religion played an important part, too. Utah was well on its way to becoming an autonomous province: the Quebec of America.

The breakdown started with the states. They couldn't afford to provide basic services anywhere near what people needed. The counties tried to pick up the slack by not forwarding their revenue to the state. In some cases they managed to provide some of service, but over time their own falling revenues ate away at that.

In theory the Feds should have stepped in but there was no money to do so. The previous administration followed a policy of "Hope for the best. Ignore the West."

That policy failed. Badly. Ignoring California meant abandoning a state whose GDP would have put it in the world's top ten if it were a country. The Pacific Northwest was ignored because its residents had turned out in huge numbers against the previous administration.

So what we had at this point were states with partially functioning services in some areas, partially functioning towns and counties, and no-go zones——areas that were run by gangs or religious or political nut jobs, or were just in free fall. The Burners ran huge parts of California, Oregon, and Washington State. Mexican gangs controlled southern Arizona, except for pockets of Maricopa County.

The Apache and some of the other tribes were also making their moves. The casino years had given them the money to make hardware purchases. The Sioux were bringing back the buffalo and beginning to burn out the AgriCorp holdings if they got in the way.

Halfway through the program, Max had turned to me and said, "Damn, we brought the 'Stan home with us." There wasn't much I could do in reply other than shrug.

Max would walk or bicycle for miles when he wasn't walking with me. Sometimes he left again after dinner. He was out talking to people. Watching the roads. Making phone calls with disposable phones.

The roads were no longer safe for us. The new administration was determined to hold and pacify the area surrounding Washington, D.C. In phone calls to old friends still on active duty Max learned more from what was not said than from what was. Often he would meet them at Top's house in the suburbs. Top was retired but he knew a lot of people from all the years he had spent on active duty.

From them, he found out that the Feds had canceled a decision to send a team to hunt us down. As long as we kept a low profile and didn't get stopped by anyone other than a sheriff or local law enforcement outside the Zone, we would be okay.

If a federal or army patrol stopped us, however, we would be screwed. The Feds no longer trusted local law enforcement with access to their databases. If the locals were good and had proved their loyalty, they were allowed access to a sanitized version. We were marked as "Hold and Notify" in the Fed version.

We planned to head south to the farm where I had recovered from my first bad wound. We were going to walk out of the Zone to a prearranged pickup point. From there we would ride the remaining distance.

We could have driven all the way or been smuggled in like the Latinos used to be, but that was risky. Plus, Max didn't want to do it that way. He said we needed to learn to move as a unit, not only in the city but also in the woods. I was up for it. I just wasn't sure if Night and I had physically recovered enough.

That night we all sat down at the kitchen table where Max had laid out a road map of Virginia. He had us study it and he quizzed us on the highway numbers, towns, and river crossings. Then he traced where he thought our route would take us, where possible problem spots were, and what our goals were to be for each day.

"I have a more detailed map," Max said. "We are going to use bike trails as much as possible. When we can't do that, we'll cut through the ghost towns and skirt people as much as we can. On the maps it looks suburban for quite a distance, but from what I understand that is no longer true."

Ninja asked, "What are these 'ghost towns,' Max?"

"They are housing developments that, for one reason or another, are empty. Well, almost empty usually."

"Oh, like Olde English Oakes?" Olde English Oakes was a local development that had housed wandering groups of homeless in ransacked remnants of luxury.

"Exactly. This is what the current political situation looks like." He took a red pencil and drew three concentric circles on the map, with D.C. at the center. The smallest included everything inside the Beltway. "The center is going to be locked down."

The second circle went out past Centerville and Sterling. "This is how far the lockdown is going to be expanded." The third circle went out another twenty miles. "This is almost locked down. My guess is that it's going to be a gray area for a few years. Word is that Special Forces has hunter/sniper teams working the second zone. Everything outside of this is still local law enforcement."

He drew another big circle around the Norfolk-Newport News area. "This is also locked down. The area around Quantico is another safe area for the Feds. The place we're headed is still in play. Once you cross the Ohio River it is all a no-go zone as far as the Feds are concerned. They don't have the manpower to bother with much except for patrolling key cities and keeping the rail and the Interstate open.

"Over here in West Virginia are our old friends led by the colonel. They are starting to expand a bit but haven't made any serious pushes outside their zone of control yet. Supposedly they are part of the new federal plan to use surrogates. They keep the area quiet in exchange for supplies and access to data. The new administration is allowing and encouraging this to happen all over. Surrogates keep the area quiet and 'render unto Caesar.' In exchange, they get to be the local warlord. If they get out of hand, or don't tithe, then a Fed team guarantees a new leader who'll cooperate."

"Who are we up against?"

"It should be fairly calm as far as us not running into organized groups. We're going to have to watch out for predator groups and local crazies. Other than that it should be rather uneventful."

In addition to gathering information, Max had made contact with a Burner cell. He had been working on trading and selling the contents of the house. I think he knew all along we would be walking out of here.

We planned to take light-weight, high-value items with us, primarily pharmaceuticals and gold. Gold had an official price and a street price. Periodic rumors that the Feds were going to ban private ownership ensured that the street price stayed high.

Pharmaceuticals were priceless if you were outside the zones. Manipulating supplies was one of the major weapons the government had left to use: Get out of line, don't embrace the new warlord, and watch as shipments of antibiotics, insulin, and antidepressants came to a halt in your area.

The Burner philosophy was simplistic, at least in the beginning: Burn down the banks, the regional headquarters of financial institutions, and fry a few bankers if they could catch them. Occasionally someone would get confused and torch a credit union. It started as a "Crash the financial system and start over with small, green, cooperative factories and farms" philosophy. It had grown since. Now it had a large green contingent, with a spiritual base rooted in Wicca and Shamanism.

Of all the coalescing factions, it was the one we all agreed was the best. Why? Because they were less likely to demand that you pledge allegiance to whatever their agenda was and to shoot you if you didn't. The Burners wanted weapons, ammo, and gold. We wanted lightweight, high-value items.

The Burners, while being anarchists of a sort, were generally nonviolent. That was changing quickly. They had been some of the first targets of Homeland Security, which hunted them from helicopters and shot them whenever it could manufacture a reason to. The current administration really, really hated them.

Max set up a meeting with the Burners and elected Night and me to do the deal with their representatives that evening. Night was the brains. She would run the negotiations, check the trade goods, and make sure everything was financially cool. I was security. The rule was no more than two in the room at the meet. We would leave the garage door open so they could pull their panel van inside.

Night was armed with a belt knife. She could shoot; she just did not like guns all that much. At first she had been okay with them. Lately, she was just not interested. Max was going to set up across the street with the Barrett. Ninja would sit in the basement, a loaded shotgun across his lap.

The Burners arrived exactly on time. I liked that. I met them in the garage. The negotiators were a woman and a man. They had hired muscle with them to do the loading: two good-sized guys in their early twenties. Both of them looked competent and I was sure they were armed, though they had no visible weapons.

Of the negotiating couple, the woman impressed me the most. She was stately, perhaps, even regal. No other words fit as well as those. In her late forties was my guess. Long hair, black with threads of silver. Clear, green eyes and loose-fitting clothing on a body that was still decent.

She caught me looking at her wrist. She held it up so I could see. "Yes, I did have one. It was removed."

She was talking about the Burner tattoo. Not all that long ago, old-timers who held a position of authority in the Burners—as much as they had authority—usually had two distinguishing marks: the flame tattoo and red hair. These badges disappeared pretty quickly when the Feds began picking up anyone who had either one. The Burners that were picked up, well, they never came back.

The male was shorter, fit, and clean-shaven. He was balding and about the same age as she. He was dressed nondescriptly and was visibly armed. It looked like a 9-millimeter of some sort. None of us bothered with shaking hands.

"Thank you for coming," I greeted them. "Any problems?"

"No. It's quiet tonight," the man answered.

The woman smiled. She had a great smile. I had better get it together or Night would kick my ass, especially if she caught me gawking. This woman had some serious charisma going on. The nipples standing up underneath her blouse were not helping either.

"Please, right this way." I let them walk ahead of me to where Night was waiting in the kitchen. I followed, trying to move sideways so I could keep an eye on the two in the garage. They had not moved. One had a faint smile as he watched me go through my contortions.

The Lady and Night clicked at once. That was obvious, and it was a relief. Night explained to them how we would do the transaction.

She and the Lady would sit at the dining room table. The man and I would go to the basement. What we had to offer was sorted and piled in groups on the basement floor. He would look at each group and decide if he wanted all or part of it. He would go back upstairs, tell the Lady what he had decided, and Night and she would work out the price. Once that was done, he and his guys, no more than two of them together, would move the selected goods into the van. Night would hand me the payment and I would put it in the backpack I was wearing.

It went well. They took everything we had. With the last load the helpers disappeared back into the garage. Max had warned me that if anything were to go wrong, this would be the time. The Lady was relaxed. She and Night had chatted the entire time. The bald man, though—he was alert, more so than when he had arrived. I guess he was their version of Max. Or perhaps he knew by experience, that this was the time to be focused.

The Lady had made no motion to leave yet. Instead she said, "I would like to put one more item on the table, if I may."

"Sure," Night told her.

"We understand you have a Barrett. In exchange, we're willing to offer you four one-pound bars of gold and two hundred rounds of ammo in the caliber of your choice."

I didn't even hesitate. "No. Not a chance."

The man really got me focused when he asked, "Is it here?"

I began to wish that Night would leave the room. I also hoped Ninja would come up from the basement. We had told him not to, but I was starting to think he and the shotgun might be needed in the next few minutes.

The Lady must have sensed the change in the room. I know Night had; her hand was no longer visible, having dropped into her lap.

The Lady laughed. "It's fine. We have hopes of acquiring one through other means soon."

For the first time, the man grinned and held up a hand. "Sorry, didn't mean for it to be taken wrong. I've just never seen one before."

I had not realized that my hand was resting on my gun butt. The Lady's glance made me realize it was—not that I moved, though.

"Well, thank you all for coming by. I hope you have a safe and pleasant trip home."

"No, thank you." The Lady gave Night a quick hug and extended her hand to me. I just smiled. She quickly dropped it, showing no sign that she felt it had been awkward. I stood in the doorway and watched them leave.

# CHAPTER SIX

We left early the next morning. Early, according to Max's plan, meant we were to have our boots on the trail by sunrise. We didn't make it until forty-five minutes into the new dawn. We didn't do a lot of miles that first day.

Max never stopped. He moved continually up and down the line, pointing out what we were doing wrong. When he wasn't doing that, he worked on getting us to respond to hand signals. The hardest part for all of us was maintaining the necessary level of alertness. Every mile carrying a pack drained away a little more of the energy needed for that.

The second morning wasn't so smooth either. We just didn't have the routine down yet. Instead it was stumble around, take a leak, and figure out breakfast. *Who has the food?* followed by *Who's going to make it?* and *Who's going to clean up?* I didn't help by insisting that we make coffee. There was a lot of sleep-stunned stumbling around just to accomplish that.

How groups of hundreds or thousands of people managed these logistics was mind-blowing. The organizational skills required just to make sure everyone would have a place to take a dump, much less have enough water to drink, were surprisingly complex, to me at least. That people had managed to progress from warrior bands to disciplined armies was amazing. It was one of mankind's greater achievements, I thought.

We had our problems on the trail, too. Max had point and the rest of us straggled after him. Within an hour we had to stop. Night's pack was killing her. The skin was still very tender where it had been burned. She had struggled with it the first day, but by the second day the pain was too intense to hide anymore. I took my towel and spread it over her back, tying it in the front like a little cape.

"Very nice!" I told her. "Super-Night."

She smiled, but I could see the pain in her eyes. I think Max did, too. We sat there for a bit, about twenty feet off to the side of trail. I transferred everything I could from her pack to mine. Ninja took what I couldn't take. The result was that Night's pack was now light enough that she could sling it from her good shoulder like a handbag, especially with the extra padding.

Meanwhile, Max gave us a lecture on how to stop. "Don't dump your packs and stand there scratching yourselves and stretching, for God's sake." He went on a bit more. It was amusing to watch him slip into his Sarge persona. He was good: He didn't overdo it or push us too hard.

We shouldered our packs and set out again. A full pack was a different beast altogether from a daypack. It did not take long to feel the weight of it. I was beginning to feel it in my thigh, where my woodie had been extracted. I did my best to ignore it and to not limp. I hated for anyone to see me limping like I was some kind of cripple. Cripples were weak, and being weak made you a target.

We were probably never more than half a mile, at most, from civilization. Sometimes we crossed over roads or saw the roofs of houses, yet it felt like we were in the wilderness. The trail, which was asphalt so far, had once been trimmed back about six feet on each side. I suppose it was to make it a little harder for rapists to leap out on unsuspecting female joggers who were wearing iPod buds in their ears. Now it looked as if it had not been trimmed for several years.

With climate change, Virginia had been getting a lot of rain. It showed. Occasionally we would see breaks in the grass and weeds where something had moved out of the woods and across the path. It could have been deer, but I doubted that. Most of them had been eaten. I didn't know really, but I was a little more alert each time we passed a broken patch of brush.

We didn't just stroll across the roads we came to. Whoever was on point would stop us. We would take cover, as much as we could find, and sit facing outward. The person on point would go across. The rest of us would wait a minute, make sure no vehicles were coming, and then one by one we'd follow and take up a covering position. It was surreal at times, sprinting across the fading white crosswalk lines. Usually there were houses in sight. The eerie thing was the silence except for the birds.

Crossing roads this way didn't feel real to me. It was like we were playing war. Yet I knew by now that the appearance of prosperity and peace was a leftover illusion of an earlier time. The reality was that half the houses we passed were trashed inside, filled with human shit and graffiti. The nice McMansion behind the trees could hold a pack of feral boomers waiting like spiders for the unaware.

We didn't see as many people on the trail as I expected. Back by the motel the bike trails had always been busy. People commuted back and forth from the Tree People enclaves to the shelter or to our little shopping center. The woods may have been hunted clean of their wildlife rather quickly, but firewood kept the people going back into them. That and water from the streams. There was also an element that naturally gravitated to the woods. For the most part they were not the most well-adjusted people.

Our first day out we saw only one man. He was out jogging, which I found rather funny. He wore a T-shirt with a blue globe and some sort of bird on it. It was pretty faded, which I guess is why he was jogging in it. When he passed, I read The Fighting 13th written inside the circle.

He was in good shape and had obviously spent some serious time in the sun. He was wearing a tan SWAT-style holster with a 1911 .45 in it. Actually, it looked a lot like the rig that Max wore.

Max gave us the FREEZE hand signal—his fist raised up in the air. We all froze, but only Ninja mimicked Max, remembering that we had been taught to pass the sign down the line.

The jogger saw it also and stopped. He was running in place but he wasn't coming any closer. Max gave the DISPERSE LEFT signal, which is a no-brainer to remember. We moved off into the grass and weeds. Max didn't move. I heard Night mutter, "I hate freaking ticks." I was going to talk to Max later. I didn't like her in front of me. I wanted her behind me, where I would be in a better position for stuff like this.

Max surprised me. He saluted and said loud enough for the jogger to hear clearly, "Semper Fi," and stepped off the trail.

The jogger nodded at Max as he passed. He checked each of us as he went by, his face impassive. Once he passed us, he turned and ran backward, moving like that for about twenty-five feet. Then he snapped off a quick salute, turned, and was gone. Max didn't say anything. He just got us back on the trail and with a brief wave of his hand he had us moving again.

The rhythm was not right on the trails, but Night and Ninja didn't seem to notice. Night had spent very little time on the trails back at the motel. Ninja had, maybe, more time than her. I had put more time on the trails in a day than those two had in a year. The flow was off.

Later, during a break, I asked Max, "What's up with nobody on the trail?"

"I don't know. We'll push for a couple hours more and then break for lunch."

I craned my head around to look at him. I knew that tone, and seeing the look on his face only confirmed it. When I stood up I made sure my Ruger was loose inside the holster and slipped the leather thong off the trigger. Night saw me do it and gave me a questioning look. I just shook my head and smiled.

I was worried about her. I wasn't sure if she was up to the grind. So far, everything was good. She was a trooper. Hell, if I had to, I would wear her pack up front and mine on my back. I hoped it wouldn't come to that, though. I was already feeling what I was carrying of hers.

Lunch was simple. Today was a no-fire lunch. We had apples and bread, with water to wash it down. It was good.

I caught Night looking at me quizzically a couple times. Something wasn't right, and now she seemed to feel it, too. I gave Max a look and got the nod in return. I was carrying my shotgun slung across my chest. I didn't like it that way. I was going to have to find a better way of carrying it. For now, though, I was going to keep it unslung and in my hand.

Ninja was busy chattering away to Night. She was not saying much in return, just a nod and a yes every two or three minutes.

"Max."

"Yeah."

"I want to take point." I thought I would get an argument.

"Sure," he answered. To all of us, he said, "We're going to change things up a bit for the rest of the day. Gardener is going to be point, but I am going to move off the trail into the tree line and walk almost parallel to him. The fancy word for this is *echelon*. I think it's French," he grinned.

"Ninja, I want you behind him. Drop back to about twenty-five feet. Night, I want you about fifteen feet behind Gardener. You have the right side. Ninja, you have the left. Night, take a look over your shoulder every ten steps or so."

She nodded her head.

Ninja grinned and said, "Cool, I am almost point."

"Yep," I told Night, "our boy is growing up." We were laughing when Ninja held his hand up in the FREEZE sign.

He whispered, "Someone is coming." The kid had good ears. I heard it about a second later.

Bicycles. They moved past us—two men and a woman, each bike towing a carrier. The carriers looked home-made, except for one that was a converted kid carrier. No kids in it that I could see.

All three of them were white. One of the males was wearing a tie-dyed shirt, which told me a lot about them: probable Burner sympathizers. The woman was not bad looking. Her brown hair was in a ponytail that bounced along behind her. All three were armed. The man in the front had a hunting rifle over his back; the woman, a holstered pistol. The guy bringing up the rear—he looked like it was killing him to keep that bike rolling—had an AR-15 look-alike over his back. He was the oldest by about ten years.

They were there and gone in a couple seconds. I noticed Ninja watching the woman's ass as she pumped the pedals. Yep, the kid was growing up. I elbowed him and grinned. Night just looked away. A faint smile flashed across her face.

That's when it struck me. Where were all the refugees? With the Feds tightening the D.C. Zone and expanding their lockdown, we couldn't be the only ones who had decided to move out. I had a good idea of what was going on. I was hoping we could bypass it.

We kept moving along, and I tried to get into the rhythm of walking. When I'm by myself, I prefer to keep the stops to a minimum. Maybe a breather every once in a while, which for me means stopping and bending over at the waist so my pack shifts enough that it feels like I'm not wearing it for a few minutes. Then it's back to moving. I liked to push until I felt like I was on autopilot.

With it came a detachment from my physical self that was pleasant.

We couldn't move that way now for a lot of reasons. My gear was bothering me. The weight didn't feel distributed right. I couldn't retrieve my water bottle without stopping and dropping my pack. Plus, my new sheath knife was interfering with how my gun belt rode on my hip. I noticed both Ninja and Night fidgeting with their gear. It was just part of the process of settling down, until your gear became as unnoticeable as the clothes you had on.

We all wore knives. Everyone in our part of town did. Max wore a KA-BAR, of course. Night wore a fisherman's fillet knife.

I could never make up my mind. I changed knives and bought knives the way kids used to buy sneakers. Then I moved from knives to daggers after a while. I thought they looked cool and they certainly were effective for one thing.

The problem was they were useless for everything else. The fifth time I found myself using a dagger to cut string or leather for tie downs, I realized how useless they really were. You couldn't use the tip for a screwdriver. Well, you could, but you ended up with a dagger with a broken tip. Cutting bread or an apple? Let's just say it was overkill. I finally took to wearing a Swiss Army knife on a leather thong around my neck. Not very cool—I felt like a latchkey kid—but very handy.

I couldn't give up wearing a belt knife, though. I had the image thing to worry about. So I was wearing a KA-BAR like Max. I was beginning to wish I had brought a machete. The sides of the trail were overgrown with Queen

Anne's lace, daisies, burdock, and other plants whose sole purpose in life was to trip me up when I needed to take a piss and to decorate my pants with ticks and burrs.

Ninja carried the same knife he had worn for the last year. He was really proud of it when he bought it at the market. It wasn't just a knife. It was the Dragon Knife. Made in China, of course. Stainless steel, with a handle shaped like a dragon's head.

He thought it was awesome. I thought it was ridiculous when he first showed it to me.

"Ninj, what the hell is that?"

"It's my Dragon Knife!"

I shook my head and handed it back to him. "It's stainless steel. You need carbon steel."

"No, I don't."

I rolled my eyes. "It's a fantasy knife, Ninj."

He pointed at the medieval dagger I was wearing back then. "What do you call that?"

He had a point. I held up my hands. "Fine. It's yours."

After he had walked away, unhappily, I thought to myself, *Wow, nice job, asshole. He's a freaking kid.* I made a point of looking him up later, reexamining the knife, and grudgingly praising it.

When I told Night about it later, she laughed and told me, "He wanted to buy a Ninja sword, but no one had any for sale."

The sun was beating down on us. Max had told us we were not going to push it past early afternoon for the first week. He also told us that after we stopped for the day and settled in, he wanted to look at everyone's feet. I had a feeling that it would probably turn into a teaching moment, which was fine. Max didn't beat his points into the ground.

Out of the corner of my eye I caught the occasional bird. I saw a red-tailed hawk soaring above us one day. That was pretty cool. On the trail I saw a lot of Virginia butterflies, also known as gypsy moths.

Maybe that was why they almost always caught me by surprise. Well, not surprise, but off-balance for a second. Probably because it was so unexpected.

I berated myself later. There was no excuse for it. Nowadays, a second meant everything.

# CHAPTER SEVEN

I was walking point and had come to a bend in the trail. I could not see around it because of the plants and a fallen tree. I should have held up my fist in the FREEZE sign and gone on by myself first. I didn't. Yet another mistake. Instead, lulled by the sun and walking on autopilot, I just kept going.

What awaited us was a little different from what we usually dealt with when we walked our beat back in Fairfax. Yet in many ways it was the same. It was always the same type of people up to the same kind of shit that they always get up to when no one is around to kick their asses.

The first thing I noticed was a fat, jiggly, very white ass pumping up and down, with a big boil or zit on it. I normally would have shot the guy just for violating the gross and ugly law, but he wasn't alone. They never are.

Also standing with his back to me was a skinny white man with a bunnytail ass and his pants around his ankles. He had long, scraggly gray-and-white hair, and even from this distance it was easy to tell that he needed a wash.

Not just his hair, either. He had a fair amount of blood on him. On the ground off to his right lay a bloody machete. He was watching Fatboy and jerking off.

About four feet away, two more white guys watched the show. One had shaggy blond hair and wore a Polo shirt and khaki pants. He held a hunting bow. My guess was that he was the leader. He was smoking and pointing at Fat Boy pumping away.

He said something to his sidekick, a middle-aged white guy who looked like every high school gym teacher I had ever seen. In his hand he should have had the AR-15 that was at his feet. Instead he had a bottle. They both began laughing.

It was easy to see what must have happened. The guy in the tie-dyed shirt had come around the bend. I'm sure he had seen the downed tree out of the corner of his eye. So when he saw the pine limb across the path it did not set off any alarms, especially since the trail dipped down to cross a stream about twenty feet further on. It had a bridge once, but it was no longer usable for bike traffic.

He had stopped, probably quickly, which wouldn't have helped him any as far as getting to his weapon. Not that he'd had a chance. He'd taken an arrow to the neck and looked as if he'd choked to death.

The woman probably narrowly avoided plowing into him. They must have been on her right away—probably two on her, with the Leader standing back and Bunnytail working his machete magic on the older guy bringing up the rear. It had been a fast and efficient slaughter.

They quit laughing abruptly when they saw me. I shouldered the shotgun. Bunnytail turned around to see what the big boys were looking at, mouth open, his hand still moving. Fat Boy either didn't hear me or was too close to the edge to care.

I took out the sidekick with the AR-15 at his feet. I didn't like shotguns but I respected them. In World War I, they called them trench brooms because of how well they swept a trench clean of anything living.

As I was racking back the slide I heard the boom of a .45 from my right. Max had taken out the Leader, his bow still at his side. That left the two in front of me. Bunnytail took my buckshot at crotch level. It wasn't pretty.

I felt someone coming up behind me. I really hoped it was Ninja because I wasn't turning around to take a look. He stood next to me. I noticed he was breathing a little hard. Night came up beside us, and together we stared for a minute at the carnage and the two survivors.

Max was moving toward us. He had moved to my right and into the brush without my hearing him. I could tell he was getting ready to say something. It was probably going to be along the lines of "What the hell you gawking at? Is this what I taught you to do?" He didn't get a chance.

I moved toward the woman. Keep in mind that everything happened in under a minute. Fat Boy was still on top of the woman, but was no longer pumping. He was also as much red as white. The red splotches, plus a few pieces of gristle, were from his buddy who had been waiting his turn.

I heard the woman moan. No, it was a keening sound. It was the sound a puppy would make if it got its nose jammed into a fan. It made me angry.

Fat Boy twisted around enough that he saw me coming. He looked ahead. The woman's clothes and holster, including the gun, had been tossed into a pile about six feet away. Fat Boy was going to go for it. That made me happy. It was considerate of him to give me a clear shot. I didn't want to hurt the woman underneath him any more than she had already been hurt.

He didn't leap as much as slither over her body. I let him get about halfway across her—unfortunate for her, I suppose. Watching his hand reaching out like a drowning swimmer for the gun, I pretty much blew it off. It looked like some of it remained—not enough for him to get his palm read, that was for sure. He rolled off her, got to his knees and then, to my surprise, to his feet.

"You son of a bitch!"

I shrugged.

"Oh, Jesus! Do something! I'm hurt!"

I heard Ninja say, "No shit."

The woman continued to shriek from where she lay.

I cycled a new round and was getting ready to finish Fat Boy when Night zipped past me.

"Goddamn it, Night!" I yelled.

I started moving toward her and Fat Boy. My first thought was that she was going to help the woman before we were done with Fat Boy. He must have thought she was coming to help him. We were both wrong.

Her hand went to her belt and the fillet knife. Fat Boy had his arm up in the air. It sprayed bright red blood like a flabby white fountain. For some strange reason I found myself thinking of the Fourth of July. He had to be going into shock.

Night got to him, reached out, grabbed his now flaccid cock, and whipped her fillet blade across it. It looked like a clean cut.

She held it up in front of his face and screamed, "Rape this, you cocksucker!" She shook it in his face, walked past him, wound up, and threw it into the creek. If he hadn't gone into shock a minute ago, he certainly had now. His eyes rolled back until all I saw was white, and he went down like a clear-cut tree.

I turned to Ninja. "You see what she just did?"

He nodded.

"That just wasn't right," I said

He looked at me surprised.

"Yep. She should have put a hook in that worm before throwing it into the creek." I grinned at him and winked. He didn't get it at first. I shook my head and started toward Max, who was looking at the bow.

Night knelt down to comfort the woman. I held back. I didn't think she needed another man in her face right then.

Ninja had disappeared in the few seconds I had my back to him. *Damn.* I looked at Max and turned back. I figured Ninja was puking his guts out in the bushes.

The woman got up and looked at the dead man with the arrow through his neck. She screamed again, a much higher-pitched scream. She took three steps to her clothes and the holster, bent over, and came up with the gun.

Time froze.

I saw Night open her mouth, the word "No" forming, as the woman took the pistol and inserted the barrel into her mouth. She pulled the trigger and dropped.

I moved quickly to Night, who had frozen in place. I think I heard Max say, "Shit." I knelt down next to Night, holding her close.

"C'mon, honey. We need to go." She resisted at first and then stiffly got to her feet. I kept my arm around her and turned her away from the woman's body. I started walking her to the creek.

I heard Ninja scream, "You motherfucker!" I looked back. He was standing over the body; in his hand was one of his shirts. He had gone to get the woman something to wear.

I didn't have time for him. That was going to have to be Max. I could feel Night shaking. I started talking to her. Nothing much. Just a string of "It's going to be okay. It's alright," as I led her away.

Max moved toward Ninja. But of course it wasn't over. I don't know if it was death throes or not, but Fat Boy started twitching like he still had some life in him. Whatever it was, it didn't last. Ninja walked up to him, pulled out his handgun, and removed the top of his head.

# CHAPTER EIGHT

We didn't have time to deal with emotional issues. Max got us moving. I realized later that it was the only sane way for regular people to cope with dispensing and seeing others suffer violent deaths. You had to get busy; keep your mind focused on the present—and the next moment.

I wanted Night away from this. She didn't need to see it. At the same time, I held her next to me, making physical contact, trying to quiet the shaking that convulsed her.

We heard Max yelling, "Night! Night!"

She pulled away from me. "Yeah, Max?"

"Get your ass over here. We got work to do!"

She paused and glanced up at me, looking for something. To this day I don't know what she expected—or wanted—to see. Whatever it was, I don't think it was there.

"Coming!" she yelled, heading toward Max and the bodies. I stood there watching her walk, shrugged, and followed her.

We walked back to where the stink of death was already drawing flies.

They always came: the big, fat, black flies. The kind of flies that crunched and squashed when you swatted them, leaving a nasty little stain.

You never saw them until blood was spilled or the latrine got its first load. Then, like magic, they appeared out of nowhere. I imagined their maggots hanging in clusters, like grapes in secret places, where they slumbered until the right smell called them forth. Then, they would burst free and, like ugly butterflies, they would take wing and follow the scent.

I hated flies. When I was bored, I would take a fly-swatter and kill every one I came across.

Max had us toss the bodies into the bushes and the bikes into the trees. He had Night fetch water from the creek to wash down the bloodiest spots.

"What about the bone fragments?" I asked him.

"Leave them. I'm more worried about what it looks like from the air. Police the brass, though."

Ninja and I tossed bodies, and Night watered the whole area. Max took over the watch. It would have been awkward to be surprised by a county park crew, if they still existed, or a random passerby, while tossing bodies. Let alone any remnants of the gang.

Ninja was bothered by the idea of tossing the woman in the bushes with Fat Boy and everyone else. "Shouldn't we bury her? And her friends?"

I could tell that "friends" was an afterthought. I bit my tongue and, instead of biting his head off, decided to try my kinder and gentler approach. "No. No time."

"Oh."

I sighed. "You want to say a prayer?" He nodded his head. "Before or after we toss her?"

"After."

"Okay."

We tossed her. He stepped forward and bowed his head. "Dear God, please look out for her. She seemed nice. Let the rest of these assholes, except for her friends, burn in hell. Amen."

I added my "Amen" to the chorus.

We silently went back to work. Afterward, I took the machete and used it cut some branches to cover up what the bushes didn't. We washed up in the creek.

We took nothing in the way of personal spoils from either group. We all decided, without talking much about it, that it was all tainted. Plus, we were maxed out as far carrying any more weight.

Ninja asked hesitantly, "Why don't we take the bikes, Max? I mean, I understand why we don't go through their stuff but …"

"Night, you want to answer that?"

She replied flatly, "Because we don't want to cover a lot of ground quickly if it means at the end of the day that we die just as quickly."

Max nodded. "Ninja, there is a time for speed, but this isn't it." He grinned at him. "C'mon, what better way to see Virginia than by humping sixty pounds of gear while you sweat your ass off? You got point. Gardener, take drag. Let's move."

We started down the trail again.

The next few days proved uneventful. We faded into the woods if we heard helicopters overhead. There wasn't a lot we could do about them. There was even less we could do about the drones that were up there somewhere.

We rolled out of our bags before dawn. We would just sit, weapons up, and wait for about twenty minutes until Max gave us the sign to fix breakfast.

When I had a chance to catch him alone, I asked him, "What's up with the morning meditation routine? I mean, I doubt if any Tree People are going to come storming into camp. Hell, they usually don't wake up until the sun pierces their hangovers."

He looked at me quizzically. "You really think we're the only people moving around out here with some kind of military training? I'm not worried about the ones we spot. It's the ones we don't that will be the problem."

Not a lot I could say to that. So I didn't. I was somewhat cranky for a while in the morning anyway.

We usually ate a cold breakfast. In the morning the only hot thing we had was tea or coffee. We ate just one full hot meal a day now, a hot lunch cooked over a backpacker's stove. At dinner, we made tea but ate our food cold. We didn't want to spend any length of time where we sent the smell of food out into the breeze.

I don't know about the others but I could now clearly identify everyone just by smell. Even their farts had become familiar. It wasn't that we stunk as much as each of us had a signature odor.

I could easily recognize Night; she had the most complex smell. It would change before and during her period. When her period was over, it would revert to what I thought of as *her* smell. I never told her, but during her period she smelled like Chinese food.

Max had a heavy smell. It was dark, with undertones of black licorice, metal, and gun oil. Ninja smelled like a sweaty kid, the beach, and a public Laundromat. Me? I don't know but I am sure there was a smell.

For some reason I didn't sweat as much as the others. Probably because I found that the heat and the load didn't bother me much, especially when I got into the rhythm of moving.

I asked Max about it, since he didn't seem bothered either. I liked getting into the rhythm, but had also noticed it numbed me to the flow. I lost a little of my edge.

"Yeah, I know what you mean," Max said. "It's actually pretty common."

"Shit. I thought I was special."

He laughed. "The only thing special you got going for you is Night." He paused and became more somber. "Some guys will get into the rhythm and then drug for the awareness edge." He shrugged. "It works until it doesn't."

"So what do you do?"

He went silent for a bit. "I'm not sure how to explain it. Nor do I know how I got there. I think it was always there for me, waiting." He paused again. We were sitting on our haunches. I had come to relieve him of the watch. He took a pine twig and used it to scratch at the ground.

"Look, don't get all twisted up about it. Think of it like this. The big *You* plods on while the little *You* rides along and does the watching and listening. After a while you will even be able to detach him and let him fly above you to watch."

Then he leaned closer to me and whispered, "It also helps if you keep your head out of your ass." I heard him laughing to himself all the way back to the camp.

Max told us that when we walked point, it was our call whether to "stop and talk" or "freeze and fade" us if we ran across other groups or individuals. This led to a discussion of what the hand signs for these would be.

I have to admit the whole hand sign thing amused me at first. Then I got to thinking about the usefulness of it. I jumped from that to wanting to invent our own secret language. I started talking about it whenever we took a break.

To my surprise, no one gave me a hard time about it or called me an idiot. Not that they had a problem letting me know when they thought I was being too off-the-wall. They just had different ways of doing it. Max would catch my eye and give a short shake of the head. Night had her public and private versions. Ninja, well, he never thought anything I said was completely stupid. I liked the kid for that.

We didn't come up with a lot of additions, probably because there were only so many signs you could remember in a day. We did create signs that could be used around strangers. We had SOMETHING IS WRONG HERE and I DON'T TRUST THEM and LET'S GO SOON.

I also liked the idea of inventing our own sign language because I figured I could create a special sign for Night and me. I planned on calling it the LET'S SLIP AWAY FOR A QUICKIE sign.

Night was relaxed about a lot of things, but asking her the question in front of the others just didn't seem like the right way to go about it. We also had the problem of standing watches. One of us always seemed to be on watch when we weren't walking.

I showed Night the sign I created. It was actually three signs done very quickly. I thought it was very subtle. She thought it was funny but she agreed to watch for it. I was delighted—and in a hurry to try it out.

The chance came soon enough. Max called a thirty-minute break the next day around midafternoon. We moved up into the woods and dumped our packs. Ninja had his boots off as soon as his ass hit the ground. Max picked a stalk of grass and began chewing it. I caught Night's eye, grinned, and let my hands speak their magic. She grinned back and I stood up.

Then Ninja, the little asshole, began laughing. "Night and Gardener are going to go have a quickie!" he said in a singsong voice between laughing fits.

Max stopped chewing his stalk of grass but didn't take his eyes off the trail. "Good. It's about time. Shut the fuck up, Ninja."

I led Night past him as we left. I planned on slapping him upside the head as we passed by. I didn't need to: Night got to him first. She kicked him solidly in the thigh, generating a nice "Woof!" of pain from him. She was still smiling when we found a flat place to lie down.

# CHAPTER NINE

As we moved further away from D.C. we saw an increasing number of signs that we weren't the only people on the move. And that we were not the only ones in the woods. We passed well-worn paths that led away from the main trail. Occasionally we caught glimpses of Tree People tarps. Sometimes we would see Tree People watching us and pacing us for a short distance, until we left what they claimed as their territory.

The Mover migration was also just starting. This was in response to the new zones and the government's carrot-and-stick program that began with the expansion of the D.C. Zone. The government announced the formation of new communities. It didn't call them "camps"; that word left a bad taste in people's mouths.

The Feds had already had a camp system built and in place for a couple years. They were essentially homeless shelters on a large scale. Designed like military bases, including the gates and fences, the camps provided services for those who needed them.

That original system had schools for children and adults. All participants over eighteen had to complete the GED certification within a year or leave. For those who already had a high school diploma, there was mandatory online training in an approved field. The system also provided job placement, including daycare and transportation.

Clothes were issued: a mass-produced, easily identifiable uniform that was a parody of civilian attire. An entire black market industry sprung up in the camps for the modification of these clothes. There was a minor scandal about the government's efforts to pay media people and others to wear the outfits—at least for propaganda videos going out on the Internet. That blew over fairly quickly.

The drawback—at least as I and many others saw it— was the price you paid. There was urine testing, which proved to be a problem for many until the prohibition on alcohol and marijuana was lifted. They replaced that with a prohibition on nicotine, as it was considered far more evil. You had to take a battery of tests, and your "profile" determined what programs were open or closed to you. And you had to supply a DNA sample. That in turn went into the national database and was part of your identification, which you had to carry at all times.

Weapons, of course, were prohibited. Possession of a weapon meant mandatory jail time. What you ate, or didn't eat, was monitored as part of the health program. Internet use was monitored. Porn sites were not blocked, but those sites whose content was deemed destabilizing were.

Now the government was touting something different with its new program, and on the surface the vision was commendable. The new facilities would provide long-term, total-care disaster relief. The future promised "open, mixed-use, planned communities with a full range of amenities."

Minus all the verbal engineering, the government's goal was to identify, tag, and transfer any wandering or lost sheep into easily manageable flocks.

People were to report to an assembly point where they could sign up for a place in a new community. They would stay in the temporary holding areas while the communities were being built. The plan was that people would participate in the building and earn stakeholder privileges. Whether the government would ever allow people to leave once the communities were done was never mentioned.

The government did not want everyone driving to the assembly points. If refugees brought their vehicles, they might cling to the idea that they could keep them and use them. When they discovered they couldn't, well, the Feds would inherit thousands of abandoned cars. Who needed the headache?

The solution was to send buses into neighborhoods to pick up the people who wanted a new life. They would be sent to the Planned Community Holding Area assigned for their zip code.

Unfortunately, the system didn't work quite as it was supposed to. Then again, it was new and it involved the potential relocation of more than a million people. As with most government programs, it soon became clear that you could game the system. What sparked the gaming was the populace's realization that certain camps were better than others. The Movers were those folks who managed to relocate to a nicer zip code just before the scheduled assembly.

We were counting on the confusion and the government's failure to execute the program as planned to help us get clear of the Zone and into what they were now calling the Badlands.

To my surprise there were more people moving into the Zones than out. For some, it was the direction of the new "promised land." But none of the Movers seemed to be well equipped for what they were trying to do, nor in shape to do it.

We began to find lots of useless belongings jettisoned along the trail. The stuff looked as if it had been dropped wherever people were standing when they decided "to hell with carrying this another foot." No attempt had been made to toss things into the grass or bushes. Some of what we came across included fancy rugs, lamps, a plasma TV, and a lot of clothes. A vacuum cleaner stood out for the total stupidity of hauling such crap. Basically, it was the contents of a yard sale, repeated over and over. The Tree People may have found a use for some of the stuff. At the very least they could resell it at a local market. We encountered a few of them working the trail for the trash.

Night had point the next time we ran into a group of Movers. She insisted on walking point. I was not happy about it, but that was the way it was. It looked to be a two-family group. They were white, clueless, and, like most Mover groups, totally unprepared. They were headed back the way we had come. Night gave us the FREEZE AND FADE sign. We did. I don't think the group even saw us until they were almost on top of us. One of the kids saw Night but didn't say anything. She just stared.

The kid—my guess, she was about seven—looked to be the only one in the group who was enjoying herself. She had been walking, skipping, and hopping her way down the trail. Her Hello Kitty backpack was not much of an encumbrance. The stuffed rabbit that poked out of it was probably the heaviest thing she was carrying.

The adults, especially the females, looked very unhappy. It was hot and they were all packing extra weight in rolls of fat around their waists and asses. So were the men, one of whom looked like a prime candidate for a heart attack. They weren't walking so much as doing a heads-down, sullen trudge to the promised land.

They wore daypacks, probably leftover school backpacks from the kids, and pulled Samsonite luggage. The little wheels had probably been adequate when the trail was asphalt. It no longer was, and one suitcase had already come off its rollers. It didn't stop the woman, who dragged it behind her anyway.

The leader, a white male in his forties, had a hunting rifle slung over his shoulder. One of the other men had a holstered semiautomatic pistol in a SWAT-style holster. As he was the one who looked on the edge of cardiac arrest, I didn't see much of a threat.

Night didn't want to bother with them. If she had stepped just a little further back into the bushes, they might have trudged past us. Then again, I doubt if the kid who had seen her would have kept silent.

The kid stopped and was almost run over by the woman behind her. She pointed at Night and said, "Hey, Mom! Look at the woman with the gun!"

The G word got everyone's attention. The entire Mover flock stumbled to a halt. We advanced to support Night with our weapons ready. Cardiac Dad put his hand on the butt of his pistol. I saw Night give him the look and shake her head. By then Max and I were facing them, and Ninja was somewhere behind us watching our backs.

The leader was the first to speak. "Hi there! What can we do for you?" This was accompanied by a wide grin.

Max answered for us. "Nothing. We're just passing through. Same as you."

. The rest of the Movers eyed us with a mix of exhaustion, apathy, and curiosity. I would say they were all glad for the chance to take a breather. One of the women certainly was.

She let the handle of her suitcase drop and sat down on it with a plop. I heard her mutter, "Thank you, Jeebus." It was as if she'd given a signal to the rest of the herd. Everyone dropped handles, packs and plopped down, too.

"Okay, everyone, let's take a break," the leader announced. I had to grin at that. One of the women, perhaps his wife, rolled her eyes and began fanning herself.

She looked over at Night. "Hey, honey. You wouldn't have a Pepsi or a beer inside that pack, would ya?"

"No." Night moved past them, watching them out of the corner of her eye, as she took up position a little further down the trail.

"I didn't think so. Damn."

"Don't mind her," Leader man said, indicating the woman. "You wouldn't have any extra water"—he saw the look in our eyes—"for the kids, of course."

In the back was a twelve-year-old boy with long brown hair. I watched as he cringed when the Leader added "for the kids." *Interesting*, I thought. Probably his stepfather. *Hopefully*.

Max just stared at Leader man. "Hey, kids, you thirsty?"

The little girl piped up, "No, but Mr. Bunny is."

"Okay. Bring Mr. Bunny over here. How about you, kid?"

The boy nodded his head.

"You got a bottle or canteen?"

"We appreciate this," Leader man told Max, who ignored him.

"Here," said the woman sitting next to Cardiac Man. She reached in her pack and pulled out a two-liter bottle of Pepsi. She drained the little bit that was left and handed the bottle to the boy. "Freaking Pepsi is for shit as a cure for thirst."

The little girl took Mr. Bunny out of her pack and held him up to Max. Max uncapped his water bottle and held the opening up to Mr. Bunny's lips for a minute until the girl pulled him away.

"Mr. Bunny says, 'Thank you!'"

"You're welcome, Mr. Bunny. Do you want a drink too?"

She nodded her head yes. "All we have is Pepsi and Mrs. Slarmy isn't sharing."

"It's *Slarami*, and yes I have been sharing, you little—" She cut off whatever she was going to say when she saw Max's look.

We had two Camelbacks that we weren't using. The problem here wasn't finding water; it was filtering it. Max took the two-liter bottle from the boy and poured about a liter of water into it.

"Keep it. Make sure you and the girl drink a lot before you let anyone else have some."

The boy nodded.

Leader man decided he needed to assert himself. "Look, you guys are going the wrong way."

Max smiled. "Is that so?"

"You should come with us. That's it!" He looked around at his group. "Nobody here would mind, right?" He got a few heads nodding except for the woman sitting on her luggage. She just shook her head and muttered something that he ignored.

"That's the ticket! Why, you stick with us and I bet I can get you in. You know they say these communities are really nice and spaces are going quickly. Why, I heard they were not going to be making a lot of these communities so you'd be getting in on the ground floor, and—"

"Save it," Max spit out.

"But—"

Max patted the girl on the head. "Take care of Mr. Bunny."

"Don't worry, I will. Say goodbye, Mr. Bunny." She waved his little furry paw.

Max growled, "Move out."

We walked away. I heard the luggage-sitter say, "Worked that ol' sales magic again, didn't you, honey?" and laugh.

His only reply was, "You heard the man. Move out!"

Max was moody the rest of the day. So was Night. Later that evening, after we had eaten and before she went on watch, she pulled me aside.

"Do you ever think about kids, Gardener?"

I thought about it a bit. It was a serious question, especially coming from her, so I wanted to answer her honestly. "Not really." I saw the light in her eyes change. "But that kid today was cute. You want to know something?"

She nodded her head.

"I wanted to kill all those people and take the kids. Mr. Bunny deserves better."

She nodded again. A faint grin appeared. "That might have been a little extreme, Gardener."

I shrugged, "I know. I'd have to kill them away from the kids and then come up with a convincing story."

"Gardener." She shook her head. "You know there are other ways."

"Sure. You can buy them."

She punched me. "You know what I am saying."

"I know." The only thing was, I had never thought of it like that: Night and me, hatching little gunslingers. Maybe a couple of gunslingers and a Mr. Bunny lover. She could be a ninja bunny lover . . . "What are you thinking?"

I told her about hatching gunslingers and a ninja bunny lover. I was surprised. Her eyes welled up and she pulled me close.

She whispered in my ear, "When?"

"When we find a safe place to settle down."

We quit talking and I became distracted. My last thought before losing myself in her was, *But I don't think I want to stop killing.*

# CHAPTER TEN

We kept moving. It took us almost a week to get beyond the heavily built-up areas, partly because the sprawl covered so much land, but mostly because Night and I were not physically up to the challenge yet.

Instead of pushing for miles, Max would run us through tactical drills. He would stop, pull us off to the side of the trail, and ask us questions: "What would you do if we began taking fire from over there?" Over there, in this case, being a creek bed. Or, "Suppose the point tells you he suspects there are people waiting to ambush us. How are you going to do a counterambush?"

We would work each scenario from the perspective of being in charge, and we'd create a plan and detail what was expected of each person when the plan was executed. There was no sense of unreality anymore about doing this. This was our reality.

We met only one organized group along the way. We came up on them from behind. They had someone watching their back, and he reacted as we approached. I got a brief glimpse of women and children ahead of them, but they moved off the trail within seconds after I had been spotted. It was tense for a minute or two.

I had point and gave the FREEZE AND FADE sign, followed by FORM ON ME. I wanted to talk to them. They must have been doing the same thing, because within a minute four more men joined the drag guy. They spread out and stared at us.

"Feel like talking?" I yelled at them.

"Yeah." This came from their leader, a black male in the chocolate-chip camo pants that were worn by soldiers in Iraq at the beginning of that misadventure. He had on a green T-shirt and a military load-bearing vest similar to what Ninja wore. So did three of his other men.

We wore regular hunting-style vests. Max and I had taken to wearing them in the city in order to tone down the GI Joe vibe. Later, when we sewed on our Fairfax City Police patches, we stayed with them. In the D.C. Zone, hunting vests were the de facto uniform of Homeland Security plainclothes types. We felt it made us more legit.

The rest of his people were similarly attired, if not in camo then in neutral color clothing. The guy on the far left looked to be wearing pleated khaki Dockers, another part of the civilian uniform in the D.C. Zone.

Like us, they were armed with shotguns and handguns. They looked comfortable with them and competent in what they were doing.

I changed my grip on the shotgun so that I was only holding it with one hand, the stock tucked into my armpit and the barrel pointed down. I started walking toward the Leader, who mirrored what I did and moved to meet me. We met in the center of the path but made no attempt to shake each other's hands.

"Let's be quick about this," he said. "I don't like standing around in the open during daytime."

Max sauntered up, looked the guy up and down, and said, "I know you."

"Sonofabitch!" the Leader yelled, grabbing Max in an embrace. "How the hell are you, man? I heard you were around and doing things. Let me guess—you got to be Gardener."

I nodded and said, "Yeah." Now we shook hands. Out of the corner of my eye I saw his people perceptibly stand down.

"Well, shit. Let's get of this sun." Over his shoulder he yelled, "We're cool. Put out security and let them take a break."

Turning back to Max, he said, "Damn, moving kids and women is like herding cats. So talk to me, bro. I figured you for a lifer and a bird at least. I was much surprised to hear you had walked away. Man, where is that medal I heard about?"

Max's smile went away. "I left it hanging on Charlie McBride's cross at Arlington. He deserved it a hell of a lot more than me."

"Ah, shit." The guy paused, shook his head, and went somber. "Yeah . . . Charlie. Too many for nothing, Max." He shook his shoulders and brightened up. "So give me some intel. Talk to me, Max, and I'll talk to you. Hell, I'll talk to you anyway. But seriously, I want to know what you're thinking."

Max gave him a quick briefing about what we had seen so far. While he talked, I was mentally shaking my head in disbelief. Did Max know every marine that had served overseas in the past decade? How did that work?

And how did he get around to killing anyone if he spent all his time socializing? I shrugged it off as just another one of those mysteries of life.

The Leader listened as Max ran things down, only asking a few questions. At the end he said, "You're moving kind of slow, Max. You should have made it this far days ago. You got anybody else out there in those trees?"

"No, just us. Call it a shakedown cruise."

He nodded. "Yeah, I hear you. I got a lot of dependents back there. It definitely changes things. My people are good. Almost all of them are vets. When they came back they got a raw deal, especially the guard and the reserve. Cutting active duty by 35 percent in the middle of this shit—no work, no anything really—has not helped. Got a lot of well-trained, pissed-off people wandering around out there."

Max nodded. "So what do you have for me?"

The Leader didn't have anything really new about the local area. But he had an interesting theory about what was going on behind the scenes.

"I think this is the first stage of a counterinsurgency operation. The Feds are going to register and render harmless everyone inside the zone of control. Right now they are picking an area and sweeping it. The Tree People are being given a choice: Go to a planned community or go to a rehabilitation center."

"What the hell is a rehabilitation center?" I asked.

"Why, it's a place that helps you, of course," he chuckled mirthlessly. "It is where you can live in an environment that will integrate you into society. They, being the government, realize that many people have suffered traumatizing loss, including PTSD, and need help to become productive members of the community again. Others need to learn or relearn basic lifestyle skills."

I laughed. "That sounded like you were reading it line for line from a government web site."

"That's because it was almost verbatim from one of their posters. I am surprised you haven't seen one. Anyway, the word is that the authorities plan to register everyone, including their DNA samples. Those who, like us, are not getting with the program are free to leave. Of course, they plan to do the DNA thing to us as we leave the Zone. Plus, run background checks, since they do not want to allow 'antisocial elements' to escape to other communities. Flush us out now and deal with the leftovers later, I figure the plan is."

Max nodded. "Yeah, that is what I see happening too. All velvet gloves until they feel secure enough to show the steel fist. So, where you going?"

For the first time, the Leader looked guarded. "We're headed into southern Ohio. There's a lot of empty infrastructure out there. What about you?"

"Pretty much the same, and for the same reasons. Probably not this year, though. This year we will stick around. I'm thinking the Stephens City area."

"Okay, Max. It's been real, but we got to roll. I get uneasy staying too long in one place now. Why don't ya'll throw in with us?"

Max grinned. "It might come down to that later. Not now."

"Yeah, that's about what I expected. We'll be around Napoleon, Ohio, probably. Listen, Max . . ."

"Yeah?"

"You always managed to come through when no one else did. So I am going to try you now and see if you can surprise me. You have any tetanus vaccine?"

Max laughed. "You're going to have to try harder than that, Dakota. Give me a minute. You need a syringe to go with that?"

*Dakota?* I thought. *Who the hell names a black male "Dakota"?*

"No shit?" said the Leader. He was incredulous. "Man, oh man. What do you want for it? We can pay in gold or ammo. I got some frags, too. Perfect for cleaning house."

"No. No charge."

"Ri-i-ight. Let me guess. Future favor?"

"Future favor," said Max.

"Done."

Dakota turned to one of the guys with him. "Jo-Jo, go with them and bring back what they give you. Don't dick around. Catch up if you have to." Then, turning back to us.

"Alright, Max. It's been real. Gardener, later."

They embraced again and he was gone. Jo-Jo followed us back to Night, who had most of the meds in her pack.

Max had us take a break after Jo-Jo got the vaccine and left.

We were sitting on a large mound about twenty yards off the trail. It was a mix of Virginia vegetation and quartz boulders, probably dumped here illegally by someone who was clearing an old pasture for building. Back where we had come from, there had been a number of ancient Indian villages or campsites. The quartz outcroppings drew them, along with the proximity of the Potomac River.

I remembered reading that the strip mall near the motel had once been an Indian village with an estimated fifty to sixty people living there. It had not stopped the bulldozers from building on top of it. Back then nothing stopped the bulldozers in Virginia.

Ninja had found wild blackberries growing off the side of the mound. They weren't ripe yet, and I didn't care for them because of all the seeds, but he was busy stuffing his face. He was supposed to be on watch, but no one, including Max, said anything. We sat there for a bit. There was a faint breeze, and since this was Virginia in the summer no one was in a hurry to get back on the trail. Plus, Max wanted Dakota's group to get a decent lead on us.

After a while Max told Ninja, "Get done stuffing your face. I want you to drag your ass over here."

"Okay," Ninja replied. He looked somewhat embarrassed but that didn't stop him from shoving a few more berries in his mouth before he joined us.

Night looked at him and shook her head. "Wipe your mouth off. Damn if you don't look like a two-year-old who just discovered jelly." He wiped his mouth off on his shirt. Night groaned.

"I have been remiss in keeping you all updated on what I've been considering as far as long-term planning," Max began. "This is partially because of how fast things have happened and partially because we are now at Plan C, which really has no planning. All I have is an outline that's been forming in my head. A lot of it is still pretty vague. All of it is subject to change. I'm going to tell you what I've got, and if you got anything to add, please do."

Night and I looked at each other, then back to Max, and nodded. Ninja just stared.

"We know where we are going. The farm should be good enough for the winter. Food is probably going to be an issue but we can deal with it." He grinned like a wolf. "There is always food if you know where to look."

We all grinned back at him. We must have looked like a wolf pack getting warmed up for a hunt.

"I just don't see the farm being viable over the long term. It's possible. A lot will depend on the town and how the Feds decide to play it out."

"Yeah, too close to the Zone, especially if they decide to push it out again," Night chimed in. "No way are they going to not patrol and police their borders."

I looked at her in admiration. She caught my look, said, "Quit gawking," and threw an acorn shell at me.

"She's right, Gardener. We are also going to have to expand. We need bodies, but people we can trust."

"Why didn't we go with the black dude?"

I knew this one. "Because, Ninja, eventually it would have come down to who was running things, and we may not have won that battle."

Max looked at me. "We would have won. Long term we might have lost, probably through betrayal. Short and middle range? Yeah, we would have won."

That made sense to Ninja, I think. At least he didn't ask anything else.

"We'll move on eventually, because we need a place far enough away that anyone will have to work to get to us. I'd like to get past Dakota, or anyone like him, before we settle down. We need a buffer for a while. Let them go through him to get to us. We need a machine shop. We need food. We need established infrastructure that doesn't require major rebuilding. I am not going to be a goatherd in the sticks for the rest of my life, and neither are you people."

Well, I was okay with that. I wasn't sure what I wanted to be. Actually, I didn't find what we were doing right now all that bad. A little boring perhaps.

"As I said," Max continued, interrupting my musing, "we are also going to need people."

"Like, what kind of people, Max?"

"Good question, Night. I'd like to say we'd know them when we see them, but that is shit for an answer. I've been thinking about it and we really need three types. God, I would give Ninja's left nut for three or four good NCOs with a couple tours behind them. That woman who manned that 50-caliber back at the shelter would have been perfect."

He paused here; we all did.

Night and Ninja's faces both sank. The female gunner and Night's parents had been in the motel when the missiles hit. We never had time to move the collapsed portions of the building to find their corpses. Night had not cried herself to sleep for the past two weeks. From the look on her face, my guess was she would tonight. Max realized that the conversation was not moving in a productive direction.

"Yeah, well . . . may they rest in peace. The other two types of people are ones with skills. Real skills. One of those skills is the ability to organize. That can be the hardest to find."

"You mean like Carol?" I said. It was petty, but I got a bit of satisfaction from the fleeting shadow that crossed Max's face.

"Yeah, like Carol." The look he shot me told me I had scored, and that he also knew why I had gone for it.

"What about computer people?" Ninja asked.

We all grinned. Most adolescent males were in heat all the time. With Ninja it was a close race between women and online gaming. He hadn't been getting either one with any regularity lately, if at all.

"Yeah, them too, Ninja."

Well, he was back to being a happy camper with that news.

"What I am hoping for are creators, not destroyers. Finding someone who will raid a farmer's corn is not going to be a problem. Finding people who can grow, store, and sell corn at a fair price will be."

"Teachers, not demagogues," Night added.

"Exactly."

"Once we find them, Max, then what? Do we invite them to dinner and let everyone take a look at them?"

"I don't know, Gardener. Probably we will all vote on inviting them into our clan."

Ninja and Night liked this. They understood clan recruitment policies.

"So, Max, when we get to our promised land, what do you see our roles being?" Whenever Night opened a sentence with *So*, I knew she wanted more than a casual reply. It was a good question, too.

"I don't know, Night. What do you want to be?"

*Damn*, I had not thought this out at all. If we created or ended up running a small town, well, then Night and I would be like minor nobility. We could have kids to keep her happy, and I would still get to kick ass!

Night frowned and paused. She was thinking this out carefully. "I'm not really interested in killing people . . . but I like figuring out what they plan on doing. I guess that would make me, oh, the S2?"

*Huh?* I didn't know what an S2 was, but Max sure did. They were grinning at each other. Whatever it was, she was now it.

"How about you, Ninja? What you want to be?"

Ninja did not even hesitate. "Head of IT. Computer king!"

Yeah, that made sense. Who was left? Me. I started thinking furiously. What was the socially acceptable job description for gunslinger?

Max looked at me and grinned. "Gardener, we already know your answer."

"We do? What would that be?"

They all answered at once: "Chief of police!"

I liked that. "Yeah. Except I want to be called Marshal."

# CHAPTER ELEVEN

We talked for a bit more. Then Max figured we might as well make camp for the night. We started into the usual routine and even had extra time to do odds and ends, like maintenance on our equipment.

When it grew dark Max called me over. He didn't say anything other than "Follow me." We went to the far side of the mound. An old SUV had been left there. The vegetation was reclaiming it but it was still recognizable. Max climbed onto the hood and extended his hand to me.

"I would try the roof but I don't think it will hold."

I looked at him quizzically.

"Just look around. Scan the horizon."

I did. There were lights in a handful of houses off in the distance. Not far from them, a few miles off to the right, it looked like a cluster of businesses still had power and a reason to be open.

"I don't get it, Max. All I see is darkness with a few buildings lit up east of us."

"Right. Happy Fourth of July." Then he jumped down off the truck and headed back to camp.

We moved out the next morning. Every morning before we shouldered the packs and stepped out, Max gave us a five-minute brief on how much distance he wanted to cover, what we would pass through—open country or built-up areas—and often what he had noticed in us the previous day that he thought needed improvement.

Today was different in that we had literally hit the end of the trail. We had run out of county-maintained asphalt or gravel a while back and had started to follow a mix of power line clearings and local paths that led in the right direction.

The utility clearings had trails. People used to hunt and run dirt bikes along them, and we saw signs that they still did. For the first time, we came across tire tracks from ATVs and four-wheel drives. Besides hunting, someone had been back here dropping trees for firewood.

Max cautioned us about hunters. We had passed a fairly fresh gut pile the previous day. "I doubt if the dumb-asses who used to shoot anything that moved still hunt around here. Whoever is hunting here now is probably good at it. Remember, if they're hunting, they are probably in camo and carrying a rifle. That means they out range us. If you're in shotgun range and they point the barrel at you, take them. If they are in a stand, and you see them first, freeze and fade us. We'll scope them and see what we see. Last thing I want to do is shoot Billy Bob by mistake."

*Who gives a shit if Billy Bob doesn't come back?* I thought. But I realized the point Max was making. Billy Bob might have a bunch of cousins. Why stir up unnecessary trouble?

Max told us we were going to change our tactics. "I want to walk the edges of the woods or follow the streambeds, which are usually wooded, if we need to cross open fields. We'll follow the power lines when we can, staying to the edge of the tree line. I want to minimize our time out in the open. In three more days we should be at our pickup point. Any questions?"

Night asked him, "This farm has showers, right?" She had asked the same question the previous day.

"Yep. You can even be first in."

She grinned. Myself? I had visions of sharing that shower.

Being off the asphalt was a lot better in some ways. Less heat, I noticed. But in other ways it wasn't. Where the bikes had torn up the trail, you had to be more careful with your footing, especially when you got tired. I didn't want to be the one to twist an ankle and delay Night from getting to her shower.

About two hours later we faded into the woods when we heard the whine of motorcycles coming up fast. We were on the power lines so I wasn't surprised. What did surprise me were the riders—just a couple of teenagers racing along the path, going way too fast and enjoying the hell out of it. One of them had a girl on the back wearing a visorless helmet. Her grin was delightful, even from a distance.

It was a bit surreal seeing them, a reminder that there was still a world out there that lived, at least partly, in the old reality.

We weren't clicking off the miles. The main reason was that we had to freeze and fade three or four times a day. We did it for light planes, helicopters, bikers, and Movers that we didn't want to deal with. Plus, we moved with the cover. Not a lot of straight paths to follow.

We learned the rudiments of land navigation using a compass. Ninja turned out to be a natural at it. We also learned the correct way to walk a hill line or rise. Basically, it came down to not silhouetting yourself. That part was easy. Online gaming had been good training for some of this stuff.

Days ago I had asked Max, "Why didn't we bring a GPS?"

His reply made sense. "Because I didn't want to raise a bunch of tech cripples."

It was the same reason none of us had cell phones. With cell phones you had the added bonus of becoming a beacon for trackers. I knew Ninja still had his iPod in the hope that someday he could put a charge on it. He'd have to be somewhere safe enough that he could relax enough to listen to it.

The Burners had a point. What use were half the electronics we owned other than being delivery systems for addictions to that all-consuming product?

We moved on. The next three days were rather uneventful. On the third day we started running parallel to a county highway.

The biggest excitement came when I disturbed a water moccasin that was sunning itself on a rock in a creek bed. It scared the living crap out of me. I was lucky. It decided not to be aggressive and faded back into the water. They can be mean. I have thrown rocks at them to chase them away and had them decide to chase me away. They usually won, unless I was feeling especially ornery. I really hate snakes.

Our pickup place was an abandoned gas station off the same county road we had been paralleling for the last day. We had camped within half a mile of it the night before.

Max disappeared around 0400 hours to take a look at the place. Before he left he told us what it looked like, how we would approach it, and where we would meet if we had to run. I hoped we wouldn't have to. I was really looking forward to that shower.

Tommy, Max's buddy from the marines, was supposed to be there every morning at 0630 for the next week. He would chalk a X on the wall of the gas station if he had been by. A circle meant go away and find a way to contact him.

We came up behind the gas station about an hour early. There was a little patch of brush and trees about a hundred yards from the station. We would stay there while Max went to wait for Tommy. We sat around, not speaking, watching the sun come up. Before he left, Max gave me the Barrett.

"Hopefully, we won't need it," I told him.

"Better not," Night answered for him, "or we are checking into a motel for the night." I was beginning to think the woman had a shower fetish.

About forty-five minutes later we saw an old pickup truck with a shell on the back pull in. I recognized the truck. It was Tommy's, and it looked like he was alone. Then Max whistled. I sent the others in while I broke down the Barrett and wrapped it up. No point in advertising that we had quality toys.

Everyone was in the truck by the time I got there: Max in front, Night and Ninja in the back. I jumped in back and Tommy pulled slowly away. His muffler had gotten worse since the last time I'd ridden with him.

Once he hit the county road, he slid open the back window and yelled over his shoulder, "Damn, you sure got uglier. I didn't think that was possible."

I flipped him off. "Fix your muffler, Billy Bob!"

He grinned. "Yeah, maybe I will when they start making parts again." He turned back to say something to Max, and I stretched out in the truck bed, elbowing Ninja to make space, and tried to fall asleep.

Our arrival was uneventful. Nothing much had changed since the last time I had been here. Tommy's kids came out to meet us. It was kind of cool to see them again. Not only did they remember me, but they also seemed happy to see me, in that shy way little kids have. We did the introduction thing and went up to his house to catch up on things.

To my delight, there was my old good nurse, Donna, who had been babysitting the kids, putting breakfast on the table. Real coffee, pancakes, and eggs. Syrup, too! My sweet tooth went into overdrive. I was really wolfing them down when it registered that the table had gone quiet.

I looked up from my plate and saw everyone grinning at me. "What?" I asked. Not waiting for an answer, I went back to eating and they went back to talking.

Night slipped into the kitchen to talk to Donna. She came back, grabbed her pack and went upstairs without looking back. I was torn for a second. What to do: Eat pancakes with syrup or join Night for a shower?

The pancakes won.

# CHAPTER TWELVE

I tuned back in when Tommy started talking about what was going on around the new homestead. He was having problems. I listened for a bit and realized that Tommy couldn't handle his neighbors.

Then again, from the sound of it, neither could anyone else in town. Oh, there were exceptions. Apparently there were a couple of guys in town who had been let go from the army when they did the great downsize.

I didn't quite understand what he was saying here. Something about it not just being them; it was the family network they were born into. Apparently they had a shit-load of homicidal kinfolk that they could call upon somewhere in the Appalachian Mountains. Or nearby trailer parks. Or the next town.

Yet it didn't ring true. If so, where were they? I didn't hear any mention of these kinfolk actually being spotted. I could picture them easily enough: white trash tweaker heads who needed to call going to a wedding by its real name—a family reunion.

I had run across a few of those peckerheads in my time. Never any obvious muscle to them, but, just like Juan from tortilla land, they could work all day. Forget fist fighting with them. You had to kill them. They were smart in a sly way. If prison or drugs didn't get them, then the Lord did. We got along well together the few times I had to hang with them. Usually it was because Mother had landed us in a neighborhood infested with them.

Tommy's neighbors, the McKinleys, were trying to fill the power vacuum left by the resignation of the local police. Funny how if you didn't pay them and provide health benefits, the police just didn't want to die protecting your F-150 from part strippers.

The evil McKinleys consisted of Ma, Pa, and two boys. One boy was a bit "slow" and the other was a nut job with issues. Supposedly he was married, but his wife had fled with their three kids two months ago. So the boys were living at home, probably back in the same rooms they had grown up in. I wouldn't be surprised if they had the same posters on the wall. My guess was Nut Job had one of Pamela Anderson. She was probably still considered hot around here.

The family also had heavy equipment that still worked. The old man was the only way people got snow removed from the side roads and the main road in town. There were locals with plows on their trucks or tractors. As long as they stuck to their driveways and service roads, then the McKinley family left them alone.

But try to plow a road in what Pa McKinley called "the Franchise" and you would come out one morning and find your vehicle didn't run anymore. Push the issue and somebody would find your body slumped over the wheel. They only had to go that far once. It was enough.

The McKinleys got their franchise because folks couldn't be sure the county and state would show up anymore. The county crews would still plow, but they wanted cash or something of equal value before they showed up. Little towns with out-of-the-way roads were especially vulnerable to this. Tommy's little town had had all of its snow removing equipment repossessed three years ago.

Every year the McKinleys got a little more out of control, so people tried to tread lightly around them. If not for the reason that they liked driving on plowed roads, then because Pa and the boys would beat the crap out of you, given the right incentive. Nowadays, not kissing their ass correctly was incentive enough.

It was typical small-town politics played out in the absence of any organized and armed authority to put a to stop it. A few frayed threads of morality and civil responsibility were the only things keeping events from getting really ugly. That and the possibility that what was happening to the local and state governments was temporary. They didn't want to push too hard, since no one wanted to explain to Homeland Security how so-and-so ended up dead, nor who was probably collecting and pocketing the tax money.

Tommy saved the best for last, as far as I was concerned. The nut job McKinley boy had taken a shine to Donna and had begun dropping by her place. He would also come by Tommy's when he saw her car there. After all, they were neighbors. Apparently Tommy's idea of discouraging him had been to hide her car in the garage. So far that had yielded mixed success. It sounded like Nut Job was not big on *no*. His type never was.

We moved outside and sat around on the porch. Night came down from taking her shower smelling good. Real good. It just emphasized how bad the rest of us reeked of sweat.

It was pleasant to see Donna again, but it was also a bit uncomfortable. I was happy that she and Night seemed to be getting along so far. At least there were no obvious claws yet.

They were both Asian, but as Night had reminded me—the last time with a smack upside the head—all Asians were not the same. I was really glad I had choked back what was in my head, which was "But you all look alike."

Seeing them side-by-side I could see a difference. Night was Chinese while Donna was a Filipina. Different body types and facial features. I was starting to go down some X-rated hallways when Max snapped me back to reality.

"Okay. Since we are together I thought we might talk about what we're going to do."

*Oh, damn*, I could already feel myself going numb and we had just started. I hated meetings. I also was not thrilled about the glare Night was shooting me. *Shit*. I sat up straighter and tried to look interested.

I managed to feign interest for about thirty minutes before I began to get restless. I really did not care about planting grains or deciding which were the best. I'd give it fifteen more minutes and then I was gone. I would deal with Night's hissy fit later. Hey, I never even touched Donna!

"I want to berm the farmhouse and outbuildings," Max was saying, "which means we're going to have to talk to Mr. McKinley."

"That should be fun," I added. That was just to let everyone know I was listening and involved in the conversation. It didn't stop Night from rolling her eyes. She was really immature sometimes.

I left the meeting when they went back to talking about cattle, goats, and chickens. Night and I had the trailer to bunk in. We were sharing it with Ninja, who had the other bedroom. He could charge his iPod but he still had no computer access, other than the half hour or so he could get on Tommy's computer each day.

I didn't even bother to ask Tommy for time on it. I realized I really didn't care if I was on the Internet. There just wasn't anything out there that interested me anymore.

I walked across the yard and into the trailer. I suppose I could have found some chores to do but I didn't feel like it. I had figured out pretty quickly the last time I was here that I wasn't a farmer, nor did I want to be. Instead I sat down in the living room and cleaned my guns. I enjoyed doing that. Plus, it looked like I might be using them soon.

At this point I had the shotgun, my Vaquero, and a black powder Colt 1851 Navy revolver. I loved that gun but I was really unsure about it. I had fired it in the backyard a couple weeks before we left. It had been in Jake's armory. I had noticed it and instantly lusted after it, more so than his later generation Colts. Much to my surprise, he had given it to me.

It felt better in my hand than the Vaquero. It wasn't as accurate, nor did it have the range or punch. It also was not a gun you could reload in a hurry. You could supposedly swap out the cylinders, but the only way I saw that happening was if you called for a timeout. Not going to happen in the middle of a shootout.

I had been carrying it in my pack unloaded. Now I decided to load it. It beat digging holes in hard-pack clay. I had to go on the Internet the first time to get instructions on loading. Afterward, I understood why cartridges were such a huge improvement in the technology for killing people. It was obvious to me every time I measured out the powder, loaded the ball, greased it, and set the caps.

I was working on the Colt when Night came in.

"Hey," I said.

She didn't reply. She just stood there in the door. I raised an eyebrow.

"Max wants to talk to you back at the house in about fifteen minutes."

"Yeah. Any idea about what?"

"My guess is it's about the same thing that has you cleaning your guns." She sat down on the couch next to me.

"So what did I miss?"

She summarized and I half-listened while I finished up the Colt. Then she sat there and silently watched me.

Out of nowhere she asked, "Did you fuck your nurse while you were here?"

I had been sitting there, tracing the engraving on the Colt with my fingernail, letting my mind idle when she dropped that verbal bomb. I set the gun down gently on the coffee table and turned to face her.

"No."

"Would you have?"

*Damn.* I really wish she had been content with a simple no. Now I had to decide whether to lie. I may be a lot of things but I am not a liar.

"No."

I am also not stupid.

She cocked her head, looked at me, and let it pass. "Don't ever lie to me or cheat on me. You understand?"

I nodded my head.

"You promise?"

"I promise."

She kissed me slowly and pulled away. "Go see Max. Your time is up."

I walked back to the house feeling like I had just gotten married.

# CHAPTER THIRTEEN

Max was waiting for me on the porch, eating peanuts and sitting in the old rocking chair that I liked. I sat down next to him and propped my boots up on the railing. He rocked and I sat for about five minutes before he said anything.

"You know, I don't really like farming."

"Yep. I don't either."

"But you got to do what you got to do."

"Isn't that 'A man's got to do what a man's got to do'?"

He flicked a peanut shell at me. "I got my lines. Get your own."

"So, what time tomorrow?"

"Well, I say early, but not too early. Don't want to catch them at breakfast and get them all upset before we even get acquainted."

"Yeah, that might be counterproductive."

"Then again, we got chores to do and I want to get moving on this as soon as possible. You know how to drive heavy equipment?"

"Nope. Can't be all that hard, pardner."

He laughed. Then he laughed some more. "Yeah, I'm getting the same vibe. You think you can get your ass out of bed and be ready to go by 0830?"

"Yeah. Leave me some of the peanuts."

He handed me the rest of the bag, stood up and stretched, and walked back into the house. I swore I heard spurs jangling as he did.

I woke up around 0730 the next morning. Night had already left. We both usually got up around 0530, sometimes earlier. Since I had an appointment I had decided to sleep in. Plus, she had kept me up late. Not that I minded.

I rolled out of bed and hit the bathroom. I spent a little longer than usual. "Look good, feel good" was my motto. I figured it gave me a little more of an edge.

I brewed up a couple cups of coffee and cleaned my guns. No vest and shotgun for this. We didn't want to present an overly threatening appearance and get their backs up right away. I skipped breakfast, just in case. I didn't want anything in my stomach. Plus, I usually was hungry afterward. At the last minute I slipped the Navy Revolver in my belt.

At 0815 I walked over to the house. Max was waiting. He was sitting in the same position I had seen him in last night. I didn't bother to sit down.

"You ready?" he asked. We both knew it was a rhetorical question.

He was wearing jeans, a ball cap, and a long shirt. I knew he had his .45 under it. He looked like he had grown up here. I looked like I always did—like I was from somewhere else. He set his ball cap so it felt right on his head, stood up, and stretched. Well, it was more of a half-stretch. He cut it off when he saw the Navy.

"You got to be kidding." It wasn't a question. It was a statement.

"Nope. Don't worry. I got a plan."

"Well, I hope it doesn't include that ancient piece of hardware. Jesus, Gardener. You worry me with this retro shit sometimes."

We were going to walk to the McKinley farmhouse. Hell, it was less than half a mile if we cut across the fields. The heat wasn't bad this early in the morning. It was probably less than ninety degrees, and the humidity was about the same. I waited until we had cleared the main house area and jumped the fence before asking Max the question that had been puzzling me.

"What's up with your boy, Tommy? I thought he was one of those supermarines."

"Yeah, good question. We talked around it a bit. The short answer is he doesn't have it in him anymore." He paused. "It happens."

"Yeah, that's what I thought. It's no big deal."

Max looked at me quizzically. "That, coming from you? I'm surprised."

I laughed. "Damn, Max. I'm not always an asshole. At least I hope not. Look at him. He works hard. He kept himself and his kids fed when it fell apart for him. He keeps a clean house. So he was once a blade—now he's a dust mop. The world needs people like him. Shit, someone has to feed us."

He laughed. "Gardener, you are such a caring individual. Next thing you know you'll be hugging people."

It was my turn to laugh. The farmhouse was close enough to make out details now. I loosened the Ruger in its holster and slipped the leather loop off the hammer that helped hold it in place. "Yep. Time to share the love, buddy."

I had read that when approaching some countries by sea, Japan for instance, you know at about four hundred nautical miles out that you are getting close. How? The amount of trash in the water steadily increases.

It was the same thing approaching the McKinley farm-house. Not that they were unusual in that. It was pretty common in this part of the world. Everybody over the past few decades had consumed a lot of stuff. On a farm, a lot of that stuff was big, too big to stuff in a trash can. You put it in your own dump or left it where it died.

The house itself was neat, with a well-tended yard. It had been painted white in the past few years. There was a garden, somewhat overgrown with weeds, and chickens running around. They had a nice-sized German shepherd chained to a steel post. He noticed us and started barking our approach to the people in the house.

Not that he had to. We had already been spotted. Two almost young white guys were standing around a black Ford F-150 with its hood up. From what Tommy had told us, we knew we were looking at the McKinley boys.

Even without a description I would have known which one was the nut job bothering Donna. The wife-beater T-shirt and can of Bud in his hand were definite giveaways. *Starting early with the breakfast of champions there, bucka-roo*, I thought when I saw him. He was wearing a black semiautomatic pistol in a black nylon holster.

The slow one was as big as he had been described. He wore black jeans and a NASCAR T-shirt. He didn't look like he was armed. Max had overdressed for the occasion by wearing a shirt with actual buttons and no silk-screening on it.

We stopped about ten feet from them. Before Max could say anything, Nut Job looked at us and said, "What do you two peckerheads want? We don't have work, food, or money."

"We would like to talk to your Paw if he is home."

*Paw?* I almost busted out laughing. Max had gone hick on me.

Nut Job must have noticed my brief grin. "What the fuck you smiling about?"

His brother chimed in, "Yeah. What you smiling about?"

*My God, it's the echo twins*, I thought. But what I said was, "Nothing. Just a nice day, and I am so happy that the Lord has blessed us." *Want to get hick, Max? I can do hick.*

Slow One yelled, "Paw!" loud enough to startle his rodent-looking brother.

"Goddamn it! Don't yell in my ear, you dumb fuck!" Then to us he said, "What you want with my Paw and what the hell are you wearing around your waist, preacher?"

Just about then Paw stuck his head out the front door and yelled, "Who the fuck are they and what do they want?"

*Damn.* This family was already starting to irritate me. I really dislike loud people.

Max said, pretty loud for him, "We want to talk to you and the missus."

Slow One started to repeat what Max had just said, but his brother punched him in the arm and told him to shut up. Then he yelled it to his Paw.

"Just a minute!" Paw went inside and came back out carrying a shotgun. As he approached us, he yelled, "You are trespassing! You sure as hell better not be selling anything!" He was a big man. When he got to us I could tell he was also one of those white men whose face always looked like they were blushing. "Okay. You got two minutes. Where the hell is your car?"

"They came from Tommy's, I think, Paw."

"I don't care if they crawled out your ass. I want to know what they're doing on my land."

It was tough to get a word in edgewise, what with all this yelling and carrying on. Max did, and it got their attention. "We have gold and we want to buy some heavy equipment."

There was the magic word. It hung in the air for a second or two, all nice and shiny. *Gold.* Gold wasn't going-to-the-market money. It wasn't buying-a-part-for-your-truck money. It was *real* money. Gold would get you land with a house on it. Enough gold, and you could buy yourself a life. Gold was serious money for serious business.

Paw cocked his head. "What did you just say?"

Slow One didn't realize it a was rhetorical question. "Paw, he said—"

"Shut the fuck up!" both his brother and Paw shouted at him.

Max grinned, slow and easy. "I hear you got some heavy equipment. We would like to buy or rent it."

"Who the hell is *we*, and it's not for sale." Paw grinned. "But I might consider renting it for the right price."

"Yeah, Paw, get him to throw in the pretty Asian girl," cracked Nut Job. He thought that was funny. He was the only one who did. When he got done laughing at his joke he chased it down with a long pull of Bud.

"By the way," Paw said, looking at me now, "what the fuck is that tucked in your belt? You just fly in from a cowboy movie?" He looked at Max. "If this is your idea of a bodyguard, then I think you need to hire my boys, especially since you have all this gold."

"No, sir. I didn't fly in from nowhere. The Lord led me here."

I have found that if you want to paralyze people like this, you hit them with the Jesus talk. It totally messes up their responses. They just don't expect violence from a Jesus talker. Maybe fraud, or their women getting knocked up, but violence? No way. We had gradually drawn closer to them, so that we were now within a foot or so of normal conversation range.

Paw shook his head and laughed. "Jesus, huh? A boy as deranged as you shouldn't be walking around with gold on him. I tell you what. You two show me the gold you got and maybe we will talk."

Slow One wasn't picking up on what Paw was saying between the lines but Nut Job was. He casually set his beer on the air filter cover and dropped his hand down next to the butt of his holstered gun. I watched his stance change with it. I didn't bother to look at Max to see if he had picked up on where this was rapidly going.

"No, sir. The Lord led me to the barn, and that's where I found this Colt 1851 Navy. I'm sure he will show me what to do with it. Take a look at this. It's almost two hundred years old, and I think it might still work." I gave them a couple more heartbeats to digest what I said while I slowly stepped up to Paw as I eased the Colt out of my belt.

"Here. Take a look at it."

Paw dropped the muzzle of his shotgun so that it was pointing to the ground and extended his hand so I could place the Colt in it. I stepped up, tightened my grip on it while I thumbed back the hammer, and shot him in the heart.

He seemed surprised—probably because I shot him, but also perhaps because his shirt was now on fire. I think it was because I shot him. Damn, that gun put some serious smoke into the air.

His sons were stunned. They had been totally unprepared due to their preconceived notions on how stuff like this was supposed to play out, which gave me the extra second I needed.

As soon as the Colt fired—I wasn't sure it would—I drew the Ruger with my strong hand and shot Nut Job. Then I pivoted and shot Paw in the head just to make sure. He hadn't moved other than to put his hand over his heart and feebly try to extinguish the flame that was consuming his polyester-blend shirt.

Slow One turned out to be not so slow—and not so predictable. Max was reaching for his .45, on the assumption that Slow One was carrying and would do the same, when Slow One decided to handle things differently. Since his training had probably come from watching the WWE, that's how he responded.

He leaped forward and wrapped his arms around Max, pinning him. Then he hugged him hard and lifted him up over his head, using Max's belt for a handle, did a couple spins, and slammed him to the ground. He stood there, chest heaving, and looked at me and grinned.

I shot him twice. He was also surprised by it. Those first few years almost everyone I shot seemed surprised when it happened.

I checked the bodies quickly using my scientific method, which consisted of kicking them in the head and listening for an "Ow." Then I turned to Max, who was holding his side and struggling to sit up.

"That big dumb sonofabitch cracked a rib or two, I think."

I was trying to think of something witty to say, hopefully to make him laugh, when Maw came busting out the front door, ripping the screen door off its hinges.

"You killed my boys! You killed my boys!" she screamed, while covering the distance between us pretty damn quick. I shot her twice, too.

As she fell I said, "Yes, ma'am, I did." Out here in the sticks, politeness counted.

# CHAPTER FOURTEEN

I walked back to Max, helped him to his feet, and walked him over to the truck so he would have something to lean against. The damn dog was barking its head off in the background.

"How are you doing, Max?"

"Damn that stupid sonofabitch. We need to burn the house down with the bodies inside. Look for keys for everything before you start lighting matches. I think I'm going to lean here for a few minutes."

"I don't see why not," I told him. "You haven't done shit since we got here anyway." I laughed. He started to, and then he stopped and winced. "You going to be okay while I do this?"

He nodded.

"What do you want to do about the dog?" I asked.

"See if you can let him go. If he lets you get close, that is. If he doesn't . . ." He shrugged.

I got a hold on Nut Job and started moving him while Max watched and tried to look like he was fine. He wanted to help but I told him, "Don't even try."

The house inside was surprisingly neat and the furniture was nice. I almost took my boots off at the door. One by one I dragged the bodies into the house, and believe me, none of them was light. I was sweating by the time I got the last one in the door. I hoped nobody decided to come by and visit. I didn't want to have to drag anyone else inside. I put the bodies in different rooms. Just in case. I didn't expect a forensics team to show up, but why be stupid.

There was a nice gun cabinet off the living room. I left it alone except for the ammunition. Guns, especially out here, were probably as recognizable as wives to the gun-owners' friends. While I was inside Max had found the garden hose and was washing down the driveway. He was hurting, that was obvious, but he was functioning. I found the keyboard in the kitchen. Each piece of equipment was labeled on the board and tagged on the key. That was a nice touch, I thought.

I triple-bagged the ammo and carried it outside. Max was done with his watering. "What did you find?"

"Ammo."

"Find a couple buckets for me and check the kitchen for matches."

By the time I came back out, he had punched a hole in the truck's gas tank. We collected a couple gallons, and I went back inside and splashed it around. I left the buckets inside the house.

"You want to head back? Maybe get them ribs looked at and wrapped?"

He looked really pissed for a couple seconds and then he grinned. "It isn't anything. Heck, I could probably carry you back if I had to."

"I know. Just looking out for you."

"Right. Before you torch the place, deal with the dog. It's not right leaving him chained up."

"Yeah. Look, Max, I know nothing about dogs. You're a dog guy. You hobble around back and let Fido go."

"Damn, Gardener. Just do it."

I shrugged and went to find Fido. He was all the way at the end of the chain, standing there, watching me as I walked up to him. He was as still as a statue.

I got to about a foot from him and stopped. "Hi, dog."

He didn't say anything. He did wag his tail twice. I thought that was encouraging.

"Okay, dog, this is how it is. If you bite me, I am going to shoot you. You won't like that. If you don't bite me, I am going to let you off that chain, and you can go be a dog somewhere else."

I waited. Nothing from the dog other than its attention. I walked closer. No growl. I held out my hand, ready to jerk it back at the first sign of teeth. The dog licked it. That scared the crap out me for a second.

"Okay, dog. I am going to take that as an indication that you and I are cool."

A wag of his tail.

*Damn.* Maybe I had some kind of magical dog power. *Maybe I was the Dog Whisperer!*

Maybe I better get my ass in gear. I reached over and found where the chain hooked onto his collar and set him free. "Okay, dog. You can go wherever you want now." I turned around and headed back to Max and the matches.

"I see you got yourself a dog," I heard Max say.

I looked back. The dog had followed me and was standing about five feet away wagging its tail.

"No, Max. You got yourself a dog. I got myself a fire to set."

I set a rag on fire and tossed it through the open door into the house. It went up nicely. When I was done, the three of us admired the flames for a minute or five, until it began to smoke enough to call attention.

"You ready?"

"Yeah, Max, I am."

I grabbed the bags of ammo, and Max and I started walking back. The dog followed.

The walk back was as uneventful as the walk over. When we came to the fence, I ripped enough of it down that Max could step over it. The dog, which was following behind us, had no problem jumping over it. In fact he looked rather pleased with himself for his leaping ability.

We got to the porch, where Tommy's two kids were playing. They were happy to see the dog—too happy. They both went running down the steps yelling, "Doggie!"

Max and I looked at each other, the *Oh, shit* unspoken. Max's hand went to his .45 and I went down the stairs after the kids.

They were standing there, staring at the dog, which was taller than either of them and outweighed the two of them combined. I made up my mind in an instant. If the dog attacked, then I would leap over the kids and hopefully land on top of him. No way was he going to hurt them. Then I would cut his throat.

The dog stood there, wagged his tail tentatively, and walked up to the kids slowly. I took a deep breath. Then the boy threw his arm around the dog's neck and yelled,

"Doggie!" in its ear. The dog did nothing. Well, actually, I swear it looked at me and smiled.

The girl yelled, "Yea! Uncle Gardener got us a dog!" Then she attacked it. The dog shrugged off her attack. He jumped so he was about five feet from them and stood there wagging his tail. They rushed him again; he let them get a hold of him briefly before jumping away. A minute later they were playing "Chase the doggie" in the yard. I let them play for about five minutes before I told them to go find Aunt Donna and tell her Max was hurt. They ran off laughing with the dog running next to them.

"So what are you going to name him?" Max asked me.

"I think I'll let the kids name him. It looks like he's going to be their dog, thank God."

Donna came running. She hustled Max into the house, chattering at him the entire time. I stayed on the porch and watched the kids, who were back to playing in the yard. The dog sat about twenty feet away, under the shade of the trees, watching them.

The boy saw me standing there. "Hey, Uncle G!"

"Yeah, kid?"

"We named the dog!"

I began walking toward them. Donna said Night was working on a project in the trailer. Maybe I could help. If not, I was supposed to weed the garden. I didn't mind weeding. I actually found it rather peaceful. It was one those jobs where you could shut your mind off and just work. It was just too hot to start now.

"So what did you name him?"

They both shouted, "Woof!"

I looked over at the dog. He was grinning. "Good name, guys."

"Watch!" They yelled "Woof!" and sure enough, the dog walked over to them, standing there as the girl pulled his ears and the boy tried to put him in a headlock. "See?"

I nodded. "You kids got yourself a dog."

The kids were happy. The dogs they'd had when I was at the farm before had disappeared. No one knew for sure what had happened to them. Eaten or killed by someone was my guess. As I walked away, I yelled over my shoulder, "Make sure he has water."

The only reply was a chorus of giggles. I looked back. Woof was standing there patiently as the girl tried to climb on top and ride him.

# CHAPTER FIFTEEN

The trailer door was open. So were all the windows, the better to catch the breeze should one decide to come this way. I called Night's name as I walked up the wooden steps.

"In here," Night answered. She was in our living room, taping road maps to the wall and sweating.

"What are you doing?"

"Making my Intelligence Command Center."

"Oh. Need any help?"

"No. Go weed the garden like you're supposed to be doing."

I shrugged and turned to leave.

"G, I'm sorry. The heat is getting to me. Let's sit outside. You look okay. How's Max?"

We went outside and sat in the shade and I told her the bare bones of what had happened. She didn't seem surprised about how it had ended. We both turned to look across the fields toward the McKinley place. There was a fair amount of smoke rising into the air. The previous night, Max had casually asked Tommy about the local fire department.

"We don't have one anymore," Tommy had said. "It was made up of volunteers, and a lot of people have left. The county came and took the equipment anyway. Or maybe it was the company they bought it from. I know it had something to do with money or the lack of it. Falls Corner has one, but you got to be on their list and pay for it."

Well, no one seemed to be in a hurry to put this fire out.

"What are you going to do about the equipment?" Night asked. I told her I had the keys and we would go back later for it. It would look a little suspicious otherwise. She agreed.

I left to go weed the garden about ten minutes later. Night had told me that she planned to unveil the new command center later that evening, and I could tell she was distracted.

It was easier to garden than it had been a few years ago. It was probably the same all over the East Coast. The deer were no longer the problem they used to be. Most of the four-legged poachers had ended up in a pot themselves. I would have to talk to Woof later about his job description. Part of it was going to act as deer and raccoon repellent.

Tommy had a pretty decent garden planted. He had planted a lot of bell peppers, eggplant, squash, and cukes. There were a couple watermelon plants that had expanded way past their allocated space, and some spicy peppers.

Too bad tomatoes had become such a rarity due to the blight. Many things I liked to eat used tomato-based sauces. Donna had Tommy plant a couple rows of medicinal herbs, none of which I had a clue about, although the coneflowers were pretty.

Whenever we cut up anything from the garden for food we had to make sure we didn't eat the seeds. They had to be set aside and saved for next year.

Tommy told us when we first arrived how important it was to save the slippery little devils. His plants produced reusable seeds. Not all seeds were reusable. He told us how the government had begun to make sure that the agricultural states that were not collecting and remitting federal taxes would now receive only one-off-use seeds.

I started hoeing and went on autopilot. It was a lot like walking the trail, leaving just enough brain running with the little man to be aware of my environment while I went to mental idle.

After dinner, Night gathered us outside the trailer for the unveiling of her new command center. I didn't know what to expect. I knew she had sent Tommy on several mystery missions. I was hoping they had involved hot oil and candles, but it looked like another dream of mine had been shattered. *Such is life*, I thought.

Before we could go in, Night gave a short speech.

"Welcome to our new command center. My hope is that from here we will all be able to understand what is going on around us and make informed decisions. Any suggestions you have to improve it will be appreciated."

Then she shot me a nervous look. I could tell by the way she had rattled that off that she had practiced it more than a few times. She was excited to show off the center, but anxious, too. I just hoped it didn't look too pathetic.

Once again I had underestimated her. It wasn't NORAD, but it didn't look like the set for a kid's play either.

The maps were the main things that jumped out at you.

The woman had maps everywhere. They were stuck to the wall, and some of them were covered with plastic. She had three road maps: one to cover the northern Virginia area, one that covered our area, and one that extended into southern Ohio. She also had a map of the town and a topographical map of the local area.

In the corner was a small shortwave radio with a long copper wire that went out through the window. That had to be an antenna. She also had a laptop attached to a nineteen-inch monitor and an old HP LaserJet 4 for printing.

Ninja lit up when he saw the computer. He rushed over and stood there, his hand caressing the keyboard. He was aching to get some computer time.

"You can use it, but"—Ninja looked at her, waiting for the rest, his face a study in apprehension and need—"you better not hog it." Then she grinned at him, and he descended on it and was lost to us for the rest of the night.

Max took his time looking at the maps. He would nod his head and look thoughtful in front of each one. The town map really caught his eye. He stood in front of it for at least five minutes, the wheels in his mind obviously occupied with something. I liked the topographical map, even though I didn't really understand it. The roads and houses were interesting. There were quite a few more houses scattered through the woods than I had expected.

Finally, Max stopped examining things. He stood over Ninja for a minute, watching whatever was on the screen, and then turned to Night.

"An outstanding job. This is going to be very benefi-
cial. In fact, I think we should talk about an idea I have.
We need to organize this town. Maybe even give it some
real law enforcement. What do you think, Gardener?"

"Sure," I said, simply. But inside I was thinking, *Yip-
pee! No more digging holes and pulling weeds.*

We never had time anymore for meetings, at least the formal ones, which was fine with me. Dinnertime turned
into the unofficial meeting time, especially after we'd
eaten. We would all sit on the porch and enjoy the breeze,
if there was one.

The kids would play in the yard. Usually they chased
fireflies and put them in an old mason jar Donna had
found in the basement. I always made them let the bugs
go before they went inside to get ready for bed.

In theory they went to bed. In reality, they would
usually sneak downstairs and listen to us talk. I tried to
be careful with my language then. Sometimes I actually
managed an entire conversation without an obscenity. It
was difficult though.

Usually everyone would have something to contribute: the status of a project, fresh deer tracks they had
seen, what was happening in the world as seen through
the Internet or heard over the shortwave.

One thing we had all noticed was that traffic was almost nonexistent on the road. We knew things, but at the
same time we didn't. We were missing the information
you normally picked up from conversations with people
who kept their eyes and ears open when interacting with
the bigger world outside our farm.

It had been two days since the fire and only once had anyone had come by to talk to us. Tommy had met them at the door and answered their questions. They were Virginia State Police and were curious if he had seen any strangers around. Tommy told us they figured that it was a robbery. Apparently a lot of that had been going around.

When he told us about it that night at dinner, Max's only comment was, "That's interesting."

I had spent some time sitting in a chair on the second floor of the farmhouse, watching to see if anyone came around. People did. They poked around the McKinley house and, when it cooled down, found the bodies. That's when the state troopers had come calling on us.

Afterward I watched as the black Ford truck and a couple of other vehicles were driven off. A different group arrived later and went through the outbuildings. They left the heavy equipment alone. Max had slipped over there at some point and done something to disable the engines, just to be on the safe side.

Our conversation that night was about the heavy equipment. Max outlined his vision, which was to build a berm around our farmhouse and outbuildings with a watch platform. That's why we needed the heavy equipment: to push dirt.

"Max, I'm puzzled," I said. "If we plan to move to Ohio, then why do all this work?" I looked around. I wasn't the only one who was wondering this.

"Well, for the same reason we always keep a watch when we're moving. Because we want to live long enough to get to where we are going. Hey, if we were Roman legionnaires, we'd be doing this every time we stopped for the night. If we have to go on the move again, you'll be digging fighting positions."

"Okay. What are we going to do with the heavy equipment when we're done?" I asked because the idea of doing snow removal and road grading was not at all appealing.

"We're going to give them to the town. It will remove any suspicion, and we're going to need to score major points right from the start. We need this town, and they are going to learn that they need us."

A few days later, Tommy, Max, and I went over to look at the heavy equipment and drive what we needed to our place. I didn't know anything about heavy equipment, but I said I figured it couldn't be that hard. Tommy laughed in my face.

"Gardener, you need to sit in the seat of one of them before you can say that. There is a big difference between knowing how to drive one of these babies and knowing how to work on-site with it. The good operators, they are artists at moving dirt." I was willing to take Tommy at his word on that, especially as he was the only one of us with any experience.

He was happy. He had something he knew about and was good at. We walked around, and I listened to him rattle off numbers and names. I wasn't really paying attention. He was right. There sure were a lot of levers and whatnot inside them things.

I looked at the various rigs and mentally called them by the names I had used as a kid. There were two scrapers, a dozer, and a digger. There was also a little one called a Bobcat and a couple of tractors. One of them had a low-slung metal thing that I had seen road crews use on grass: a bush hog.

The McKinleys also had an underground diesel fuel tank and a pump just like a gas station. Max saw that and said, "I really hope they topped that off not too long ago."

He pulled a piece of paper from his pocket and spread it out on an oil drum. It was a sketch of his plan to fortify our living area.

"I'm not really happy about this. We don't have time to build a berm around the entire area. Hell, in some places we can't. It just isn't practical from the way the buildings are laid out and the number of people we have. We are going to have to put in motion detectors here and here," he said, indicating spots on his sketch. "That is, if we can find them. I want to do a couple things. We can't have the road running straight up to the farmhouse. We need a dogleg in it. I want to berm the front all the way from here to here. Regardless, we are going to have gaps by the outbuildings."

Tommy was busy nodding his head and pointing at the design. "Yeah, that can be done. Maybe a short wall here and here. Dig the dirt out and push it up. It will go quicker." Then they started talking about berms they had both known and loved in the 'Stan.

"Hey, guys. What are we defending against?" Nobody had clued me in on that. I figured it was because it was so obvious that everyone knew but me.

"I wish I knew for sure," Max said, shaking his head. "What I want to do is make us look formidable enough that the drive-by types will move on. But I don't want to go overboard and draw Fed attention. I want to make it difficult, if not impossible, for a swarm invasion."

I think I knew what he was getting at but I wanted him to spell it out. "That would be . . .?"

"A crew with a couple of four-by-fours and ATVs racing in from different directions and taking us by surprise. I think that and a park-and-sneak-the-perimeter are the most likely scenarios. It depends on how crazy it gets."

We stared at each other for a beat. Yeah, it could get crazy. It already had.

Max and Tommy talked for about ten more minutes and then Max slapped him on the shoulder. "I know you got it. We'll be back in time for dinner at the latest."

"*We*? You forget to tell me something?"

"Yeah. It's time for us to go into town and introduce ourselves to the locals."

We walked back to our farmhouse. Tommy stayed behind to get the dozer running and drive it over to the house.

Night had set up a chalkboard by the front door. Everyone was supposed to leave notes to each other. They were to include where we were. Sometimes I forgot. That made Night very unhappy with me, so now I tried to remember.

I waited for Max on the porch. Night had signed out to go to Donna's house to pick up a sewing machine. She had taken the kids and the dog with her. I bet that was a fun trip. Hopefully Woof didn't get carsick.

Max came downstairs. I heard him pause to read the board before he joined me. "I see you signed us out. That has to be a first," he laughed. "You got what you need?"

"Yeah." I got a flashback of walking the neighborhood around the motel with him. *Going on patrol* is what we called it. Damn, that seemed like a million years ago.

We took Tommy's old truck. I let Max drive. He always wanted to drive. I didn't mind. We had worked all this out a while ago. He drove and I ran the radio. Not a digital radio, either. Digital had really killed the quality of FM programming. There was not a lot to listen to out here. It was classic rock, praise Jesus, and country music, that was for sure. At least it was in English.

Max honked as we passed Tommy. I leaned out the window and flipped him off. He had the dozer on our property and was starting to scrape the ground.

"So, we got a plan, Max?"

"Yep. Go into town first and get a feel for it. You spent some time here. Got any suggestions?"

"Drive around, see what we can see. But we should go over to the diner for lunch. Anybody who is somebody— or wants to pretend to be somebody—will be there. We can order hamburgers and apple pie, and I can shoot a few people to get their attention."

"Naw, wait a bit on the shooting part. We don't know who we need yet."

I thought about the girl I had met at the library for a few seconds and then quickly shut down that line of thought—nothing but trouble down that road. Even an idiot like me could figure that out. We passed a few vehicles. Max gave them the wave. They returned it.

I told him, "If you want to tour the residential areas, you need to make a left at the light. Then we can do downtown. Not much worth seeing on the outskirts, but we should do a drive-by just to take a look anyways."

He nodded. "Anything like a machine shop or anything industrial out here?"

"I don't think so. This was a dead town when I was here, and it already looks deader every minute we drive."

The residential sections weren't much. There was the good neighborhood, the not-so-good, and where the foreigners and blacks lived.

The good neighborhood covered all of three streets. There were a few brick houses, but most of them were frame, with fading paint. At least a third of the houses looked empty. The vandalism looked minor. Most of the places needed extensive yard work. No one was out on the street here. I caught a couple glimpses of people moving around their yards, and one person was actually sitting on the porch in plain view. I waved. He didn't wave back.

The not-so-good area was a little livelier. A couple of kids playing. A woman hanging laundry out to dry. Two guys standing around an old but freshly washed BMW. Windows were open to let in the breeze, if and when it decided to arrive. I could hear music coming out of a few of them. There was a tired, sullen vibe in the air. It wouldn't take much of a spark to create a fire. Domestic disturbances would be the primary call here, if there had been a police force.

The downtown was there in name and material only. A stab had been made at making it shiny again. We were still close to D.C. At the height of the boom, the waters of prosperity must have lapped close enough to here that the speculators and dreamers had hoped to make this a destination town—a Berkeley Springs or a Woodstock.

For a few months in 2005, it looked like it might actually happen. But it didn't. Just like it didn't in a lot of other little towns that had smoked the same brand of "hope-ium." A lot of bed-and-breakfasts began dying in 2008. Their carcasses littered the landscape up and down the Eastern Seaboard.

The town still had a few open stores: a bar, a lottery ticket and beer store, a used clothing and antiques place, a storefront church. The town hall was closed, and the park in front needed mowing. Cracked sidewalks and a lot of windows boarded or soaped up. No place to get coffee that I could see.

The churches were still in business. The Episcopalian one had a cheery message. The Baptists had a sign advertising their Come to God and Feed More Than Your Soul plan. The Catholic church had a sign listing Mass times. At the bottom an arrow pointed to the location of their food bank.

We drove on, headed toward the land of big boxes. Big Box Land once had a Wal-Mart, a couple of fast-food restaurants, including an upscale one, a couple of car lots, two gas stations, and a Southern States co-op. One gas station was still open.

Everything else was closed—boarded up or just abandoned. The Wal-Mart parking lot already had weeds coming up through the asphalt. The car lots didn't have any weeds. This puzzled me until I realized that all the oil and what have you dripping from the vehicles over the years had effectively sterilized the land.

"Pretty fuckin' sad," Max said. We had pulled over and sat there, the truck engine idling.

"Yeah, but you know what?"

"What?"

"I don't really remember anymore what it was like. I mean, I do—but it all seems like a dream."

"Yeah, well, that's because it was."

# CHAPTER SIXTEEN

We pulled into the diner parking lot. It was busy. This was the only decent place now to buy a meal for six miles. I got out, stretched, and took a look at the vehicles. Nothing unusual. A couple of trucks and a Toyota Camry that had been hit several years ago in the passenger side door. I guessed at the several years because of the rust that was bleeding through. One bicycle and an SUV. Nothing weird in the vibe as I followed Max inside.

Taped to the door was a hand-lettered sign:

No Barter Unless Arranged First!
No Checks.
Weapons to Remain Holstered at ALL TIMES.
We Can and Will Refuse Service to Whoever We WANT!

Someone had added a Burner logo in pen underneath, but it was crossed out.

As I walked through the door, the odor of grease, meat, and potatoes slapped me upside the head. I like that smell. Also noticeable was the sound of all conversation coming to a halt. We paused in the doorway near the cash register. We stood there and looked over the crowd while they did the same. There wasn't a welcoming face among them.

The waitress, a tall white woman with pale skin and red hair that was starting to gray, greeted us cheerfully enough. We weren't strangers to her. We were money in her pocket, hopefully.

"How can I help ya'll?" She was a local. If not a local then she had grown up within a hundred miles of here, all those miles in the opposite direction of Northern Virginia.

Max grinned at her. "Yes, ma'am. We would like to get something to eat."

"Well, help yourself to a table or sit on up here with these no-accounts." She laughed. "As you can see we have a few open tables." She waved her hand in the direction of the roped-off section and turned in response to a call of "Shelli, more coffee here, please."

We took a booth next to a window that allowed us to look out over the parking lot. I looked around. This wasn't a real diner in the sense that it had been here for fifty years. It was a copy of a diner that someone had built in order to cash in on the feel-good, small-town vibes during the boom. The red pleather covering the booth seats had begun to crack. My rip had been patched with duct tape, which would probably outlast the pleather. The ketchup and hot sauce bottles had no caps. I had seen that before. That was to prevent anyone from pocketing them. My guess is they still lost a few bottles. We picked up our menus. Across the top was written Please Ask for Salt and Pepper!

I looked over the menu at Max. "You do take me to all the finer places, big guy." He ignored me.

The conversations began again, this time at a lower volume and punctuated by sidelong glances at us.

Shelli came back, order pad in hand. "You decide on anything yet?" I ordered coffee and pancakes. Max went with a burger and coffee.

We sat there waiting for our order and checked out our fellow diners while making small talk. There were three men sitting at the counter, with empty stools between them. The one closest to us was wearing a blue blazer over a Polo shirt and a pair of khaki pants. He had on brown-tasseled loafers. A salesman—or, more likely, a former salesman still clinging to his uniform out of habit or wishful thinking.

I had learned to check out people's footwear when Max and I did our stint as officers of the law. Actually, Max had pointed it out to me, and I had worked on it since. The theory was simple. Shoes, more than anything, told you what was really going on with a person. A disconnect between shoes and attitude was always a warning flag. Age was also important.

For example, here's an obvious one. Say I stop a male, any color, who is fit and in his twenties to forties. He is dressed passably well except for tan lace-up work boots. He will usually be wearing sunglasses, probably Oakleys. If he isn't, good. If he is, I tell him to take them off.

Why? Because nine out of ten times I am dealing with a vet who is armed and has more experience and training in violence than your average civilian. If his boots are scuffed and sun-faded, he is almost certainly a vet. I say *almost*, because I sometimes ran across guys—especially in urban areas—who didn't have the experience but wanted to project the image. You could count on Homeland Security types to be wearing the same sort of boots, only in black.

Tassel Man's shoes were shined, which told me he had either driven or walked a very short distance to get here. He had a house or decent place to live. He once held middle-class status, and in his mind he still clung to it. He would be armed—I assumed everyone was now—though he didn't carry every day. It was too heavy and uncomfortable. Plus, at least in his worldview, things weren't that bad, and he just knew the old days were coming back. One just had to keep a positive attitude.

The guy next to him was sloppy—sloppy body, sloppy clothes, unshaven face. His Nike running shoes had seen better days. He wore a black nylon holster with a Ruger Blackhawk in it. That was the only point in his favor. Even his hair was sloppy and greasy. He was comfortable on his stool, which indicated he was a local. His left forearm had a tattoo of an eagle.

I watched Shelli, the waitress. Her body language changed subtly around him. She didn't like him.

The third guy was old but alert. I noticed that he was studying us while trying not to be obvious about it. He wore work pants and a clean shirt with a collar. He had on a pair of work boots: Sears brand, old. Sears was gone now, but a few of its products lived on. He wore suspenders and had a Leatherman looped onto a plain wide belt. My guess was he had some heavy iron hanging off the other side. He looked competent. He was wearing a John Deere ball cap.

In a booth in the back was a middle-aged couple. He looked like a math teacher with a bad comb-over. He was also wearing a collared shirt. *This must be the rich people's diner*, I thought. I didn't really understand then how hard some people clung to the old ways. Partly in denial, partly in the hope that if they acted and dressed as they always had, everything bad would go away. I had no idea about the woman. Her back was to me.

I noticed that the short-order cook kept an eye on us. He'd pop his head up in the window where the completed orders were stacked, look around, and disappear.

There weren't any young people in the diner. In a town like this, the young ones usually bailed as soon as possible, with only a handful staying behind. That flow had reversed a bit in the past few years as some returned to Mom and Dad, broke and towing a couple of grandkids behind them. They didn't have the money to eat out, and most didn't have the skills to create anything to barter with.

When Shelli returned to find out how we were doing, Max asked, "So do you have a mayor or someone in charge here?"

Before she could answer, Sloppy barked out a laugh. "Well, the man who thought he would be king got himself baked like a Purdue roaster right next door to you."

Shelli frowned, her expression saying, *What an asshole.* Over her shoulder she said, "I think he was talking to me, Gillian Rogers." She answered Max, "No, sir. We don't even have a sheriff, let alone a mayor."

"Hell, we don't even have a post office anymore or a fire department. This town ain't much of a town. Shit, we don't even have any good-looking women." Gil thought this was pretty funny. He held up his hand. "Sorry, sorry. We do. I forgot about that niece of yours, Fred."

The old guy down from him stood up like he was going to do something, or at least wanted Sloppy to think

**139**

he was. "Shut your mouth about my niece, Gil." Then again maybe he was. Firearms were just as deadly in a sixty-year-old's hands as they were in a twenty-year-old's.

Shelli said sharply, "Enough! Gil, you need to watch your mouth."

The cook had appeared in the window and was watching intently. I looked at Max. He was sitting sideways in the booth now, watching it all calmly.

*Damn*, I thought, *come in for some pancakes and we end up in the dysfunctional family diner.*

Gil held up his hands, "Sorry, sorry. Just funnin' ya'll." Then he smirked and spun his stool around.

"So there's your answer, mister. Would you two want some more coffee? I'm going to have to charge you for an extra cup. Coffee is getting tough to find in quantity lately."

"Sure, I would love another cup, ma'am." We grinned at each other, and she turned and headed behind the counter to get the pot.

Gil spoke into his coffee cup without turning around. "See you got his equipment running just fine in front of Tom's place. Kind of convenient, since the old shithead never would have shared."

*Okay*, I thought, *showtime!* I reached down and slid off the leather thong that held the Ruger by the hammer and started easing out of the booth. Max caught me with a glance and a tiny shake of the head. Then he slid forward and stood up.

Very quietly he said, "Hey, Gil."

Gil spun around, smirking again. "Just funnin', strang—" He would have finished the —*er* part if Max's open hand hadn't connected with the side of his face. The sound of a nicely landed smack filled the air.

I slid out of the booth and moved to Max's left, leaving him room to work. I was grinning. Gil had just been bitch-slapped. I bet it was the first time he had seen it done outside of cable TV, let alone felt it.

Gil sat there for a second, stunned. His face had gone white, which highlighted the imprint of Max's hand. He touched the side of his face and almost got to his feet, but then decided it wasn't such a good idea. Max looked at him and cocked his head.

"Damn, mister. I was just—"

"I know," Max cut him off, "You were funnin'. You got something you want to accuse me of?"

Gil shook his head.

"Cause, being that there isn't any law around here, I figure we can settle this ourselves"—he paused and then added—"like men."

"No, no. I'm good. I was leaving anyway."

*Damn*, I thought, *bitch-slapped again.*

He was off the stool, eyes down and moving past me, and out the door in under three seconds.

In the silence that followed his departure, I asked Shelli, "Ma'am? I see he didn't pay his check. You want me to go remind him?"

She laughed; a shaky sounding laugh, but a laugh. "No, I'm sure he'll be back. I'll get it then. Thanks."

Max looked around slowly, addressing no one and everyone. "We are using the equipment because we need to. We will not keep it. I asked if there were any local authorities because I wanted them to know of our equipment use, and that we plan to return it. I apologize for disturbing your meal. Thank you."

He sat down. I wanted to applaud but decided not to.

The diner slowly returned to normal. The buzz of conversation resumed. Heck, we had probably given everyone within a couple miles something new to talk about for the next week. We sat there. I was enjoying my coffee. Max was working on eye contact with Shelli when the old guy came up to our table.

"Excuse me. I just wanted to say thank you for putting Gil in his place."

"Not a problem. Care to join us?"

He did, which meant I had to move over to give him room.

"Gil wasn't always an asshole," he continued. "He just hasn't adjusted well to not having any money." As an aside he added, "A lot of us haven't."

Max nodded. "Yep. It's been rough."

This was what Max was good at. Talking to people. He could project a strong, nonjudgmental, and caring attitude at the flick of a switch. People ate it up, especially the scared and lost ones.

Old Guy paused. Even I knew he had something he wanted to say. You could tell he was trying to control both the flow of his words and the naked need behind what he had to say. He almost did, too.

"Well, I am a pretty good operator. I learned in the Seabees way back when. And, well, I could use some work and . . ." He stopped. His hands were on top of the table. They looked old, brown, ropey, and scarred. No wedding ring either.

"Seabees, huh?" Max said pensively. "You know anything about building berms?"

The Old Guy grinned. "Some. Did a year in Kuwait in '05 with KBR. We did some of that. Pushing sand is a lot different than pushing clay. It don't stay put. That was some good money that year."

"Okay, I tell you what. Find Tommy and tell him I said to start you up. We will see how you work out today, and then we can dicker about how expensive you are going to be. Sound like a winner?"

He stood up. "Yes, sir! You are going to be surprised! I'm damn good. Thank you!" He reached over the table, shook Max's hand, nodded at me, and left.

Shelli walked up to the table "Well, you guys are good at one thing, that's for sure. You sure can empty out a diner."

# CHAPTER SEVENTEEN

The next week or so passed fairly quickly. The Old Guy was as good as he said he was. Between him and Tommy, the main part of the berm that ran in front of the farm-house and the dogleg in the approach road were done in a week. They started working on the side berm. Old Guy said he knew where he could get some gravel. Making the dogleg had required creating a short stretch of dirt road, and we needed to lay gravel on it.

I was helping out where I could. I built the watch plat-forms and walkways on the interior side of the berm. I used wood salvaged from different places to frame the platforms, most of it from an old barn down the road. I found out pretty quickly that the muscles I'd developed while walking here weren't the same ones used to run a shovel. I was sore for days.

It was a good time despite the heat and labor. We would break for lunch, made for us by Night. We ate it sitting on the porch and washed it down with sun tea. Tommy and the Old Guy would talk about heavy equip-ment and lie about fish they had caught at the pond over by Route 235. Night would talk about her day. I would sit and listen to her and to my body talking to me.

I was drinking a gallon of water a day working out there in the sun. Tommy and Old Guy weren't far behind me.

The kids would come out in the late afternoon to play on the hills or just watch Tommy run the equipment. Woof would investigate and sniff-check everything ahead of them. By the second day Old Guy had started staying over to have dinner with us.

Max was around, but never for long. He would spend a few hours working with us and then head into town. I asked him what he was up to and his reply was "Politicking." He was also making phone calls. The day after we finished the main berm, he pulled us off the side berm so we could provide security for a deal.

A couple days earlier he had explained to us after dinner that he was going to have to sell a significant part of the trade goods, especially the medicine, to raise enough gold to buy the stuff we needed. We needed ammo. You could never have enough ammo. Plus, we needed some other hardware and food.

Night was handling our logistics. She had made up a list of non-weapon-related items. She called it her "shopping list." We spent valuable time in bed discussing how many pairs of underwear and socks we might need. Nothing was too trivial for the shopping list or for discussion. I felt like screaming, "Damn! I don't care about an adequate supply of toothbrushes! I just want to get naked!"

The night before the deal, Max told us, "These people that we're dealing with are somewhat iffy as far as what I know about them. They are outside-the-Zone types and have been vouched for. The person who connected us up is known to me, but I heard a bit of hesitation in his voice that I didn't like."

We didn't hide the discussion from Old Guy, nor did we ask him if he wanted a piece of it. It was up to him.

He volunteered. "Hell, I can help you out. You're going to need another body that can point a gun. Plus, it beats pushing dirt in the summertime."

Max asked him what he had in the way of weapons. He had a bolt-action 30.06 and the .45 he wore on his belt. A lot of older guys and a fair number of the vets preferred the .45 to the 9-millimeter. I had asked Max about it once and he had told me, "If I pull the trigger on someone, that means I want him to die." He didn't offer any more and I knew him just well enough by then to let it slide.

"I got maybe forty rounds for the rifle. I do a bit of deer hunting now and then. Used to be I would carry it in the cab of whatever I was running. You would be out there doing site work and scare up deer all the time."

Max asked him to bring it the next day. Before the light went bad and we broke for dinner, Max had him run ten rounds through his rifle. He was right. He was a deer shooter—competent at a hundred yards, but he wasn't going to be a sniper.

We did a walk-through that night on how we were going to handle the deal. Old Guy would get the Barrett and a seat at the second-story window looking down on the yard. Tommy would have been a better choice, but you work with what you have. Instead, Tommy would be on the porch with a shotgun. Night and her shotgun would take the other side but at an angle; we didn't want to shoot our own people. Max would do the talking and wear his usual weapon. I would hang back a bit and watch from the top of the berm. I was going to tote a shotgun also. The kids and Woof would head to Donna's house for the day.

Max told us not to be surprised if they came in government vehicles or if we saw a uniform or two. They may have been based outside the Zone, but the weapons they were trading were government bought. Local law enforcement that worked the Zone, or the area just outside of it, got a lot of free ordnance courtesy of Homeland Security. Apparently they weren't averse to selling some of their older stock. They had also begun hiring out as mercenaries to guard conveys and for personal security. Their IDs came in handy in case of a surprise checkpoint.

This swap was to be pharmaceuticals for weapons.

I asked Max, "What happened to the part where we trade for gold?"

"Gold is in real demand now. No one wants to give up any. They want it but they won't spend it."

"Why?"

"Because it's a supply and demand thing. Weapons are not a big deal to get now if you have the right trade goods. Decent pharmaceuticals are harder to find than weapons. Gold is the hardest to get because everyone thinks it's going to be worth a lot more, and soon at that."

"What do you think, Max?"

"I think they're right. The only problem is it draws a lot of attention. Soon it will be Fed-level attention. We don't need that."

"Why's that?" I was genuinely puzzled.

He didn't say anything. Night answered for him, "Because the Feds are running on paper with nothing behind it. They have been running on bullshit and yesterday's habits for the past few years. We accept it because we can't conceive of not accepting it. The rest of the world doesn't have that problem. We believe in it because to not believe in it is too freaking scary. It's all make-believe and has been for awhile."

"Oh, okay." I didn't really give a damn about the dollar. Money didn't make me happy. Night did.

We sat on the porch the next day waiting for them. Tommy had the binoculars and was upstairs watching the road. An hour after they were due to arrive he yelled down, "They're coming!" He came leaping down the stairs, and Old Guy passed him, going up to his post.

I went up the ramp I had built on the inside of the berm, moving to where I could look down on the cars after they cleared the dogleg. They had to slow to a crawl to navigate it. I realized while watching them approach that we should have a log or something we could drop across the entrance. Just because they slowed down didn't mean they came to stop. The dogleg bought time, but it wouldn't be enough time if we were attacked, especially at night.

Max walked out and stood in the middle of the yard about twenty feet back from the berm entrance, waiting for them. They arrived in two black Chevy Suburbans, the three-quarter-ton model—the SUV of choice for nine out of nine Homeland Security-equipped agencies. The blue lights on the dashboard confirmed it.

The lead vehicle stopped about a foot short of Max. He didn't flinch. In fact, he looked bored.

They had the windows down and guys sitting in the sideways Secret Service-style seats looking out. The rear doors opened on each side of the lead vehicle. From the left-side passenger door a white male stepped out wearing a blue T-shirt with POLICE printed in white on the back. His handgun rode high on his hip.

Two seconds later, another male stepped out from the opposite side. He was wearing a white dress shirt and black dress pants. He had his weapon in a black leather FBI-style holster. While the other guy had on tan boots, this guy wore dress shoes—wing tips would be my guess. He had to be management.

The passenger doors opened on the other vehicle, but nobody exited. The two who had just gotten out didn't bother to shut their doors.

"Hey, Max! Everything cool?" Wing Tips called out.

Max walked around to meet him. "Yep, so far, Sheriff."

Police T-shirt had circled around and was now standing behind Max. I was not thrilled about that. Max did not even seem to notice.

The sheriff held up his hands. "It's cool, Max. How do you want to do this?"

"Why don't you unload what you brought and we will see what we can do."

He nodded. "Sounds good. My people are going to get out of the vehicles and start unloading. I want to do this quickly. We have approximately one hour and ten minutes before the next drones pass. I want to be five miles east of here by then. Where do you want it?"

"Stack it by the stairs going up to the porch. That would be fine."

"Alright, people! Let's unload." He walked over and stood next to Max. "After this, maybe we can be more civilized the next time. You know, you could invite me up on the porch, and we could drink something cold and talk shit for a while."

"Yep. Right now let's talk about what you got coming off the truck."

The sheriff sighed. "Okay, man. This hardcore thing is going to make you old before your time." He nodded toward the first crate two guys were bringing out. "You can keep the crates. We made them special for this at no extra charge."

Max just stared at him.

"Okay, moving on." He looked at the taller of the two guys at the crate. "Pop the top, and let's do show-and-tell."

The guy walked back to the SUV and returned with a short pry bar. I really dislike the sound of wood and nails being separated.

"What I got for you, Max, is old. Everything is old. It's functional to the best of my knowledge, but what you are getting is armory clearance stuff. The Feds won't support it, so we might as well dispose of it. What you got there is the M-14. I have no clue why we had them. Probably bought or given to the department by the government in the late 1960s, just in case the Russians came. They were supposed to be destroyed back during the Clinton administration but someone overlooked them."

Max had already pulled one from the crate and was looking at it. He nodded. "Not a bad weapon. Better than the M-16 in some ways."

"Well, you got ten of them. I can probably do ten more. We aren't the only department to have them buried in the back. The National Guard destroyed all of theirs a while back. I couldn't get you a lot of what you asked for. No night scopes. No M-60s. Actually, anything manufactured later than 1970 or that can generate serious firepower is not going to happen. At least not from me. I got Fed accountability problems and I got my own people to look after. So, you want to see the rest?"

Max said, "Sure."

"Good. I thought you would."

What he had were five pump riot shotguns, two flak jackets, and ammo for the shotguns and the M-14s. For handguns, he had six Colt .357 revolvers and six cases of .357 ammo.

"The Colts are the only things I got for you made later than the seventies. I think they are left over from when the department switched to the Beretta in the early eighties. Or was it the Glock? Hell, I don't remember. That was five sheriffs ago at least."

Max brought out what we had. While they went back and forth, I checked out the two guys who had done the heavy lifting.

They noticed and one said, "What are you looking at, Tex?" They both thought that was funny.

"Oh, I don't know, Deputy Dawg. A couple of dipshits probably."

"You want me to come up there and kick your retarded little cowboy ass?"

"Sure, why not. We got more dirt to move. Wouldn't be any problem to put you under it."

His buddy smacked him in the arm and said quietly, "Not now. Not here."

I grinned and watched the first one turn red.

Then the sheriff unveiled a surprise for Max. At his nod the two guys dragged a crate out of the back of the SUV and gently set it at his feet. They popped the top and stepped back.

"I know you recognize these, Max. Probably made in the early seventies. And don't ask me where I got them."

"Nice."

I agreed with Max. I had never seen real ones, just the virtual models from online gaming, but I knew what they were: claymores.

They went back to haggling and struck a deal. The guy who had been behind Max had gradually wandered away and around. He tried to be casual about it, but it was obvious what he was doing. He tried talking to Night but got nowhere. As his boss and Max finished up he asked Tommy if he could come inside and use the bathroom.

Max broke off what he was saying and answered him. "No. Piss in the woods or shit in town."

The bodyguard shrugged and muttered something. The sheriff raised an eyebrow but didn't say anything. He and Max shook hands and they were gone. Deputy Dawg flipped me off as they drove off. I winked at him.

Afterward, we went over what had happened, what could have happened, and what we would have done. Then people started to get up and go back to their work.

"Hang around, Gardener," Max said. He pulled the box of claymores over to his chair. "So what's your intuition telling you?"

"Well, the sheriff is a used car salesman with a badge. His bodyguard has a clue and was busy checking us out. The two other guys were spear carriers. I never got a good look at the drivers."

He reached into the box and pulled one of the claymores out. "Ever seen one of these before?"

"Just online."

He snorted. "Ah, yes. Tell me what you see," and he handed it to me.

It was lighter than I expected. I looked at it, shrugged. "A claymore?"

"Yeah. You're close." He set the plastic case on the floor, knelt down next to it, and drove his knife into it. He worked at it a few minutes and then pulled the case apart. He reached inside and pulled out a black sock filled with sand.

"I'm guessing that isn't what it is supposed to look like inside," I said.

"Nope."

"And we paid for these with our meds, didn't we?"

"Yep."

"So we going to go find them and kill them? Maybe even get our drugs back?"

"Nope. I'll tell you why, too. You may be right about it just being a rip-off. Then again, why did he keep telling me how important these would be for our perimeter defense?"

"Because we don't need to find them. They'll be coming back."

"Yep."

# CHAPTER EIGHTEEN

At dinner, we explained to everyone what we had found out about the claymores and then talked more about it on the porch. People were pissed. I think I even saw Tommy's nostrils flare in anger.

Yeah, I am being a jerk, but the man had skills, experience, and—you would think—motivation. He just didn't have the will to use it anymore. Oh, he would pull the trigger if someone shot at him, at least I hoped he would, but we needed more than that. We needed him functioning like he did with Max during his first deployment.

The one who surprised me was Old Guy. "The hell with sitting around here waiting for them to decide when they are coming over the walls," he barked. "I say we find them and drag them down a gravel road naked for a while."

I laughed. Everyone laughed. I even heard one of the kids snickering in the other room. He looked at us like we were crazy for a second and then he laughed.

"No, we get them alive, then, well, I say we leave them with Night. What do you think, honey?"

"I think they will find the sun is very hot when they don't have any skin." She wasn't kidding either. I don't know about anyone else, but that sent a chill down my spine.

The rest of the conversation was a lot more pleasant. Night wanted to buy a cow and a steer from someone Donna knew outside of town. The cow would provide milk for the kids. The steer would be for meat. She planned on drying most of it.

Everyone seemed to be waiting for Max to tell us what the plan was. He was being a little more quiet than usual. He startled me when he began talking about something completely different.

"So, Gardener . . . how do you feel about going back to law enforcement? I mean, I know how much you love farm work and all."

Everyone thought this was funny, which pissed me off. I pulled my weight. Then I realized they were right. I hated farm work. I did it, but it was not what I wanted to do. I began laughing. I felt Night's hand on my leg. She gave me a quick squeeze and then pulled her hand away.

"Sure. I think I could probably work that in."

"Yeah, well, you're even getting a promotion." Night clapped. I waited for the hook. "You're going to be deputy chief, and you're going to have a couple of deputies."

"Okay. But we don't have anyone to spare. Wait—who did you hire?"

"You met them last time you were in town. They say they owe you for 'the library,' whatever that means. It will be good for you. You can practice your leadership skills."

That made me laugh. I wasn't a leader. I wasn't a follower either. I never did get around to telling anyone about the library incident. Tommy must have snitched me out to Max.

"Yeah, Max, I think I remember them. So, are we going to talk about what we're going to do about today?"

"Yep. I got to tell you all that we are going to have to roll the dice on this one. I think I know what's going to happen. If I'm right, then we are going to have to go medieval on their dead asses to make a point."

I looked at Night. "You have a problem with going medieval?"

"Nope. I'm already there." She turned to Old Guy. "How about you?"

He grinned. I liked that grin. He was an old dog, but he had some wolf in him too. "No, ma'am." He also had good manners.

We all looked at Tommy.

He grinned. "I might surprise some of you."

I realized as I was getting ready for bed that no one had thought to question Max over his intuition about what was going to happen and what our chances were. I didn't. The only question I had is why he gave first watch to Night and last watch to me.

Max had us stay close to the farmhouse the next day. He also had us resume carrying our shotguns. Tommy and Old Guy kept working on the last part of the berm. Because of trees and outbuildings we couldn't berm everything without stretching our perimeter to an unmanageable size.

Old Guy was running the Bobcat now. He was an artist with it. He reminded me of a cowboy riding a rodeo horse the way he whipped that thing in, out, and sideways. Tommy told us that they would be done in two days at this rate.

Max left early and came back after a couple hours with a large bell and a post. He dug a hole for the post and set it up, while I dug holes and set posts in the gaps between the berms. When I wasn't doing that, I worked on the freshly completed part of the berm.

We needed rain, but I was glad we hadn't gotten it. Most of what we were pushing was hard-pack clay. A little rain and we would have had to stop.

One problem that we kept facing was the amount of work that needed to be done versus the number of hands we had to do it. Night worked on the garden and tried to keep an eye on the kids, while also doing the cooking and laundry. It struck me as a bit sexist, but at a hundred pounds she just didn't have the upper-body strength required for the heavy labor. Plus, someone had to make sure I had clean underwear. I kept that comment to myself.

At lunchtime Max rang his newly rigged bell. Of course Tommy and Old Guy ignored it. I had to go fetch them. We ate lunch while Max told us about the bell. It was now our "Alarm Bell." Tommy's boy asked, "Can I ring it?"

Max told him, "Sure. I made certain the rope was long enough for both you and your sister. You have to understand"—here his voice grew very serious—"that it can only be rung for fires, strangers, or if Woof starts barking a lot. Oh, and for lunch and dinner."

Tommy added, "If it isn't serious, then I am going to whip your butt so hard you won't be able to sit down for a week."

Both kids nodded their heads solemnly and agreed that they would ring it only in case of bad men and fire.

The boy made me laugh. He asked Max, "Can we ring it one time for fun?"

"Sure. If you ask Aunt Night nicely, she might let you ring it for her at lunch and dinner time." They loved that idea. "But not now. We need to talk, so why don't you go make sure Woof has water."

They knew what that meant. They climbed down from their chairs and went out the door arguing over who should get to ring it first.

"After we get done talking we're going to break out the M-14s and do some target practice," Max said. "I stripped and cleaned them all last night. They look good. When we're done shooting I am going to show you how to take care of them."

I saw the frown that fluttered across Night's face. Max's idea of learning how to take care of weapons meant learning how to strip them and put them back together in what he considered a respectable time. She hated doing that, which was surprising since she was the fastest of us by far. She caught me smirking and kicked me under the table. Max ignored our little drama timeout.

"This is what I think is going to happen. We are being set up for a raid. We should have been able to get better weapons and more of them. Eventually we will, but that is something for another day. I can tell you that when Gardener and I go back to law enforcement, I am going to make sure we are federally recognized."

"For the weapons we can get?"

"Yep. Exactly, Gardener. We are going to become 'marcher lords,' albeit minor ones for now. The Feds don't call it that. They may not even know their history well enough to understand what they are doing. But that is what they are creating in the areas near the Zone border, which comes back to why we are being set up."

He paused. "Tell me, Night. What's your analysis?"

I had forgotten about her self-appointed role as our group's intelligence officer. She did work on her maps, and we all found time to stop by and look at them. For me it was just something to keep her happy. But she took it seriously. At dinner she would give us an overview of what was happening in the world. Max had not forgotten.

"I believe there are three possible answers," Night said. "One: It is the Feds—a payback for the food-for-the weapons confiscation fiasco at the shelter. Two: It's the colonel and those assholes in West Virginia. Three: The sheriff is thinking along the same lines you are, Max, and he wants this area to be part of his domain. Of those, I'd go with the sheriff. Though I do believe he has Fed support at this point."

Max replied formally, "I agree, Night." She grinned. "I don't think it's personal for the Feds. They are just letting the dogs fight until the survivors shake themselves out and they know who to throw the bones to." Night grinned.

Old Guy muttered, "Assholes." I agreed, but then the Feds were always assholes.

"This is the way I see it happening," Max continued. "They're getting a feed from the Feds on our progress here. They also have eyes on us. They'll watch until the berm work ends. That's when they figure we will set the claymores out. Then they will wait a day or two to let us settle in and get comfortable behind it all.

"When they come, it will probably be a little before sunrise. They'll spread out a bit, probably a team of six, and come in fast. Four will split up to take the front and back door at the same time. The other two will clear the trailer. My guess is they will spray the bedroom area of the trailer with a burst and then come in to clean up. Then those two will join the other four for a final walk-through. They won't be planning to let anyone get out alive. Finally, they will burn down the place and blame it on the 'same bandits' that hit our neighbors. They'll follow that up with an offer to provide law enforcement to the town."

I nodded. *A nice plan*, I thought. It was how I would do it.

"I'm going to need to get the kids out of here."

"No, Tommy, you are not. They are going to sleep in the basement."

The steel in Max's voice was obvious and unusual. He wasn't fucking around. Tommy was stunned. Night looked puzzled.

"We're being watched, Tommy. There is a guy in a blind on the next hill. You pull the kids and by the time you get back from dropping them off, your farmhouse will be gone and so will we. They will come in fast and hard then. If they don't, they will pay the Feds to use a drone to take us out."

Night was nodding her head in agreement.

Tommy looked around the table. He didn't see any support. He shut his eyes for a minute. When he opened them again I was pleased to see a different Tommy looking out of them. Now if he could just maintain it.

"So be it," he said very softly. "Bring it on."

# CHAPTER NINETEEN

Three days later, Old Guy was finishing the little berm. Ninja and I were building the watch platform on the main berm. Max told us to build the sandbag base and then stop. His logic was that the attack would come after the berm was done but before we had finished hardening everything. The claymores would keep us feeling secure until then. That meant we could expect them tomorrow or the morning after.

We had been practicing with the M-14s. I liked them. They were solid, heavy weapons. Night hated them. They kicked. And what I liked in them were liabilities to her. Ninja turned out to be a pretty good shot. I was too. But Max was the rifle marksman among us. He shrugged off Ninja's compliment with a comment about how he just had more training and practice.

On the morning we finished the berm, Ninja asked Max, "What if they don't come?"

"They will."

He didn't look very convinced so I added, "Ninja, if they don't come, we will go find them."

"Okay. Cool." He grinned.

"Damn, when the hell did everyone turn into blood-thirsty killing machines around here? I thought that was my job."

"You're not the only one who hates digging post holes."

I turned to Max. "You know, you haven't shared your plan on how we are actually going to deal with this."

He looked at me. "That's because I haven't figured it out yet. Don't worry, I'll have something by lunch. Meanwhile you can help me with the addition to the chicken coop."

I looked at Ninja. He rolled his eyes. *Exactly*, I thought.

We worked until we heard the sound of the lunch bell. We headed back, passing the kids, both of whom were pulling the bell rope and grinning like maniacs.

As I passed them I said, "Great job, guys, but you can stop now." They did, reluctantly. It also silenced Woof, who was barking like a dog possessed. Damn kids.

We ate lunch. It was bread and some kind of vegetable lentil bean soup. I never asked. I just ate the food and praised it. I learned to do that after watching Night's reaction when Ninja had asked, tactlessly: "What the hell is this shit?" We didn't hang around to talk after that particular meal. We just got the hell out of the house and went back to work.

Max asked for a second bowl of soup, much to Night's delight. I didn't bother to tell her that Max would eat two-day-old, cold roadkill if he was hungry. I was starting to get the hang of this relationship stuff, I thought. Max finished drinking the broth from the bowl. Then he leaned back in his chair and stared at us. We knew it was talking time.

"Okay, here's the plan. I do not want to fuck around and take casualties. This is not a gunfight. This is a slaughter.

My goal is zero rounds fired by them. No mercy. We all on the same page here?"

Everyone nodded.

"After I go through the plan, we will do a walk-through. Oh, but I do have a surprise for them."

I grinned. "I knew you would."

"You see those two boxes over there, next to the car batteries? They're airbags, one from a 1999 Dodge Caravan, the other from a Chrysler P/T Cruiser. Those are our improvised claymores. They won't kill them, especially if they are wearing vests. They will, however, inflict a great deal of pain and pin them long enough for us to finish the job. We will kill them."

Ninja had a pained look on his face. "Max . . . American cars?"

I snickered. Max ignored it. "Yes, Ninja. American cars."

Ninja shrugged. I thought it was a good point. I guess you go with what you got.

He told us where we would be. "Night, I want you in the basement with the kids. If they get that far, then I know I can count on you to make them pay. Old Guy, I want you outside in a blind on the back hill. Ninja, you've got the back door. Gardener, you get the front. Tommy and I will deal with the trailer trash and sweep the outside perimeter. I want you all to call out when you take them down. If I don't hear from you, Tommy or I will be coming."

We talked some more about it and went over other possibilities.

Max added, "With the M-14 you can take body shots. Their armor won't help. Remember, what do we do?"

We all answered as one: "Head shots."

"What?"

This time we answered louder: "Head shots!"

He shook his head sadly. "What?"

We screamed: "Head shots!!!"

Juvenile, I know, but I loved it. I was pumped.

Then Max showed us the improvised claymores. Each one was in a brown cardboard box. Wires ran to a battery and a simple switch. Complete the circuit and the bag exploded, hurling steel ball bearings, glass, and rusty metal bits into their faces. If it didn't kill them, I figured tetanus would.

After that, it was just doing the walk-through and getting ready.

It was still dark when I took my post, sitting at an angle to the front door. Max had explained how they would enter. "The first one is going to come in low and move to his right. The other one will stay high and step directly in. Shoot the low one first."

So I sat there waiting. It was quiet. I could hear Ninja near the back door, shifting his weight in a chair. It creaked. I amused myself by exercising my fingers.

My hands felt stiff. Probably from all the pick-and-shovel work. I didn't like that. It could mess up my timing and speed with the Ruger. That could be fatal. Fatal was bad. I was tired. Working outside really wore me out, especially in the heat.

I woke up in a hurry when they came through the door. Jesus, they startled the shit out of me! Luckily—and that's what it was—luck, I clicked the claymore switch.

They were dressed all in black with masks, just like in the movies. Their eyes were very white in the dark. The low guy was just swinging his gun around to center on my head when the airbag blew. His eyes were just starting to widen when the metal and glass reached him and his buddy. It shredded his face. Literally shredded.

I leaped to my feet. I didn't even think about the M-14. Actually, when I jumped up it had dropped to the ground. If I hadn't been deafened by the blast and the first guy's screams of anguish, I might have heard it clatter. The blast from Ninja's claymore didn't help. Instead, I reached for the Ruger. It had never failed me and it was what I knew best.

I shot the trailing guy once in the head and cocked the hammer while I swung back to catch the first one in. He had dropped his handgun and had both hands pressed to his face. He was trying to hold a large flap of skin in place that had been almost completely sliced off his face. I remember seeing a nose where there shouldn't have been one He was bleeding, a lot. Or maybe he was having an *Oh, shit* moment. I don't know, and never will, because I blew his brains out right there. I remember thinking, *Oh, damn. Going to have to prime these walls before we repaint.*

I yelled, "Clear!" Then I turned and scuttled quickly toward the back door. My mind had registered the sound of Ninja and his M-14. It had also picked up the sound of a handgun being fired. That was not good. I was going to be really pissed if Ninja got himself killed.

I yelled, "Ninja!" as I rounded the corner into the kitchen. He was crouched in the doorway leading outside. His face was splattered with blood. He had his rifle locked into his shoulder and was tracking something. Next to him was a sprawled black-clad body.

I was about to yell, "Where's the second?" but I didn't want to mess up his concentration, so I grabbed a piece of wall to put my back against and froze in place. The boom of the Barrett was punctuated by a body going rapidly backward, past the open door. Well, now I knew where the second guy was.

Ninja looked back at me. "Hey."

I didn't like the tone of his voice, so I asked, "You okay, Turtle?"

"Yeah." He grinned for a second. It disappeared. "I didn't want to shoot him in the back."

"That's cool. Don't go darting out that door yet. I don't want Old Guy removing the top of your head in front of me." He nodded. "Hang on. I'll be back."

I went back, grabbed the M-14, and holstered my Ruger. No way did I want to listen to the shit I would catch from Max if he found out I had run off and left it behind. While I was doing that I heard the *zip-burr-r-r* of an automatic weapon followed by the heavy return of at least one M-14. It sounded like the trailer boys were a little off on their timing.

I yelled, "Clear" from the kitchen, since Ninja had forgotten to. I stuck the barrel of the M-14 out the kitchen door and waved it a couple times. Then I slapped Ninja on the back and said, "Let's go!"

I darted out the door, moving low with Ninja right behind me. We were going to have to circle the back end of the house to see the trailer. I went out at an angle until I had a clear view of it, and dropped to the ground. Ninja had gone past me to crouch behind an old oak tree that shaded the house.

Max, moving at a crouch, was headed toward us. Tommy was barely silhouetted against the side of the trailer, where he was crouched and covering Max. They both saw us at the same time. Tommy didn't move.

Max made it to the kitchen door. He pointed at Ninja and then the door. Ninja ran and ducked inside. Max said something to him and then signaled to me. We were going to sweep the area. Ninja would stay behind to cover the house. Old Guy was still out there covering us.

We began moving leapfrog fashion until we had swept our perimeter. Max signaled Tommy and me into him when we reached the dirt movers. He was still staying low and alert.

"I'm going out wide. I want to make sure we don't have anyone in the woods. Tommy, I want you to move toward the neighbor's old house. I want their vehicles. If you find them, drive them here, and put them in the garage for now. If they left anyone behind to watch, put them in the trunk. Gardener, get Old Guy to dig a hole and bury the bodies."

He didn't need to tell me to strip them. This wasn't our first time.

Tommy looked at me. "How're my kids?"

"Untouched."

He nodded.

Max said, "Good work, guys. We got to move, though."

We did. We disappeared them. The bodies went into a hole right outside the front of the main berm. We covered them with a layer of dirt to hide them from prying eyes in the sky, while we dealt with the SUV they'd come in.

The SUV sat in the garage until it was time to whack it. We had a piece of equipment with an end like a claw; it smashed the bejeebus out of the car. Then we pushed it on top of the bodies. We did a pretty good job of minimizing the time that anything identifiable was out in the open. It wasn't perfect, but sometimes perfect isn't possible. Only fast was.

First, though, we harvested their weapons and body armor. The body armor was good quality and easy to clean. I volunteered to hose it all down and hang it in the garage to dry.

The rule was, if you killed someone, you got to keep what they had. I donated the armor from the guys I shot to the house armory and gave Night the handguns. My plan was to sell one of them around Christmas, so we would have some spending money of our own.

# CHAPTER TWENTY

It was after lunch when I rode with Max into town. I was to be introduced to the town council, who was going to vote on whether or not to contract with us to provide law enforcement services to the community.

"You really think they will, Max?"

"Sure. We are cheap. All I asked for was half-priced meals at the diner and an equipment allowance. They have one functioning car left, the old police building, which has two holding cells, and not much else. Once we get done with the formalities, you'll get to meet our deputies. We will find or make some uniforms, and we'll be set."

"Anything I need to know for the meeting?"

"No. Just be brief if they ask you anything. Tell them you consider it an honor to be asked to serve the community. Hell, you know what to say."

"So who is on this town council? Anyone an asshole?"

"No—kind of amazing that way. The head of it is the pastor at the First Baptist Church."

I had to raise an eyebrow at that.

"No," Max said, "he is actually all right, at least so far. I think he's worried that if his flock leaves town for somewhere safer, then he'll have to get a real job."

"Yeah. Who else?"

"Shelli from the diner; Bob the builder, except he doesn't build anymore; and an old lady who is on it because, as far as I can tell, she has nothing else to do."

"Okay. So does our half-priced meal at the diner include dessert?" I liked dessert.

"It should. If not, I'll add it to the contract."

"Then I'm good with it."

The meeting was held in the town hall. It was an old, redbrick building with white pillars and chimneys from when they heated it with fireplaces. An engraved sign on a post in front let you know exactly how old and historic it was. They had unlocked the front doors for the meeting.

It was quiet inside, and a faint film of dust covered everything. We walked through the unmanned X-ray and search area without stopping. I was getting a strange vibe—a "hum"—from the building. I got it from every old building I walked into, especially ones that had been open for public use for a long time.

The chamber where we met looked like it had been renovated fairly recently, probably during the boom. Nice wood paneling, red velvet upholstery, and marble floors. The only spoiler was the brown water stain on the ceiling that had not been fixed. The paint around the edges of the stain was already starting to curl. Either the roof had leaked or a large squirrel had taken a piss up there.

I sniffed the air. It occurred to me that if it was squirrel piss, I might be able to smell it. I wasn't sure exactly what squirrel piss smelled like, though.

Max gave me his "Knock off whatever crazy shit is going on in your mind and focus" look. I really hated meetings, and this one had not even started.

They were waiting for us, sitting in high-backed, black leather executive chairs. The council table was solid looking and very heavy. I bet if they flipped it over and took cover behind it, we would have a hard time digging them out.

I knew Shelli and nodded to her. The rest I had seen around. The pastor turned out to be the guy who had been sitting in the diner with his wife when we met Old Guy. His comb-over was looking very sharp today. We even had an audience of five people. You got to love concerned citizens. I was surprised to see Old Guy in the audience.

The other woman on the council looked like every old white lady I had seen around here. The only difference was, she wasn't carrying an extra hundred pounds. I realized then that the real fatties were disappearing. Maybe poverty had turned out to be the best diet ever. I added that to my Ask Night Later list. Some days it grew to be almost as long as the list of things she wanted me to do.

The pastor sat in the center. The two women flanked him, and Bob was on Shelli's right. The pastor and Grandma had plastic bottles of water and notepads in front of them. In front of Shelli sat a silver metal reusable water container with a hand-painted scene of something flowery.

They had set up two chairs in front of the table, facing them. I knew where we would be sitting.

"Please take a seat, men." Pastor had taken charge. I bet he was a meeting person.

We settled in. I winked at Grandma, who grinned back at me. That caught me by surprise. I had expected either no response or a frown.

The pastor steepled his hands on the tabletop. "We have considered your proposal and we have several questions for you." I groaned inside. "We will begin with Mrs. Edna Jacobson on my right. Mrs. Jacobson?"

She leaned forward. For a second I saw her as she was when she was younger. She must have been a hellcat and a lot of fun at the rodeo—or whatever the hell they did around here back then.

"Taxes. We need money. You boys going to collect them?"

Max answered, "Yes, ma'am. As long as they are fair."

That set her back a bit. "What do you mean by that?"

"I mean this: We will not assist in collecting unfair or excessive taxes. We are not going to be used as tools for one person's, or several persons', enrichment."

"What makes you think anyone here would be interested in doing something like that, young man?"

Max looked around the room. "Pretty fancy meeting place for such a little town."

Someone in the audience snickered. I thought Shelli was going to bust out laughing. I thought, *Oh well, back to digging holes. At least this meeting will be shorter than I expected.*

She stared at Max. "That was then; this is now. Please answer my question." Then she softened. "We need to fund a couple teachers and a list of other things that don't concern you. Else my town will die."

"Ma'am, I understand. I just wanted that out front."

"Thank you. You also answered my other questions with that answer. I have no desire to see my town run by gangsters. That is all." She nodded at the pastor.

"Miss Shelli Peterson will now ask you her questions."

Shelli asked boring questions about patrol coverage and whether we were familiar with the town's rules, ordinances, and the laws of the county. She asked Max questions about specific ones, and he had an answer for each one. So they had been doing more than chowing down on apple pie and messing up her sheets while he was visiting her.

The pastor snapped me back into the moment when he said, "Please explain your policy about the use of force." I was really glad that Max was doing all our talking.

"I don't believe in using more force than is needed at the time," Max said. He went on a bit more with some high-sounding bullshit and finished with, "Like the police force I once was a proud member of, I plan on using 'To protect and serve' as our primary guideline in all situations."

Someone in the back began applauding. A few others joined in briefly, then it died out.

The pastor waited for quiet, then he said, "You have proven that to your country before. While never having served in the military myself, I respect your courage and devotion to duty, especially as you are one of the few to have been awarded the Medal of Honor. Now, if you'll just leave the room while we make our decision."

We went out and stood in the hall. I leaned against the wall by the door. "How long do you think it is going to take them to make a decision, Max?"

"Oh, I expect they already have."

He was right. The door opened about thirty seconds later. We had the job.

We left the town hall as a group, including our audience. Old Guy was walking and talking a mile a minute with a couple of the old guys he had been sitting with.

Everyone had hung around to watch Miss Edna Jacobson swear us in. To my surprise, she was the local judge. I was going to have to ask Old Guy about her. There was more to her, and her role here in town, than I had first thought. She was walking side by side with Shelli, and they were chattering away.

We all headed to the diner to celebrate with a free meal provided by Shelli to mark the occasion. Max and I walked together. He had hung back a bit as we left so I had waited with him. As a result there was a decent bit of space between the others and us. I wasn't all that savvy about the political stuff that had just happened. But I knew enough to know that we had waltzed into a done deal, and that Max had made it happen somehow.

I didn't really care about the details. I was curious about the power structure, though, and what we would really do versus what was said for public consumption.

"So, Max, what's the deal with Miss Edna and the tax thing?"

"Miss Edna thinks the lights have gone out for the town, but it is only a matter of time before 'the authorities' get them all turned back on. She wants to raise enough money enforcing, and maybe bending, a few of the old rules until that happens."

"She doesn't get it, does she?"

"No, and I would have been really surprised if she did. She will. She's a sharp old gal."

"And when she says *taxes*, how do you translate it?"

He looked at me, grinned, and said, "Tribute." That I understood.

"So when do I meet our two new deputies?"

"They're at the diner. Got to make sure our people get fed."

"Yeah. Don't forget the dessert."

We both laughed. Then we picked up the pace so we could walk in with everyone else.

The new deputies were waiting for us. I recognized them right away. They were the two that had rescued the girl at the library when I was here before. They recognized me, too.

Max was in a good mood. "Gardener, this is Diesel and Hawk."

We shook hands, and each said, "Hey. Pleased to meet you." Then we scanned each other from head to toe.

Diesel was the brother of the girl in the library. He was white, six foot two, one hundred eighty pounds, with brown hair that was streaked by the sun. He was wearing it longer than the last time I had seen him. There was a skull tattoo on his left forearm with writing that looked Arabic underneath it. He had a black semiautomatic holstered in a faded camo rig and an old Palin T-shirt that had achieved the washed-out look a few years ago.

Hawk was his cousin. They looked a lot alike. The difference seemed to be that Hawk liked lifting weights a lot more. He had his hair cropped short and was wearing faded desert camo pants and a T-shirt advertising Pabst

Blue Ribbon. Hawk had the same kind of gun rig as his cousin. His arms were covered in tattoos, and he had a metal stud in his eyebrow. Both guys were wearing faded and scuffed brown boots.

I thought to myself, *Shoot Diesel, move right a step, and then shoot Hawk.* Then repeat, because these two were not going to die easy. I began running through it in my head, picturing different scenarios—a habit of mine when I met people like this.

I guess I had kept eye contact for a bit too long. I tuned back into an uneasy silence broken by Max's overly loud, "Alright! Let's get some food." I let them walk in ahead of me.

Shelli unlocked the door and let us all in. Then she hung out a sign that read Closed—Private Party and started cooking.

I ended up sitting with the new deputies. I wasn't sure how that happened. I know Max had a lot to do with it and I just went with the flow. Also, it was a four-person booth, and no one else joined us. It felt like I had been set up for a blind date. I am not the most sociable person in the world. I have gotten better at it over the past few years, but it's not anything I search out or look forward to.

We had two menu choices. That's how it usually was at the diner. Today, Shelli had hamburgers and stew. The hamburgers resembled what I remembered of real burgers in name only. A Shelli-burger consisted of fried venison with onions between two slabs of homemade bread. No tomatoes or ketchup because of the blight. No lettuce because it was the wrong time of year. No cheese because there had not been any available for the past couple of weeks.

I ordered mine with fried jalapeños, even though I knew I would be dancing on the outhouse seat tomorrow. For a beverage we had our choice of several kinds of flavored water that never seemed to have enough sugar.

I tried to make small talk while waiting for my food. "So, you guys were in the army?"

"Yep."

"Where?"

"The 'Stan, and a short stint in Africa." So far only Diesel was answering my questions. Hawk just sat there, looking bored.

I thought, *Screw it*, and waited for my food. I ate it and liked it.

Shelli had someone helping her serve. She was plain looking but had a nice body. It was clear she knew and liked the guys I was sitting with; she took the time to greet them with smiles. They exchanged banter about people and events I knew nothing about. And Hawk thought he was bored?

The noise level built to a point that made quiet conversation a little difficult. Apparently one of the old guys was spiking drinks with a flask he had. I was sure I heard the word *moonshine*, followed by laughter. *Shit*, I thought, *the meth of the postcollapse world*. I had really hated tweakers. Shit-faced drunks were a lot easier to deal with.

This was when Diesel decided he wanted to talk. "You remember the library?"

"Yeah?"

"Me and Hawk had to clean up the mess afterward that you created."

"How's that?"

"Them boys you killed had family—a lot of family around here, family that went looking for us when they came up missing."

"Yeah. So what's your point?"

Hawk had quit looking bored.

"My point is I appreciate what you did. I just wanted you to know that it created a mess. One we had to clean up."

Hawk was nodding his head.

"Well, I want to thank you for sharing that. You need to know something important, though." I leaned forward like I was about to whisper a great secret. He bent his head forward to hear it. "I don't really give a shit."

Then I laughed in his face.

# CHAPTER TWENTY-ONE

Me and the deputies didn't talk after that. I thought about getting up but I wanted to eat my apple pie. Instead, they got up and left the table. We were all supposed to meet at our new office—I called it "the Headquarters," to Max's minor irritation. Max caught my eye as the cousins left. I just shrugged and ate their apple pie, too, when the girl brought it. He came over just as I was finishing the last of the pie. Shelli did know how to bake an apple pie.

"You ready?"

"Yep."

We headed out, with Max yelling goodbyes and comments to people even as the door shut behind us. His demeanor changed as soon as we got outside.

"What the hell was all that about?"

I shrugged. "They wanted me to know that I owed them."

"How so?"

"You remember when I was here last? The deal at the library?"

"I heard about it. Now I want to hear your version."

"Some punks decided to give this girl at the library a hard time. She is Diesel's sister, by the way. I backed them off while she texted her brother for help. He and his cousin arrived, saved her, and drove off into the sunset. I left. The bad guys followed me into the woods. I shot them."

"So what was his problem?"

"It seems the bad guys had friends and family who blamed it on them. I guess stuff happened as a result. Or as they put it, 'We had to clean up after you,' which seems to have bothered them."

"I'm surprised. I have never known you to leave anyone alive to be cleaned up. Buried, yes." He laughed. "Don't worry about it. We'll straighten it out."

Max had laughed, but I could tell he really didn't think it was funny. Max and I had been together for a while now. I could read him pretty well, maybe better than I could read Night.

Just before we entered our office, I undid the leather thong that held the Ruger in place. I didn't even realize I did it at the time.

Max did not open the door so much as he made an abrupt entry. The two deputies were in what was left of the outer office. Diesel was sitting in a chair, tipped back against the wall. His cousin was on the couch, holding a magazine that had been left behind and laughing as he read aloud to Diesel.

When Max burst through the door they both leaped to their feet. Max kept going. He didn't lose a step or slacken his stride. When I saw that he wasn't going to stop at conversation distance, I quickly sidestepped and turned so that I could watch Diesel out of the corner of my eye while focusing on his cousin.

Max stopped maybe an inch from Diesel. Then he said, very slowly, "When you accepted my offer, you enlisted in my own personal Marine Corps. This is not going to be your air-conditioned, goat-fucking, Starbucks coffee–drinking army of one that you are accustomed to. You will not make decisions until I think you are ready to. You will do what I tell you, when I tell you. You bring nothing to me that I cannot replace. You will leave any attitudes, thoughts, or beliefs that are contrary to that behind you. Do you have a problem with that?"

"No, sir!"

"What about your sheep-fucking cousin? I want to hear him."

"No, sir!"

"Good. This is going to be your only chance. You want to step outside with me? Maybe both of you?"

"No, sir!"

"I didn't hear you, sheep-fucker."

"No, sir!"

Interesting. I saw a bead of sweat form and slowly drip down from Diesel's hairline. I looked at Hawk and grinned. He stayed stone-faced. I don't think he liked me.

"Good. Because if you ever decide to question my or Gardener's authority, you will be shot on the spot."

Max held eye contact for a couple beats more and then stepped back. He kept stepping back until he was almost at the door. He stopped and said, "Gardener."

I may suck at social situations but I lived for this. I grinned at them and said, "Care to try your luck, gentlemen?"

They did. If it had been just Diesel, nothing would have happened. Hawk didn't know any better, or he was pissed enough to think he could beat me. They went for their sidearms.

They simply did not understand. I lived for this. While I worked on the farm, digging holes or whatever, I practiced in my head. I would take a break every hour or so and practice for ten or fifteen minutes. Every other hour I changed my reps. I practiced my draw standing, sitting, sideways, basically every position I could think of.

After dinner I would sit on the porch and listen to the conversations until there was about thirty minutes of daylight left. Then I would go down to the berm and shoot fifty rounds. I practiced with the Ruger and the Navy revolver. The kids came with me. They would sit about ten yards behind me in a row: Woof, the boy, and the girl. They would clap when they felt like it, and Woof would bark.

I shot at playing cards, the thin edge turned to me. My goal was to split the cards six out of six times at ten feet. I had six broomstick-size pieces of wood with laundry clips attached to them. Each one held a card. With the Ruger I could slice four out of six on average. With the Navy revolver I had hit six out of six twice now.

One evening Night got pissed at me: "You are freaking obsessed with those guns! What the hell is the matter with you? Why can't you ever give it a rest?"

I didn't know what to say. I thought she knew. "Because . . ."

"Because is not a fucking answer!" she screamed.

I shrugged and told her, "Because I want to live so I can come home to you every night."

She stopped and gave me the strangest look, then rushed into my arms and cried and cried. I will never understand women.

So they went for it. I had my gun out, cocked, and pointed at Hawk about the time he reached the butt of his weapon.

"Bang!" I said. Then I pointed it at Diesel. "Bang," and grinned at him.

They froze and slowly moved their hands away.

"Care to try for two out of three, gentlemen?"

Both of them shook their heads.

Max laughed. "Okay. Are we done sniffing each other and growling? I hope so. We have work to do."

# CHAPTER TWENTY-TWO

We spent some time talking about patrol schedules, and Max gave us his Five Commandments:

*You will not steal or extort money from the citizens of the town, or from strangers passing through, for your personal use.*

*You will be polite.*

*You will not verbally or physically abuse anyone in public.*

*You will not take shit from anyone in public while in uniform. This includes your mom, wife, and pastor.*

*In any situation involving a local and a stranger, you will take the local's side over the stranger's.*

He added, "For God's sake, try to use some common fucking sense."

Then he handed each one of us a small spiral-bound notebook and a pencil. "Use them. I will be looking at them. I want each man who goes off watch to update the incoming watch on what happened, how it was handled, and anything else of interest. I don't want to be surprised, and I don't want any of you surprised. I want to know about strangers as soon as you know, especially if there is more than one of them."

He paired me with Diesel for the next three days. He told him, "I want you to show Gardener as much of the town as possible in those three days. I want you to knock on every door and introduce yourselves. Talk to the people. Find out if anyone is really hurting. Do they have any special needs? How do they look? I want to know every crazy and near-crazy in town. I want to know who is really hungry."

Diesel asked what I was thinking: "Why?"

From the look Max gave him, I was glad I hadn't asked.

"Because if they are starving, we want to get some food to them," Max said. "Same thing if they need medical attention. From now on these are our people. I expect them to be treated as such."

He went on. "I also want to know the address of every house you think is vacant. We're going to have to go back later and check each one of them." He didn't wait for us to ask why. Instead he kept going. "Think about it. We don't need fire hazards. Plus, we might find some useful stuff that's been left behind.

"Hawk, you have the night shift for the next three days. Here's what I want you to do—" He paused and looked at Diesel and me. "Okay, you two, hit the streets. Gardener, I want you to come and talk to me before you go home."

I nodded. Since he was my ride back to the farm I thought that was already the plan. Instead I replied, "No problem, Chief." I turned around and hit the door before anyone could see my grin.

Diesel and I started walking side by side. It was hot out. The sun hitting the concrete sidewalk bounced back hard. We didn't have official shirts yet, but we had badges. I pinned mine to my belt loop for that Fed look. Diesel followed suit.

I decided to reach for new levels of maturity. I was on a roll. Hell, I hadn't shot them. "You know the town," I said. "Where do you want to start?"

"I don't know. I'm thinking we do the better neighborhoods first."

"They have more shade?"

He grinned. "Yeah. Plus, who knows? Maybe we'll get invited in for cookies and iced tea. That sure isn't going to happen in Trailer Town."

"Look, Diesel, I'm sorry if you caught the blowback from what happened that day." I bit off what I really wanted to say, which was *Hey, asshole, they wanted to kill me. Get over it.*

He waved it off, literally. "Like the man said, it's history. We need to cross the street here. There is a path behind the old auto parts store that puts you out on the street."

He started telling me about what used to be in the empty buildings we walked past. "I never understood why anyone wanted to start a gallery or a coffee shop here. But I tell you, it sure brought in a better class of women. Even better was, when it went sour, you didn't have to worry about their cousins, brothers, and uncles."

"Yeah. I got a feeling that not only am I going to need a mental map of the town, I'm going to need one for all the relationships and family trees."

He laughed, genuinely, "Just assume we are all related somehow, and you'll know all you need to know."

The first house looked vacant. Dead lawn. Dead vibe. I wrote it down. I thought about asking Diesel to do it, but I knew who was going to be getting the information, so I did it. My guess was Night would be updating her maps over the next few days. We rattled the doorknob. It was locked, and I peered in through the window. Empty.

"You know who lived here?"

"Naw. Most of the people I know live near or in Trailer Town. People my age, when we were getting out of school, they usually got out of town. We couldn't afford a house here and we couldn't afford one wherever we ended up."

The second house looked occupied but no one answered.

"You think they're at work?"

I looked at him and laughed. "Yeah, right."

I realized we were going to need to make up some fliers. Let people know we weren't there to serve papers or evict them. The suburban setting was beginning to lull me into complacency. "Look, Diesel. When we walk up to these doors, I want us to approach as if there is a crazy on the other side with a shotgun in hand and a belief that we are coming to evict him."

"Yeah, makes sense. How do you want to do it?"

"I'll knock on five doors. Then you knock on five. The other guy will hang back at an angle to provide support. You know, just in case the door explodes. Watch the windows, too."

"I know, I know. I've done this before."

I just stared at him thinking, *Why do people have to make everything so complicated.* I waited until he looked away. My glow from being so mature earlier was rapidly dissipating.

The next house looked empty, too. "Sweet Jesus. Anyone still live in this town?" I rattled the doorknob. It was unlocked. I looked in the window. I could see some furniture, but the house had that empty feel.

I opened the door and the stink hit me. I turned around and gave him the hand sign DANGER without even thinking. God bless military standardization. He knew the sign, and I saw his body language change.

"I think the place is clear. I'm going in." He nodded and jumped up on the porch with me. I went in first. Nothing. I yelled, "Hello! Police!" Still nothing. I did it the way Max had taught us. Diesel had been to the same school, which made it fast and a lot easier.

We found the source of the stink in the kitchen. Whoever had lived here had left their dog behind. It had died of thirst, probably trying to get to the sink. I don't know. I hoped they had stuck around. I would like to talk to them.

We backed up and out.

Diesel said, "Assholes."

I nodded thinking, *Hey, the first time we actually agreed on something. We both dislike dog killers.*

"We are going to check upstairs and the basement. God knows what else we will find."

"Probably grandma," was his reply. It was almost funny.

We didn't find grandma. We didn't find much of anything. I noticed that out here in the country, the houses seemed to remain in the same state the owners had left them. No trashing of the property or stripping of the appliances. The owners just decided one morning to load up the car and go somewhere else.

These people had forgotten the family dog. I saw evidence of kids, so I wondered what they had been told. Something like, "Sorry, son. Rover is going to stay here and watch the place for us" or "Someone is going to come by and take care of him."

I don't know why it bothered me so much. It wasn't like I didn't know firsthand how a lot of them would discard their own kids if they felt they needed to.

A couple of houses later, someone actually answered his door. He was a white guy, tousled hair, stained T-shirt. He hadn't shaved for a few days. When he opened the door, he just stood there blinking at us like we were apparitions.

We were a little off-balance ourselves. Since finding the dog we were a bit edgy. I think we would have been quicker to respond if a shotgun blast had greeted us. So we all stood there for an awkward couple of seconds, staring at each other.

"Can I help you?"

Diesel was doing the door knocking at this point, so he got to answer. "Hello, sir. We are from the local police and, um, we are new, so we, um . . ."

"I know you," the man said. "You're Frank's kid."

"Yes, sir."

"Come on in. Don't mind the mess."

His front room was a disaster. Clothes lay wherever he had tossed them. Shoes were scattered across the floor. Dirty glasses and a bottle without a label sat on a side table next to his La-Z-Boy recliner. The room didn't smell too bad, always a plus.

"So how's your dad? I haven't seen him in months."

They spent a few minutes chatting about Diesel's father, and what a shame it was that the town wasn't what it used to be, but that he had heard the fishing was good.

"And who's this?" Meaning me, of course.

"This is Officer Gardener. Officer Gardener, this is Mr. Morris." We shook hands and said our howdies.

"He's on the police force with me. We are walking around and introducing ourselves, seeing if folks need anything. Seeing if there are any problems."

"When did we get a police force? I thought they left town because they didn't like getting paid with promises." He thought that was pretty funny.

"Yesterday." I decided to join the conversation, mainly in the hope that I could bring it to a swift end.

Jeebus, if everyone who answered the door took this long to get to the point, it would take us a month to do this. Of course, then I had to answer where I was from and listen to him tell me about his cousin Mel who had taken the family to Northern Virginia to look for work six months ago. *Did I know him?* Yep. This was going to take a while.

I was hoping to wind it up so we could move along when the guy surprised me.

"Well, sounds good to me," he said. "What can I do to help? I'm getting tired of sitting around here on my ass."

That is when I had a minor burst of inspiration. Diesel was saying, "Oh, we have it under control—" when I cut him off.

"Actually, Mr. Morris, there is something you can do."

His whole face changed when I said that. This guy really wanted to do something.

"We could use your help. We need a block leader for this street."

"What the hell is that, son?" He wasn't being hostile or a smart ass. He was genuinely curious. So was Diesel.

"Well, a block leader makes a list of the houses on his block: which ones are empty, which ones aren't, who lives there. If they don't know about us, you could tell them. If you know anybody who is really short on food or medicine, let us know. I don't know how much we can do but we can try. And you can tell us if anything suspicious is going on."

"You're asking me to spy on my neighbors?"

"No, sir, not at all, Mr. Morris." This was Diesel. "Actually we were hoping you would lead them. Be the point of contact. I think Officer Gardener meant to say 'block manager.'"

He liked that. I liked that too. *Block manager* sounded white-collar and much more American.

He was getting excited. "That's a good idea. We need to get organized. The damn government ain't doing shit." He looked at me. "I thought you were talking about spying at first. Like some kind of Zone shit, but this is good." He was nodding his head the entire time. I also noticed he was standing a little straighter. Five minutes later I had us heading out the door.

"An Asian woman named Night may get in touch with you about this," I told him.

He grinned. "I do love Asian women."

"So do I. She's going to be my wife." That wiped the stupid grin off his face. We left him standing in the door, waving goodbye to us and yelling how we would hear from him soon.

I walked away somewhat stunned at what I had just said. I wondered how Night would feel about it.

# CHAPTER TWENTY-THREE

The next evening we were all sitting around on the porch after dinner when Max rolled in late. When he walked up to the house he wasn't alone. Shelli was with him. They walked up the stairs to the porch with Max trying to play it off like it was no big deal, but it wasn't working.

Old Guy turned to Tommy and in a falsetto voice, said, "Looky, our boy done grown up and got hisself a woman!" They fell over laughing. Of course, Old Guy had to repeat it a few more times.

Night got up, hugged Shelli, and welcomed her to the house. Then she went inside and came back with a couple bowls of what was left over from dinner.

Max turned it down at first. He changed his mind when he saw Night get that glint in her eyes. Shelli had no problems with eating it. I am sure she had eaten earlier, but she didn't act like it. She praised it repeatedly, which was a big deal for Night.

I think it was bunny stew with carrots, which was pretty funny, if it was true. I decided not to share that with everyone. Usually, when I tried to be funny people looked at me like I was from another planet. Night would often laugh at my attempts at humor, but anything to do with her cooking was off limits.

I was also in the mood, and I wanted it reciprocated later. Plus, I had something I wanted to ask Night, and it would help if she wasn't glaring at me.

I sat back trying to figure out how I could find a ring. Wasn't I supposed to wait until I had a ring? Maybe Old Guy could help me.

Meanwhile, Night was sitting next to Shelli, and they were talking about spices, and how they missed tomatoes. Max was finishing off his dinner. He caught my eye.

"I got a surprise for you."

"Yeah?"

He wiped his lips with the back of his hand, set the bowl on the floor, and said, "Hang on." He went to the truck and came back with a stack of blue shirts in his hands. He counted off the top four and tossed them to me. "You're almost official."

Night clapped. "Let me see!"

Everyone else was making a big deal of it except for Ninja. I knew he really wanted to be a deputy. I took one off the top and threw it to him. "Save it for when you turn eighteen, Turtle Boy."

He was grinning, and so was everyone else. I had not realized until lately that it didn't take all that much effort to make someone else happy.

"Thanks, Sport!" He knew I hated being called *Sport* as much as he hated being called *Turtle*.

"But they're blank," Night said. Where are the usual patches? The—the U.S. flag. And the city patch?"

"Sorry. No patches to be found. We can get someone to make some up, I'm sure."

Then Ninja asked, "Why are you going to put the American flag on there? We aren't Americans anymore."

His statement hit like a bomb that exploded in silence. Then everyone tried to talk at once. Old Guy went a little nuts. He was the most vehement and also the one who, from my perspective, said nothing other than clichés.

I think everyone was stunned because no one could wrap their mind around the idea that America might cease to exist. Or that America wasn't everywhere anymore, and that it was shrinking every month. Much less that we might no longer even be in America.

This led to more questions: *What is America? Is America only inside the Zone? Is it a government? A religion?* Everyone had a view and everyone wanted to voice it. No two people seemed to have the same view either.

"My God, boy," Old Guy shouted, "What about the Bill of Rights and the Constitution!"

Ninja looked at him puzzled. "What's that? I mean, I've heard of them—but what are they?" He looked at me as if I knew.

I shrugged. "Beats me. I think they were around a long time ago, probably back in Old Guy's day. I think they got rid of them or something. I know it had something to do with guns."

Everybody started chiming in with a different interpretation. I was right about the guns part. Tommy said, "Freedom of speech." Max added, "Searches. I know it has something to do with searches." Shelli was trying to tell everyone about old white guys and slaves, which didn't make any sense to me.

Then Night stood up, walked to the center of the porch, and began reciting the Constitution of the United States of America. She stood there, her eyes closed, speaking each word slowly and clearly. It was easy for me to see her doing the same thing in front of the class, or on stage at school, not all that many years ago.

When she finished, she opened her eyes, smiled at us, and said, "I had to learn it for 'What America Means Day' in fifth grade." Then she sat down quickly and, I think, a bit embarrassed.

I applauded, as did everyone else a second or two later. To no one in particular I said, "That was awesome. What happened to it?"

No one seemed to have an answer for that.

We decided to put the flag on the uniform, especially after I reminded everyone that Fed security troops expected to see it. The absence of it could get us relocated—or shot as terrorists.

Ninja still was not satisfied. "Okay, if we are going to do that, then I think we should have our own flag below it."

"Huh?" we all gasped.

"Ninja," I said, "we don't have a flag."

"Yes, we do. I designed it."

I looked at Night and Max. Night just arched an eyebrow while Max looked amused.

He told him, "Okay. Let's see this flag."

"I'll be right back," Ninja said and took off at a run for the trailer.

Max asked, "Anyone seen this flag?" No one had. Ninja was back in under two minutes, breathing a little harder than when he had left. He also looked really nervous. In his hands he held a folded green square.

"Alright, let's see what you got," Max told him.

Ninja looked over at me, and I nodded yes. I was thinking, *Kid, I really hope this doesn't have space ships or dragons.*

It didn't. It was a green square of cloth with a white square added to the center. Inside the white square was a bird that had been colored in with a black marker.

"A crow?" Night spoke for almost all of us. I was glad she had. I thought it was a blackbird. "Why?"

He answered proudly, "Because that is what we are."

Max sighed and rubbed his face. "I'm not following you."

"Max, don't you see? We are a family. Crows are a family. We take care of each other. Crows take care of each other. Crows are smart. They are survivors. So are we. The green is for the world. The white is because we are the good guys." Then he stood there, his flag held in front of him, but emotionally naked to all of us.

"Sure. Why not? I like it," Max said. "Hell, why not!"

Ninja grinned. We had a new flag.

Everybody began drifting away after the decision on the flag. I had missed my window of daylight to practice shooting. We said our good nights, and Night and I started toward to the trailer holding hands. Ninja walked with us.

I was struck suddenly by how much we had all changed—how different we were compared to when we were living in the motel. "Night, have you noticed that people talk more now?"

Ninja replied before she could. "Duh."

She smacked him in the back of the head. He didn't have a chance to evade it either. The girl was fast when she wanted to be.

"What was that for?"

"Because I felt like it. Now shut up." Then she said something to him in Chinese. It was the first time I had heard her speak Chinese since her parents died. She turned to me and switched back to English. "Yeah, it's because we are our own entertainment. I spend some time online still, but when was the last time you did?"

"Damn, I can't remember."

"We don't listen to the radio. No one here watches TV. Outside of me, this idiot, and Tommy, who does?"

"Yeah. You got a point." I thought about it. I wasn't standing still long enough or in a vehicle often enough to listen to a radio. I sure wasn't going to walk around with an iPod distracting me. Television? What was on that was worth watching?

"Hey, Ninj."

"What?" He sounded a little surly. Night was laying into him for some reason.

"Nice flag."

That brightened him up. "Thanks, G."

"I got one request, though."

"What's that?" he replied somewhat hesitantly.

"Can it be a raven? They are a lot cooler."

He shrugged. "Sure."

Night looked at me, grinned, and shook her head. "Yeah. We couldn't have a bird that's not cool, could we?"

"No way. At least not on my shoulder."

When we walked in the door Ninja went directly to the computer and logged in. We kept going, headed for the bedroom.

"Hey, Night. Can I talk to you before you kick Ninja off the computer and start checking what's going on in the world?"

"Sure. Let me do a few things first and I'll be in."

I unlaced my boots and hung up my gun belt. Night frowned on me sleeping with it on. I was okay with that after I jammed one of my spares between the mattress and the headboard.

I sat down on the bed. *Jeebus. How was I going to do this? I didn't even have a ring.*

About five minutes later she came in and sat down next to me on the bed.

Hesitantly, I said, "Night—"

"Okay. The answer is yes."

I almost fell off the bed. "What—? Wow! Really? How did you know?"

She grinned at me. "I still want to hear you say it."

I swallowed hard. "Night, will you marry me?"

"Yes!"

About ten minutes later I got out of bed long enough to close the door. By the time I woke up the next day, Ninja had already hoisted our new flag underneath the faded Stars and Stripes that we flew.

# CHAPTER TWENTY-FOUR

I woke up that morning with a smile on my face. Night was already up and in the bathroom. I listened to her singing softly to herself and thought this economic crash stuff wasn't as bad as everyone was making it out to be.

"Better hurry up, sleepyhead. I got to go make breakfast. The shower is yours."

I got up, showered in lukewarm water, shaved, and got dressed. Then I inspected and strapped on my gun belt, slipped the Navy revolver through the belt, and slid the bayonet in and out of its sheath three times for luck. I grabbed my daypack and filled my water bottle from the tap. When I got to the house Old Guy was sitting on the porch eating a bowl of oatmeal.

He laughed. "He's running behind. Just like you." He thought that was really funny. He was still laughing when I came back out with my oatmeal.

"Hey, Old Guy."

"What, buddy?"

"Any ideas on where I can get a ring?"

The spoon stopped halfway to his mouth. "What kind of ring?"

"An engagement ring."

"Alright! Say, Gardener," he lowered his voice, "what is Night going to say when she finds out you and Ninja are getting hitched?"

I choked on my oatmeal, swallowed some of my coffee, and then set the bowl down slowly on the porch deck. "No, asshole. I asked Night to marry me, and she said yes. I thought you might be able to help me…buddy."

He stopped laughing and cleared his throat a little. "Look, I'm sorry. I'll ask around."

"No problem," I told him and rolled my eyes. I went it, said goodbye to Night, and told her to tell Max I was down at the range waiting for him.

I stopped by the trailer, stuffed twenty rounds in my pocket, and went on down to my practice area. The morning was cool for summertime in Virginia. The last few summers had been that way. We still had days when going outside and moving around was like swimming in a hot tub. But the summer was just not as hot as it used to be. Weird considering I had grown up listening to people talk about global warming.

I was working on weak-arm shooting. What I liked about the long barrel of the Colt was that it pointed well. At the same time the barrel length and weight were problems. My right arm didn't have the same degree of muscle control and strength as my left.

Max came up behind me as I fired the last two rounds. I didn't hear him but I felt him.

"Hey, Max."

"Hey, Gardener. Ready to roll?"

"Yep."

"I'll be in the truck."

I joined him about five minutes later. I didn't rush my practices for anyone. He was waiting where he said he would be. We hit the road into town.

As we pulled onto the main road Max looked over at me. "You okay?"

"Yeah. So you know I asked Night to marry me?"

"No! Congratulations! When is the big day?"

"We don't know yet. I got to buy her a ring."

"Ask Diesel. He probably knows someone."

Max and I talked about different projects until we pulled into the station parking lot. Inside Diesel was waiting for us. Hawk had night shift and was home by now. Diesel came in early and covered for a couple hours until we came in. In turn, he got off earlier than I did, at least in theory.

Diesel went through what had happened during the night, as told to him by Hawk. "Not much. He was flagged down, and had to tell his cousin to shut the hell up. He lit up some people drinking in the park. They left and he didn't pursue them. There is an RV parked at the diner— probably a sleepover, but we might want to check it out. Oh, and he saw a gray Honda Accord driving around town. He didn't recognize the car or the driver, but he saw it twice, and that was from a distance each time."

"Good. Good report. I'm going to try to find us some kind of communication equipment. You and Hawk have cells?"

"Hawk lost his a while back. I got one, but reception is worthless most of the time. What about y'all?"

"Naw. I'm going to see if I can find us some walkie-talkies. I got a meeting next week with some people from Homeland Security."

Diesel snorted. "What do we need with those assholes?"

"We need them because they have all the cool toys. I don't know if you noticed but we are a little short on hardware these days."

"Yeah, Max, I understand, but don't their toys come with strings attached?"

Max laughed. "Everything comes with strings attached. That doesn't mean we can't cut them. Don't worry about it. Take the vehicle, gas it up, and run the town perimeter. Check out the RV. Then come on back, walk some streets, and get me some more block managers."

"Alright." I grabbed the keys off the hook and tossed them to Diesel. "You can drive."

Max yelled at me as we left, "Tell Ninja when you see him I want the crow patches in black and silver for us."

"It's a raven."

"Whatever—" and he waved us off.

We got into the car and Diesel asked, "Raven patches?"

"Yeah. You'll see." This was going be interesting. *Would he qualify for a bird?* I wondered.

"What do you want to do first?"

"I don't know, Diesel. Let's go check out the RV. Maybe they'll be giving away free cookies to law enforcement."

Shelli must have had Max drive her home late last night. The diner was open, and I could see her moving around inside. She waved at us. The RV was sitting in the diner parking lot, taking up two spaces, not that it was going to cause any problems. Nowadays for Shelli, four people coming in to eat at the same time was rush hour.

The RV looked okay, especially since it had to be fairly old. I had seen far worse on the roads. I think RV production in the states had stopped completely in '08 or '09.

"Too bad we can't run the tags."

I agreed. Even back when Max and I patrolled the motel area, we couldn't run plates unless a real city cop was nearby with his car. The RV had current in-state tags. The windows were tinted, but I knew there were people inside. I could feel them.

I pushed open the patrol car door; it had a tendency to stick. "I'll knock," I told Diesel.

*Damn.* On the door was a USMC globe-and-anchor sticker. It was another one of Max's fraternity brothers. I knocked on the door and stepped back and off center.

It opened quickly, almost like the guy had been waiting. He probably had been. He was turned sideways so I could not see his one hand. I did a quick DANGER hand sign to Diesel.

"Hello, Officer." He was one gnarled, leathery, bald-headed old coot. Maybe five foot ten, a hundred seventy pounds. He didn't have any shoes on. He was wearing a pair of running shorts and a blue T-shirt with Jesus Saves screened on it. On his left forearm was a tattoo that matched the door sticker.

"Sir, this is just a simple stranger check, but if you don't drop whatever it is you're holding behind you, I am going to shoot you dead. You have five seconds to decide."

"Five . . . four . . ."

"Give it to me, Darrell, before the officer shoots you for being paranoid."

The voice was female. It sounded like it had been cured in smoke and whiskey. I saw a white-haired little woman in a print dress appear behind him and take a heavy revolver back into the darkness of the interior. As she did, I heard her say, "Clear!" and gasp out a crackling laugh that ended in a coughing jag.

"Sir, your license and vehicle registration please." I was glad I had watched lots of old *Cops* reruns when I was a kid. The training I received watching them sure had come in handy the past few years.

He slowly reached for his back pocket. "I am getting my wallet," he said. "The registration is in the glove compartment." He handed his license to me. As he turned, I glanced at it and tucked it in my shirt pocket, making a mental note to return it once we were done.

"Thank you, sir."

He dug out the registration and was getting ready to hand it to me when the woman said, "Darn it, Dar. Ask the young man in, for Pete's sake."

I could tell he didn't want to. "Why, thank you, ma'am." I said, stepping up to the door.

He hesitantly moved aside. She was sitting at a table behind the driver's area and door. A cup of coffee and a pack of real cigarettes were on the table in front of her.

"Come on in. Dar, step away from the door. He doesn't want you behind him."

The old guy mumbled something and moved back. He looked at me, sighed, and sat down at the table with her. He said, "Come on, sit down. Invite your partner in."

Diesel came in. He didn't sit. He just leaned against the driver's seat, his arms crossed, and watched.

"So, you men want some real coffee and cookies?" We most certainly did.

"No, ma'am. That's not necessary." I had to say that. Pride made me say it, and I figured it was just people protocol. I would say *No, ma'am*. She would ask again and I would say yes. I was hoping I had guessed right.

She smiled and asked, "You sure?" I could hear the hint of humor and teasing in her voice when she did.

I replied, "Okay. Sounds good." She had a deep, throaty chuckle. After my eyes had adjusted, I saw she was a couple of shades darker than her voice.

"Well, okay then." She got up and poured Diesel and me each a cup of coffee and pulled a bag of real Chips Ahoy out of the cabinet. She laughed when she saw my eyes widen. "Yeah, I imagine they are tough to find outside the Zone."

"Is that where y'all are coming from?"

"Yep. Getting out while the getting is good." They started telling their story. Well, she did. He interrupted to ask a question about our community. *Were we churched here?* We were. *What kind of church?* I listed the churches I knew were open and he left it at that.

It was an interesting story. They were coming from the D.C. Zone. They had both retired from Homeland Security about two months ago. Now they were heading to Pennsylvania to a Born Again compound they had bought into. They had no problem telling me why they had left the Zone.

"The government has been taken in by Satan's minions." She paused for maximum effect while we took that in. "They are going to embed Satan's mark in everyone who lives within the Zone!"

"No way!" I replied.

"Yes, way!"

Her husband added, "Plus, if you don't, then you don't eat."

They went on some more about it. How it was going to be tied to your bank account, your labor card, your medical records.

"So when is this going to happen, and how come y'all know so much about it?"

She looked at me like I was an idiot and said, "It's in the Bible."

He smiled and said, "Our department was doing the logistics part of it. You know, the ordering and processing stuff." She was nodding her head. He added, "It's not going to be real popular. Give it a couple months and you are going to have a lot of people coming your way."

"You think they will bring cookies?"

"I doubt it. Just trouble."

We talked a few minutes more, gave them back their papers, and left them to continue on with our duties as guardians of the peace.

We took the squad car over to the gas station. Miss Edna had made arrangements so we could get gas without paying for it. I asked Diesel how she had managed that.

He replied, "Not a surprise, since she owns it." That came in handy, I suppose.

We drove into town afterward to the "business district," which was a stretch considering how few places were doing business. Once we found a shady place to leave the car, we parked and walked.

This, according to Max, was going to be part of our daily routine. Stop in and say hello. See if there were any problems. Talk about the weather and listen to whatever idle chitchat and gossip got served up. I let Diesel do most of the talking. He was good at it.

At one of the stores, an antiques place, he brought up that I was looking for a wedding ring. We had been talking to the old woman who owned the place, and she got all excited.

"Oh, yes! You must be fixing to finally marry that Asian girl of yours! Why, yes, I do have some rings you might like." She disappeared behind the curtain that closed off the storage area from the main part of the store.

I looked at Diesel and raised an eyebrow. He shrugged. Just another reminder that small towns are small worlds.

She reappeared a few minutes later with a tray. "I keep these in the safe. They're the only real valuables I have now."

I looked at them. Yep, they looked like wedding rings.

"Are you going to get an engagement ring also? This is a nice set." She pointed to the one she meant. She must have seen the expression on my face. "That's how it used to be done. You don't need to do it that way if you don't want to."

I shrugged and looked at Diesel. He shrugged. They were pretty. They matched. They had lots of shiny diamonds. I didn't see how I could go wrong.

"How much?"

"Oh, my. I don't know. I mean, I know what we could have sold it for a few years ago." She paused and her brow furrowed. "Hmm. Once upon a time, I would have sold it to you for five thousand dollars. I could let you have it for two and a half ounces of gold."

We dickered back and forth. I ended up paying an ounce and a half. I had a one-ounce Canadian gold piece in my wallet that I dug out and gave her. It was funny. I set it on the countertop, and as far as Diesel and the old woman were concerned, it was all that existed in that moment. Gold really does have a power all its own. Diesel asked me if he could look at it.

"You've got to ask the lady. It's hers now."

She nodded, and he picked it up and held it in his palm for almost a minute. Then he set it down gently. "Damn. I didn't know law enforcement paid so well."

I laughed. "It doesn't. I am a careful saver."

We left the store. I was feeling pretty good. She wanted to let me take the rings, but I told her to hold on to them instead. I told her I would be by to pick them up in the next day or so. As I hit the door I turned back and asked her, "You have any CBs or walkie-talkies hidden away in here?"

"Hmm. I don't think so, but I think my late husband had one. It should be in the garage."

"If you can dig it out, we would appreciate it. If you know anyone who does have any, let them know we're buying."

She walked us to the door and waved as we left.

"So you decided to do it the old school way, huh?"

"Yeah. It seems like the right thing to do."

Laughing, he said, "I hope you know what you're getting into."

# CHAPTER TWENTY-FIVE

I was getting ready to ask him if he was or had been married when we both saw it: the gray Honda Accord. It was sitting two blocks down and parked on the side of the road facing us.

"Foot or back for the vehicle?"

"Just keep walking." We were almost at the corner, where a side street intersected Main Street. "We're going to make a right here. I'm going to run parallel on the next street and see if I can walk up to him in his blind spot. I want you to head back to the vehicle and come in fast. Block him if you can."

By then we had made the corner and were out of sight. "Go!" I yelled and started sprinting for the parallel street. As I did I pulled the Ruger. In no time I had hit the intersecting road that marked where he was.

I had a choice. Go down another block and come up behind him or pop out about twenty yards in front of him. I had been working it out in my head as I ran. I wanted to come up behind him, but I got the feeling I didn't have time.

I went with my gut and I was right. The Honda was just finishing a U-turn. I wasn't the only one who trusted his instincts. He must have sensed something, too.

I could hear Diesel roaring down the street behind me as the Honda accelerated. I stopped in the middle of the street and thought briefly about sending a round after him. It would have been pointless.

I holstered my weapon as Diesel pulled up next to me, the passenger door already open. I jumped in, pulled the Ruger, and set it between my legs as I buckled in. Diesel had already covered ten yards while I was doing this, and the Ford Crown Vic was just starting to gain momentum.

Whoever it was in front of us was not driving a factory issue Honda Accord. The car was pulling away from us with ease. That's when the Crown Vic's oil light came on.

"Fucking Ford piece of shit!" Diesel screamed, slamming the wheel and taking his foot off the gas as the engine made extremely unhappy sounds.

He looked over at me: "Go or no go?"

"No go." I had no desire to walk five miles back to town after what would likely be a futile chase anyway. "See if you can nurse it back to the gas station or a garage."

He started to turn the Ford around but couldn't even do that before it died. He slammed the wheel again and yelled, "Shit," to emphasize the point.

"Well, we learned one thing about whoever is driving that car," I told him as I put my shoulder into the door to pop it open. Diesel was out of the car on his side. We looked at each other over the top of the cruiser and then down the empty road.

"Yeah. They're not friendly."

I nodded and grabbed my bag out of the back. Time to go find Max. Something was up. I could feel it.

We walked back to the station and found Max in the office sitting at the chief's desk staring unhappily at a stack of paperwork. He brightened up a bit when he saw us.

"Hey. What's up?"

We told him about the gray car. He grinned, swept the paperwork back to a corner of the desk, leaned back, and put his boots up on the desk. "So, tell me what you think is going on, Gardener."

"Someone is watching us."

"And you, Diesel?"

"Same. Seen it before."

"Yeah, we have, haven't we?" he replied pensively. "Going to have to do the same thing here that we did about it there."

Max must have noticed I wasn't following their shared unspoken conversation. "In the 'Stan," he said, turning to me, "we saw the same pattern. Usually it was scouting before someone drove a car into our area with a load of explosives and a high-definition vision of naked virgins playing in his head."

"Oh, yeah. That always puzzled me—the whole naked women thing. I thought a lot of those guys liked naked boys. Is there a separate heaven for them? Or do they spend eternity walking around, looking for the little skinny ones and asking them to roll over on their stomachs?"

That threw a wrench into their reminiscing. I think Diesel was having trouble parsing what I had just said.

Max laughed. "You're going to have to ask the next mullah we run across that one, partner."

"So, we go find them first and kill them?"

"Yep, Gardener. That's what we need to do."

"Well, I hope it's no one I'm related to," Diesel said.

We talked some more about where the gray car might have come from. Diesel pointed out nearby towns on the road map we had pinned to the wall and made some suggestions. "Of course he could be coming out of some farmhouse in the woods," he added.

"Before I forget," Max interjected, "you both need to be at the VFW hall for a meeting at 1800 hours. Night is going to talk about the block manager program, and I am going to make my pitch to the vets about a town militia."

This was news to me. "When did this get planned?"

"Oh, about two hours ago—when I found out they were having their monthly get-together."

Diesel grinned. "They gonna have food again?"

"Yep. I think the Ladies Auxiliary is doing something."

Diesel looked at me. "You're going to like this. Some of these women can cook!" We talked a bit more about the Ford. Diesel said he knew a guy who could fix it.

I never made it to the meeting. Just as well. I hate meetings. The food would have been nice. Watching Night do her thing would have been nicer. That would have taken care of the first thirty minutes and then it would have gone downhill fast.

There is always some idiot at this kind of meeting who feels the need to talk and talk. Then I would have to fight the overwhelming desire to pistol-whip his ass because even I am smart enough to know that would set back our community outreach program.

I was sitting in the office with Max. We were getting ready to head to the VFW hall; for Max, an appointment at 1800 meant arriving at 1745. Diesel had already left. He and Night were going to meet us there.

Then a concerned citizen came in. He said he had been driving into town from West Virginia to see family. About ten miles out of town he saw an RV off the side of the road and on fire. As he passed it, a white Ford F-150 and a gray, foreign-make car had pulled out and gone the other way. He didn't stop.

"I saw that RV on fire and them boys staring at me through that truck windshield, and I hit the gas. Them boys sure didn't look like Good Samaritan types to me, let me tell you. Thank God, I've driven that road a million times, because I was flying."

"They follow you?"

"No, sir. And I'll tell you what, I am taking the long way back when it's time to go home."

We asked him some questions but he couldn't give us a good description of any of them. Max thanked him, told him we would get right on it, and sent him on his way.

After the door shut, I looked at Max. "We?"

"Yeah, well, you and Ninja need to run by and take a look. I need Tommy and Old Guy at my side for the meeting—they being local and all."

"Okay. So, we take your truck, see what we see, and report back. That it?"

"Yep. And Gardener—"

"Yeah?"

"Make sure you pick up a couple M-14s. You may need to put some holes in steel."

"Okay. Give me your keys and I'll be on my way. Make sure you tell Night what happened."

He handed me the keys and as I walked toward the door he added, "Body armor. Get the good stuff for you and Ninja out of the armory."

"Yeah, yeah."

I grabbed the armor and two M-14s and headed to the farm to look for Ninja. Of course he wasn't where he had signed out to be. Instead I found him on the far side of the berm horsing around with the kids and Woof. I walked the kids back to the house while Ninja ran into the trailer and got whatever he thought he needed.

We headed back toward town and about fifteen minutes later we were moving down Route 235 West. We were probably going to run out of daylight, which would hamper our look-see. I figured we'd have to come back and told Ninja as much.

"Then why are we going now? Can't it wait?"

"No. There might be hurt people waiting for help. Plus, how can we be the law enforcement around here if we never go out on calls?"

"So where's our medic kit?"

"Shut up, Ninja."

He laughed. "I thought so."

We talked about farm stuff and some girl he had seen when he had been in town. We saw the smoke right about where we were told it would be. It was coming from a dirt pull-off picnic and rest area. I stopped the truck. No one else was around. I saw a trailhead at one end of the pull-off with a couple of state signs next to it.

"Is the Appalachian trail around here?"

Ninja replied, "I have no idea." His tone left no doubt that he thought it was a stupid question. He was right; it was.

"Okay, hop out. Take the M-14 and cover me. I am going to roll right up to the RV. Get off to the side in the bushes."

He gave me a look that clearly said, *Idiot, I know what to do*, and jumped down out of the cab.

I rolled up to the RV and got out. The camper had not completely burned. I could still make out the sticker on the door. It was the couple heading to the Born Again compound in Pennsylvania, all right.

I didn't like the smell of the smoke, though. Burnt RV should not smell like pork barbecue.

I gave Ninja a hand sign: CLOSE ON ME. Then I walked around the RV. That's where I found the old guy. He was lying in the dirt. It looked as though they'd had him kneel and had shot him in the back of the head. There was a spent brass casing on the ground about five feet from him. I picked it up and looked at it. It was a 9-millimeter. I dropped it into my pocket.

About then Ninja came around the corner. I looked at him. He looked curious instead of like he was going to barf. He was starting to get hardcore, but I thought I would spare him seeing the toasted grandma I knew I was going to find.

"Ninja, start making a circle around the RV. Work your way out and see what you find."

He nodded. One last backward look at the corpse and he began walking. I went around with him and stood in front of the door. It was open and I could see stuff scattered over the floor inside. It looked like the contents of a purse.

I stepped inside. The cabinets in the kitchen were all open, and everything was gone, even the cookies. The refrigerator was also empty.

I walked back toward the bedroom. That's where she was, or what was left of her. She was curled up on the bed—what was left of it. She had been set on fire. I hoped she was dead first. The bed was smoking, and she was crispy. It was not a nice crispy. It was a red-and-black-with-glints-of-white-from-bones crispy.

I backed out of there. I walked about ten yards away from the RV and took a lot of deep breaths. The smell would not go away. It was as if it had crawled up my nose and made itself at home in my sinuses.

I shrugged and turned around. Ninja was standing there looking at me. He was getting pretty good at moving quietly.

"There was someone in the RV, wasn't there?"

"Yeah. It was an old lady. They set her on fire."

"Why? To hide what happened?"

"Yeah, probably."

"Then why didn't they drag the old guy in there too?"

I took my eyes off the road long enough to look at him. "Good point, Ninja, good point. Maybe they were just assholes."

"Yeah."

"Should we bury them?"

"Not now, Turtle. We don't have any shovels, and I am not sure how Max wants to handle it."

He was quiet after that. I was thinking to myself, *No way am I going back in there and hauling Crispy Grandma out.* Just thinking about it gave me the willies.

We headed back. I dropped Ninja at the house. Night wasn't there so I headed into town. Old Guy would have given them a lift back, but I was restless. If I could have, I would have headed for the Interstate and driven for a while. Instead I figured I would go to the station, park the truck, and walk the town.

Nobody was at the station. Still at the VFW hall talking, I guessed. I decided to leave a note to let them know what I was doing. I went to Max's desk in search of paper and a pen. Curiosity got the better of me and I thumbed through the paperwork. Nothing exciting. Fed paperwork for law enforcement grants. Town census notes. Financial projections by tax revenue. He was welcome to it.

I walked the town. It was a quiet night. The cicadas were out, and I noticed how the stars were a lot clearer and there seemed to be more of them. I also noticed that I still smelled like pork barbecue. I hoped I had some clean clothes back at the trailer because I wasn't going to be able to get my usual three days out of these.

I passed a couple of people out walking and said, "Evening, folks." It was returned with a smile and a hello. I was glad I liked watching westerns as a kid. It was great training for this. I headed back.

They were all at the station, waiting and buzzing with excitement—Night especially. I sighed inwardly. I knew I had a few hours of listening to her analysis of the meeting ahead of me.

I won't bore you with what was said. We talked for the next two hours. I told Max about what I found, and he called the state police on our newly installed landline. It worked most of the time.

One day Miss Edna told us that she had talked to the woman who took care of the telephone lines for our sub-region. If we were willing to pay a small fee, the woman had said, she would see that our phone service worked most of the time. She could not guarantee it, because the phone company was no longer doing maintenance on the equipment. She would try to keep the line up and running as long as they could scavenge material. She was even willing to take payment in food or other items. I had been there when Miss Edna came by the station to talk to Max about it.

"Max, I don't mind paying them their 'maintenance fee.' I'm not sure how we are going to come up with it, but I will figure something out. What I am worried about is if they try to squeeze us for more once they get the first payment." She paused and then added, "After all, this is the phone company we're taking about here."

Max laughed. "What are we going to do if they try that, Gardener?"

I thought for a few seconds. "Hmm. How about her, or one of her employees, hanging from a tree with a sign around their neck? I think something like 'I got greedy and tried to Banker this town' would get the message across."

Miss Edna looked at me. I watched thoughts flit across the surface of her eyes. "Yes, that would do just fine."

Max came back from making the call and pulled me aside. "The state police don't want anything to do with it. They said bury them and e-mail them the victims' information. If we could do that, he told me they would owe us one."

"Shit, Max, I am not burying her. You can count me out on that one."

"Don't worry. I got a couple of people from the meeting who will do it for silver. It will also help focus them on why they need us."

"Well, I hope they don't eat a big breakfast before they go. That was nasty."

"Oh, and don't bring up the militia. Old Guy won't shut up about it, but I want to talk to you about it in private."

"No problem. We are going to have to find these people."

"Yep. All in due time."

We went back to join the others, and Night told me about the progress the block managers were making. She would soon have a complete census for us that would include who had Internet or phone service, where the vacant houses were, and much more. She also wanted to talk to me later about the RV incident. She wanted to look at the topographic map to see if she could figure out possible places where they might be based.

Max was right. Old Guy was talking nonstop about the "new unit." I sighed. I was trapped for at least another hour.

# CHAPTER TWENTY-SIX

Two uneventful days passed. I showed up for work on the third day expecting the same. I stopped by the station to get Diesel. Hawk had decided he liked working the night shift. Eventually we would go to three shifts, with Diesel and me trading off on the swing shift. That way I could still do chores on the farm. It made for a long day, but hey, everyone else was putting in some serious time, too.

I didn't know Diesel really well yet, but from his grin I knew something shitty was in the wind. "Hey, Max. Hey, Diesel. What the hell you grinning about?"

Diesel laughed. "You'll see."

"Yep. Come on, Gardener. It's time to introduce you to your new patrol car."

I followed Max outside. I had noticed a blue minivan parked in front and was going to ask about it. It looked like I wasn't going to have to.

Max handed me the keys. "That's it."

"You got to be kidding me. What am I going to do, take people into custody and then drop them off at their soccer game?"

Diesel started snickering in the background.

"What're you laughing about?" Max asked. "You got to drive this piece of shit too."

"I know, I know."

I opened the door. There was a blue bubble light on the dashboard. I pointed at it. "Oh, now that makes *all* the difference in the world."

"You didn't think I was going keep letting you drive my truck, did you?"

I slid the back door open and looked around. On the floor was a DVD case. I picked it up and read the title: *Veggie Tales*. "So what were you using this van for before, torture?"

"Very funny, Gardener. It's only until we get the Crown Vic back from the shop."

"Right. I suppose this starts today?"

"Yep, as soon as you get briefed. You're on your own for a couple hours. Diesel is going to help me put in a tollbooth. Didn't Night tell you?"

"No." Actually she had started to, but I had changed the subject to something that didn't require as much talking.

I rolled out in my blue 2001 Chrysler Town and Country. I hit the business section, parked, and did my rounds. I stopped in and picked up my rings. I had to slice my last remaining gold piece in half to pay off the balance. Then I got back in the minivan and started doing my drive through the residential areas.

That's when I saw the Accord. It had pulled out of one of the side streets and was heading toward the outside of town, where it could pick up Route 235 to West Virginia.

I swept the bubble off the dashboard and turned to follow him. I saw him checking me out in the rearview mirror, but he didn't pick up speed. Why should he? I was in a freaking minivan.

He was going to have to stop at the four-way stop in three blocks. I put on my turn signal, turned right and then left, so I could run parallel to him.

Three blocks up, I hit the intersection, made my left, and was picking up speed as he rolled to a stop. I didn't. I floored it and was moving about thirty-five mph when he started through the intersection and I T-boned him.

*Wham!* My airbag blew. Oh yeah, that hurt. I fumbled for my belt release and stepped out of the van. The other car's airbag had not deployed. I was out of my car a few seconds before the driver of the Accord was, not that it meant all that much. It took me that long to be sure that all parts of me were going to function correctly.

He stood shaking his head and holding on to the edge of his car. Since I had T-boned him, I had to go around his car. That was going to take too long.

I yelled "Insurance!" at him and stepped back up into the minivan. From there I put one foot into the shattered side window frame and pushed off, trying to leap across the top of the Honda.

I think he figured out about then that I wasn't some dumb-ass who was taking a short cut to him with my in-surance card. He dropped his hand from the car and went to draw his weapon.

I didn't make it all the way across. I came down hard on top of the car, my chest hitting right above where the driver's head would be. I didn't have time to draw. I should have drawn when I jumped. Instead, I reached out and grabbed his head with both hands and smashed it against the car where the door joined the roof. Then I pushed him back and did it again.

I wanted to kill him, but I also wanted to talk to him. So I shoved him back hard. He lost his balance and fell onto his back. I pulled my legs up under me, jumped off the roof, and fell on top of him.

He was moaning. He wasn't happy, and neither was I. My chest hurt and my right hand was bleeding. I must have scraped it on the shattered glass or metal.

I put the barrel of the Ruger in his face and said, "Don't. Fucking. Move."

Blood poured from a gash in his head. I reached down, pulled his weapon from its holster and tossed it about ten feet away.

"Get on your knees and take off your shirt."

"Damn. Call 911. I need help."

*911?* I thought. *Is this asshole in shock or did he just drop in from Zone central?*

"Get on your knees, asshole. You need to take off your shirt so I can wrap that head wound."

He struggled with getting it off. I let him struggle. Damn, he had bled on it, too. We needed to get some gloves for this kind of shit.

"Toss it to me." I took it and walked behind him. "If you move, I am going to hurt you."

"Like you haven't already."

I wrapped it around his head and knotted it tight in the back. "Stay there."

I looked up to see Max and Diesel flying down the street toward me in the truck. Max braked hard and was out the door as soon as it stopped. Both he and Diesel had their weapons drawn. Diesel had an M-14 and was scanning the rooftops and houses.

Max yelled, "You got any more, G?"

"We're good. This is it."

Max holstered his .45, but Diesel did not relax. If anything he was getting even more tense. He kept watching the rooftops.

Max walked over and looked at the minivan. "Damn, Gardener. If I knew you felt that strongly about driving this, I would have let you take the truck." He walked over to where the dipshit was on the ground. "You know this is going to be a little embarrassing for you if it's the wrong guy."

"It's the right one. I remember the tag." That wasn't entirely true; I only remembered the first three letters. Close enough.

*Where was Diesel?* I expected him to be standing here giving me a hard time. I turned and spotted him crouching by the back of the minivan. I didn't like how he looked.

"Sarge, where are the rest of the guys?" he said, searching around. Diesel was with us physically, but I wasn't sure where the rest of him was.

"Sarge, we need a pickup. Those fuckers are somewhere around here. They always are when they set this shit off."

The sense of urgency in his voice was palpable.

I wasn't the only one who noticed.

"Hey, buddy. I think your man there is losing it." The Dipshit followed his comment with a malicious chuckle that ended with him crying in pain and pitching forward. A kick in the kidney hurts, especially when you're wearing boots like mine.

Max was next to Diesel now. He was talking to him softly. I couldn't hear what he was saying but I flashed back to when he had done the same thing for me when I was hurting really bad.

I knelt next to Dipshit and did my own version of a soothing whisper in his ear. "When I get you alone in about thirty minutes, I am going to hurt you so bad you are going to beg me to stop." He didn't say anything but I knew he was listening. "Then you are going to find out that I'm just getting started."

I stood up. Max had his arm around Diesel. They had their backs to me. Dipshit was on his knees still, both arms on the ground, with his head hanging down. He was still moaning from my kidney shot. I stomped the hand closest to me and watched him go flat on the ground, shrieking. Max and Diesel didn't even turn around.

Diesel seemed to be back from wherever he had gone. I could only guess where that might have been, but I bet it involved the sun and friends dying. He was embarrassed about it, I could tell. Max had him go through Dipshit's car while we stood over him.

"Did you search him?"

"No, I thought I would just shoot him if he twitched wrong."

"That's not how we do it, Gardener. You got to search him."

So I patted him down while he whined about how he needed medical help. The only thing I found on him was his wallet. I started going through it.

"Hey! Dipshit has a name. He also has a Zone pass." It was an old pass, expired three months ago, and the photo was a few years old. "So, Casey. That is you, right?"

"Yes, Damn. You going to help me?"

"In a minute. Maybe."

Diesel had found a Motorola walkie-talkie and a cell phone in the car. "Check it out." He held them up for us to look at.

"Nice. Stomp the shit out of the cell and bring me the walkie."

He brought the walkie-talkie to Max, who said, "Roll Casey over."

I rolled him over. "Damn, Casey, you are going to have a couple of gorgeous black eyes."

Max knelt down next to him. "Okay. When is your next check-in time?" Casey looked away. "Okay, Casey, I am going to ask you one more time. If you don't answer, I am going to ask Officer Gardener to break all the fingers on your other hand."

"Prick!"

I drew my foot back to prompt him, but Max shook his head no.

"Alright—at four o'clock if I have any problems."

"And if you didn't have problems?"

"I would just show up."

"Thanks, Casey. I appreciate it. Okay, put him in the back of the truck. We'll take him to the station and get him fixed up."

Diesel grabbed his feet and I got the head.

"Remember what I said, Casey? We are not done caring and sharing yet, not by a long shot."

# CHAPTER TWENTY-SEVEN

We dropped him in the back of the truck. Max and Diesel had their shovels and a tamp bar in there, so he was a bit unhappy about that also.

"Jesus Christ! Wait until I tell my dad about this! He is going to have your balls."

I climbed in the back with him and slapped the side of the truck cab to let Max know I was ready. "Really? Is it okay if I save the rest for your mother?"

"Fuck you. You're a goddamn whack job."

I didn't say anything. I just smiled and stared at him until he turned his head.

When we got to the station, I stood him up, and we walked him in. We had two holding cells. One was filled with boxes of paper and who knows what from the previous administration; the other was guest-ready. We put him in there.

"Am I going to get a doctor? I want to make a phone call."

"Yep, we'll get right on it," I told him. We left him mumbling to himself in the cell and went back to the main area of the station.

"Diesel, take the truck and see if you can get Donna to come by and take a look at him, will you?"

"No problem." He didn't hesitate, either. I think he was still bothered by losing it in the field.

We waited until the door had shut. Max put his boots up on the desk. "So, how do you want to do it, G? I think you have established a rapport with him—not that I would mind beating the snot out of him."

"We might not have to, Max."

"Do tell."

"Well, let me tell you his backstory. I'm guessing on this but I bet I'm pretty close. He's young, probably not more than nineteen. His dad is someone back in the Zone, probably military. He's gay. Dad didn't like it. He ran and ended up with whoever the hell he ended up with."

"The wrong crowd?"

We both laughed. "Yeah. Those people. I think he has a lover in town. That shouldn't be too hard to find out. There can't be more than four gay people in this town."

"Actually five, but two are a lesbian couple, so I think we can rule them out."

"You got an idea who then?"

"Yeah. He's in the militia. I doubt if he has any connection to what happened on the road. I'll talk to him anyway as soon as Diesel gets back."

"So we make Casey here an offer," I said. "We tell him he can go home—that is, if Daddy will pick him up—but he has to tell us where his buddies are. We go wipe them out. Maybe Daddy shows his gratitude in a tangible way."

"Sounds like a plan. You want to make the offer?"

"Sure. If Diesel comes back before I come out, you might have him take Donna for a walk."

Max grinned. He knew what I meant. Donna was a healer, not a pain-giver. She might get upset if I had to resort to physical attitude adjustment tactics.

I walked back into the holding area, past the sign that read Check Your Weapons Before Entering! I checked mine. It was still there.

Casey was huddled in the corner. He didn't look at me.

"Hey, kid."

"What?"

"I don't care if you are gay."

That got a reaction from him. "Who said I was gay?"

"No reason to get defensive. Like I said, I don't care."

"Fuck you."

"How's the hand?"

"It hurts. Hurts bad. My ribs and head do, too."

"Well, we got a nurse coming."

"I don't need a nurse. I need a freaking hospital, thanks to you."

"We don't have a hospital. We don't have a doctor. We don't have pain meds."

"You don't have shit, do you? I want to make a phone call."

"To your dad?"

Silence. Then, grudgingly, "Yeah."

"Let me explain something to you. Just to make sure we're on the same page and all."

"I'm listening. Hey, can you at least get me some aspirin?"

"No. Not until you listen to me and pick a scenario. You do know what a scenario is, don't you?"

He rolled his eyes. "An outline or synopsis. I'm not stupid."

"First, I give you the backstory. You were seen killing those two old people." He twitched at that and started to say something. He changed his mind and looked away from me. "The ones in the RV." Just in case there were others. "Well, them people you killed?—Grandpa was a Marine Corps vet."

That hit home. *Interesting*, I thought.

"Okay, now that I have your attention, let me present Scenario A. We have an eyewitness. We have a shell casing from Grandpa's execution."

I liked the part about the shell casing. Thanks to *CSI*, which was probably still running somewhere, everyone knew that any evidence found on the scene would identify anyone who was within fifteen feet of a crime.

"I didn't shoot him!"

"Kid, I got your gun. I can walk outside and fire a round in the dirt. Then I pick up the brass. We got an eyewitness and a brass casing that I will say I picked up at the scene of the crime. Then, I get a pair of bolt cutters and I come in here, sit down all nice and cozy next to you, and start cutting off body parts until you confess."

He was staring at me wide-eyed. "You wouldn't."

"Kid, in this town I can do whatever I want. If you have not figured that out yet, then I am wasting my time talking to you. Am I?"

"No-o-o-o!"

"Look at me, kid. Look me right in the eyes. Do you think you can tell when someone is lying to you?"

He nodded his head.

"Good. I don't care if you are gay. Truth?"

He nodded yes.

"I don't care who your dad might be. Truth?"

"Yes," spoken very softly.

"I have no problem with cutting off your fingers, toes, and cock if I have to. Truth?"

He just swallowed.

"Truth?"

"Yes!"

I figured later that threatening to cut his dick off was what tipped him over. Hell, it gave me the willies.

"You have any other scenarios?" This was tentatively asked. He wasn't sure yet how much wiggle room he had.

"Did you kill those people?"

He shook his head slowly, then the words started coming. "I'm just a spotter. I spot people I think might have something good. Then I follow them and call in. I give the description of the car and who's in it. They did the rest. Honest!"

I shook my head. "You want Scenario B?"

"Yes!"

"Tell me about your dad. Who he is? How I get hold of him?" He was nodding his head with enthusiasm now. "Then you tell me all about your friends. I mean how many. What kind of weapons. Where they are living. Anything you can think of. You got it?"

He got it. He was liking this plan.

"So talk to me, kid. Oh, one more thing. If it isn't like you say—or if any of my friends get hurt—then I am going to dig a hole in the ground, put you in it, and set you on fire. Truth?"

"Yes. Oh, my God. Truth."

"Start talking."

He did. One thing I noticed was that I could remember more than I could before. I don't know if it was because I was no longer feeding my brain a constant stream of stimuli or it was the memory trick Max had taught me a million years ago. Probably both.

Casey's short version was there were four men, two women, and a couple of pit bulls. Two of the guys were a couple. That was who had recruited him. I didn't ask if the pit bulls were in a committed relationship.

They called themselves the Bunker Busters. I thought that was interesting. They took the name because they originally planned to prey on people in bunkers. They had done a couple, but lost two of their original people in the process, and decided to go for softer targets.

They used the women as decoys. They would wave down the mark and claim to have mechanical problems. Then the women would pull their weapons at the right moment and whistle up the men. They usually left two people at their safe house to keep an eye on things.

They had AR-15s, a Ruger Mini-14, and a shotgun. The women had handguns only. All the handguns were semiautomatics. Glock and Beretta was all he knew. Two of the men had armor.

"Are there any veterans?" I asked.

"Yeah. Glenda was an MP. She's a real bitch, too. I think Jonesy was in the air force. My friends, Merle and Chad, told me they had been in the national guard. Darlene is just there for decoration. I don't know about the other guy. I don't think he likes me. He calls me Little Bitch, if he talks to me at all. Chad said that he really likes me, but I don't think so."

"Yeah, kid. I doubt it, too."

"So when is this nurse getting here? I hurt!"

"One more thing. Your dad have a personal cell?"

"Yeah. Supposedly only three people have the number, but I doubt that." I looked at him.

He sighed. "I suppose you want it."

"Yep."

"It's 202-456-1414."

"One more thing. Daddy got a name and a title?"

He told me and then he grinned. The grin faded when he saw it made no impression on me.

"Alright. I'll go see if the nurse is here." I got up to go.

"Hey! You're not going to hurt them, are you? I mean, for real. My friends—"

"Kid, they are all dead men walking now."

# CHAPTER TWENTY-EIGHT

I walked back out into the bullpen area. Donna was there. Everybody froze what they were doing and looked at me expectantly.

"He's ready for you, Donna."

She gathered up the bags she had brought with her and walked past me. As she passed she said, "Hey, Gardener."

I laughed. "Hey, Donna."

Max asked, "So what did he have to say?"

I ran down what Casey had told me. Max looked off in the distance for a minute, thinking it through.

"So who's his daddy?"

"You are going to love this, Max. His daddy is Robert Case, the current National Security Adviser."

"No shit?" We both started laughing. The laughter was tinged with an undercurrent of *Oh, my God.*

"How do you want to handle it, Max?"

"Well, hell, give Big Daddy a call. Don't lie to him. He should have the resources to do this quickly. Arrange for a pickup ASAP. We got a couple of hours of daylight left.

Meet him outside of Centerville, where Tommy picked us up. Then get back here. We got a house call to make."

"Alright. You got any requests for the man in case it comes up?"

"Naw. Play it by ear. Do what you think is right. Hell, take my truck. We don't want the little shit dying on us."

"Okay. I'll give 'Bobby' a call. Then I'm going to the diner to get something to eat. By then Donna should have Casey patched up and ready to travel. Let Night know what's up."

Max and I stood there and stared at each other for a handful of seconds. Then I shrugged and said, "Life's a bitch," and laughed.

He didn't. "I can go with you—"

"No. I doubt if it's going to be a big deal. I mean, what did we do wrong?"

Max thought that was funny. "Yeah, really. Just tell the kid to keep his hand in his pocket. If it will fit."

I went into the other office, which had the working phone. I picked up the handset and got a dial tone, took a deep breath, and punched in the number.

It rang three times before the other end picked up.

"Hello." Brusque. A deep voice. A command voice. The kind of voice that, just by the tone, you knew you were going to have to make a real effort to satisfy.

"Mr. Case?"

"Yes."

"My name is Officer Gardener. I am with the police department here. We have your son in custody."

Silence. Then, "What are the charges?"

"Murder. Assaulting a police officer. Littering. Probably about five or six more that I can't think of off the top of my head."

I could hear him inhale deeply and slowly let the air out. "What do you require from me?" It was a good connection, which was unusual nowadays.

"You want him back?" I asked.

"I'm sorry, what is your organization, and who the hell are you?"

I laughed. "If you are who your son says you are, you already know who I am, where I am calling from, and my favorite color. So let's not fuck around, okay?"

Silence. Then, "Very well. How do you want to do this?"

"Your son was in an auto accident and sustained injuries. He is currently receiving medical care, but we do not have the facilities here to do more than the minimal patching."

"How bad is he?"

*Finally*, I thought, *a note of actual concern. Or was it just guilt?* "Casey is all right. He has some cracked ribs, a broken hand. His forehead is messed up, and he probably has a broken nose. More than that I can't say because—"

He cut me off, "Because you do not have the facilities."

"Correct."

"Fine. I will meet you—"

It was my turn to cut him off. "Good. I'll give you directions." I did. But the phone sounded dead. I wasn't sure if he had cut me off, the line had dropped, or he had muted it so he could talk to someone on the other side. Then, "I'm back. Fine. We estimate we can be at the pickup spot in forty-five minutes."

"Make it an hour and a half. I'm hungry and he is still getting his boo-boos kissed."

"Fine." This was hissed. Then the line went truly dead.

I had left the door open. When I turned around, Max was standing there shaking his head.

"Damn. I'm glad you turned me down on my offer of backup. I'm not really sure now that letting you have my truck was a good idea."

"Lighten up, Max. We both know if he wants his pound of flesh, he is going to take it even if I spend a half hour groveling and kissing his ass."

He laughed. "Yeah. You really polished his knob on that call. The kid will be ready in fifteen minutes."

I went over to the diner. The selections were getting limited. Shelli was trying to fill in the holes by using local foods and minimizing the meat offerings. At least that was what she told me. I figured it was more of the Burner vegan crap. The only choice I found appetizing was a medium well-done goat burger. I didn't even bother to ask what the goat had done to end up on the menu.

My waitress was the same girl as the day of the swearing-in ceremony. She was civil but a little distant. I shrugged it off.

I headed back to get the kid. Max was gone. Casey was out of the cage and sitting with Donna talking. He did not look as enthusiastic about going home as I thought he would. "You ready, kid?"

"Yeah."

Donna told him, "See you. I hope you feel better." She turned to me. "I gave him a pain-killer. He's going to be groggy before too long."

"Thanks, Donna. Come on, kid, I'm not going to cuff you." I grabbed him by the elbow and steered him to the door.

We settled into the truck, and I put it into drive and headed down the road. Traffic was light and the sun was starting to set. Summer was fast disappearing, and the maple and oak leaves would soon be changing in their annual display of color. My favorite time of year, by far.

The kid had slumped against the door and his eyes were shut. He was still breathing, so I left him alone. *I better make sure he is breathing a couple miles out from the pickup*, I thought. I doubt Big Daddy would be very happy with me if I delivered a corpse.

He surprised me a couple miles further down the road when he started talking. "You know, you could drop me here and no one would ever be the wiser."

"Kid, if that happens, you won't know because you'll be dead."

"Yeah. That's what I thought."

"Let me guess. Daddy gives you a hard time about being gay."

He laughed. It was bitter one. "You don't know the half of it."

"Kid, I don't want to know."

"Yeah. That's what I thought. Wake me up when we get there."

I didn't need to; his dad's security team did. I pulled into the gas station. It was empty. Casey's breathing was heavy and slow. I rolled down the window. The smell of trees, old oil, and grass drifted in. Across the meadow next to the lot I saw three deer burst out from the tree line and move east through the wild grass.

*There's one*, I thought to myself.

That's when the black Suburbans came roaring in. Where the meadow and the parking lot met in front of me, two men rose up from the grass. Even their weapons were camouflaged. The Suburban doors swung open, and about a second later I had a pistol pressed against my head and was being dragged out of the driver's seat and dropped, hard, to the ground.

"Lay flat and spread them." They patted me down quickly and professionally, first relieving me of my Ruger. "Roll over!" Then it was the Colt. I had left the bayonet back in a desk drawer in the office. They even took the little penknife I wore around my neck. "Roll over." Back I went onto my stomach. "He's clean!"

I couldn't see but I heard the sound of an inbound helicopter. It came down in the middle of the meadow. I bet it scared the crap out of the deer. I heard the truck door open on Casey's side.

"Got him. Go! Go! Go!" Wow, his daddy really did love him. He had ordered up a medevac.

The helicopter's rotors had slowed but never stopped spinning; now I listened to them increase in speed and I knew he was gone. I just lay there facedown in the asphalt, waiting for their next move or the bullet, while I watched an ant travel past my nose.

Five minutes after the sound of the departing helicopter had faded into the twilight, I was jerked upright and told, "Time to talk to the man." They frog-marched me to a black Suburban that looked no different than any of the others. The passenger doors were open on both sides. I was jerked to a stop about five feet from the open door.

"Wrists!" someone yelled. I held them out and was flex-cuffed. "Okay. In you go."

I was alone. It was starting to look like Plan A might need some modification. I was trying to remember what Plan B was when I heard footsteps approach.

"Thank you. I have it from here. Post them out twenty feet and tell Major Debose that this should not take long."

He climbed into the seat beside me. He was six foot two, in shape, fifty years old plus or minus a couple, and a hundred ninety pounds. He was wearing black jump boots with a mirror shine. I knew he didn't polish them himself. He was in khakis—the most popular power suit of the current administration after camo BDUs. His hair was the color of professionally polished silver, and his tan had been color coordinated to accent his blue eyes. I still didn't recognize him.

"Officer Gardener?"

I nodded. *Who the hell else was he expecting?* I thought.

"Thank you for coming. I just got off the phone with the medic team. My son is in good condition. They confirmed your diagnosis. There is the question of the injuries to his hand and forehead. It is their opinion that those are not consistent with a car crash. My son also confirms that."

"It is extremely important that he is not allowed any outside communication, including access to a cell phone."

"Why would that be?"

"We are not done cleaning up after him."

He stared at me and then activated his Bluetooth and told someone to make sure his son had zero access to any type of communications device until further notice. He looked at me. "Satisfied?"

"Can you confirm he has not had access up to this time?"

He had never closed the link. He muttered something into it. He waited twenty seconds and then replied, "Thank you."

"No. He asked to call his mother. They told him to wait until they landed because of the noise."

"You're very polite," I told him.

"I can afford to be." He shifted in the seat so he could look directly at me. "What do you want?"

I almost said "a cheeseburger," but the smart part of me slapped my brain in time. Instead: "Recognition."

"That's it? What do you want: a statue? A medal?"

"No. I can also offer you a guarantee."

"First tell me about the guarantee."

"By this time tomorrow morning, if you can keep your son isolated, I can guarantee that there will be no witnesses left alive who can put him at the scene of the murder. Or anything else."

"Tell me about what my son has gotten himself into."

I told him about the old man and his wife. And what had happened to them after they were jacked. That his son had been working as a spotter. That I knew he would flee again and I would not be able to catch him, so I rammed him. That he tried to draw on me and I dissuaded him of that. That he was a smart-mouthed punk who didn't know when to shut up.

His face remained expressionless throughout my tale. His eyes narrowed slightly when I ended. Then he laughed. "Tell me about the recognition."

"My guess is the area outside the Zone is a concern. We are not separatists. We are Americans—Americans who are also outside of the Zone. With support, we could provide you assistance in the way of intelligence gathering, policing the area, especially the roads, and perhaps trading the food we raise for money, goods, or both. We wouldn't need to enter the Zone. We could set up a trading post in a neutral area to transact our business."

He looked at me. After a period of time that almost became uncomfortable, he replied. "Make a list. Someone will be in touch." Then he left.

I sat there for about five minutes until a soldier filled my side of the door. "Wrists!" *Jesus*, these guys were big into shouting. I stuck out my arms, and he cut the cuffs.

"Out of the vehicle!" He and another soldier assisted me out and then frog-marched me back to where I had started.

"On the ground. Face first!" I could hear the vehicle engines turning over. They were leaving.

The soldier who cut my cuffs told me, or rather my backside, that I was to stay in this position for ten minutes. If I moved, I would be shot. After the ten minutes had passed I could get up and go about my business. *Did I understand?*

"Yes. I did." That's what I said. I don't know what it sounded like to them, as I was planted facedown. I don't think they cared. They left without saying another word.

I waited twelve minutes. Then I stood up and stretched. My weapons had been emptied and left on the hood of the truck. I got in and headed home.

# CHAPTER TWENTY-NINE

I swung by the station in town. Once our patrol car was repaired, we planned to install one of the CBs we had scrounged up. Max would get one for his truck, and the farm would have one. We already had a set of walkie-talkies, but we didn't have the batteries for them.

The station had POTS—plain old telephone service—as did Shelli's diner. Our communications didn't bother me as much as it did Max and Night. They were used to a functioning system, and our half-assed patchwork of CBs, POTS, cell phones, e-mail, and notes stuck to doors made them crazy.

I didn't expect Max to be back at the station, but he was, along with everyone from the motel, plus Diesel and Hawk.

Night ran to meet me and gave me a big hug, which surprised me. She was not much into public displays of affection. It reminded me that I still had the rings in my pocket. I did the greeting thing and kicked Ninja out of my chair. Night sat on the desk next to me.

"So, are you all here just to listen to me talk about my exciting adventure at daycare?"

"That and to plan a house call."

"Oh. Well, Max, you'll pleased to know that in exchange for my being released with all my body parts intact, I agreed to the stipulation that you will return to active duty."

Dead silence and jaws dropping. I loved it. I waited a couple seconds and said, "Just kidding."

"Gardener, you're an asshole."

I laughed. "No, really all is well. Big Daddy agreed to Plan A."

Night asked what I knew Max was thinking. "What was Plan A again?"

"We get to give him a list of goodies we want. We get recognition as the civil authority in this part of the world and trade rights with the Zone."

We talked about the ramifications of that, and whether or not Big Daddy would actually come through. Night liked my part about guaranteeing the cleanup.

"He'll never know for sure that we aren't holding back on some crucial piece of evidence."

Diesel's reply, which I had not thought of, was, "So then he just comes back and kills us all."

"No," Max shook his head, "he would never be sure he got everyone. Plus, he may be powerful, but I think wiping out small towns for personal reasons is a bit of a stretch, even for him. No, that was well played, Gardener."

Night reached over and rubbed my back. I thought, *Well, I guess I'll skip the part about how I didn't think of Plan A until I was staring at him.*

Then Ninja asked the question we had all been avoiding. "So the little shit gets away with it?"

Night started to answer him but I cut her off. She was coming to my defense, but I was really the one he was addressing.

"He'll be back, Ninj. He can't help himself. He doesn't fit in the Zone, and he thinks he can survive out here. Plus, he thinks Big Daddy will always have his back. No, he and I will definitely talk again."

Ninja looked at me. I mean, he *really* looked at me. He knew. Truth. He nodded his head and smiled. The smile reminded me of Night when she knew she had me backed into a corner.

Casey was a dead man.

While I was with Big Daddy, Night had gone back to the trailer and printed a Google map of the address Casey gave us.

It was a farmhouse, a lot like Tommy's, with the usual scattering of outbuildings, except this one had a barn. A lot of rural houses didn't, which surprised me. It had taken me a while to grasp that rural didn't mean they had a herd of cows. This was an older house; these older farmhouses usually had barns. At one time barn wood was in high demand for new construction. I doubted if that was still true.

The last part of the nearest road was dirt, running for almost half a mile before it reached the farmhouse turn-off. It continued on for a number of miles until it crossed back over a paved county road. They weren't alone out there, but they were on sixty acres, which is about as close to alone as you get in this part of the world.

Night had printed a zoom of the house and then another one so that we could see the lay of the land.

"Very nice," I told her.

"Thanks. It's also the last one I'm going to be able to do. We're out of ink."

"Really? I thought we had spare cartridges."

She reached over and slapped Ninja upside his head. He didn't move, other than to look down. "Some idiot has been printing porn." Another slap.

I just shook my head. "We'll get some more, or get a printer that still has good cartridges. Sounds like a job with your name on it, Ninja." I looked at him. He checked to see if Night was looking at him; she wasn't, so he rolled his eyes.

"So, Max, how do you want to do this?"

"It's your call, Gardener. I'm not going."

That surprised me. I waited for the *Just kidding* but it didn't come.

"Gardener, while you were out, we talked about the militia plans. We are going to split it into two groups. The town guard will be just that. They will also handle the tollbooths and do limited patrols around the outskirts of town. The second group will be rangers. That will be the younger men and woman. They're going to do deeper patrols and serve as the muscle when needed. You're going to lead them."

I was stunned. Truly freaking stunned. Night was beaming at me, and so was everyone else. I was genuinely touched. "Why thanks, Max—I think."

"Yeah. Try not to fuck up too bad. So, let's hear your plan for this op."

I had looked at the photos and on the way back I had thought about how I would handle the Bunker Busters, so it wasn't hard to tell everyone what I had in mind.

My idea was along the same lines as what the sheriff—who was still on my to-do list—had planned for us.

"We'll approach on foot. I want to do this right before dawn. Hawk, I want you on the Barrett as overlook. Kill them fucking dogs if you see them. I think these people deserve something special other than a bullet. Diesel will take out the front window with the shotgun. Then I toss a Molotov through it. We hit the door with another. We each fade right and left of the house and take cover. Ninja—damn, we're going to need Old Guy. You two got the back. Torch the door. Fade back. Watch the second-story windows. We kill them all. We go home. We stop at the diner, and the goat burgers or whatever's on the menu are on me."

Everyone, including Max, thought it was a good plan.

I gave Night her engagement ring and hid the wedding ring in the bottom drawer of the chest we shared. I didn't get any sleep. She was just drifting off when it was time for me to get up.

Old Guy was now living on the farm, and he had the bedroom next to us. He snored, loudly. I never mentioned it to him because I didn't want to hear him complaining about the noise we made. And we did make some noise.

I knocked on his door and heard him grunt. I did the same for Ninja and then went into the kitchen and started the coffee.

Getting ready for a new morning was not the same as it once was, especially a morning like this when full dress was required. Once upon a time it was: Pull on some pants, grab a shirt, and go. No longer, especially for something like what we were doing today.

I was going to be wearing a battle dress uniform in the Woodland pattern. I called it my GI Joe suit. I already had my underwear on. I put on a cup over them and then I pulled on the pants. Next came a brown T-shirt that was borderline—it almost failed the sniff test. I shrugged and pulled it over my head. Socks came next. I skipped the sniff test with them.

Then I put on my armor. Luckily, it was getting cooler and this op would be over by 0830. Otherwise, wearing armor in the summer really sucked. I wiggled it around and adjusted it. Next was the belt for the pants and then my gun belt. I was wearing the bayonet now, so I slid it in and out of the sheath three times for luck.

I put my kneepads on next. Max wore only one knee-pad when he got geared up. Most of the time they ended up around my ankles, but I liked wearing both. I would never admit it, but wearing them and everything else made me feel like a medieval knight.

I slipped the Colt into my gun belt. I stuffed my BDU pockets with a water bottle, an apple, and a piece of bread. In another pocket went my personal wound kit, which fit inside a metal Band-Aid box. Then it was time to pull on my boots and lace them up. Finally, my fisherman's vest went over the armor. All I had to do was put on my hat and I was ready.

The others were doing the same thing, just not to the extreme that I carried it. Old Guy wore a vest and a gun belt, and slung a daypack over his shoulder. Ninja wore a load-bearing vest that he always kept ready to go. He had a ballistics vest under it, and he usually took forever to lace up his boots.

I poured coffee for everyone. We didn't eat. When everyone was ready and had taken that last piss, we headed out. We took two cars—Max's truck and Old Guy's Chevy—just in case one of them broke down. Tommy stayed behind to keep an eye on things at the farm, and Max was doing the same in town.

We picked up Hawk and Diesel and hit the road. There was no other traffic. I couldn't get used to that. Roads were supposed to have traffic, a lot of it. No traffic always creeped me out; it was as if everyone had been abducted by aliens, or had all gotten the secret memo that I never got.

We stopped about a half mile from the turnoff. We parked the vehicles off a road being reclaimed by Queen Anne's lace and burdock. It led to a lot that still had an old Don's John on it. The land had been scraped a couple of years ago in preparation for site work that had never happened.

We walked single file, with Ninja at point and me next in line, carrying a cooler with the Molotovs in it. It was awkward to carry. We walked on the opposite side of the road from where the house was. There was a bush and tree line running parallel to the road on both sides. It was thick enough this time of year that I felt comfortable approaching the farmhouse access road this way. It was also easier in the darkness.

From the access road to the house, it got a little trickier. Hawk dropped off to find a place to set up in his blind. Ninja and Old Guy continued on the road a bit and then started working through the woods, which stopped about seventy-five yards from the house. From there they would have open ground to cross, not quite a lawn, in order to get behind the house. I told them to watch for the dogs, as that would probably be where they were.

Diesel and I were going to cut along a streambed and come out about fifty yards in front of the house. Ninja and Old Guy had the advantage of old cars, a shed, and whatnot that were strewn between the back of the house and the barn. The only thing we had for cover was the slope of the ground as it headed down toward the creek.

We synchronized our watches before leaving. I always felt like I had stumbled onto a cheesy movie set when we did that. I handed Ninja his Molotov cocktail and made sure he had matches. I had almost forgotten about them until Night reminded me to take some.

Now I was lying there in the weeds bothered by something. The vibe just didn't feel right. The house didn't feel right.

I mean, it was a piece of crap farmhouse, but that was no surprise. The truck that the witness had seen was parked next to the barn. Another truck, an older F-150, was parked next to it. Off in the distance a dog was barking, but that wasn't anywhere near here.

Diesel was stretched out in the weeds about fifteen feet from me. *Shit.* I wanted to crawl over and ask him if he felt it too, but we were running out of time. The guys in the back would be going in two minutes.

# CHAPTER THIRTY

I opened the cooler, pulled out two Molotov cocktails, and set them in front of me. Then I got to my knees, slung the shotgun over my shoulder, and looked over at Diesel. He was staring at me, waiting for me to move.

I grabbed the bottles and started running for the front window. While I ran I scanned the house, checking the windows for movement. I stopped and set one of the Molotovs at my feet.

The boom of Diesel's shotgun was simultaneous with the window exploding. I extended my arm back for Diesel to light the Molotov I held. Through the ringing in my ears I heard him yell, "Up!" In a beautiful arc, I tossed it through the window.

On the other side of the house I heard the blast of Old Guy opening the back door for Ninja. I was already moving to the front door. Diesel fired double-aught buckshot, slug, and double-aught again, repeating through the load. He hit the door right below the knob. *Shit! It didn't open!*

I ran up the steps leaving the other cocktail behind while I pulled the shotgun off my shoulder. I got it down and had a decent grip on it two steps before I hit the door sideways with my shoulder. The door popped open, no resistance at all, and I kept going, fighting to keep my balance.

The smoke from the fire in the next room was already picking up. It didn't stop me from registering the fact that the room was empty. *Fuck!* I spun around. For a microsecond, Diesel and I stared at each other. Then we bolted out the door. Already I could hear gunfire from the back. *Shit!*

Diesel was in the lead. I stooped as I went by and grabbed the Molotov, tossing it away from the house and me. About three strides from the corner of the house, Diesel went airborne like a ballplayer diving for second base. He came down right at the edge of the building, his upper shoulders, chest, and head extended past the corner. The shotgun was at his shoulder, his cheek against the stock.

I was outside of him by two feet and didn't stop. I came around the corner moving fast, knowing now that Casey, the little fucker, had conveniently neglected to mention how they all slept in the barn.

Him and the fucking sheriff—if I had to take a vacation to do it, I was going find both of them and kill them.

In front of me and to my right was the barn. One truck was parked in front of it; the other, on the right side. The barn had huge double doors, almost the height of the building. Set into one of them was a normal-sized entry door. That door was open. In front of it, I could see someone shooting toward the back of the house with what looked like an AR-15.

At least that little shit had gotten something right. Off to the shooter's right, at the corner of the barn, another male with a similar weapon was firing at the house. I could hear handgun fire from the side of the barn but I couldn't see who it was.

Diesel got their attention with a blast from the shotgun. I didn't see anyone go down or even look mildly discomforted. *Should have brought an M-14, dude*, a voice inside my head scolded. The shotgun blast from Diesel also let them see me hauling ass in their direction. I cut to the right and headed toward an outbuilding that I hoped I could get to for cover.

That was when I saw or sensed a movement out of the corner of my eye. The barn had a loft with a window that was open. Someone was up there with a rifle. I was moving fast at an angle when he shot me.

My armor vest had ceramic plates in it. I got lucky, if you want to call it that, in two ways. The shot hit a plate, and it hit at an angle. Later, I realized it was an impossibly lucky angle. It still hurt plenty and it knocked me off-balance and stride. My momentum carried me forward in a tumble that ended with me going down hard to the ground.

I heard the boom-bam of the Barrett just about then. As I hit the ground I remember thinking, *About fucking time, Hawk.*

The good news was I had gone down behind the outbuilding I had been trying to get to. I was sitting up and working on clearing my head when I heard the sound of dogs barking. *Jesus*, I thought, *the shit just keeps coming.*

I got to my feet with difficulty and slung the shotgun. My intention was to pull the Ruger, go around the side of the outbuilding, and kill every motherfucker I saw.

I took two steps and got hit by seventy-five pounds of muscle and teeth.

The beast knocked me on my ass again and then clamped its teeth down on the outside of my right leg. The hungry sonofabitch was growling and shaking its head and wouldn't let go.

The trouble was, I am left-handed and I was pinned down on my holster side. The Colt was gone, probably shaken loose in my first fall. Life is a bitch—but sharp carbon steel can fix a lot of problems

I grabbed the hilt of the bayonet, pulled it from the sheath with my right hand, and passed it to my left. Cujo was sending intense flashes of pain through my nervous system, and his eyes, which I had no problem seeing, stared at me with evil doggie hate.

I cut off his head. A K98 bayonet is sixteen inches long, and mine was made early on in the war, so it was quality steel. I kept it sharp, too. The hardest part to get through was the spinal column, but that only took an extra couple of seconds and a few more pounds of pressure.

After I safed the shotgun, I tried to stand up, unsuccessfully. I reversed it, used the shotgun as a crutch, and tried again. Then I started to circle the outbuilding. Damn, *I hurt*. I grayed out for a second but stayed on my feet.

About fifteen yards from me a man behind one of the trucks was exchanging rounds with someone near the house. I blew his head off with the Ruger. There were two bodies lying in front of the barn. One had a pair of mangled legs.

I saw Diesel coming toward me at a run. He was moving pretty fast for someone running crouched over. I kept walking toward the barn, giving a quick look to the house. Someone was down. It looked like Old Guy. I stopped at the white truck, dropped the shotgun, and used my free arm to brace myself against it.

"Hey, Gardener! You have a dog's head attached to your leg!"

"Yeah. No shit. It hurts, too. So what do we have?"

He tore his eyes off the dog's head. It was still staring at me and, if possible, looked even more pissed than before. "Old Guy is down. He's still alive, I think. Ninja is somewhere in the trees. I think he's covering the side door. I'm pretty sure he is okay."

"Okay. Go get Old Guy and drag him around that tractor. Do what you can for him. I'll cover you."

"On it." He took off running again. I slid down to the cab, using it to steady my shooting arm. The barn was quiet. I heard a shotgun boom from the trees. Ninja was on the job. I watched as Diesel slowed down enough to grab Old Guy by the collar and drag him to safety.

I turned and started walking toward where I had tossed the Molotov. It was maybe fifty yards away, but it felt like two miles. I bent over, almost fell over, grabbed it by the neck, and started back to the barn. When I got about twenty feet from the main door, I let the shotgun fall to the ground. I dug into my pocket for the lighter I had brought, flicked the Bic, tossed the Molotov through the open door, and waited.

About a minute later, maybe less, two men came running through the flames inside the door. They had AR-15s at their hips and were firing as they came out. I shot one in the head. The other stopped like he had run into a wall and then went flying backward. The Barrett had spoken. I did the math in my head twice and came up with five both times.

Diesel was headed toward me, moving fast and looking the other way so he could keep an eye on the barn. We stood there for a minute watching the flames. Behind us, the house was further along in the burn-to-the-ground race. I noticed for the first time how hot it was standing there.

"Diesel, you okay?"

He nodded his head.

"Get Old Guy and move him down toward the creek. Be careful. We still have one unaccounted for."

He was halfway there when Ninja came out of the woods pushing a woman in front of him with the barrel of his shotgun. My face was starting to feel like it was sunburned from the heat of the fire. I knew I should move but I wasn't sure that I could still walk. I let him come to me.

"Holy shit, Gardener! You have a dog's head hanging from your leg!"

"That's King!" the woman screamed, looking at the head.

"Lady, the King is dead. Ninja, get her in front of us and help me walk." I put my arm around him and we headed down the front yard until I told him to stop.

"Hey!" I yelled. The woman looked back at me. "Get on your knees and put your hands behind your head." She sank to her knees, her back to Ninja and me. "Ninj, I need you to police the area. Don't take any stupid risks but try to get those rifles."

"What about—"

"I'm fine. Go before it gets too hot and the rounds start cooking off."

As soon as he left, the woman said, without turning around, "I think me and you could work something out."

I would have kicked her in the kidney but I knew I would have fallen over. Instead I just told her to shut up. Diesel arrived about a minute later with Old Guy. He set him down gently.

Old Guy looked at me. "Damn, Gardener, you need to get that dog's head off your leg."

"Well, I guess it's unanimous," I said. "How are you doing?"

"I'm okay." He was awfully pale for being okay. Diesel looked up from where he was working on Old Guy's leg. "One to the leg, one to the hand."

Old Guy held up his hand, which was bandaged and bloody. "Can you believe it? They shot off my finger!"

I would have had a witty comeback, but this wasn't a movie and I hurt too much.

But the woman found some words: "At least he didn't cut your dog's head off!"

"Shut up."

What was taking Ninja so long? Old Guy grunted in pain as Diesel put pressure on his leg to stop the bleeding. I fished inside my pocket and tossed him my med kit. "Here. I'll use Ninja's when he gets back."

A couple of minutes later Ninja was back. He dropped two ARs and one vest next to me. "Sorry, it's getting too hot to get to anything else."

The house had partially collapsed, and the fire in the barn must have found some ammo because it was exploding. It was time to go.

"Turn her around so she can look at us."

Ninja got her to turn around. She wasn't bad looking. Blonde hair with black roots. Brown eyes. A little pudgy, early twenties. A nice rack.

"So, you arresting me? Don't you got to read me my rights?" More than a hint of a sneer in her voice.

"Sure," I replied. "Tell me, first, though. When was the last time you had some really good Chips Ahoy cookies?"

She looked at me like I was nuts. "A couple days ago. Why?"

"Because." Then I shot her between those brown eyes.

"Alright. Let's go home, guys."

# CHAPTER THIRTY-ONE

"Can you believe this shit?" Max said, looking at papers in front of him. He had been going through the "requisition options" that Casey's Big Daddy had sent to help us make our wish list.

"You mean it doesn't get any better than this?" I asked him. "I did like the part that you read about the free flags. I feel there is a real need for American flags and traffic cones these days. The free BDUs sound okay. Maybe they'll include boots."

"What do you make of the fine print, Max? Whoever wrote this had a twisted mind."

"Not quite what I expected, Night. I knew there would be hooks, but I thought we could nibble off more meat than this before we hit metal."

"Slide it over here." I scanned a few sections. Sure enough, all the goodies were booby-trapped. "So let me see if I got this right." I began reading aloud:

"Level One weapons. Okay, they will give us M-16s, four magazines per weapon, one hundred rounds for training purposes, and five hundred for reserve. That's *per year*, and we need to be certified as qualified to use them. Oh, and we must demonstrate that we have secure storage facilities. Also under Level One, we can get Colt .45s, 9-millimeter Berettas, and shotguns under the same restrictions. We can be issued Type II body armor, although vests issued must match the certifying officer's audited number of authorized users."

"Yeah, keep reading," Max told me.

"Level Two. Ah, now we get into the goodies. Oh, no wonder, we are also at the end of the standard package. Night-vision goggles. First-generation rifle scopes. Better vests. Helmets. But here's the hook: All personnel will have to pass a background check and urinalysis test. All law enforcement or certified auxiliary personnel receiving said equipment will then be required to pass a three-week training course. Sites are available throughout the United States. Housing and food cost per participant must be paid for by the sponsoring agency."

I stopped. "Do I even need to read the Level Three requirements?"

"No," Max replied. "They want an on-site advisory team when they issue Level Three gear."

"What the hell is their problem?" Night snarled. "Damn. You should have shot the little asshole and buried him in the woods."

"Hey! We are still going to come out ahead on this," Max told her.

"Yeah, plus I plan to shoot his scrawny little ass the next time I run across him," I added.

She nodded, but I could tell she was still pissed.

"Look on the bright side, Night. Under 'Miscellaneous' we have a selection of pamphlets with titles like *Know the Dangers of Fireworks* and *The Dangers of Drunk Driving*."

"Check the vehicles section," Max said.

"The realistic level?"

"Yep."

"Crown Vics with a hundred thousand miles, some repair needed. Suburbans. High mileage again is my guess, though it doesn't say. So what are they trying to tell us, Max?"

He laughed. "They want to keep us on a short leash. If they can't do that, then they want to be damn sure they can win any encounter with us."

"So what was up with the 'blank check' bullshit?"

"If the history of this country has not taught you that bureaucrats lie every time their lips move, then nothing will. G, we can and will ask. But I say nothing above Level One if it has strings attached."

I looked at Night, who nodded her agreement, adding, "I want to ask for a LaserJet with paper—a lot of paper and toner."

"There's always more than one way to do this. What we need is a crooked supply sergeant. Most of all, we need hard money."

Night agreed with Max. A pensive look came across her face. She added, "With hard money, my old clan would be willing to help."

"Order a lot of flags. We can fly them from the toll-booths," I suggested.

We all grinned at each other.

We came up with some more additions to the list. We were going to ask for two thousand battle dress uniforms, boots, long underwear, and gloves. Night said, "We can always drop it down if they balk at the numbers. I want to ask for coats also. A clan always takes care of its members, no matter how little they actually contribute."

I looked at her and grinned.

"What?" she replied.

"You are just so freaking smart," I told her.

"You two done with your moment?"

"Yeah, Max."

"Good. Okay, we'll take what the government is giving. We don't have much choice."

"Yeah."


I was killing time before I was scheduled to go look over the people I was supposed to lead now. I had mixed feelings about the idea. I'd never seen myself as a leader. Hell, I don't even like people all that much. Plus, I didn't have a clue about the military stuff I figured you needed to know. Diesel or Hawk would have been a better choice. Shit, I didn't even know how to march and I didn't really want to know.

Max was sitting across from me, going through paperwork, when he looked up and asked, "Have you given any thought to how you are going to review your team?"

"Not really. I figured I would walk over to the park in front of the town hall, and Diesel would have them there. Then I would say my hellos and tell them to be back there the next day at 0600 to start their training."

Max and Diesel looked at each other and shook their heads. "No good, G. You're an officer. You have to make an entrance. Diesel and Ninja will turn them out. Diesel will present them. There may even be a small crowd."

"A small crowd? What the hell?"

"G, think about it. This is a big deal for these people. They will have invited their parents, boyfriends, girlfriends, friends, and pets to this. Damn, what else is happening in town?"

Night added, "That's something else we have to think about. Entertainment."

"One event at a time, please," I told her. "Then what, Max?"

"You've watched the movies. You do a troop review."

I was starting to get the picture. "I show up. They are presented. I walk the line, ask them their names, maybe a question, and then go to the next one. Wait! Then I make a speech, don't I?"

"Yep."

I glared at Max. "Thanks."

He laughed. "You want to do this, well, it comes with a lot of obligations."

I looked at Night. "Want to watch *Patton* with me tonight?"

She rolled her eyes.

"That's what I thought."

The next morning we met at the station. Diesel and Ninja were already over at the town hall.

Night handed me ten city crest patches. "You give each person one of these after you inspect them."

Max added, "Giving them a Raven is up to you. When you do hand them out, I suggest you use the same criteria for everyone."

"Yeah, I got a few ideas for that."

"Max, what are you going to do for the militia?"

"I don't know yet. Probably a city and an American flag patch."

"You okay?" Night asked me when we were alone for a minute. She knew the speech was making me very edgy.

"Sure." I told her. The reality was I had no idea what I was going to say. I had played the game, but this was a little different.

The three of us left a few minutes after that. It was only a few blocks away, but Night drove us over. My leg had been bandaged. The damage was bad, but nowhere near my prior experiences with pointy objects becoming embedded in my body. After she parked, Night kissed me and wished me luck. That caught me by surprise.

"Where are you going?"

"This is a you and Max show. I'm going to join the crowd."

We got out of the car. There really was a crowd. I watched Night walk away. That was more enjoyable than watching the crowd watch us.

Max was carrying a small leather case. He set it on top of the car, carefully opened it, and with both hands took a medal suspended from a blue ribbon and hung it around his neck. At first I thought, *Why is he wearing a Euro award?* Then I recognized it. I had forgotten about it, and this was the first time I had seen one in person.

When Max noticed me watching him, he said, "No, it's not the original. Word got around about me leaving the medal at McBride's grave site. Next thing I know I'm being handed a box one day. Apparently, the commandant thought it was the right thing to do."

I nodded.

Max looked at me. "You ready?"

"I am always ready. Let's do this."

Diesel had wanted to give me a thumbnail report on each of the people in the squad. I told him, "Maybe later." I wanted to form my own impressions first. They were lined up in front of the park bandstand.

The bandstand had seen limited use, mostly as a prop for the Fourth of July celebration that the town had once run to suck in tourists and their money. The council was already standing on it. Someone had found red, white, and blue bunting and woven it around the bandstand railing. The flagpole had the flag of the United States run up.

There were at least eighty people watching from behind a rope barrier, maybe more. Folding chairs had been set up around the bandstand to seat the block managers. Some of the militia strolled around with weapons, supposedly for crowd control. The reality was they were enjoying the chance to show off. If they weren't related to the graduates, they probably knew someone who was. The recruits were in formation—two rows of five. A dog ran up to one of them and stood there wagging its tail until a kid ran out and grabbed it by its collar.

We were noticed as we approached. One of the block managers trotted over. He was a little short of breath but managed a formal "Good morning."

"Morning, Mr. Jacobs."

"Y'all want to hold up right there. We got some music to play as you walk up." He looked around for someone. I didn't see the person he was looking for in the crowd but he did. He waved, and from two black PA speakers came the Star-Spangled Banner.

Max was not facing the flag, nor were Jacobs and I. At the sound of the first notes, Max stiffened, did some kind of footwork that spun him around to the flag, and saluted. I didn't even try to match his maneuver. Jacobs and I faced the flag, and I did my best to look like I had spent my life snapping off salutes. The recruits had even saluted in unison. In the back of my head, I hoped Homeland Security had a drone in the area taking this all in.

When the music ended, Max continued toward the recruits. I kept a beat behind him so I could mimic his moves. He walked—*marched* might actually be better—but that doesn't quite describe it. His entire bearing had changed, yet his movement was neither stiff nor robotic.

I was surprised at how I felt. I was proud to be with him. Proud to be associated with these people. It was pride shot through with a fierce sense of belonging, of righteousness.

Max stopped at a line only he could see. As the officer in charge, Ninja was the sixth man in the front row. He was standing stock-still, straight as an arrow, looking into the distance. Diesel was in front of the recruits and staring straight ahead at us.

He shouted, "Atten-*shun!*" and they went from what I later learned was parade rest to standing tall and rigid. He then shouted, "Recruit Squad A is ready for your inspection, sir!" and saluted. We returned the salute. At this rate I was going to get pretty good at this saluting stuff.

Max strode off and began with the first man in the first rank. He stopped briefly, looked him up and down, nodded, and stepped over to the next. A lot of my life has been spent pretending I know what I am doing, and this was just another instance of it. I read the first recruit's name, which had been written on his pocket in block letters with a black Sharpie. Then I looked him up and down.

"Johnson, welcome aboard." I stuck out my hand and we shook hands. I handed him his city patch and told him, "Wear this with pride." I repeated this without variation for every recruit.

I had ten recruits. Two were black males—unusual since the town was only 4 percent black—two were white females, one of which I was sure was lesbian, and the rest were white males. The oldest was perhaps twenty-two, at most. One of the youngest had a huge zit on his chin.

We finished and walked back to where we had started. Well, I walked; Max and Diesel turned the corners like they were squared off. The two of them took a step back, and I was left hanging out there in front. I addressed the recruits:

"These are unsettled times. They are not of our making. Yet we have no choice but to persevere through them. All of us are called to do different things with our lives. You have made your choice today—a choice that has been made by every generation in history. You have chosen to protect and serve the people of your community against those who would destroy it. I and the people of this town commend you on your choice. Welcome aboard!"

Diesel shouted, "Squad dismissed!" They yelled and threw their hats in the air and ran off to meet whoever was awaiting them. I just stood there. I felt Max step up to my side and whisper, "Not bad," before he turned and went in search of Shelli.

# CHAPTER THIRTY-TWO

The next morning Ninja and I were up early, getting ready for the first phase of training. I went fully geared up, as did he. We were meeting the squad in the park and planning to run two miles to an empty house Diesel and Max had selected as our training property. I wasn't sure if I was I ready for a two-mile run yet. That stupid dog had dug in deep with his teeth.

I said I was going to run anyway. I felt like I had to. Ninja disagreed, saying that I already had established my cred. Night put her two cents in, telling me I was a macho fool.

None of what they had to say dissuaded me. I knew I wouldn't believe or trust someone with my life until I had seen him perform when the shit hit the fan. The recruits may have heard stories about me, but I wanted them to see with their own eyes that I was hardcore. It would do no good to have me pull up in a car at the end of their run.

Diesel had them form up in two columns. When he saw me arrive all geared up he just shook his head. I gave the order and we took off running. It wasn't bad at first.

The end of the second mile was hell. I gritted my teeth and concentrated on putting one boot in front of the other until we reached the house. I wasn't winded and neither were they.

From the look of them we could have gone for miles. That was an exhilarating idea. Just running and running like an unstoppable machine. Of course, they would have left me behind by the end of the fourth mile.

We spent the next week working on basic training: how to come up on an occupied house or trailer while on patrol. How to knock on the door and talk to the people. What to ask them. How to do an inventory of what people had, and how to do it without being obvious. How to read a paper map—none of them knew how. How to get out of a truck or car and approach another vehicle.

We also burned through precious ammo at the range. We still did not have a standard battle rifle for all of us. There weren't enough M-14s to go around, so we issued shotguns to some of them. Low-scorers at the range with the M-14s got to carry the shotguns.

Toward the end of the first week we took a training break to help unload a semi sent by Homeland Security. This was our "Community Policing and Freedom Assistance" package—and, hopefully, the extras we had ordered. A two-person security team in a black Suburban accompanied the truck. Our certifying officer was Eddie. He didn't look happy about it.

He got out of the SUV, and we did the small talk thing with him while the driver parked the semi in front of the station. We were going to unload it directly into our building and use the empty holding cell as an armory for now.

A drunk and disorderly local who was supposed to go home that morning occupied the other cell. He had asked if he could stay for lunch and Max told him, "Okay, but you'll have to trim the bushes at the town hall." He was fine with that for about an hour and then he drifted back to watch the unloading. So did a handful of other locals.

Eddie gave Night the manifest and went over to Shelli's to get something to eat. He took the security team with him. The driver unlocked the doors and disappeared back into his cab. Night was speed-reading the manifest while we waited.

She looked up after flipping through the pages. "We got the standard package. Nothing extra."

I shook my head and avoided looking at anyone as I threw open the doors.

The trailer was packed. It smelled like BDUs and grease. All I could see were uniforms, baled and stacked to the ceiling of the trailer. There was about two feet of space between the end of the load and the door. I climbed up into the space; so did Max, to my surprise. I reached up and pulled on one end of a bale as he pulled on the other, and we let the weight and gravity tumble it to the ground.

"The town is going to look like an army base from 1987 once all this gets handed out," Max said as we sent down another bale. Night already had some of the squad breaking up the bales and sorting them inside. Unloading the two bales had exposed what looked to be a wall of wooden crates.

Max turned to me and grinned. "I think we got a bonus."

"What are they?"

"Well, the manifest said we got ten M-16s. This is a lot more than ten. Don't pop the lid on this. Let's just put it in the cell."

The first crate was heavy, but Max and I got it down and moved it to where the squad could pull it off the truck. I told them to take it directly to the cell. I also told one of them to get Night and have her come out to the truck. While they did that, Max and I pulled down another crate so we could see what was behind it. It turned out to be another wall of crates.

Max read the stencils. "It's ammo, and not just any ammo. They're fifty-caliber belts."

Night vaulted up into the trailer. Sometimes I forgot how athletic she really was. "What's up, guys?"

"Guns and ammo, Night. Guns and ammo."

"We don't want to advertise? Is that why we're not opening them?"

"Yep," Max and I answered at the same time.

The trailer proved to be a cornucopia of stuff. The squad got the job of distribution. The block managers accompanied them as they went around passing out the goodies. Night wanted the townspeople to associate goodies with Max, the block managers, and the rest of us. It was good PR, hearts-and-minds stuff.

We still hadn't popped open the bonus crates in the cell. One of the things we noticed right away, though, was that some of them were stenciled in Spanish. The best explanation we came up with was that Big Daddy had managed to divert a minor drop to some South or Central American warlord. The quality was up to Third World warlord standards, but not good enough for drug lords or actual state-sponsored troops. We were as grateful for them as the warlord would have been, and for the same reason: Beggars can't be choosers.

We sat in the station talking about the load. We had cut the squad loose and Max sent Ninja to fetch Eddie. It turned out Eddie was smashed. Shelli had started serving drinks to her clientele along with food, and Eddie must have been drinking the "fortified" wine. He weaved in the door, not quite staggering. "So you got it all unloaded?"

Night answered him, "Yes."

"That's good. Real good. I need Mr. Max to sign these papers." He opened his briefcase. I looked over his shoulder. Other than the paperwork, the only thing in there was an envelope with my name on it.

Max handed the papers to Night to look over and asked Eddie, "What am I signing?"

"That you received the standard Community Policing and Freedom Assistance package and all is well. Also, you are stating that you have trained on these weapons and have a secure storage area." He paused, "What the hell is in the wine here? Oh, never mind." He swayed in place for a minute. "Oh, and that you will not use them against any lawful agent of the U.S. government and that you swear to be good. Or something like that."

Max looked at Night, who nodded that it was as he said. Max picked up a pen while Eddie stood there swaying and blinking.

He focused on Night. "Hey, you're cute."

She was watching Max sign his name; she didn't bother to look up when she said, "Fuck off, Fed boy."

Eddie, to his credit, laughed. "Yep, that's me."

Max looked up at me from the paperwork for a second. I smiled, and he went back to the papers. When he was done he gave them to Eddie, who tossed them in the briefcase.

"Well, toodle-oo, people." He turned to leave, bumped into a desk, backed up, stopped, and turned to me. "Oh, my God! I forgot something."

He set the briefcase down on the desktop, opened it, and handed me the letter with my name on it. "Here. I can't believe I almost forgot that. I got to go. I don't feel good."

Max shot the security team a look and they closed on Eddie. Each one grabbed an arm and they hustled him out the door.

Diesel said, "I pity those guys. You know he is going to barf before they get back. That is going to be one nasty-smelling Suburban."

I laughed. I had yet to inhale the smell of a squad car that someone had puked cheap wine in. Max had, more than once. He didn't laugh.

Once they were gone I opened the envelope. Inside was a single sheet of paper. It had one line of text, which I read out loud: "Go to Bruxton, West Virginia, and take a look around."

"Well, that's interesting," I said. "Anyone know where Bruxton is?"

To everyone's, amazement Diesel did. "It's about forty-five miles from here."

"You know what's there?"

He shrugged. "I've been through there before, I think. Not much probably."

Night was not to be deterred by my letter. She was still focused on the truckload and the crates. She pulled out her notebook and told us to start opening crates. She was dying to know what we had.

That was the last time we opened crates from the Fed with all of us present. If one of them had been booby-trapped, it would have been the end of our experiment in collective survival.

Diesel and Ninja went to work on the crates with pry bars, starting with the ones stacked in the bullpen area. We had run out of space quickly in the cell. Max wanted to keep the other cell open for police business.

The first two crates were each half-full of green metal boxes. We all recognized them: ammo boxes, a surplus store mainstay. Max opened one, and we gathered around to stare inside. I don't know about anyone else, but I always thought of new ammo as jewels, each one a beautiful golden work of art.

"M-16 ammo. I hope they remembered magazines."

"Damn, Max. It's the Fed. You know they have to screw up something," Diesel replied.

The next four crates were the same. But the crate after that was filled with M-16 magazines. It looked as if they had been tossed in by the handfuls. Max and Diesel rummaged through them. They would pick one up, look at it, and toss it back in.

"Tommy is going to need to go through these one by one."

Diesel agreed. "Yeah. A lot of these have seen some use." He looked at Max, "Maybe we even used one of these."

"Yeah." Neither one seemed too thrilled at the thought.

The next four crates were M-16s. Each one had been wrapped in a green trash bag and laid in the box.

"Not bad," was Max's only comment. Watching him and Diesel unwrap and examine them, it would have been obvious to even the densest bureaucrat that these two knew M-16s.

The word *knew* doesn't convey the depth of familiarity that they displayed. It was like watching professional musicians pick up the instrument to which they had dedicated their lives. Without even hearing them play a note, you knew they were going to be artists.

I was getting bored. I was trying not to. Max and Diesel were in their element. Night was in hers; she loved acquiring and keeping track of stuff. Ninja watched Max and Diesel work and was dying to get his hands on the hardware. Meanwhile he soaked it all in. He was the apprentice in a field they had already mastered.

"You know, Gardener. You should help Tommy strip and clean these. You're going to need to be able to do it. If not for you, then for someone in your squad."

"Yeah. Sounds good, Max." I got a look from everyone. I guess the tone of my reply spoke volumes about how I felt. I knew he was right. I was to going to have to know every weapon we stocked.

The next two crates I recognized. They were the heavy ones. Inside we found they were filled with loose ammo, damn near to the top.

Max picked up one of the rounds, looked at it, and then tossed it back into the crate. "Interesting."

It was what came out of the next crate that caught my attention. The top was popped, and as soon as the first item was unwrapped and set on top of a crate, I fell in love. It was ugly. The metal was darker, deeper, more real looking than anything else I had seen so far. It had dark solid wood where it needed it. It looked like a tank compared to the M-16s.

"That's mine!" were the first words out of my mouth.

Diesel was staring at it. "*Damn*, is that what I think it is?"

"Yep. The corps still had them around when I first came in."

"You guys were always a couple decades behind everyone else in weapons procurement."

I had no idea what it was, but I wanted it. I didn't want to ask what it was in front of everyone. Thank God for Night.

"Okay, so what do I write it down as?"

"That, Night, is a BAR, a Browning Automatic Rifle. It's no surprise G likes it so much. It was the automatic weapon for rifle squads about a million years ago. The Marine Corps usually assigned two to a squad. It runs out of ammo pretty quickly. Go on, G, take it, and set it aside. We probably have someone in the militia who knows how to use it."

"Yeah, we just need to find the oldest living one," Diesel replied.

I picked it up to put it aside. It was heavy.

The rest of the crates held more ammo, including some for the M-14s, .357 and .45, plus magazines and bandoliers for the BARs, and a couple of cans of loose fifty-caliber, including armor–piercing shells.

"Look at this," Max said, holding up a round. "See the tip? That's how we tell what it is." He held up another. "This is a tracer."

"So they know we have a Barrett?"

"Yeah, and for now it seems like they approve."

The final crate held cleaning kits and a box full of parts.

Next we started on the cardboard boxes. We had boots, ALICE packs, plastic canteens, folding shovels, cases of

MREs, and a carton that had twenty smaller boxes inside. Each box contained civilian-made night-vision goggles. We also had a box of night-vision scopes—old ones, according to Max.

Ten boxes of copier paper perked Night up. "Yea! Maybe my pony is in here somewhere." It was—in the form of two HP LaserJet 3400s and seven toner cartridges. She was ecstatic. There was also a box of slings, canvas belts, load-bearing vests, and three pairs of wool socks.

"Not bad," Max said after stifling a yawn. "You know what's weird?"

"Diesel?"

Everyone ignored me except for Diesel, who flipped me off.

"No," Max laughed, a tired laugh. "No helmets, no comm, no vests."

"Yeah, they should have sent more green BDUs. Then we could field a well-dressed, vintage 1980 rifle company. Still, not bad. We never planned on going head to head with the U.S. military anyway," said Diesel.

"What about the note?" Ninja asked.

"Tomorrow, Turtle. Tomorrow," I told him.

The note stuck in my head. It pissed me off. It was obvious manipulation. I talked about it with Max, who told me to blow it off. "You start running errands for Big Daddy and he will run you into the ground."

"Yeah. What about the payoff, Max?"

"Did you see any guarantee of a payoff?"

"No." That was a good point. Still, it stuck in my head. We needed more of everything.

# CHAPTER THIRTY-THREE

The tollbooths were up and running. While I was out in the field we had received three Crown Vics so we had vehicles again.

We also had a protected parking area for RVs and cars. These same vehicles paid to use the town campground which also included an escort for ten miles when they left town. The campground proved popular, so popular that Night told me they were considering a commercial vehicle area only. A lot of small trades and craftspeople on the way into the Zone liked having a secure area to park. They were usually coming from within a day's drive of us. Parking with us kept them safe, and within a few hours of the Zone for an early morning check in.

The state police liked what we were doing. They had a lot fewer officers; budget cuts had hurt their force badly. Those that were left found that they were getting pulled into local policing, which they hated. So we set up an informal information-sharing agreement. The state guys would cruise by every other day and stop in at the station. If Max had anyone he was interested in, they would run it through their car communications for us. In exchange, they got a free meal at the diner and the knowledge that we would never call them into areas we claimed.

We were locking people up now. For petty crimes, we would hold people overnight to sober up or cool down. Miss Edna would lecture and fine them, and we would cut them loose.

We also were getting an increasing stream of people who wanted to stop and settle here. That was going to make for an interesting town meeting next time.

Night ran a town update that was open to the public every Thursday. Miss Edna and the pastor ran the town meeting once a month. Finding out what the town wanted to do with settlers was up for discussion at the next meeting. Night told me the general feeling was to "move them on."

Her plan was to make people apply for residence. "That way we can look for medical professionals and any-one else we really need. They can pay a 'resettlement' fee. If they can't afford it and we really need them, well, they can pay it off with community service." I thought it was a damn good idea.

The squad spent the next month running exercises at the training house and in the nearby woods. Twice we flushed deer and were able to kill a couple each time. The first time there was no way to decide whom the kills belonged to, as almost everyone had fired on the small herd.

After that we devised a plan. The second time, Diesel was on point and flushed them, and I took the shots with the BAR. We cut up the meat there, and everyone got some. I initiated the rule on the spot: Regardless of who took the shot, everyone got a piece. The only thing the shooter got was first choice.

The other rule I devised was that everyone could change their name—with my approval—if they wanted to. But it had to be a one-word name. I added that part after Zit asked to change his name to Wandering Dark Death Wolf. He ended up going with Darkness.

It turned out that our lesbian, Grace, was an herbalist. She was also our only female now; the other female recruit had broken her ankle during training. She slipped on a rock, trapped her foot, and then fell wrong. We were wearing packs, which didn't help. She was good, but I was glad to see her go. She was very hot and a bit of a distraction for me. I think she was to the squad, too.

I found out Grace knew her stuff about plants when she flashed the S\ TOP sign and motioned for me to come to her. She was excited.

"Look! We are in the middle of ginseng patch. A good one too!"

It turned out everyone in the squad knew something about ginseng. We took some roots from the oldest plants back with us. Grace made sure I took a big piece for Donna, whom she apparently knew. After that, I had her teach us plants we could eat and use for medicine whenever we had a chance.

The squad and I also practiced using the night-vision goggles. At first that was fun. Darkness—I really had to work at not calling him Zit—made infrared flashlights for us using a regular flashlight and a remote control. That was very cool.

One night when I came back to the trailer I didn't light the kerosene lantern. Instead I took off my clothes and slipped into the bedroom, intending to surprise Night. Instead I almost lost Mr. Winkie. She came awake fast, pulling her fillet knife from where she had it stashed at the head of the bed. She carved air in front of me and had me stumbling back calling her name: "Night! Chill. It's me."

After she got over being pissed we took turns with the goggles and invented a couple new games.

My time after the field exercises was spent doing and learning. I ended training at 1500 hours every day after multiple requests. Many of my team had responsibilities elsewhere. Some had family who needed them on the farm. Others were needed to do community service projects Night had come up with.

She had them distributing rain barrels to collect fresh water. She managed to get a truckload of food-grade fifty-gallon barrels from her clan. They got them from the Chinese restaurants they owned or protected. She also wanted to start a community food bank. So far that had not happened. Time and people who could organize were both in short supply.

The day after I got the BAR, Max brought an old guy around to meet me. He said the guy had been a "gunny"— a gunnery sergeant—and Max made sure I knew that was a big deal. Anyway, Max said, he was now our armorer. I never did ask his real name.

Gunny and I would meet at the station, which is where he hung out most of the time anyway. He taught me how to fieldstrip the BAR and insisted that I do it every day. So after I cut the squad loose I would go by the station, clean the Browning, and talk to him about the exercises. He would then tell me stories about some young lieu-tenant he had known and some incident or situation he had been in and how he handled it—sometimes correctly, sometimes not. It took me a week to realize he was teaching me, not just talking for the hell of it.

Gunny knew his stuff and he liked to talk. I liked to listen. I learned to fieldstrip the BAR blindfolded. Then I learned the M-14 and the M-16. Next we started on the handgun inventory. He was partial to the Colt .45 but he thought my Ruger was a fine weapon.

What he kept coming back to in his stories was the need, if you're a leader, to have people believe and trust you completely. They had to know you cared about them, and you had to demonstrate it. It was important that I train them hard and never let up on them or myself.

Once I would have walked away muttering "stupid, corny, old doddering asshole." Now what he was saying rang true to me. I had never understood what motivated men to stand in disciplined lines, and take and give brutal life-taking blows. I understood the desire to inflict pain; I just had a hard time grasping why I should do it at someone else's command. Now I understood that you did it because the people around you were your family.

I hadn't forgotten about the sheriff. He may have lost the team he sent to kill us, but he himself had not paid the price. The feeling of loose ends in my life bothered me. I still had the sheriff, Casey, and the trip to Bruxton, which I felt obligated to do.

If I was going to do it, I was going to have to do it soon. We had been asking around about the town, mostly with the people who passed through ours. Bruxton was near the farthest outpost of the guy we knew as "the colonel." The colonel's territory had expanded rather rapidly.

Night charted the growth on a map. He had quietly set up outposts in towns that sat on half of the secondary roads into the D.C. Zone. He stayed away from the interstates, which made sense. They were considered priority mini-zones and a lot of resources went into policing them.

The next day when we all were at the station I mentioned I was going to pay a visit to the sheriff soon. I had already told Night. She wasn't happy about it but she understood. Our power had been down for two days. I was waiting for it to come back up so I could get some Google maps of his area. I told them I was going in soon regardless. Fall was coming, and the temperature was dropping. I wanted to do it while I still had ground cover.

They were fine with the idea. They were not fine with me going alone. Some said I should "make it a team exercise." Ninja claimed he had just as much right to go as me. I told them I would think about it and get back to them.

Later, when I came in from the field, I sat with Gunny to clean the BAR and my handguns. We were talking about nothing when he asked me, "You going tomorrow?"

I looked at him. I hadn't even told Night yet. All I had was an address and the knowledge that the sheriff and his family lived in a farmhouse.

"Yeah. That I am."

He nodded his head. "I thought so. Doing it alone too, aren't you?"

"Yep."

He started to say something but stopped. Then he shook his head and said, "Son, you were either born too late or just in time for something I am too old to want to see."

# CHAPTER THIRTY-FOUR

I woke early the next morning. Night got up to see me off. Ninja came out of his bedroom when he heard me putting on the gear.

"You're an asshole, Gardener."

"Yeah, I know."

He just stood there staring at me. It seemed like minutes.

"Alright. Gear up, ya freaking Turtle."

He grinned. "Yes, sir! Don't go anywhere." He disappeared into his room.

Night came out of the bedroom wearing one of my uniform shirts. "You taking him?"

"Yeah."

"Good." She stood there staring at me. I hated the goodbye scene and she knew it. She did a little wave and went back in the bedroom. I was tempted to follow but Ninja popped back out.

"Almost ready, bro. How much food?"

"Three days should be good." I knew he kept that much in his pack. We always kept our packs loaded and ready to go. The required food minimum was three days.

We had a rendezvous point about ten miles away, in case we got separated. We also had plans to set up a cache there someday soon, in case the helicopters came again.

I finished dressing. He was lacing up his boots. I slipped my bayonet in and out of the sheath three times for luck and I was ready. "Bring it all, Ninja, and bring your best."

He nodded. He had switched to the M-16 for no apparent reason other than it was cooler looking. Max had shown him how to tape two magazines together so he could reload faster.

We left the trailer. Our breath was smoke, and a touch of frost was on the ground. It glittered in the moonlight. I could smell the leaves. It was beautiful.

It was good to be alive. *Damn good.*

"Let's go headhunting, Ninj."

He grinned, and I stepped off across what passed for a lawn. We waved to Old Guy as we crossed the berm. Within five minutes we were in the woods.

I liked to believe I could live in the woods forever, especially at this time of year. I had read a poem in school by a guy named Frost that captured it perfectly. I had no idea what deep woods were like then, but I understood exactly what he meant. It was "Into My Own" time.

We had approximately twenty-five miles to go as the crow flies. A lot of it was uphill and then back down again. We followed deer trails, old logging roads, and paths that should not have existed for any reason I could imagine. These were not the trackless woods I had read about in the West. People had been walking them for centuries, if not a millennium. We passed house foundations and stubs of chimneys in the middle of nowhere. We scared deer in places that were still barely hunted. We saw a black bear cross the trail a couple hundred yards in front of us.

We made wide detours around any house or trailer we saw. Most of them were occupied; we usually could tell from the chimney smoke. A couple of times distant dogs barked at us, or we heard shots from someone hunting. At night we made a fireless camp. The only time we made a fire was at lunch.

Ninja and I didn't talk a lot. Well, I didn't. He did. I would listen, make appropriate responses, and let him ramble. He wanted to discuss the mysteries of the universe. I didn't care about them anymore. I had once, I suppose. We all do at some point in our lives.

I didn't define my world, or myself, by what I was looking for. If anything defined me, it was what I was running from. I had no desire to discuss that with anyone, not even Night. I wasn't even sure I wanted to think about it. Ninja enjoyed talking, though, and I was okay with that.

Late in the afternoon of the second day we came out on the side of a ridge and saw the town below us in the distance. The scattered farmhouses grew thicker. In the distance we could see a newer development that looked to be from the boom years. The shells of fast-food places and gas stations stood at intersections. Then it thickened into a town about three times the size of ours. It was the county seat, so the downtown section had a few more blocks of business and housing.

A large trailer park sat at the opposite side of the town from us. The state had purchased a number of FEMA trailers and set up temporary housing; that was at least four years ago. They wanted to run their own state camps for those in need, but the money for the program dried up after the first year.

I pulled us back a bit, and we sat down to look at the map. There was only one main road in and out of town, which made the orientation easier. We were a bit off from where I wanted to be, so we kept going for another hour until I thought we were in a good place to scout from without being spotted.

I was secretly impressed we had come out as close as we did. Deep down inside I would not have been surprised if we had wound up ten miles from where we wanted to be. Navigation by map and compass still seemed a lot like magic to me.

The house I hoped was the sheriff's was below us and in the middle of a cornfield. The hills were clear-cut to about a quarter mile from their tops. This was pasture-land down to the start of the flat land, which had all been planted in corn, ready now for harvest. This town was at a lower elevation than ours. Back home, our corn was already in. We had timed it right. Another week and our cover would have been gone.

"So how are we going to be sure that's the house, G?"

I had been looking the house over with the binoculars. "Well, there is a sheriff's car parked in the driveway. Damn, it looks like he has someone posted outside." I was also not thrilled to see a couple of kids running around. It hadn't stopped the sheriff from raiding our place, but I didn't want to go shooting into a house with little kids in it. I passed Ninja the glasses.

"He has kids there, G."

"Yeah, I know. We're going to have to move down to the intersection and check the street signs."

"What if they're down?"

I had to bite off the irritation that I was starting to feel. "Then we watch and see who gets in the car tomorrow morning."

I could hear the defensiveness in his voice. "G, look, I just want to make sure, okay?"

I laughed. "I know. So do I." He looked relieved to hear that. "We should also plan some kind of exit strategy. They are going to be pissed off after we kill his dumb ass."

"Yeah. Then again, we might be doing them a favor."

"That kind of luck I don't want to count on."

We waited until nightfall to hike through the cornfields to the intersection to check the signs. We wore our night goggles, which was cool but also very weird. After the novelty passed, I found I didn't like them, so I took mine off. I felt I could see better without them. Plus, they messed with my depth perception and made me feel disconnected from the world. Just more plastic gun shit.

The corn was over our heads and I swear it was talking. There was no wind, yet a constant barely audible crackling and popping surrounded us once we got into the field. The combination of the corn hemming me in and the sound of it talking spooked me. I was beginning to feel claustrophobic, and I was very happy when we came to the end of the field.

The street signs were still there. We were in the right place. When we got home I was going to suggest that we pull all of our signs down. Why make it any easier for people who weren't local?

We turned around and headed back without talking. Max had impressed on me that if we used more than a few words once we started an op, then we had talked too much.

When we got back, I could tell Ninja was tired and I let him sleep first. I sat up and watched falling stars and thought about how we were going to do this.

When it was time I kicked Ninja's boot and told him he was up. Then I crawled into my bag and went to sleep. It wasn't a peaceful slumber.

I dreamt I was being hunted through a cornfield and the corn kept reaching out to grab me. I would slash my way through it but it was slowing me down. Whatever was coming for me was gaining on me, and I knew when it caught me I would be torn asunder. That is exactly what I heard in my head. A voice like crackling electricity warned, *They will tear you asunder!* I was glad when Ninja kicked my feet and whispered, "Get up! We got something!"

He handed me the binoculars. I saw the sheriff step out of the house and climb into the back seat of the squad car that was parked there. The same deputy we had seen walking around outside yesterday got into the driver's seat. They pulled away, and the driver switched on the lights. I checked my watch: 0645. The sheriff was an early riser.

I told Ninja, "We go on half rations starting now. We are going to have to bag some squirrels or waste a lot of deer meat on the way back." Inwardly I was kicking myself. We should have hunted on the way here, but I was in too much of a hurry. Or we should have brought more food. *Was I even fit to do this?*

Ninja interrupted my self-hate session. "So what's the plan?"

"We set up at the intersection." I watched the squad car stop at the four-way stop. "We ambush them. Kill them. Take the car and drive home."

He nodded. "Okay. That sounds good. What if he doesn't come by at the same time tomorrow?"

"We pull back and see if we can bag a deer. This is a cornfield. There have to be a few survivors wandering in to graze. Then we come back and wait."

"Okay," he shrugged, "whatever. I know you got it under control."

The next morning we set up in the field. The plan was so simple I didn't see how it could fail.

There was no traffic. None. It was entirely possible that the clip-clop of horse hooves would become more common than the sound of automobile engines in the next few years. The sheriff was on time. The rotating lights were easy to spot through the rows of corn.

I yelled, "Go!" and we popped out of the cornfield and opened fire. I'd had us sit back about eight feet in the cornfield so we wouldn't be seen. Ninja was to my left. But we were too far back and had to take too many strides to get to the road.

The driver saw us and punched the gas.

He accelerated and was already fifty feet down the road when we cleared the corn. I had to take an extra step to clear Ninja, who was firing three-round bursts into the back of the car.

I took an extra second and aimed at where the driver's head should be. Then I started walking toward the squad car, pulling the trigger with every step. The car slowed suddenly and rolled to a stop after crossing into the other lane. That BAR sure was a showstopper.

I looked over at Ninja, who looked back at me and said, "Well . . . shit."

We approached the vehicle slowly, separating just in case. I heard the engine hissing and thought, *Not good.* The back window was completely blown out, as was the front.

That's when the sheriff rose from the dead—or at least from the back seat. He got off two rounds before I blasted back and he disappeared from sight. I charged the car, vaulting from the bumper to the trunk, and put two more rounds into his body.

I stood there breathing heavily for a couple seconds. Then I realized there was no Ninja.

*Where the hell was he?*

I turned around. He was sitting in the middle of the road holding his right arm, his M-16 lying where he had dropped it.

"Shit!" I leaped from the car and raced over to him. "Where're you hit, Ninj? Talk to me!"

"My arm. It really hurts, G."

"Don't worry, Turtle, I'll fix it. C'mon, let's get you off the road and out of sight." I helped him into the cornfield and sat him down. Then I raced back to get his weapon.

"Okay, let's get you out of the armor so I can take a look at this." I eased off his vest, wincing mentally as he winced for real. The shot had missed the bone, which was good. I tried to remember what Donna had taught us about treating this kind of wound. *Shit.* I knew I had to stop the bleeding and watch for shock.

"How bad is it, G?"

"Not bad. Not bad at all. Probably have a cool scar."

"That's good." He tried to smile.

Looking at him I suddenly realized he wasn't even eighteen yet.

"You're going to be alright." I fished out his med kit and started to work on stopping the bleeding. We had some fancy blood stopper in a foil envelope. It was effective, but hard to find and expensive. When I finished, I had him lie back and raise the arm above his head.

"Hold on. Let me see if I can start the squad car." I ran back, opened the driver's door, and dumped the deputy on the ground. Then I slid behind the wheel and turned the key. It was already turned. I switched it off and back on. Nothing. Not good. I smelled gas, too. *Very not good.* I got out of the car and hustled back to Ninja, trying to think of a viable Plan B. Hijack a car? Run for it? Both?

"C'mon, Ninj. I need you to sit up. I am going to put your vest back on."

"We going to make a run for it?"

"Going to have to. At least get away from here and find a vehicle. Then get you home."

I went through his pack and got all the food. Then I quickly dug a shallow hole and buried his pack. "Don't worry," I told him. "We'll get you another one."

He grinned wanly. "I did pretty good, didn't I?"

"You sure did. Without you it wouldn't have worked."

I slung his M-16 over my shoulder and gave him a hand getting to his feet.

"Okay, we are going to head over the hill and start looking for a farmhouse with a car. With a little luck we will be home in an hour. We just have to get across that pasture before anyone comes."

He nodded. I took one more look at him, and then we started back through the cornfield. We were taking the fastest way, which meant going back the way we had come. It also meant leaving an obvious trail, especially since Ninja was not really worrying about where he put his feet. He was moving, though; that's all I needed of him right now.

We had cleared the cornfield and were halfway across the pastureland when we had to stop. Ninja was looking a little gray. We decided we would sit for just a minute. We heard the sirens at the same time.

Ninja spoke what I was thinking. "We're fucked, aren't we?"

"No. We just got to move."

He nodded his head.

I put him in front of me.

"Head for the tree line and don't look back, bro." I was the one doing the looking back and not liking what I saw.

Three squad cars pulled up to the scene. Two deputies jumped from each of the first two cars. The third driver was alone, probably the supervisor. They checked the deputy on the ground and peered into the car, where the sheriff lay.

"Freeze, Ninj!" If they didn't see us, they might think we had driven off. One car raced down the road toward the sheriff's house. Then I saw one of the deputies point into the corn. He went to the trunk of his squad car and reappeared with a pair of binoculars. I watched as he started sweeping back and forth.

"Please, God," I prayed, "let me get Ninja home." God, as usual, was not listening to me. What a surprise. I watched as the deputy swept across and then came back to us. We stared at each other across the distance until I flipped him off and put away my binoculars.

"Time to run, Ninj."

# CHAPTER THIRTY-FIVE

We were almost to the tree line when I heard gunshots. We were not the only people in the world with M-16s, and they were using theirs. It gave us the extra jolt of energy we needed to get to cover.

*Fuckers*, I thought. I steadied the BAR on a tree branch, compensated for shooting downhill, and shot Binocular Man in the chest with the third round. They were all wearing vests, but the BAR would pierce everything but the best quality. Plates might stop it, but wearing plates was rare. The weight was just too much for day-to-day work. I hit the next deputy low in the throat. That was a spectacular mess. The other two dropped behind their vehicle. I put a couple rounds in the engine and it was time to move again.

"Come on, Ninj. Got to roll."

We began making our way back along our path. For the next hour or so I kept up a steady stream of encouragement to urge him on. Then he stopped.

"Sorry, G. I'm just really tired and cold."

"Don't worry about it," I told him. "Let's get you comfortable."

I set him down and elevated his arm again. Then I start digging clothes out of my pack to cover him. We had just come up a slight hill and were about three quarters of the way across a meadow. We had stopped next to a quartz outcropping.

"Ninja, I am going to brew you up some coffee. How's that sound?"

He nodded, smiled, "Sounds good, G."

I was willing to chance a fire at this point, especially when I heard dogs barking far in the distance. I got a small fire going next to the outcropping and moved him near so the heat would bounce back on him. I had enough coffee left for one more cup. It was instant anyways.

While the water got hot I tried to calculate when they might get here. On the other ridge I saw a glint from steel or glass. I pulled out the binoculars. It was a four-wheel-drive truck moving really slowly. They must have come up on one of the old hunting or logging roads. It made sense that they would have people who knew these woods.

"Am I going to die, G?"

"No, you are not going to die. Though it would be nice to have the extra room in the trailer."

"You're an asshole, G."

"So I've been told."

As he drank the coffee I came up with Plan B. It wasn't much of a plan. Basically it was to kill as many as I could before they killed me. Hopefully they would take Ninja into town and fix him up. Max would figure something out to get him back. I mentally shrugged. I had nothing else.

"You know, Turtle, if this was the movies, an F-18 or a Blackhawk would appear just about now."

"Yeah. The Blackhawk would be cool."

"Sorry I messed it up."

"You didn't mess anything up. Shit happens."

I took a deep breath. "Yeah."

The dogs were getting louder.

"Those dogs for us, G?"

"Yep, I'm afraid so."

"You going to cut their heads off, too?"

"Naw. Probably shoot them if they come too close. Otherwise they can just hang out with us."

We spent the next twenty minutes reminiscing about the good old days. By then the dogs had gotten closer. I could hear the truck. It looked like everyone was coming together. This promised to really suck.

I got up and took a kneeling position behind a chunk of quartz. I put four magazines for the BAR where I could reach them, then pulled my bayonet out and set it next to them.

"You only put out four of your magazines, G."

"Yeah. I doubt if there are more than eighty of them."

He thought about it for a second and grinned. "I might as well go to sleep, then, if there's less than eighty."

"Yeah, you do that."

That's when the two dogs appeared at the foot of the meadow. They looked at me. I looked at them. I shot them. "Sorry, doggies," I whispered. Then I waited.

"Give me my weapon. I will help."

"Stay put. I may need you to reload." That seemed to satisfy him.

There were, by my count, maybe only ten of them. They were not that good at moving in the woods, and the department uniforms did not work well as camouflage. They were using shrubbery as cover, which was not real smart.

"Come out with your hands up! You're surrounded," someone yelled. It went through my mind that, in so many ways, my life was becoming one bad movie. *Who the hell really says shit like that?*

I didn't bother to answer. I just shot the two guys on my left. Then it was time to try to become a turtle inside my vest as they proceeded to chip away at the quartz outcropping that I huddled behind. I got as flat as I could and poked my head out near the ground. I couldn't see anything because of the grass and weeds, so I just started shooting from one side and worked my way across, hoping to hit something.

From the scream of pain that I heard, I think I did. Then it was their turn to mow the grass where I had been. I reloaded the BAR. The five or six seconds it took felt like a year. By the time I got that done the return fire had stopped. Either they had all decided to reload or they were getting ready to rush me. I knew it was over regardless.

I set the BAR down, looked at Ninja and winked, and then slid backward, keeping the outcropping in front of me. I got my legs under me and sprung up. I landed awkwardly in a crouch on the lower part of the outcropping. My leg was still not completely right. I stood up and saw that the deputies were out of the cover and moving in a line toward me. I shot the two in front of me.

Then I leaped off the outcropping, aiming at one on my left as I dropped. I was hoping to kill a hole in the middle of the line and roll into it. But his head exploded before I got a chance to pull the trigger. I landed and did my roll, crossing my arms so my pistols pointed away from my body. Doing that also made it easier to extend my arms into position to shoot when I came back up. My unseen helper made it easy for me to decide where to focus my fire.

I took out two guys on my right. They were trying to compensate for my new position, but they were too late. The tree line behind me exploded with automatic rifle fire. The guys to my left didn't have a chance. Another BAR was in there somewhere punctuating the M-16 bursts. The last guy on my right wasn't bringing his rifle up; he was just staring at me wide-eyed. I shot him, too. Just to be safe.

People came charging out of the tree line. At least two of them were screaming something.

It was my squad, with Diesel yelling at them to push out a perimeter. Max strolled out from the woods behind them, carrying the Barrett. Even from this distance I could tell he was pissed. The squad streamed past me, giving me some seriously weird looks.

*What the hell was going on?*

Diesel was checking the downed bad guys. "I got a live one here! Medic!"

Max said, "Forget it, Diesel. She is taking care of Ninja. Get someone else to take care of him."

The perimeter team found the ones I had shot in the bushes. When Max reached me, he just stood there and stared at me while I reloaded. I finished and slid the Colt into my belt.

"Hey, Max. What's going on?"

"Get in over your head again, Gardener?"

"What's with this 'again' shit, Max?"

"We'll talk. We need to find that truck, get Ninja on board, and clear the area."

That's exactly what we did. It wasn't easy. The wounded guy was coherent, and after we told him he might lose a leg if he didn't help us, we got the directions to the main road. We were packed tight in the truck. I rode in back with Ninja.

I asked the squad, "How did you end up saving our asses?"

The story, it seemed, was that Max found out I had left with just Ninja. A day and a half later, he rolled the squad out after us. They had no idea why the delay.

I asked, "What's up with everyone and the attitude change?" It was like a sudden distance had sprung up between them and me.

Grace answered for them. "You don't know? We saw you jump up on that rock and start shooting. Then we saw you just leap at them with your guns blazing and kill even more. We spread out the perimeter and we find more dead bodies. Plus, there are probably more further down. You're like . . ." Her voice trailed off.

Zit finished it for her. "We've all heard stories about you, and we were there at the house, but —you get rolling and everyone dies." He sounded amazed, awed. But I heard something else, too. Disgust? Admiration?

Once we hit the main road and started making time, it was too difficult to talk. We dropped Ninja and the other guy at Donna's. She was going to need a bigger house at this rate. Diesel and the rest of the squad were dropped by the town hall, leaving Max and me to ride back together.

He barely had the door closed and the truck in gear, when I asked, "What's the problem, Max?"

"The problem is this is your second op. This is also the second one you have screwed up."

"Wait a minute. What screwup? All the bad people are dead. Ninja is going to live."

He stopped the truck hard and slammed it into Park. "Look at me. Look me right in the eye and tell me you think that went well!"

I didn't answer. He put the truck back in gear and started driving. Neither one of us said anything for a few minutes.

"Look, G. I don't doubt your courage," he said, finally. "The squad we left back there, they are going to make you a legend. They will also follow you wherever you tell them to go. The question is, can you lead them? You're a fucking cowboy, not an infantry officer."

That cut deep, really deep. What made it really hurt was the possibility that Max was right.

Night was waiting for me. She was sitting on the trailer steps, her head propped up on one hand as she stared out into the darkness of the yard. I stood there, looking at her. Without turning to look at me she said, "The fireflies are gone."

"I know. It's getting too cold, I think."

She turned and regarded me solemnly for a couple seconds. Then a big grin split her face and she jumped into my arms. "Oh God! I am so glad you are back!" Then she suddenly pulled away, still holding on to me, her eyes wide: "Where's Ninja?"

"He got hurt, Night." I added hastily, "But he is going to be okay. He took a round through his arm. Donna says he'll be fine. He just needs to rest."

She pulled me close again. "Damn! You two scare the hell out of me sometimes."

An hour later we lay side by side in bed. I was tired, but there was something I wanted to know before I went to sleep. "Night, why did Max wait so long to send out the team? Why did he send them at all?"

"Because I told him if he didn't, and you and Ninja died, I was going back to the clan."

"Why? And when did you tell him?" I had propped myself up on one elbow and was looking at her. My mind was screaming at me, *Let it go, doofus; let the woman sleep.* But I couldn't.

Her eyes popped open and she took a deep breath. Her voice, when she spoke, was a whisper. "I told him two hours after you left."

"Oh." I paused to digest this. "Did something happen? What took so long for the squad to assemble and move?"

She moved her head just enough to make eye contact. "I'm not sure. I'm not sure I even want to be sure. I know what I heard in my head."

I had the feeling I was not going to like what I was going to hear, but I had to ask. "What was that?"

"He who would be King can tolerate no rivals."

I looked at her for a couple seconds. Then I put my head down on my pillow and rolled over. Sleep did not come easily that night.

# CHAPTER THIRTY-SIX

The next day I went into town. I found Diesel and told him to let the squad know they had a three-day leave. Then I went back to the station. I was looking for Max and found him sitting at his desk talking to the two patrol officers who were now working the morning shift. I sat on the edge of my desk, which Night was using in addition to hers. Gunny was in the back; we waved to each other.

I listened to Max tell the patrolmen what he thought they needed to know. "Now I don't want you two slacking off and sitting on your asses in the diner or parked under a tree. Make a visible tour through the campgrounds. That means get out and walk and talk to people. I want to know where everyone is coming from and where they think they are going. That's it."

They nodded politely to me as they passed by.

One of them stopped long enough to fist-bump me. He grinned and said, "Stone cold, Gardener, stone cold." Then he was out the door. I looked at Max, waited until the guy cleared the door, and laughed.

Max grinned at me, "We cool?"

"Yeah, but I want to talk."

He paused. "Private talk?"

"No, Gunny can listen if he wants. We have anyone in the cell block?"

Gunny got up and shut the door leading to the back. "Better?"

"Better. Thanks, Gunny."

"It's like this, Max. I've been thinking about what you said last night. I'm not an officer type. I am not even an army type. Not only that, I don't want to be. You called me a cowboy. Well, I am. This world of plastic guns, night-vision goggles, thermal sights, and what have you—I don't understand it and I don't really want to. I do understand killing a man and doing it so he can see me. I understand that breaking the law is something that can't be tolerated. That the strong should not oppress the weak. That 'to protect and serve' means just what it says.

"I don't like all that black plastic, Darth Vader shit for a reason. It's just another part of the fucked-up system that got us living here. Expensive killing toys for people who don't want to look someone in the eye and recognize him as another man. They are banker weapons. They are 'suck the money out of the poor' weapons. It stinks of corruption, evil, and destruction for the sake of greed." I stopped.

Max sighed. "You done?"

"Yeah."

"You going to be lighting bonfires next?"

"I hadn't planned on it. Why? You hungry?"

"Yeah, actually I am. Look, what do you want to do?"

"Be a cop: Kick doors in, shoot bad guys—and maybe a few not so bad. You know, that kind of thing."

"Well, I don't think we're going to run out of bad guys anytime soon. You're still the assistant chief of police. Order yourself back on patrol if you want."

I grinned. "I think I will have a meeting with myself and do that."

"Good. C'mon. I'm going over to the diner and having some pancakes. I'll even buy you breakfast."

"Wow. I'm impressed, especially since I know Shelli lets you eat for free."

"Yeah, there is that." We both laughed.

"Max, I'll meet you there. I need to give Gunny something."

He cocked his head as if he was waiting to hear what it was. Then he shrugged. "Sure, no problem."

I walked over to Gunny and set the BAR on his worktable. "I don't think I am going to need this anymore. You want to check it back into the armory for me?"

"Sure, G. No problem."

"Thanks." I headed for the door to catch up with Max.

Just as I put my hand on the knob I heard Gunny yell, "Hey, G!"

"Yeah?"

"Don't sweat it. Anyone in town who's worth a damn knows that you're the man when the shit hits the fan."

"You know what, Gunny?"

"What?"

"You just sounded like the lamest rapper I ever heard." I could hear his laughter even after I shut the door.

I caught up to Max at the door of the diner, and we headed for the back booth that Shelli somehow always knew to hold for him. We sat down after working the tables. That meant stopping and talking to people we knew—or, rather, mostly people Max knew—and eyeballing anyone we didn't. Max was good at this. He exchanged insults with some and chitchat with others. I heard him ask one woman, "Did you get any tomatoes to grow?"

The answer was a sorrowful "No, damn blight is still at it."

Business was good at Shelli's, and it got better at night when she served her "wine." She was talking about opening another place to handle the nighttime traffic. She was calling it a dance hall. It was going to feature local bands and serve drinks. Miss Edna saw it as a tax generator. I saw it as a busy night shift.

Max and I talked about it while we waited for breakfast. "I got mixed feelings about it. They get that fortified brew flowing, and get young men and women together, and we are going to have trouble."

"Yeah, well, isn't that what we were hired to take care of, Max? It can't be much different from what we ran across before."

"I'm not worried about us. I am worried about the people who normally wouldn't cuss in public, worried about them getting loaded and shooting their best friend."

"Why does Shelli want it so bad? Other than the obvious answer?"

"Not much past that really. It would bring needed money into town. Create a few more jobs. Put some life into the place. I told her that if she does it, she'll have to pay for security inside and out. More shit starts in the parking lot of places like that than you could imagine."

"Put it further out. Use the old RV place. Keep it out of town but near enough to keep an eye on. Maybe run a small pub in town for locals and have it close earlier."

"Yeah, Night suggested the same thing, except she wants all the bartenders to be working for us."

"I know, Max. She wants us to buy in, become part-owners."

He grinned. "Might as well. It's not like anyone is offering a retirement plan that is worth anything these days. Plus, someday you are going to have to be buying new shoes and gun belts for little gunfighters."

"Ah, let's not get carried away, Max."

He just laughed. "You got the tip."

After breakfast, which was very good, and before he went back to the station house, Max told me what else was new.

"I got a spotter sitting on the road with our best walkie-talkie. She is going to holler if she sees anything coming up the road from the county seat. We got the old civil defense siren hooked up. If you hear it go off, head for the park by the town hall. Of course, there is the problem that we can never be sure the electricity will be on to run the siren. What we need is a bell. Anyway, that's the rally point."

"Then what?"

"I don't know. We got to figure out some signals and a plan. Never enough time, G, there is just never enough time. Since you're back I am going to give you some of this to work on."

"Sure. It's better than digging holes."

I decided to walk around town. I felt pretty good as I stood there in front of the diner. I tasted pancakes again with a burp a teenage boy would be proud of. Outside of the weight, the body armor was welcome on a morning like this.

After walking the town I planned to pick up Night. I figured we could ride over, see Ninja, and then maybe, just maybe, get some early quality time back home.

Max had mentioned the need for helmets. Sitting behind that quartz outcropping while it got chipped away had made me realize that they made sense. I just didn't want to wear one. I suppose if I had lost the tip of my nose, or had gotten a chunk of quartz embedded in my face, I would feel differently about them. I knew eventually I would be wearing one. But eventually was far enough away from today that I wasn't going to sweat it.

The town had changed. I could feel it. More energy was flowing. People were out and about. They were happier. I decided to head over to the north tollbooth first. I walked down Main Street to the far end of town, going slowly, just taking in the scene.

I was even passed by several cars headed for somewhere other than here. I could tell because they just stared at me. They were probably pissed at paying the toll.

The tollbooth was a small wooden shack. There was a steel post in front of it designed to slow down anyone who might want to avoid the toll by driving through—or over the toll collector. It was a two-person operation. One person took the toll based on vehicle type; the other watched, in case there was a problem, and inspected the vehicle. We didn't want any Trojan horses rolling into town. Plus, Night thought it was a great way to get a read on the world based on what kind of people were moving around.

The tollbooth had a CB radio. We had standardized on CB radios for almost everything. We used twelve-volt car batteries to power them. The problem was finding enough solar-powered chargers. Each tollbooth had one charger plus three batteries: one to charge, one to run on, and one for backup.

We kept all the radios on the same channel, and Gunny monitored communications back at the station. Gunny was now our armorer, dispatcher, and desk sergeant. He wanted a raise, too.

The guys manning the tollbooth saw me coming. They had been sitting in the shade talking until they spotted me. I saw the watcher say something to his buddy. By the time I got up to them they were trying to look busy.

"Hey, guys. What's up?"

"Hey, Gardener. Not much." This was from the toll collector. Both of them were militia, which meant they were over forty years old but had prior service.

I waved the watcher over. "Come in out of the sun."

He had to be three hundred pounds, which was getting to be unusual around here. None of it looked like muscle either. The tollbooth roof extended enough to provide shelter for them if it was raining and a little extra shade on a sunny day. He looked like he couldn't handle more than ten minutes in the sun before all that fat would be talking to him. I didn't want him keeling over just because I had shown up.

"How's traffic?"

"Light. The middle of the week is usually slow. Tell him about the big excitement of the day, Junior."

The watcher, whose name I now knew, laughed. "You tell him, Bill. You tell stories better."

"Well, we had this couple in a BMW. You know, one of them high-dollar cars."

Junior interrupted. "It was beat up. I bet it had been seven or eight years since it could be called a high-dollar automobile."

"You going to tell the story or am I?"

Junior held his palms up. "Sorry." He looked at me. "He's a bit touchy when he tells stories."

Just shut up, Junior. Anyway, they wanted to go through. Told me it wasn't fair. Said there was no toll marked on the map. So we go back and forth. The guy says they are broke. Looked like he wanted to cry. Then the woman says, 'If I show you my titties, will you let us through?' I told her, 'It depends.' So she pulls up her shirt and shows us these saggy titties. Junior here looks at them and laughs. He says, 'You call them titties?' Then he shrugs off his vest, pulls up his T-shirt, and shows them his."

"They are pretty nice," Junior said. "Want to see?"

"No. So then what happened?"

Bill and Junior started laughing. "We told him that her titties didn't qualify for the special discount!"

They were laughing their asses off now. I chuckled a bit myself.

"And then what?"

"The woman started screaming shit at us as her husband put it into reverse."

"You know, guys, that is pretty funny. How many times have you let people slide for a tit shot?"

Bill said, "None," at the same time that Junior said, "Three."

I watched as Bill shot a glare at Junior, who hung his head contritely. I just stared at Bill. He tried to match me and then decided to look away after five seconds or so.

"So, G, I guess this isn't the best time to congratulate you on killing the sheriff and a hundred or so deputies."

"No, it's not, Bill. And don't call me 'G.' Only my friends call me that. I don't consider you or Tits here my friends." I paused. "In fact, I am wondering what else you need to confess. You know, get off your chest."

"Nothing else, I swear! Isn't that right, Junior?"

"Bill, if you say one more word, I am going to open your head like a melon. Do you understand me?"

He nodded that he understood. His face was ashen.

I said, "Good. Now go stand over there and watch for BMWs."

I watched him go. I waited until he got about ten feet away before I said, "Junior . . . Junior, look at me." I waited until he did. "It's okay. I am not going to hurt you. I just want you to answer a few questions."

He looked at me. I had not realized it at first: He wasn't country; he was slow. *How the hell did he get into the military?*

"Are you going to hurt Bill?"

"Only if he has been bad, Junior."

He thought about that and nodded his head. He understood that.

"Did you and Bill let anyone go for free?" He tried looking over at Bill. "Junior, I want you to look at me when I talk to you."

"Mr. Gardener, we only let friends go. Does that count?"

"Hmm . . . were they good friends?" I smiled at him. He keyed on the smile, just as I thought he would.

"Yes! Bill has lots of friends." He smiled. I smiled. We were in love.

"Does Bill always collect the money?"

"Yes." Here he looked down. "I'm not so good with money. I mean we don't have pictures on a machine to push."

"Yeah, that makes it harder. I hate that. You did good, Junior." He looked up at me like he couldn't believe it, like he was waiting for me to drop something nasty on him.

"Really Junior. We're cool." I patted him on the shoulder. "Just stay here while I go talk to Bill. Oh, hand me the magazine on your weapon."

He did. I knew Bill saw it and was drawing conclusions about my conversation with Junior. I took the magazine and stuffed it my belt, making sure it didn't get in the way of the Colt. Then I started walking toward Bill.

Bill had put on his sunglasses so I couldn't read his eyes. Instead I was going to have to read the angle of his M-16.

"Bill, we need to talk."

"About what?"

I kept walking. "About that woman. Did you find out who she was?"

"What? What are you talking about?" I wanted him off-balance and thinking it was no big deal. "Gardener, you need to slow down." I guess he had a guilty conscience.

"Bill, I see you raise that barrel up another inch and I am going to have to hurt you."

He was undecided on what to do. Not being able to make a decision is the same as making one. I didn't stop until I was in his face. He was holding the M-16 across his body, barrel pointed down. Now he had no room to swing it up without stepping back or pushing me. Neither was a good option for him.

"Bill, I want you to drop your weapon on the ground for me."

"Why should I? What's up, G?"

I drew and went upside his head with the Ruger. He crumpled. I looked down at him and shook my head. "Bill, you got to learn to listen." I picked up his M-16 and walked back to Junior.

"It looks like me and you are going to be working together for a bit, Junior."

He had a bit of a frowny face. "Why did you do that to Bill?"

"Junior, he was bad, but he will be okay. Go drag him into the shade here so he doesn't get hot or run over." I smiled at him. "He'll be okay. Go on now."

I went in the booth and got Gunny on the CB. I told him to send the patrol officers to my location ASAP and to have them bring a med kit. He asked if everything was okay.

"Yeah. Just a minor mishap." I hung up the mike and took a look at Bill. I pulled his handgun. "Thanks, Junior. I appreciate it."

He started to walk over to his watch post when I called out to him, "Hey, Junior. Were you in the army?"

"Nope. Semper Fi, Gardener."

I nodded and went inside the booth, where I could laugh my ass off in private. I was still laughing when the patrol officers showed up.

# CHAPTER THIRTY-SEVEN

I rode back with the two patrol officers, who had shown up in one of our functioning Crown Vics. It dawned on me that we should look into golf carts for transportation. They would be a lot cheaper to use on these short runs.

I'd had to wait for the patrol officers to show in order to restrain Bill, not that he had moved any. They had restraints; I didn't. Yet another thing we were running low on. I made a mental note to call the state police barracks and ask if they had any they could drop off. We needed to find some old-fashioned metal ones or see if come-alongs would work for us.

At the station, I told the officers to charge Bill with theft, log it, and arrange his hearing with Edna. He was already showing signs of coming back to life. They left him in the cell after a quick head wash and wrap.

"So, you getting soft, G?"

"No, Gunny. I figure shooting strangers is one thing. Locals, well, that could cause some resentment."

He laughed. "Hell, that peckerhead is my sister's nephew, and I wouldn't have grieved too much if you were in the right."

"Yeah. Thanks. Anything happening other than that?"

"You're supposed to be at a meeting in twenty minutes at the town hall."

"Says who?"

"Says the calendar on your desk that you never look at, that that girl of yours fills out every day for you and reminds me to remind you."

"Oh. That calendar."

"Yeah. That one."

I walked over to my desk and looked at it. It had way too many meeting entries. "I got ten minutes to kill, Gunny. Tell me something good."

"Well, Shelli lost her freezer again 'cause of power failure. She got some of the church ladies to help her try and preserve the meat."

"You mean the Bible thumpers are jerking the meat?" I started laughing.

"Yep. Actually it is mostly the Baptist ladies helping, so they should be done in no time."

"Thanks. I need to wash my head out now." I headed for the door. "On second thought, I guess I will get there early. Thanks for sharing, Gunny."

"No problem."

I walked into the town hall and headed for the meeting room. Everyone else was already there. Everyone in this case meant Night, Max, Miss Edna Jacobson, the pastor, and a really old lady who was sitting next to a much younger woman—meaning she was in her early fifties. I said my hellos, squeezed Night's shoulder, and grabbed a seat next to Max.

I got the nod of approval from Miss Edna. She hated it when I was late or went to sleep.

"Very well. Please, someone close the doors." The pastor got up and took care of it. I looked at Night. She had on her most serious face, and Max was looking a little more grim than usual.

Edna wasted no time. "Thank you for coming. We have two guests whom I will introduce in a few minutes. Ms. Night brought something to my attention early this morning and I thought we should discuss it immediately. Would you like to explain the situation or should I?"

Night shook her head. "You go ahead, Miss Edna."

"Thank you, my dear. Based on her calculations, and checked again by me, it is pretty much certain we will be starving to death in about three months."

Apparently, this came as news only to me.

She continued, "I will summarize what we know and what we don't know, and then we will discuss what we can do."

She began reading from a sheet of paper. "As of today we have approximately 875 people living within the town limits. Of those, 373 are between the ages of forty and sixty, and 202 of those are women. We have 102 people over the age of sixty, and 71 of those are women. The remaining 400 people include 52 children under the age of fourteen; the rest are adults—190 women and 158 men.

"Our official unemployment rate is not even worth mentioning. The reality is that this town lived off of tourists, people commuting to nearby towns for work, and government checks that arrived every month. All of that has dried up, in that order. The town is our biggest employer, and it's broke. Our food problem is not just from one cause." Here she paused and looked around to see if everyone was paying attention. We were. I didn't even feel like sleeping.

She started again. "Our food problem stems from many different things coming together all at once. First, our people have limited funds to buy anything. We have been making up the difference with the church food bank, hunting, and gardens. The problem we have with the electricity randomly failing is not helping. Food storage is yet another major problem. It is also getting colder, and the gardens have not produced enough this year to feed the gardeners, let alone everyone else.

"Hunting is not going to work. A year ago, deer were everywhere. Now you have to be a good hunter to get one. Same with anything else you can cook in a pot. What is available in the stores costs too much, especially when too many of us in town are living on a fixed income that, for the most part, isn't coming in. When it is does, it buys a week's worth of groceries at most.

"In addition, we will have problems keeping people warm. We are fortunate that a lot of people still have fireplaces. The problem is our demographics. We don't have enough people to do the work needed to support everyone. If the older people do not get deliveries of wood and food, they will die—not that they aren't dying as it is. The lack of insulin and blood pressure medicine, or the difficulty in getting it, is killing off a handful every month.

"I have invited Ms. Faith Weiss and her granddaughter, Sarah, to this meeting because they are going to be our food experts. Faith, because she is, well, knowledgeable—"

Faith interrupted her. "Oh, say it, Edna. I'm older than dirt." She laughed a raspy, dry, old person's laugh. "Because I am older than the hills, I remember stuff about living here that just about everyone else has never learned. My granddaughter here is smart because she majored in agriculture at Tech. Isn't that right, Sarah?"

Sarah did not relish the sudden attention. "Yes, well, it was not quite agriculture—"

"It's close enough," her grandmother cut her off, "especially as most of these people think corn grows on trees."

"Grandma, you know that's an exaggeration."

Edna cut in before they could get rolling. "We need to come up with a plan. Otherwise this town won't survive. People will go to the Zone camps before they let their kids go hungry."

The old lady knew a lot. It was just that it took her a while to get to the point. She loved the attention. Plus, she and Miss Edna had known each other for a million years, and they were suddenly tripping down memory lane together. Even the pastor was getting into it.

I wasn't. I knew this was some important shit, but what happened sixty years ago at the prom was not.

"Excuse me. . . . *Excuse me!*" I was pretty loud the second time. I figured if they didn't stop talking, I would just bust a round through the ceiling. That would get their attention. But they actually fell silent.

"Look, I am glad your son Adam got a seven-pointer back in 1968, but that isn't going to feed anyone today." I watched Miss Edna start to puff up and then sigh and deflate.

"Sorry, Mr. Gardener, you are right. This is not why we are here. Do you have any suggestions?"

"Send out teams and hit every store in a twenty-mile radius. They are going to have what we need, and, hopefully, we will be a little bit ahead of the crowd. Me, I am hitting the road to Bruxton tomorrow. If what you say is true, and I believe it is, then we're going to need more than beef jerky to get through the winter."

"Bruxton? No, Gardener. That . . . we . . . no."

*Why was Night getting so upset?* I wondered. "Night, we can talk about it later, but seriously, who else is there? Who else was asked? Besides, I'm just going to take a look."

Night laughed. It was a mirthless laugh. An odd laugh. One that sounded too close to the edge of a sob. "You never *just* look. I know you."

"Don't worry. I'm going with him."

I looked at Max. Surprise and delight shot through me. "Well, alright!"

Night stood up. Her fists were clenched at her side. She screamed, "You're an idiot! Do you want to get killed?"

I spoke my "Not really" to her back as she exited the room. She was moving fast. But she stopped at the door long enough to look back and scream, "Assholes!" Then she left.

The silence was, well, silent. Miss Edna got up and glared at me. "I'll go see if she is all right."

I looked at Max. He shrugged.

"Tell Night I'll be back at the trailer. Dawn is going to come early." I looked at Max. "Dawn's good?"

"Yeah. We'll take my truck most of the way. I figure four days' rations should do it."

"Good night, ladies. Good night, pastor." I could hear Max's boots clicking on the floor behind me as I left.

Just as I cleared the door I heard Ms. Weiss say, "Bruxton? Of all places. Even Wal-Mart wouldn't go there."

I was asleep when Night came home. I had spent about an hour cleaning weapons and getting my gear together. I could have done it faster, but I dragged it out in the hope that I would hear her car coming in.

Ninja was still over at the "hospital," otherwise known as Donna's spare bedroom. He didn't seem in any hurry to come back and was suspiciously cheerful when I visited him. The Old Guy was asleep and snoring loudly in the room next to ours. Sometimes, when he really got rolling, Night would pound on his door or on the wall and yell at him to roll over.

One night we were lying there and she told me, "Between his snoring and Ninja's cheesy farts, I feel like I'm living in a frat house." I thought it was funny. She didn't.

I woke up when she came in but I pretended to be asleep. She grabbed my foot and shook it to wake me up. We always woke people by kicking or shaking their feet. In the field people had a tendency to wake up ready to go, so it was a good idea to stay at arm's length until they focused.

After she shook my foot she said, "I know you are awake, so open up them eyes and look at me."

I sat up, stuffed a pillow under my head, and stretched back out. "Hey. What's up?"

She sat down on the bed and looked at me. Her hair had grown back nicely and it hung like a silk curtain, the tips brushing my chest. "I'm sorry. I am . . . well, I am just a little more emotional lately."

"Why? What's bothering you?" I was surprised at the rush of protectiveness I felt. I didn't say it, but inside I was thinking, *Who's bothering you?*

She smiled and brushed her fingertips across my face gently. I loved it when she did that. "Well, I think it has to do with me missing my period."

It took a bit for me to process what she said. All the time she was looking at me with a half smile.

"You mean?"

She nodded.

"Holy shit!"

"Yes. Exactly."

"This is great!" I sat up. "When do we start thinking of names?"

She laughed. "Not now, silly." Then the silk curtain came down to cover me.

# CHAPTER THIRTY-EIGHT

Max and I headed out the next morning. I dumped everything in the back of his truck except my weapons and I climbed into the cab. He greeted me with a sardonic, "Good morning, sunshine."

"Yeah, whatever. Wake me up when we get there."

"Damn, G," Max said, shaking his head. "We're going to be looking for a place to hide the truck in less than an hour."

I didn't reply. I wadded up my coat, stuffed it in the corner of the cab interior, and went to sleep. I woke up when my head slammed against the window. Max had decided to drive through, rather than around, a pothole.

"Damn." I rubbed my head. "I know you did that on purpose. You're really an evil freaking asshole sometimes."

He laughed. "I need your eyeballs. Look for a turnout or a side road. Maybe an abandoned gas station"—he cut the wheel to the right—"like this one."

It had been a country store and gas station once; now it was just another empty building in a country full of them. The front door was boarded up, but the back door had been opened with a sledgehammer—the official key of the new millennium.

Max took the truck to the edge of the parking lot in the rear and began backing up. He didn't stop when he hit bushes. He just kept going until he found a spot he liked. Then he shifted into first gear and drove out.

"Just checking." He backed into the spot again. We got out, stomped down some bushes to make room to move, and stretched. "Hang on a minute."

He popped open the tool box and pulled out a brown sheet that had black and green stripes spray-painted on it. "Give me a hand." We draped it over the front.

I cut off some branches and threw them on the hood. I looked at him, shrugged, and asked, "What do you think?"

He stepped back, squinted at it, and said, "Close enough for government work." We grabbed our packs out of the truck and got ready to roll.

"You ready to do this, G?"

"Yeah. We got a plan?"

"I do," Max replied. "I am sure it is more detailed than whatever the hell you had planned."

"So, you going to let me in on it?"

"Yeah. Let's move into the woods a bit. Then we can go over the topo map I peeled off the wall in the trailer."

"Uh-oh. Night is going to kick your ass when she finds out."

"Yeah, well, I think we should blame it on Ninja."

"He's not even here. He's never here anymore."

"Exactly."

We walked past the ring of trash. It was the rare building out here that didn't have a ring of plastic bags, oil cans, beer bottles, and the ever-present, rusted fifty-gallon drum. We kept moving past it all, the low-growing brambles grabbing at my boots. A squirrel peered at us as it clung to the side of an oak.

Max kept going, the leaves crunching under his boots. I was looking around for ginseng. Actually finding any was about as likely as winning the lottery was a few years ago. It would be nice if I found some. Night could send it into the Zone to her clan contacts. They loved it.

I was thinking about what kind of gun to get the baby when Max held up his hand for HALT. We had only been walking about twenty minutes, all of it steadily uphill, yet we could have been a hundred miles from civilization. I never understood how people could get lost and die a mile or two from civilization until I started doing this. Hell, left on my own, I wasn't sure I would do much better.

"Okay, G." Max dropped his pack and dug the map out. Sometimes I wondered about Max's pack. It was almost magical how much stuff came out of it. Sometimes I imagined peeking into it and seeing a black vortex. I would be sucked into it and deposited on the floor of an army surplus store in Oregon. Scary stuff.

He shook out the map and picked up a twig to use as a pointer. "This is where we are. This is Bruxton. We are getting into Appalachia here. Whatever we are supposed to see is probably tied into the coal mines. A lot of shafts were sunk around here. You ever been in a coal mine?"

"No."

"Neither have I. I'm not sure what we are looking for."

"Yeah. I keep picturing the gates into NORAD or Mordor."

"Well, my guess is it will be a little more subtle than that. This is the route I want to take. It will put us up high enough to look down on the town without going into it. Plus, it's an approach from the back. They may have motion sensors and sentry posts with thermal imaging on the main approaches. Hopefully this way we can avoid all that shit."

I looked at the map more closely. The little squiggly lines were awfully close together. I knew what that meant: serious sweating despite the chill in the air.

"How long do you estimate to get to your observation point?"

"Maybe a day and half up, a day back. We are going to push hard going in until we get within three klicks of where I want to be. Then we'll take our time."

"These little black squares are houses, aren't they?"

"Yeah. We'll stay away from them. Could be bunkers. Or it could be Jed Clampett, Junior, and his crew of inbred meth-shiners. Whatever. I don't want to jack around. This is a pure recon mission. We go, we look, we go home. Any more questions before we button up?"

"Yeah, Max. Why are you here with me?"

He looked at me quizzically and then grinned. "Because this is what I do. Because you're an idiot. Because I have been sitting around on my ass in meetings while you have been out gathering the garlands of a hero. But mostly because I know you get lost just going to take a piss in the woods."

I stared at him. "You know what?"

"What?"

"Try to keep up."

"Right."

We started walking. About two hours later I began to feel it. By that afternoon I was definitely feeling it. It hadn't been that long since I had done some distance with a load, but all uphill felt like I was using an entirely different set of muscles. Also, the thigh muscles on my bad side were starting to talk to me. So much for being 100 percent rehabbed.

There were breaks in the tree cover, either logged areas or a lot of gray rock breaking through the surface. We never walked through them, always around them. When we stopped for the night, we cold camped. No conversation. It was all hand signs. I got the midwatch, which I spent with my sleeping bag wrapped around me. It was quiet, very quiet, out here. I didn't wear night-vision goggles. I had not even bothered to bring them.

As usual Max woke me up right before dawn. I pissed, snacked, and packed. By midday we approached what he had thought would be a good observation point. It wasn't, but we found one about thirty minutes later that satisfied him. We set up on the side of the mountain, very near the top, in a rocky outcropping.

The place was not too uncomfortable. We wedged ourselves into a space that was more of a crack than a cave.

Once we had settled in, Max pulled out a camo space blanket, yet another accessory that had been customized by spray paint, and draped it over us. I was almost comfy. He handed me the binoculars, gave me the Two sign, rolled over, and went to sleep.

I had done some research on Bruxton and coal mining after receiving the note. As best as I could tell, there were two ways to mine coal. The old way was to tunnel into the side of a mountain and follow the coal seam wherever it went. The new way was to cut the top off the mountain and dump anything that wasn't coal down the side.

Bruxton had made a living off the old way a long time ago. It even had a railroad spur that ran directly into the mine back in the fifties. But the town gradually died off. I wasn't sure why. Maybe the coal ran out, or perhaps the need for high-sulfur coal disappeared because it burned so nasty.

In the eighties, the town made a bit of a comeback. They even began taking off the top of the mountain they had burrowed into. But that must have never been very successful, as most of the mountain was still there. Then about fifteen years ago, the town had slipped back into its coma.

Information on it had been scanty on the Internet. My casual questioning had not turned up much more. Then again, I got the impression there was nothing to talk about. It was just another little town that time passed by.

The town had never gotten very big. The older part of it was built right up to a large metal building that covered the entrance to the mine, where the railroad tracks led to the mountain. The mine entrance was at the point of a V, with the town filling the space. Surrounding it were other mountains. Across the widest part of the V, the road went by on its way to somewhere else. There were fireplaces burning down there, so someone was at home.

It wasn't Currier and Ives, but it wasn't the gates of Mordor, either. Then again, there had to be something here. I dug into one of my pockets and pulled out my notepad and pencil.

That was one thing I had liked right away about military dress. You got lots of pockets to put stuff in—maybe too many. If I didn't always put the same thing in the same pocket, I could never remember what I did with it.

I swept the area twice before I caught the first anomaly. Doing this reminded me of looking at two supposedly identical photos and finding the differences between them. The old mine area entrance was fenced off. No big deal. You don't want people wandering in there looking for free charcoal for their grills. Yet the entrance had a very nice gate and guard shack with two guards. The railroad tracks were shiny too, which meant they were being used. I got excited about that one. Then I noticed that an SUV I saw driving through town never parked or came to a stop.

I watched for another hour but didn't see anything else. I woke up Max, handed him my notes, and went to sleep quite pleased with myself.

When I woke up he handed me his notes. He had written, "You missed the dishes and antennas on the roof by the mine shaft entrance. Also the cell tower by the trailer. It isn't one. We leave in five minutes."

I nodded that I understood and I got up to stretch the muscles in my legs. At least it would be downhill on the way back. I knew Max never went back the same way he came in, but damn, we would have to go downhill eventually.

I was puzzled by something, though: Why had we been sent here? A drone could have seen the same thing. Hell, a man in Big Daddy's position could have sent a real recon team here to do this. Oh well. It was better than digging post holes or going to meetings.

I was right about our route back. Max went further away, rather than in the direction we needed to go. It was only after a couple of hours that I felt we had begun to curve back toward the truck. By then it was getting dark. We made another cold camp. The next day, if we pushed hard, we would make it home by nightfall.

# CHAPTER THIRTY-NINE

I woke the next morning without Max having to be my alarm clock. He was already up, alert and scanning the woods around us. He looked at me and nodded. I didn't move. Something had changed. I just breathed deeply and waited.

Sometimes, especially when I had the watch, I would imagine sending a part of me out to look around, a piece of me that would drift slowly like smoke and scout while I remained seated. Sometimes I was sure I was seeing things I would not have normally been able to see. Other times I thought that maybe I had slipped a gear.

I wasn't seeing or hearing anything now. I did feel a profound sense of urgency. We had to go. *Now*. I did the BAD STUFF hand sign followed by GO and FAST. He looked at me. He felt it too, but he was asking *Where?* I didn't know. I just knew it was time to go.

It took us less than three minutes to get ready. I looked at Max. He shrugged again, so I took the lead. I started heading back to the truck. That didn't feel right. I stopped, breathed deeply, and waited. Nothing but the *Go!* feeling. I started back toward Bruxton. No, that was wrong.

*Shit.* Of course—uphill. I should have known. I looked back at Max. He nodded. I was already getting twinges of pain in my thigh. I disregarded it, telling myself, *Come on, body. Why bother? We know what pain is. This is not pain. The pain that can hurt me does not exist.*

We moved fast and we moved like ghosts. We were in the zone. The last time I had felt like this was the day of the food distribution shoot-out at the shelter. Whatever was waiting at the end of this was in for a surprise.

I went cold as we approached another rock outcropping. I froze in place. Max did too. That is when I heard the sound of male laughter from the other side.

I looked at Max and quietly dumped my pack and the M-14 I was carrying. I didn't need it. I didn't want it. Max hit the snap release on his pack. He had left the Barrett at home and brought an M-16 instead.

He nodded and I went. I hit the side of the rock and went up without hesitation. There might as well have been stairs carved in the side. I felt good. *Damn good.* This is what I was born to do and I loved doing it.

I hit the top of the rocks, cleared a knee-high chunk that was sticking out and in my way, and went over the edge into the light, soaring like a bird. I didn't even look down at what was waiting. I didn't care. I was also sure, sure as a man could be, that it was going to be alright.

Instead, I looked into the sun and screamed with pure fucking joy.

I hit the ground, rolled, and sprang to my feet. In front of me were six guys in full gear, including black plastic rifles. They stood in a semicircle around a blonde-haired, blue-eyed girl who looked to be about twelve. She had a fresh bruise on her cheek and a bolt-action wooden stock rifle about four feet from her. A large black male was standing off to one side in front of her. He had just finished saying, ". . . sick shit."

She looked up at him calmly. The paleness of her face made her blue eyes really stand out. She had on a yellow dress. They wore helmets.

"Hey there." It's always polite to introduce yourself when you drop in on folks unexpectedly. They had heard the thump of my landing. They had seen the black guy's eyes widen.

I heard the voice that runs my world at times like this tell me, *Don't stand off. Move into their personal space.* At the same time, I registered that Max had come around the other side and had the M-16 up and ready.

"What the fuck?" one of them said. "What the hell?" screamed another. They had turned toward me. Not all of them in full body profile, but at least now I had single-shot targets.

I drew on the two in front of me and shot them in the face. I kept moving toward them and didn't stop. I had both guns drawn. I wasn't even aiming. It was as if I had 360-degree Panavision. I just pointed and pulled the triggers again. That was four.

The guy standing by the girl didn't move a muscle. I looked at him. I looked into his eyes. I saw resignation in them as Max shot him through the neck a microsecond after shooting the man to my right. He didn't go down. He just jetted blood like a fountain from the bullet entrance. I shot him between the eyes. It was over.

"Hey, kid. Anyone else we should know about?"

She shook her head no.

Max had come up. He was looking at her, "You okay?"

"Yes."

"What's your name?"

"Freya."

She was staring at me intently. "You are what I thought." She turned to Max. "As you are also."

"That's nice, Freya. Where are your parents? And your house? We need to get out of here now."

"I know. I was coming to meet you. My parents are dead and I am alone."

For the first time I noticed a small camo daypack at the foot of the tree behind her. "Okay. What do you think, Max?"

"Outside of this being some seriously weird shit, I say we move. These guys are probably body-monitored and a whole bunch of screens just flat-lined."

"Freya, you are going to have to keep up."

"No problem. I will wait while you get your packs."

Max looked at the dress. "You got any pants in that pack? You're going to need them."

"No, I am fine." She smiled at us.

"Okay." Max and I went to get our packs. We were not touching these guys. I had no desire to get near them now, let alone claim anything.

When we turned the corner of the rock outcropping Max told me, "We don't even have to talk about this, do we?"

"Nope." I knew that fact with as much certainty as I knew that I'd be okay when I jumped off that rock into the sky.

As he pulled his pack on, I heard him mutter, "This is going to be really interesting."

We headed back. Moving downhill with gear strapped to you is entirely different than going uphill. I had done it before for short bursts, but never for a prolonged period like this.

If anything, it is worse than going uphill. It requires a completely different set of muscles and a lot more attention to what you are doing. Screw up—or just get unlucky—and there goes an ankle or a leg. It didn't stop me from feeling like we were flying compared to the speed we had made going in the opposite direction.

What added to our need for speed was the knowledge that we were racing the clock. Even if that patrol had not been hooked to a command center, or weren't having their vital signs monitored, someone would be expecting them to call home eventually.

Any minute I expected a helicopter to pass overhead, hunting us like some prehistoric predator. I hated them. Soulless dark machines run by mirrored-faced automatons who thought they were actually engaged in combat. They were nothing but button jockeys running a video game—a game in which the humans had become mere images, losing any degree of individuality. In fact, that probably made it even more fun and exciting for the button jockeys. Assholes.

Freya was flying, loving this. Max had to shush her. She laughed as she went down one particularly steep slope, riding it like a downhill skier. After that I quit worrying about her and concentrated on not breaking an ankle or pitching headfirst down the mountain. Thank God, it hadn't rained lately. The leaves were slippery enough.

We sure as hell were leaving a trail that even a condo-dwelling grandmother from Boise could follow.

I was beginning to think we might be all right when I heard the helicopter. As soon as the thought hit, *Hey, we might do this*, I should have started expecting trouble. I needed to add that to my mental list of things to never think. Probably right above *Never assume the last few sheets on the roll will be enough when it is time to take a dump*.

We froze in place. I looked over at Max. He wasn't watching the helicopter; he was trying to sense if it was working with anyone on the ground.

Freya and her yellow dress didn't stand out as much as I expected. It was fall, so yellow, gold, brown, and red were the predominant colors. If they had thermal imaging gear, it wouldn't matter anyway. We would just be vaguely human-shaped targets. *They probably always get their limit in deer season* passed through my mind. I had given up wondering where the weird crap that floated across my consciousness came from.

Either they didn't see us or were pretending not to. Whatever, we kept pushing on when they didn't head our way. We had to be getting close to the truck. Max had taught us never to just stroll into a pickup point. Always expect that an ambush may be possible.

Using universal hand gestures, he told Freya to stay. We dumped our packs next to her and split up, approaching the abandoned store from above, moving parallel to each other. I watched Max out of the corner of my eye. When I saw him freeze and take a knee, I did so also.

I didn't have to look. I could feel it. Uninvited guests. Max gave me the sign to pull back. I knew he was pissed. He really liked that truck.

We got back to our packs. Freya looked at us expectantly. We shook our heads, shouldered the packs, and started walking. We had a ways to go before we could chance the road and catch a ride. We made a cold camp and ate the rest of our rations after making sure the kid got enough to eat. She had some bread, which she contributed. It was quite good, with a very subtle taste of honey.

I know I wanted to ask her a few questions and I am sure Max did, too. The primary one being, *Where the hell did you come from?*

She didn't have a blanket, so I gave her my bag and used Max's while he was on watch. After I took over the watch and had been sitting there for a while, she began talking in her sleep. It sounded like the same words over and over: *"Elden och svärden har blitt grunda fader."*

I had no clue what language it was, but the hair on the back of my neck stood up, and a cold chill ran the length of my body.

The next day we kept going. At lunch I dug into the bottom of my pack and gave the kid my reserve, an expired PowerBar. I wasn't the only one holding back. Max came up with a pack of Skittles for her, which I thought was pretty funny. She was pleased.

We heard a helicopter again, but it was some distance away. Max showed us the map, pointing out where we were and where the road was. We were taking the long way home. The helicopter was working the area of the road, so it made sense. It was just a bit inconvenient.

The next day was more of the same until it wasn't. I noticed a pair of hawks had joined us. That was pretty cool. I liked watching hawks.

Years ago there was, or had been, a place off of Route 7 that was not much more than a dirt parking lot. It was there only because it was directly under a raptor flight path. It used to be cool to go there, walk into the woods to where there was an outcropping of rock, and lie back and watch for them. I had taken Tiffany there once. She was not impressed. That may have been when she began to realize I was a bit odd.

We didn't see the hawks constantly. The canopy wasn't thick like a jungle, but we were not hiking in the Great Plains, either. What made it weird was I felt certain that Freya was talking to them; I just had no idea what she was saying.

I caught Max giving her the eye, but she was keeping up and she sure as hell was quiet. She literally made no sound that I could hear. Then again I doubt if she weighed more than ninety pounds. She could step on a stick and it wouldn't break. I would step on the same stick and it would snap, loudly.

We were getting hungry—well, I was. You burned serious calories moving like this. We would have to take a break soon. We still had some tea, and it would be nice to get off our feet. My leg wasn't talking to me as much today, which was a relief.

We came to the edge of a large clearing with a small stream running through it. Max stopped at the end of the tree line after giving us the HALT sign, but the girl kept going. We had been keeping her between us as we moved. I stopped and was trying to keep an eye on the direction we had come while I waited for Max to figure out what we were doing next.

Max looked at her and pointed for her to move back, but she shook her head and pointed at the sky and the hawks. I could see them both looking up, and then it rained bunnies. Well, only two, but they came thumping down in front of Max and Freya. She looked at Max and smiled. He looked at her, his face expressionless, and just turned and began walking off the trail after giving me the FORM ON ME sign. She ran out, grabbed the bunnies, and joined us.

They were pretty good eating. Max and I exchanged looks over her head while we munched on them. We had worked together for a while now. I didn't feel threatened by her. He did not seem to be either.

We both were at a loss. She was not a threat, and weird had become commonplace. Well, maybe not this kind of weird. I just wondered if she could arrange for an airdrop of pizza.

After lunch Max unfolded the map. We were going to begin the curve toward home.

# CHAPTER FORTY

We made it back and we arrived hungry. Coming into town we were greeted as soon as we passed the first handful of houses. People came out, waved, stared, and wanted to hear the story. Some asshole yelled out to me, "Hey, Gardener! How many did you kill this time?" I couldn't tell if he was being sarcastic or not. Regardless, I filed his face away for future reference.

The girl got her share of attention, too. Hers was of the stare-and-quiet-comment variety. Max traded insults and greetings. A couple of kids started tagging along. It was turning into a parade.

I hate parades, and I really hate this kind of attention. I also hate clowns. Thank God, a patrol car showed up and took us the rest of the way home.

Diesel was driving. It was good to see him. After we rolled a bit and got the "How are you" crap out of the way, he asked Max, "You want to talk about your trip or do you want to hear what happened yesterday?"

"When you put it that way, I guess you should tell me what happened."

Diesel told us the story of how Old Guy had died. A Chevy Malibu had shown up at the station. Two guys went inside and began asking about Max and me. They told Gunny they were Feds and needed to talk to us about an "ongoing investigation." He told them that we were in the field.

They got threatening, and Gunny pulled a sawed-off shotgun that he had clipped underneath the desk and asked them to leave. After they left, he called the farm on the CB and told Tommy to expect visitors.

Tommy only had Old Guy, Woof, and the kids there. When the Malibu rolled up to the gate, Old Guy was waiting. Tommy was still rounding up the kids and getting them inside.

"We don't know exactly what happened. Probably they got pushy again. Anyway, Tommy heard shots as he was coming out of the house. He saw the gate up and Old Guy lying there as the car passed through. He hosed the car. The guys are dead. Tommy is fine. Their bodies are in a hole out back, and their car is roasted. Old Guy is going in the ground tomorrow."

Max sighed. "Damn. He was a good man. Any family?"

"No. According to people at the VFW, the hall and the farm were his life. He has a son somewhere on the West Coast, but nobody has seen him in years."

"You get IDs off the bodies?"

"Yeah. I didn't recognize the agency, but that don't mean squat."

"Anything else?"

Diesel looked at me and grinned. "There is a warrant out for G for murdering a dozen or so citizens of the burg down the road. I don't expect they are going to do anything about it. You probably got a million or so meetings lined up, Max."

"Lovely," Max replied.

As far as the warrant went, my attitude was: "Well, fuck them."

"I knew you two would like that part of the news. So what's the story with the kid? Hey, kid. You got a name?"

She smiled and said, "Freya."

I told Diesel, "We found her along the way. We're almost at the farm. You might as well wait for the telling of the tale."

We pulled in and were followed by laughing, running kids and a barking dog after we cleared the gate. Night and Tommy were waiting. It was minor chaos for a bit. It was fun, too.

The kids stared solemnly at Freya, who stared back.

"Alright, everyone. This is Freya. We found her in the woods. You can hear the rest after we clean up and eat."

What was interesting was Woof's reaction. He stood still when Freya got out of the car. He usually ran up to me and Max to give us the sniff test and get his head patted or his ears scratched. Instead he hung back, standing very close to the kids.

I wasn't the only one to notice how he acted. In fact, I had been curious to see how he would behave toward her. Freya stood there, alone and separated from us by about three feet. I don't know a lot about twelve-year-olds, but I would have been uncomfortable to have everyone staring at me. But she was unfazed. She looked at us and then extended her hand to Woof.

Woof looked at her, whined, and approached her hesitantly. She said something. I have no idea what it was, but it sounded reassuring. Woof moved forward just enough to lick her extended hand; then he turned quickly and resumed his position next to the kids. He seemed more at ease now. His tongue was hanging out, and I swear he was smiling.

That relaxed everyone. The Woof seal of approval was important—enough so that if Woof didn't like her, she would not have been allowed to stay. No vote or discussion would have been needed.

Max and I flipped to see who would get to use the shower first. I won. Our shower was outside by the garden. We had taken one of the rain barrels, painted it black, and set it on a platform. The shower floor was a wooden pallet, and the water drained into the garden. It worked well during the summer, but we were going to have to come up with a better idea soon. We took navy showers. That meant get wet, turn off the water, soap up, and turn on the water to rinse. It worked.

I went in the trailer. It was weird without Old Guy. The energy in our little tin can of a house had changed. I peeked in his room. Someone had cleaned it out already. Just like that, he was gone. I felt a moment of existential angst, but it passed. Shit happens.

I mentally shrugged and went to see what Night was cooking for dinner. Plus, I just wanted to say hello again. People had started drifting in. Almost everyone was sitting on the porch talking. I stuck my head in the kitchen but she shooed me away. She took cooking seriously. Actually, she took everything seriously. We were definitely a case of opposites attracting each other.

The rule was, if you had a story to tell, you had to wait until dinner to tell it. That way everyone got to hear it.

But until then, gossiping and general bullshitting were acceptable.

Freya was sitting in the corner. She was so still that had she been someone else she would have been invisible. But she was one of those people that you found yourself watching, looking away from, and coming back to. She didn't talk. I was beginning to wonder if she spoke English beyond a few simple phrases.

A lot of people in the old days had been like that, especially in the food service business. They would fool you. You would say, "Hello, how you doing?" They would respond. Then you'd ask them something else, and the conversation would flounder. Their entire vocabulary consisted of rudimentary greetings and the menu, and half the time they couldn't get that right.

Max usually told our stories when we had one. I would just sit back, listen, and watch people's faces. It was going to be interesting to see how he handled the bunnies from the sky.

We also had to discuss what we would ask for when I called Big Daddy. I planned to tell him what we'd found in Bruxton and ask for some goodies. Since we had not found anything of importance, it would be interesting to see what the payoff would be. Probably a big nothing burger with a side order of unreturned calls.

The gossip, if you want to call it that, was about the town's accelerating death rate. Getting insulin on a regular basis was fast becoming a problem. It just wasn't happening anymore. Almost any medication that required a daily dosage was difficult to find.

As supplies dried up, the problem worsened. Scarcity meant that prescriptions shipped through the mail often did not arrive. Postal workers probably made more money selling Grandpa's blood pressure medicine than they got in pay.

There were reports that the big pharmaceuticals didn't even make medications in North America anymore. On top of that, ever since the dollar got the big slap-down, manufacturers wouldn't ship products unless the distributor could pay in a "real currency." And prices got marked up to the point where if you didn't absolutely need it to live, you went without. If you needed it that badly, then you had to decide how far you were willing to go to stay alive.

There was also the growing problem of people migrating to and from the Zones. Or just floating, unable to get into a Zone but unwilling or unable to do what was needed to survive outside of one. These people were not predators. At least I didn't see them that way. Rather, they were jackals and professional victims—people who were at a loss how to survive and who, increasingly, got no tolerance or sympathy from the rest of us.

Max told our story the way he usually did. He skipped over the actual killing unless he thought a point needed to be made. Instead, he emphasized the terrain, what we saw and didn't see, and the town itself.

He mentioned the communications array and the indication that something was going on. That the setup screamed the Feds was a given. What they were doing was less clear.

I noticed that Max omitted the bunny drop. I caught him later and said, "What, no bunnies from heaven? You skipped the best part."

He stopped, looked away for a second, and then faced me. "I did it on purpose. We don't need to be starting anything with people that the kid can't finish. If it wasn't a fluke, it will happen again. If not, well, such is life."

I thought about it. "Okay. I agree, but I still am going to tell Night."

Max laughed as he walked away and said, "Fine. She would have gotten it out of you anyway."

The next two weeks flew by. I called Eddie—our contact on the Community Policing and Freedom Assistance package—using the landline at the station.

I called him right after calling the number Big Daddy had given me. Big Daddy hadn't answered. Instead I got a female who gave me only one-syllable responses after I started talking. She also hung up without saying good-bye. Rather rude of her, I thought.

Eddie was noncommittal about providing anything more. He told me everything was scarce at the moment, but that anything was possible. He also said it was important for us to submit our monthly status and crime reports in a timely manner, and asked if we had gotten the spreadsheet he had e-mailed us. We needed to update that for him as soon as possible, he said.

I told him we would get back to him on all of the above, and gave him our order list. Of course, he wanted me to e-mail him a copy and fill out the special request form available on their web site. I gave him the order over the phone anyway.

We wanted vitamins, chard seeds, MREs, helmets, ammo, more weapons, feminine care products, antibiotics, insulin, socks, underwear, generators, cloth diapers,

and all of Clint Eastwood's and Monty Python's movies on
DVD. We had decided to ask for the world and hope that
at least we'd get Latvia. I added the movie request while
I had him on the phone. Once Night got bigger, I figured
we would need something else to do in bed.

Food storage and distribution was a major headache.
Damn, I had to fight back the desire not to hurt some
of these people. You'd think in a town this small people
would see the need to pull together, shut the hell up, and
do what I told them. No. We had to talk about it, argue
about it, and compromise.

Night pulled me aside at one point and explained win-
win negotiating to me.

I listened and then asked her, only partly kidding, "If I
can't shoot them, can I disappear a couple of them?"

"No. That is not an option."

The food distribution and storage was running
aground on control, power, and political issues. I listened
to people claim it was socialist, that we were outsiders
trying to take over, that we were alarmists, and that everything was going to be okay "real soon."

I think the speakers actually believed what they were
saying most of the time. I understood that. It was when
they started talking shit just to camouflage their real
agenda that I got pissed. The worst ones were the preachers, which came as no surprise to me, and we had a lot
of them.

We had six churches in a town of less than a thousand
people. When news got out that the pastor of the Episcopal Church was going to run the new food bank, the
other pastors decided they needed to host one also. Why?

Because they saw it as a source of power. Forget about feeding the hungry; it was about feeding their egos.

Who would have access to food also became an issue. What about those Pope-worshiping Catholics? Didn't they have their own? Or the illegal immigrants? Never mind that we only had a handful of those, and they were already starving. One dumb-ass wanted to feed only those who had been "saved" or who would agree to let the Lord into their lives, preferably as a member of his congregation. I was really, really tempted to shoot him on the spot.

Night came up with the idea of treating the food bank as an actual bank, which created a new problem. Each resident could pay in cash, gold, or labor to the food bank; in turn they would be guaranteed enough food for a meal every day for a period of time.

There was no way in hell we were going to be able to grow or hunt enough food for everyone. Night figured that with cash we could buy the basics in bulk whenever we found them and store them for later use. It was a good idea, but more than anything, it convinced the preachers even more that they needed their own food banks.

We ended up compromising. Each pastor could start a food bank. Anyone in their congregation who signed up was their responsibility. If they ran into difficulties or it didn't work out, that was their problem. The town committed itself to providing one meal a day for children under fourteen and adults over seventy.

I asked Night later, "Why are we feeding the really old? I mean, I understand it is good and noble and all, but why?"

She replied, "Don't worry about it. Most of them will be dead by the new year anyways."

We had to stop locking up locals for petty offenses. Public drunkenness, domestic disturbance, possession of minor amounts of drugs except for meth—those sorts of things only got a warning. The warning was just a little different now. Usually we would say something along the lines of, "If I have to come back here again for the same shit, I am going to kick your ass." After we did that a few times, most of the locals learned that we were serious.

I never threatened anyone with an ass-kicking, although I did bust a barrel across one drunk fool's head just because he thought that he could get away with talking shit to me. I did not tolerate that. Generally, locals were polite to me and I was polite to them.

If a man was a wife-smacker, then we usually told the woman, "Next time shoot his ass. We don't care. If you don't want to do that, then leave." So far we hadn't had any woman tell us she had no place to go. If one did, we would have found a place for her.

If the man pushed it, I told the patrol officers to kick his ass. If it seemed like someone was escalating things, they had orders to shoot his ass on the spot. No one got shot over that. I didn't expect them to. They were all related or had known each other for years. They knew that if it got ugly enough, I would find them. That seemed to work.

If you were not a local, we would put you in holding. Depending on what brought you to our attention, we might call the state police and have them run your background. Most times we didn't bother. If it wasn't a crime of violence, you saw the magistrate, paid a fine, and were moved on. If you smacked a local and were at fault, then you resisted arrest, paid the fine, and were moved on.

We finally got our town alarm system working. The Episcopal church had a bell, which we convinced the pastor to donate. It sat in the front of the church as a historical artifact, and it was one heavy piece of metal to move. We ended up having to use the front-loader, which we had donated to the town after building the berm. We had held back the Bobcat, though.

It was Night's idea to ring the bell once every four hours. She figured it would get everyone used to hearing it. Plus, it let everyone know that someone was alert and watching. The system was simple: One ring meant all was well. Two rings meant all available officers and militia were needed at the station. Constant ringing meant all block managers should get their blocks ready and armed; all militia report to the town square and all officers to the station.

The people who thought we were alarmists began to reconsider as they watched friends and family die from lack of medications. They also became more appreciative of our security efforts when stories of carjackings and raids at isolated farmhouses began making the rounds with more frequency. Cattle rustling was coming back in a big way, too.

# CHAPTER FORTY-ONE

Freya did not speak English. Well, not much. That put a bit of a damper on finding out who she was, why she was in the woods, and how she got hawks to deliver bunnies on demand. Initially, we left her with the kids at the farm, the idea being that she could watch them, help with chores, and learn to speak English.

That did not work out very well. After the second week, the kids wanted to know if Auntie Night or I could take her into town with us.

I asked them why. All they said was, "Uncle G, she isn't a kid. She's old." I asked them to explain but they couldn't. They just kept saying, "She isn't a kid."

The squad came back from its second foraging trip to the surrounding countryside. They brought back a couple iron stoves, some lanterns, and some old tools. One of the tools was a hand-cranked drill. We passed that around and stared at it. The rest, as far as I could tell, was junk.

When I got a chance to talk to Diesel alone I asked him, "What was it like out there?"

"Weird, G, and probably going to get weirder. We're not finding much of anything. Hell, a couple places we pulled into, we were coming in as other people were leaving."

"That had to be a bit tense." I laughed.

"Yeah, well, we showed them ours, and they showed us theirs, and we both decided it wasn't worth it."

"So what were the people like? Talk to me, Diesel."

He rubbed his face and reset the faded ball cap on his head. "People were hostile. Of course, we didn't look like a bunch of bicycling Mormons."

I nodded. That made sense. A handful of warriors armed with rifles and sawed-off shotguns would tend to make people standoffish.

"We saw a lot of stupid shit. Houses burned out for no reason we could see. Whacked-out people. Bizarre shit spray-painted on billboards. People are hungry, pissed, and feeling like they got the shaft. They just haven't figured out who did it, how it happened, and why it happened to them personally."

"So you telling me it's not worth it?"

"Yes and no, G. We can't just go out there and drive around. Eventually we're going to end up in a situation where we lose people and have nothing to show for it. We need intel. We need a destination and some idea what we'll find when we get there."

"Yeah, that makes sense. The problem is we haven't figured out yet if we want to be farmers or the Golden Horde."

He laughed. "G, between me and you, the hell with farming. I'll go with the Golden Horde option."

I agreed with him but I played it off. I didn't want to encourage the idea. We were here, and that was how we were going to play it.

Later I told Night about what the kids had said about Freya.

"So did she drop bunnies on their heads, too?" she asked.

"Night, what's the matter? You don't like her?"

She sighed, looked away, and looked back at me. "It's not that I don't like her."

She paused and brushed her hair back. "It's more like she scares me. No, that's not right. Sometimes I look at her, and it's like I see her but I don't. She is . . . I don't know how to say this. . . It's like she's shielding herself. Like her body is really a cloud or a . . . I don't know. I do know that she is far more than she seems—and that, I think, is what scares me the most."

"So this means tomorrow it will be 'Take the kid to work day' for me?"

She smiled. "I think it would be better if you did. I suppose I should be worried about her safety, but you know something? I'm not."

"Have you heard her talk?"

Night shook her head. "No. She says hello and she's friendly, but no, she's not a talker."

"Woof seems to like her."

"Have you watched Woof around her? No, you've been in town every day. Woof watches her. He is not scared of her—it's more like he's waiting for her to do something. He tracks her with his eyes wherever she goes."

We talked some more about how she was feeling. She had vetoed Freya going into Old Guy's room. It was to be the baby's room. Damn, *did that sound strange to me*. It was tough even to connect the two. Me. Baby.

Night was not showing yet. Well, I thought her breasts were a tad bigger. That was good. I could live with that forever if need be. I decided it would probably be a good idea not to mention that.

Freya was ready and waiting on the porch the next morning when I got up. Night was busy throwing up in the bathroom and told me to go on without her.

I was driving an old Chevy truck that had shown up at the station one day. It was an automatic. Max had once told me he refused to own a truck with an automatic, so he gave this one to me. It had probably belonged to someone who had not survived the insulin shortage. I didn't ask, and no one told me.

"You ready to go to work, kid?" Freya nodded and followed me out to the truck. The keys were in the ignition and the doors were unlocked. I wasn't worried about someone stealing it, and I did like knowing it was ready to go.

Gas was becoming difficult to come by. I was going to have to find out if there were any golf courses nearby—or a golf cart dealership, if there was such a thing. I had been on a golf course only once in my life and that was to go deer hunting. I didn't think I could go back to riding a bicycle; that just seemed so undignified now.

Horses might be cool. I had never ridden one, but it couldn't be that hard. I was daydreaming, picturing myself on a tall black stallion, the sun setting behind me. I looked pretty damn cool.

The daydream ended abruptly when I heard Freya say, "Helikoptern."

"Excuse me. Did you just say *helicopter*?"

"Yes. They come." She must have seen something cross my face that disturbed her. "It is good. They go to where you found me."

I rolled down the window. I didn't hear anything.

"Other big plane"—she cocked her head—"a BUFF." She frowned. "It drops death eggs . . . no, bombs." She smiled. "Yes. Bunker busters. Bad." She laughed. "No, good. Very good."

I thought, as I had before: *That is not a kid's laugh.*

I heard them now. I stopped the truck and got out to watch. Two flights of three. They were moving low and fast. *Damn, I hate helicopters.* Thank God, they were not headed to my town.

Watching them fly over was a reminder that the Feds may be diminished, but they were far from toothless.

Freya had gotten out of the truck, too. She was watching them disappear into the distance. Her hair was braided and held together in the back with a silver brooch made to look like an oak leaf.

"So, Freya, you speak English?"

"Yes, of course. I am learning."

"I see. And where are you from?"

"Vanaheim."

I had my suspicions about the kid. Normally I would have found her reticence irritating but I understood it. It fit with what I was beginning to believe. She had been abused, run off, and then almost raped. She would not give up herself, or any information about herself, until she felt I could be trusted. I also guessed she had watched *The Lord of the Rings* one too many times.

"Is that a town? A country? What, exactly?"

"You do not know this name?"

"Ah, no."

More to herself than to me, she said softly, "So much has been lost."

"Yeah, well, you got that right. Come on. Get in the truck. I'll buy you a pancake breakfast."

"Are pancakes good?"

"You'll see. I think they are almost as good as cookies."

Freya liked the diner. She told me as we entered, "This is a nice inn. It smells good."

"That's the pancakes, kid."

Shelli was working the tables. That meant Max was already at the station. I noticed lately that Shelli's hair was getting a deeper shade of red. She must have been feeling more confident about her safety. The Feds hated Burners, and red hair was one of the ways Burners identified themselves in the early days.

She had her back to us when I grabbed a booth away from the door. Freya sat across from me. Getting to meet Shelli and taste her pancakes would be a double treat for the kid.

Shelli hadn't been to the farmhouse in a while. Max usually walked her home, ate with her, did whatever, and came back to the house, where he had a room upstairs. Sometimes, lately, he didn't come back. He told me Shelli felt safer when he stayed the night.

When Shelli came to take my order, she said, "Hi, Gardener!" Then she turned and got a look at Freya for the first time. "Holy Goddess," she whispered.

Freya smiled at her and nodded her head.

Shelli looked at me. "Max wasn't kidding. The bunnies thing. Oh, my God."

"Get a grip, Shelli. We're hungry, and I'm running late. Pancakes: a short stack for the Shorty here and double for me, please."

"Ah, yeah. Sure." Shelli walked away and collided with a chair. You should never walk forward while trying to look backward. It can hurt. I shook my head and wondered what the hell that was all about.

We sat there waiting. Freya didn't talk and I didn't mind. When Shelli brought the pancakes, I noticed Freya's plate had a tiny cat made out foil next to her pancakes. "Hey, nice touch for the kid, Shelli."

She ignored me. She was watching the kid, who picked up the trinket, held it to the light, and set it by her plate. Freya looked at Shelli and said, *"Min välsignelsen."*

Shelli smiled as if she had just won the diner lottery. "Thank you, Freya," she whispered and backed away.

*Jesus*, I thought, *the kid must remind her of someone.*

Freya liked her pancakes. She ate them all. Just before we left she asked me, "Cookies are even better?"

"Yep. But it's hard to find good cookies these days."

"We must find."

"I'm with you on that one, kid. You know, Shelli had no clue what you said."

"I know. It does not matter."

I took Freya over to the station. Max and Gunny were there. I introduced her to Gunny, who said, "Hey, kid," and went back to tearing down an M-16. Max looked at me with a WTF?

I shrugged. "It's 'Take your goddess to work day.' What can I say?"

"Well, read the log and tell me what you think."

I had been remiss in doing this for the past few days. I scanned the pages.

One drunk—I recognized the name. A domestic dispute. Next to it was written "Dealt with" and a smiley face, in Hawk's handwriting. Someone had gotten his ass kicked.

Unknown vehicle. Toll paid but acting suspiciously. Called in by Block Manager Flag—no details other than it was white.

Toll payment argument. Suspicious noises. Flagged down by Block Manager Gibbons. Were some kids getting drunk in an empty house? Note: Day shift, take a look. Not the first time they had been in there.

Suspicious car. White. Virginia license plate partially obscured. Followed but not stopped. Why? Flagged down for bitch session by a local.

Then the white car again. Followed and stopped. Two men, armed, polite, with a bullshit story, but no reason to hold.

The final entry was a drunk-and-disorderly at the diner. I had heard about that one. Max had broken the guy's arm.

"We're being scouted?"

"Yep. Looks that way. Do me a favor—"

I held up my hand, "I know. Don't T-bone them."

"Yeah. Call the station and have them ring the bell twice. I want you to have backup, and I want them out of the car alive. We need to chat with them." He grinned.

"Yeah, I got it."

We went over the projects that were going on. Max wanted a fast react squad.

"I want you to come with me. We're going to run through scenarios with the squad in the park, such as how to respond in force to a situation involving multiple hostiles in town. I think we'll also do a tollbooth, a food bank, and a market square situation."

"Market square?"

"Yeah, last night the town council decided to run a flea and farmers market in the park every Saturday. We'll provide security and charge a table fee. No toll during it if you are participating. It will give everyone something to do."

"Sure. I get overtime?"

"Yep. I only want the best on duty for this. They get rewarded, and the odds of a problem getting out of hand diminish. Oh, Night called in. She's on her way. She'll be at the food bank and wants to meet you at the diner for lunch."

Night was working on canning groups. Each church usually had a ladies group of some sort. In that group you found at least one person who knew how to can. Each church also had some kind of food preparation area. The Catholic and First Baptist churches had full kitchens with freezers; they were now being used as root cellars. The old ladies loved it, and they loved Night. She was exotic. They were doing something useful, and they got to hang out and gossip. There wasn't a heck of lot happening in town for them to do otherwise.

I think one of the reasons we had such a low crime rate was that we had given almost everyone in town a goal and a role. The goal was survival, and the work to make it happen involved everyone.

"Okay. Tell her noon, Gunny." He nodded. I knew he had been listening to every word.

Max added, "We haven't had any traffic from the direction of Bruxton all day. Someone said it sounded like thunder over there. We should send somebody to take a look if we don't get any traffic by tomorrow."

"I don't think there's any point, Max. Freya told me the Feds were dropping death eggs, and we saw helicopters overhead, moving fast in that direction."

"Death eggs?"

"Yeah, probably hard-boiled."

"Damn, G. At least they didn't drop one on us. Yet."

I shrugged. Like we had any control over what the Feds did or did not do. "That about it, Max?"

"Yeah. Let's gear up and go play SWAT."

"Hey, kid. Want to watch us play SWAT?"

She shrugged. "Okay."

We walked over to the park, Freya in tow. Max and I talked about how we wanted to do this. There were usually a few old men sitting on the park benches. They liked to watch the squad train and yell the occasional comment at us. In many ways it reminded me of high school.

We decided to do the market scenario first.

"I think that if we have any old guys watching, we should use them," I told Max. "They'd get a kick out of it, and the squad would be more careful with them."

I had noticed once that when the squad was geared up and matched against each other, they had a tendency to get rougher more quickly. When I mentioned it to Max, he had called it the "pads syndrome." I must have looked totally blank at that, because he shook his head.

"You know, scrimmage?" Still blank. "Let me guess," Max said, "You didn't play football in high school."

"Nope. Let me guess. You did."

"Yeah. Quarterback."

"Wow. What a surprise. I never would have guessed."

What I didn't tell him is that I had wanted to play. But it was a little tough, seeing as I went to seven different high schools in four years and had to work every night for the last three of them.

"Pads syndrome," Max went on, "is, well, when guys put on the pads and helmets and they begin hitting for real, even if you tell them to go easy. Hang some flags on them, and it's something else entirely. Then it's just a game."

"Okay. Makes sense."

Diesel had the squad members all standing in ranks waiting for us. Both Max and he put a lot of stock in formalities, something I never did. A handful were wearing their Raven patch. It was awarded like a medal. Kick some ass. Show initiative. Get in with the Raven Clan.

Ninja was with them. He looked pretty good. He said his arm was still stiff, but he didn't show it. I knew from personal experience, though, that he had to still be feeling it.

Freya ran past us and stood there, staring at everyone. As we walked past her, she said, and there was no mistaking the delight in her voice, "You have warriors!"

We practiced different scenarios for the market: the drunk who makes a scene, the rowdy group of locals, the rowdy group of outsiders. That took most of the morning. We put off the other scenarios until tomorrow. Even keeping the squad this long was difficult. Their labor was needed elsewhere. Half of them would be splitting logs and stacking wood after lunch.

Freya had watched everything from the sidelines, sitting cross-legged in the grass quietly. So quiet I almost forgot about her. She came up to Max and me after everyone had been dismissed and we had told Diesel and Ninja to meet us at the diner.

"Those are warriors? That was not warrior training," she said. "You have a woman warrior. This is good."

Max looked at me, "So she can talk?"

"Yes, I can talk. I am learning. Your word order different is strange."

"She like pancakes," I told Max.

"Yes. Pancakes I like." Then suddenly she froze. "Badness comes quickly." She cocked her head, slightly. "Very quickly."

"Where, Freya?" Max and I never discounted people's intuition. Hell, we lived and killed by ours.

"They move too fast. The gate place."

# CHAPTER FORTY-TWO

Max and I looked at each other and simultaneously said, "Tollbooth." Then we heard gunshots from the north end of town.

I told Freya, "Quick, get inside the town hall." I realized she did not understand what I meant. "In there!" I yelled, pointing at it. Then I took off to catch up with Max, who was already moving toward the sound of the gunshots.

The bell in front of the station began tolling and didn't stop. *Shit!* I thought. Max held up his hand. We could hear more gunshots. Closer. Quick staccato bursts.

"Go back. Get the squad. They should be at the park in minutes. As soon as you get a handful, move them to where you hear gunfire."

"Got it." I turned and almost tripped over Freya. That kid could move quietly, that was for damn sure. "Get your ass in the town hall!" I screamed at her.

I ran back to the park. The gunfire was picking up. I could hear someone using a BAR near the diner. *Shit!* That was too close to the food bank. The bell had gone silent. I was getting a bad feeling, a very bad feeling.

The squad started to arrive at the park. One of them came hauling ass on a bike. A car sped up the street and didn't stop until it was on the grass. Two more squad members jumped out. They all huddled around me. Thank God they were silent—watchful, but silent. I heard murmurs of "What the fuck?" and "What are we waiting for?" but no one spoke directly to me. I was getting itchy. I wanted to move. *But where to go first?* Ninja came running as fast as I had ever seen him move, yelling something. Maybe he knew which direction we should move. I looked around; with Ninja I'd have a squad of nine, plus myself. "Teams of three. On me!" I yelled.

Ninja came to a breathless halt. I didn't like how pale he looked. My bad feeling intensified. "G! Night's down! Night's down!"

"Where?"

"By the diner! There are truckloads of them!"

I took off at a run. Ninja could lead the others. I had shit to do. I sprinted toward the station. Behind me I could hear boots pounding on the pavement.

My heart was screaming, *Night's down! Night's down!* My head was whispering, *Think. Don't react. Think.* My heart replied, *Fuck that. Kill 'em all.*

Then all thoughts were pushed away. An image flashed in my head in black and white: the area around the station as seen from above. The detail was amazing. *Where did this come from?*

I saw Night, down by the bell. A body lying across her—Gunny. Night's head on the grass, her face slightly turned toward me. Blood from her mouth traced a red tear down her cheek.

A voice in my head whispered, "She lives. The child is gone. Go! I will protect her! Go! Kill them all!"

Another image. A hundred yards from the diner, men deployed in an L-shaped defensive position, the trucks and vehicles they had come in forming the long side of their defenses. A dump truck pointing at me formed part of the short side of the L. From the back of the truck, behind the steel sides of the bed, several troops fired on the station.

Bodies lay scattered. Some behind the trucks, some lying in heaps in the open. From their clothes and the body types I knew those in the open were unlucky civilians.

I was past coherent responses. I moved far deeper into the killing zone than I had ever gone before.

I welcomed it. I wanted it. I screamed in joy and rage just to hear myself. I screamed so they would know I was coming. I wanted them to know. Just like I wanted to see their faces when I killed them.

I came out of the side street and saw the dump truck in front of me. Next to it was Miss Edna's Prius, miraculously undamaged. I leaped, landing on the hood of the Prius, and felt it crumple under my weight. I adjusted for it and leaped again, landing on the hood of the dump truck. Then again, up to the top of the cab. It was red. That was going to be the color of the day.

I looked down into the truck bed. Three shooters. I screamed and jumped into their midst. As I landed I went to my knees with the impact. They were turning toward me but they were slow. So very slow. I was not. They wore armor. Good armor. I could see where the ceramic plating protected them. I could also see where it did not.

As I came out of my crouch I pulled the K98 bayonet from its metal sheath. Sixteen inches of Solingen steel designed to be used just the way I was going to use it. I hit the man in front of me, turning him away from me, and drove the steel into his kidney. I yanked it out.

I screamed again and stepped forward. The second man had pivoted to face me. I drove the blade in low, jamming it into his abdomen, and then yanked it up.

The third man tried desperately to swing the barrel of his M-16 around to center on me. But the poor guy whose breakfast I had just spilled was blocking the barrel. The third shooter was too focused on his rifle. This was not a rifle fight, not in such close quarters. I hit him with a forearm to the face and drove the blade into his throat. As I pulled it out, I heard a voice in my head whisper, "Good."

I looked across the street to where Night lay with Gunny's body draped over her. Freya and one of the teams of three were protecting her. They had formed a triangle with her in the center and Freya off to one side.

Behind me, Ninja and the other five had not progressed past the dump truck. One of ours was down—down hard, it looked. The others were returning fire like this was a freaking tennis match. You shoot. I shoot. Pause. That's right, it's my turn. Bang.

Out of the corner of my eye I saw Freya raise her arms and scream. A wave of homicidal fury swept through me like a shot of the best dope ever known. I leaped out of the truck and ran toward my squad. I was beyond pissed.

"Get off your asses and MOVE! Kill them!" I roared.

I could hear the gunfire behind me increase, rounds passing me by, buzzing like angry bees. I walked to the trooper closest to me and ripped the Raven patch off his uniform and tossed it in his face. He recoiled from me in obvious and total fear. Then I yelled "Move!" in his face.

*Screw this*, I thought. I turned around and faced the assholes that were trying so hard to kill me. I slipped the bayonet back in its sheath and screamed, "Night!" Then I started walking toward the enemy. Fuck running.

I drew the Ruger and the Colt and started picking targets. I would shoot a couple, scream, "Night!" and kill a few more. "Fuck them." I was laughing. "Die, mother-fuckers, or run!"

I heard the burst of an M-16 behind me. Someone from my squad was back in the game.

I wasn't killing them fast enough.

Plus, I wanted to smell their blood. I wanted to see them twist. I didn't even bother to holster the Colt. I just let it drop and pulled out the bayonet. It slid easily out of the sheath. Blood made for good grease. Then I charged them. They broke. Some ran and were dropped.

The few remaining threw their weapons down and raised their hands in surrender. They thought it was over now for them. They were wrong.

It was Ninja who had been behind me. Diesel and Max were headed toward us. Max was limping.

"Ninja, search them. Give them medical care only after our people are taken care of. I need to see Night."

"Sure thing, G."

I started to walk away, stopped, and turned back to him. "Hey, Ninj."

"Yeah?"

"Good work."

People moved out of my way. *Scurried* would be a better description. I wasn't sure why. I also didn't give a damn. I could hear their comments as I headed toward Night.

"Did you see what he did? That was freaking amazing." And, "Did you see his eyes? I ain't ever going to get him pissed at me."

*Maybe if they had moved, instead of sitting on their asses, they would be running their mouths about each other's exploits rather than mine,* I thought.

The three troopers protecting Night were still there. They saw me coming and moved back a couple of feet. Freya was on her knees next to her. She must have had them pull Gunny off as soon she saw the others break and surrender.

I knelt down near them. "How is she?"

"She is fine." This didn't come from Freya.

"Night!"

"Hey, G," she said weakly. "Some asshole hit me with a car door. It hurt."

"I bet it did." I brushed a strand of hair out of her face. "Did you see who did it?"

"No. Is Donna coming?"

I didn't know for certain but I was sure she would be.

"Yeah. I'll make sure."

"Good. Hey, G?"

"Yeah?"

"You think the baby is okay?" Her eyes were scared. I didn't like that. She was never scared. Ever.

"I don't know, honey. I really don't know." I knew I should have said something reassuring to her but I never lied to her, mostly because she always knew as soon as I did.

Freya said softly, "I am a healer. Let me look after her until this person comes."

"Night, Freya will take care of you for now. I got things to do for a little bit, then I will be back." I bent down and kissed her gently. "Okay?"

She nodded her head and then whispered softly to me, "No mercy."

"No mercy it shall be, then."

"Alright, guys, move her into the station. She doesn't need to be gawked at." I gave her hand a squeeze and told her, "I'll be back." She nodded and shut her eyes.

I knew she was hurting. She wasn't going to be the only one.

I walked back to where my troopers held the ones who had survived by surrendering. Diesel had had them strip off anything of value and pile it in front of themselves. Then he lined them against the brick wall of what had been a travel agency. I thought that was funny in an ironic kind of way. Max was leaning against a car, watching.

"You okay, Max?"

"Yeah. Just a scratch. What about you? My guess is that's other people's blood you're wearing."

I looked down. Red had definitely turned out to be the color of the day. "Yeah. I'm fine."

"Night okay?" He asked this casually, but I also knew what he meant without saying it.

"Yeah and no. She lost it. Is Donna coming?"

"Shit. Sorry, G. Yeah, she's on her way." He looked away for a couple seconds and then back to me.

"How do you want to handle this, Max?"

"I can't have people coming into my town and killing my people." His voice was gray, cold, and flat. When Max sounded like this, it meant someone was headed for a flat line. In many ways we were direct opposites. He was cold, and just got colder when the shit hit the fan.

He thought ahead, planned, and had that gift of being able to anticipate what would happen several moves ahead. He was also a mean, merciless son-of-a-bitch when he got rolling. People had seen me when I was on. I had seen Max. He was far more than what he had shown so far.

The difference, I was beginning to believe, was that I could shut mine down. Or maybe it just left me. When Max got rolling, it didn't shut off. It had to burn itself out. That was why he was reluctant to let loose the beast.

He asked, "You know who hurt Night?"

"No. I plan to find out."

"Fine. Leave one alive for me to question. If they are local, we ride."

I walked over to where Diesel had them standing. "Hello, gentlemen. We seem to have a problem."

No one spoke. I looked at them. Starting on my left, I looked each one in the eyes. One returned it with defiance; the other two, with apprehension and fear.

I started with the defiant one. "Who hurt the woman by the bell?"

"What woman?"

"Wrong answer." I shot him. I looked at the next one. "Who hurt the woman by the bell?"

"Jesus man! Are you fucking crazy?"

I shot him. I looked at the remaining guy. He had pissed his pants. "Strike two. Are all the men raised to be stupid where you come from?"

He shook his head. "Please, mister—"

"Hopefully you've figured out how this works by now. I doubt it, but I can dream. Where are you from?"

"Meadow Mills. Please, mister, I got family and—"

"Shut up."

He started nodding his head yes and wouldn't stop.

"Quit nodding your head," I told him. "It's making me dizzy."

He nodded his head to that, realized what he was doing, and stopped.

"Thank you. So, who hurt the woman by the bell?"

"It wasn't me! I swear! It was Danny. We were pulling in, going too damn fast. That little gook was yelling at us, and Danny headed for her. She jumped out of the way. He threw open the car door and hit her with it. It wasn't me!" He wailed the last part more like a child than a man.

I smiled at him. "Not bad. Which one is Danny?"

He pointed to one of the bodies by the car. "That's him. Please, mister."

"Shut up. Listen, you did pretty good. What's your name?"

"Jimmy."

I saw the flicker of hope in his eyes. "Only one problem, Jimmy. You called my woman a gook." His eyes widened, the flicker of hope disappeared as quickly as the bullet I sent into his head.

I walked over to where Danny's body lay. He had not been wearing a helmet, which had made it easier for me when I shot him earlier. It would also make it easier for what I was going to do next.

I grabbed him by the hair and pulled him away from the car. The bayonet was sticky now. I had to reach back and hold the sheath in order to pull it out. Then I bent over and cut Danny's head off. It was a little messy. I heard someone vomit. I didn't look to see who it was. I was glad Danny had long hair. It gave me a better handle.

# CHAPTER FORTY-THREE

Max limped over to me as I finished. "Well, I guess you decided to kill them all and let God sort it out." He laughed. "At least you got the name of the town. No surprise there."

"Yeah." Meadow Mills was the sheriff's town. "How many did we lose, Max?"

"Three civilians, none of them skilled. We'll probably lose the two who were working the tollbooth. That's a loss. One of the squad—that's a real loss. Losing Gunny is a pisser. Other than that we have three minor wounds. Not bad."

I was bummed about Gunny. "He was a good guy."

"Yeah. Plus, he knew what he was doing, which is rare these days."

We had begun to gather a crowd. We could hear the comments and crying from where we stood. The three downed civilians had family, and they were still showing up. The pastor and Miss Edna had arrived. The militia had mustered. They were talking shit about what they could have done, but it was obvious to me that more than a few were glad they were late.

People would look at us, start to approach, see what I had swinging from my hand, and decide it could wait.

"So tell me, G, did you have Freya in your head during all this?" Max asked.

"Yeah." I thought for a couple seconds. "It was not a problem like you'd think it would be."

Max grinned. "I'm surprised you noticed her—what with all that space she has in there to run around."

"You're a funny man, Max." We laughed, him more than me. I didn't realize until later that he hadn't said whether she had been in his head.

"G, what are you planning to do with it?" It took me a second to realize he was talking about Danny's head.

"Put it on a pole by the tollbooth. Maybe right next to the sign that says Welcome and lists all the clubs in town that no longer exist."

He shrugged. "Sounds good. Go get cleaned and gear up again. After I deal with the grieving families and the town council, we're going for a ride."

I let Max deal with the politics of the situation. I started walking to the station when I remembered I still had Danny to deal with. Or at least his head. I yelled at the militia who were standing around in a group. They had gone silent when I had walked by.

"Come here," I said, pointing at one.

The one I yelled at looked and silently mouthed *Me?*

"Yes, you."

He walked unhappily toward me. I waited until he got about fifteen feet away and tossed him the head. "Catch."

His hands went up automatically. He caught Danny cleanly but then dropped him.

"Make sure he gets cleaned up. Then I want you to put him on a stick by the Welcome sign next to the toll-booth." As I walked away I heard him throwing up.

*Must be some food poisoning going around*, I thought.

I headed to the station to clean up and see how Night was doing.

Donna met me inside. "She's asleep, G. I gave her a sedative."

"How is she?"

She reached out and touched my arm. "She lost the baby. I'm sure of it."

"I know. Can I see her?"

"Sure. We have her in the conference room. Try to let her sleep. I'm going to spend the night here. Just in case."

"Yeah. Thanks."

I went in. They had spread some of the army surplus blankets on the table to pad it for her. She was asleep. I sat on the edge of the table watching her breathe for about five minutes. Then it was time to get ready.

I gave her a light kiss on the forehead. "Sleep tight, Night." Saying that used to crack me up for some reason. It didn't today.

I left the room. Donna was waiting in ambush. "What about you? I know that can't be your blood or you would be dead."

"I'm fine. Where's Freya?"

"I'm right here," the kid said. Donna jumped. I was getting used to it.

"Want to go for a ride after I clean up?"

"Sure."

"Donna, do me a favor?"

"Sure, G. Name it."

"Go to the diner and have them make up some sandwiches—at least four. Freya, are you hungry?"

"For pancakes."

"Take her with you. I need you back soon."

"Sure, G. Not a problem. Come on, Freya."

I went to the storage room and got a clean BDU. Then I hit the shower room that was set up for prisoners and turned on the water. To my amazement I actually got hot water. It had been a long time since I had taken a really hot shower.

When I got out, I realized how much time I'd spent. I needed to pick up the pace.

I tossed my dirty stuff in the corner, where it would probably remain until I picked it up. I took my gear over to Gunny's desk and cleaned my weapons. Someone had come in and left my Colt on my desk. I got a rag and wiped down my armor. Then I sharpened my knife.

I was strapping stuff back on when Donna and Freya came back.

"Pancakes good the second time?"

"Yes. Will Meadow Mills have cookies?"

"I doubt it."

One of the militia guys—I think it was Leroy—stuck his head in the station door, "Mr. Gardener, the chief is waiting for you."

"Fine. Tell the big guy I'll be out in a minute."

"Okay."

"Take care of Night, Donna. Are those our sand-wiches?" Freya was holding a plastic bag, recycled at least twenty times by the look of it.

"Yes."

"Let's go sightseeing, kid."

Freya and I walked out of the station. There was a weird moment when everyone stopped what they were doing to gawk at us.

I paused to gawk back and asked the kid, "So when did you become a superstar?"

"I am a goddess."

"Kid, all twelve-year-old girls think they are goddesses."

"I am not twelve years old!"

"Well, then you are a runty sixteen-year-old." I could tell she was getting ready to say something. We really didn't have time for it, so I started walking. The gawkers quickly went back to what they were doing.

I spotted Max standing next to the dump truck. The truck bed had been elevated, and there was a pale red puddle underneath the back end. My guess was they had washed out the bed.

"Hey, Max. What's the plan?"

He looked at Freya but didn't say anything about her. "I asked for volunteers. We are going to do a drive through Meadow Mills and let them know that it's time for them to reconsider."

"Reconsider what?"

"You know, I really got to stop letting you talk to the prisoners." He held out a folded paper. "Take a look at this."

I took the paper, unfolded it, and began reading. There were two pages, an arrest warrant for each of us for murder. Mine had more details, as I had apparently been far more evil. I handed the warrants back to him.

"You're slacking off, Max. It's not often anyone wants me more than they want you."

He grinned. "That will change shortly. I'm going to make some calls later. I don't think it's a big deal. It looks like a county judge signed it, which doesn't mean shit, especially as this isn't his county."

I didn't really care. I figured if they really wanted me, they were welcome to try. "So what are we doing?"

"We are going to burn as much of Meadow Mills to the ground as we can."

I looked past Max and saw that he had about three dozen Molotov cocktails. The wicks were sanitary napkins. I shook my head and asked, "Jeebus, what was harder to come by, the napkins or the gas?"

He grinned. "You don't want to know."

The plan was to drive the dump truck back through Meadow Mills. Anyone who saw it would think it was the boys returning from the raid. We would take Route 11 right through town until we hit Lee Street. Then we'd turn right until we hit Black Mountain Road. That would be where we started heading back home.

Once we entered the town, it would be light and toss until we ran out of cocktails. Max was going to ride in the back with Freya and me. We would have a couple of the squad with us to provide security and toss Molotovs out the other side.

We filled another stakebed truck with volunteers, all of them either part of the squad or kin to the people who died. The entire squad was going. Apparently they felt they needed to redeem themselves for their poor performance earlier.

Max was already in the truck and yelling at people to mount up. I told one of the militia to find me an empty metal trash can and put it in the back of the dump truck, pronto. Fortunately, he didn't have to go far to find one.

"There you go," I told Freya. "Stand on that and you can see the world."

We hit the road. The locals we passed waved to us. "Hey, Max"—I had to yell in his ear to be heard—"does everyone in the world know what we're doing?"

"No. Why?"

I shrugged. He was the planner. But I wondered, *How did the kid know, then?*

I figured we had about an hour and a half of sun left. We would be coming home in the dark. It was windy and a bit chilly. I liked it. So did Freya, who was clinging to the side of the truck bed. It was too windy to talk, which was also nice.

Once we got about ten miles out of town I noticed that a lot of fields were fallow. There should have been corn or something in them; instead there was nothing growing in at least half of them. Also, a lot of the farmhouses looked vacant. I am not a genius, but if this was what the rest of the country looked like, then cookies were going to be scarce everywhere.

We passed the green Welcome to Meadow Mills sign, and Max handed me a lighter. He yelled in my ear, "Don't lose it. It was my Dad's!"

It was a Zippo with a crest on it—blue with stars and a red "1" on the field of blue. Inside the red number, there were faint letters. I tried to make out what they said in the fading sunlight, but they were too worn. I'd have to ask Max about it later. I thought it might say "Guadalupe," which didn't make sense. Maybe it was his mother's name? But I didn't have a lot of time to think about it.

Max had already pulled one of the Molotovs out of an ice chest. He braced himself, held the bottle out for me to light, and tossed it overhand into the front of an old building. It went *who-o-omp!* spectacularly.

The guys from the squad started tossing theirs. We were cruising through what looked like the Meadow Mills version of a historic district. At this rate it was going to be the site of the place once known as the Historic District.

Max was laughing; he loved this. So did Freya. She was giggling, clapping her hands, and singing a song in whatever the hell her native tongue was. I wasn't smiling. This didn't feel right to me. There was no honor in it.

I understood it, but I didn't like it. This would break their backs. Their food supplies were probably elsewhere, but this and the death of so many of their warriors would shatter their resolve. That was the point. This was "no mercy."

We ran the entire town with only minimal resistance. A squad car came whipping down a side street and pulled in behind us. That did not turn out to be a good idea. Max shattered a Molotov on their windshield. We had a few scattered rounds thrown our way, but nothing intense enough to matter. It was over for them.

Somewhere on Lee Street I handed Max his lighter. He was high—high on fire and destruction. Looking back, we could see smoke and flame. Given the condition of most local fire departments, Meadow Mills was going to burn for a while.

We passed a silver sign that the state used to mark historic sites in Virginia; one of the squad busted a couple rounds through it.

He and his buddy thought it was funny until I yelled, "Knock that shit off." The world was filled with fucking idiots.

I leaned over and yelled in Freya's ear, "Having fun?"

Her reply startled me: "I prayed to my Father for this."

I pointed at the fire that was receding behind us. "For that?"

"No. Fire and Sword. For the rebirth." The way she said the last part, her tone, sounded like an explanation for an idiot.

"You know what my Momma always told me?"

She shook her head.

"Be careful what you pray for. You might get it."

# CHAPTER FORTY-FOUR

I spent the night sitting in the station. Night woke up around 0400 and I helped her get to the bathroom. On the way there, she said, "Damn, G, you smell awful. Somebody sell you unleaded aftershave?"

"No, I was busy earlier burning a town down."

"Not ours, I hope."

"Nope. Meadow Mills."

"Oh, I guess that's alright, then. Don't go anywhere." She shut the door. When she came out she clutched my arm. "Damn, my ribs hurt."

I got her back to bed, woke up Donna, and asked her to check on her. Then I went in the storeroom, picked out a jacket, and went outside to sit.

I had never seen so many stars in the sky as I had in the past few years. I wasn't surprised when Freya sat down next to me.

"Couldn't sleep, kiddo?"

"I do not sleep now. I slept for too long before."

"So you want to tell me who you are? I mean, if it's painful, we don't need to talk about it. Plus, where is your coat?"

"I do not need a coat for the same reason I do not need to sleep. I am not human. I am a goddess."

"Okay." I thought about that for a bit. "Is that how you get inside my head?"

"Yes."

"Are you there now?"

"No."

"Why not?'

It was her turn to pause. "Most of the time it is boring."

"Oh—sorry about that. I'll see if I can do something about that."

"No." She was serious now. "I like you the way you are. You remind me of someone I knew a long time ago."

"Anyone I would know?"

"Perhaps. Perhaps not. You should go back in. I think Night is calling you."

I went back in. Night was asleep again, and Donna was going back to bed. The kid had blown me off like a pro.

The next few days were busy with the usual mixture of the mundane and the irritating. Night was badly bruised, and she probably had a couple of cracked ribs. That was on top of the run-of-the-mill aches.

She had woken up the next morning crying. She knew the baby was gone. She knew it earlier, of that I am sure. She just hadn't wanted to admit it. I climbed up on the table, hugged her carefully, and asked her if she wanted to go home. I got back an emphatic yes.

Around noon a Prius with a crumpled hood pulled into the farmhouse yard, and more stout old ladies than I could have imagined got out of it. They all seemed to be balancing casserole dishes, a good thing since I had no idea what was for lunch. They had me announce them, and when Night was ready, they went in to keep her company.

I waited a few minutes and went in to help myself to a plateful of beans with badly cured venison, mac-and-cheese, and some kind of weird bread pudding with cinnamon. As I finished I heard laughter coming from the back bedroom and decided to go walk the berm. Nobody was keeping watch. We didn't have the bodies.

Woof didn't know it, but he was our primary alarm system for now. He followed me as I walked the line. I had no idea where the kids were, probably in the house. If they were loose outside, then I would not have had the pleasure of Woof's company. He saw his primary job as "kid shepherd."

I sat for a while on the main gate berm, just watching the clouds and smelling fall in the air. A hawk circled above me. I watched it ride the air currents and hunt for lunch. Not a single car passed by. I knew I should go into town, check on things, and deal with whatever needed dealing with. I just didn't feel like it, at least not right away.

I sat there, just watching the world go by, until the ladies left. They honked and waved as they drove off. I waved back and went down to make sure they had shut the gate properly. I could hear an axe chunking into wood, which told me where Tommy was. Woof must have heard or smelled the kids, because he ran off in that direction without even looking back.

I walked back into the house and was surprised to see Night up and about. She was in a much better mood. The first thing she did was to give me a hug and tell me how much she loved me. I don't know if she felt better from the old ladies' visit or their casseroles, but they were welcome to return anytime they wanted.

She shooed me out and told me to go be useful; she was going to boil some water and take a bath. That reminded me, I was supposed to check on propane availability two days ago.

I was also supposed to be finding us a house in town to move into. Night had given me a list with three addresses to look at. I couldn't understand what the problem was with the trailer. She very rarely got angry with me, but my questioning her decision about moving was one time she did.

I knew Max had talked about relocating some of the married squad members who lived in Trailer Town to empty houses. The problem was finding houses that no one in town had a claim on. Generally that meant newer ones.

The ones Night had on her list were older and smaller, but made of brick and with wood-burning fireplaces. I knew of each one, but I had only a vague memory of what they looked like and approximately where they were. I figured I would find the block manager for each street, spend some quality time with them, and see if they remembered anyone complaining about problems with any of the houses.

I decided to bicycle in. Going uphill was a workout, but coming down was worth it. With no cars on the road I could fly. I had forgotten how much work it was, but I had not forgotten the thrill. I arrived in town in a good mood.

I parked the bike in front of the station and had started up the steps when a woman burst out the door. She was in her fifties, gray-haired, skinny, and clearly angry.

She looked my way and it got even clearer: She wasn't pissed in general; she was pissed at me. "You're the one I wanted to see!" she screamed. "You are a killer! When the country gets back on its feet, I will see to it that you are tried for murder! You wait! Things will get better and you will be hunted down like a dog!" Then she stormed off.

So much for a constructive, caring dialogue.

I went inside and asked the militia member who had taken Gunny's place who the old lady was.

"Sorry about that, Mr. Gardener. She was a bit upset."

"I got that part. Why? And why me?" He looked a little uncomfortable. "Come on, just tell me."

"One of them men you killed from Meadow Mills was her nephew."

I thought about how to answer that, especially as I knew my answer would be repeated. The old me had one answer.

The newer, politically aware me had another. "Well, I am sorry about that. She have any more dumb-asses in her family I should know about?"

His mouth dropped open. I didn't wait for a reply.

I went for a walk around town for a couple reasons. One, it was my job. Two, I wanted to see the reactions I got from the people. For one of the few times in my life, I was actually interested in what people thought of me.

At the diner it was a mix of reserved greetings, fawning, and "How is Night doing?" In the business district, it was, "Hey! How are you?" and "Nice work. How's Night?"

I noticed two new storefronts getting cleaned up to open for business. I went into the first one and interrupted the family inside.

They went silent when I stepped through the door, then they lit up with smiles. I had seen the older man and woman around, but knew almost nothing about them. The same went for a young pregnant girl who was engrossed in doing the lettering for a sign. The young guy I knew. He was a squad member. *Come on, brain! I* thought, *Give me his name!* It spit it out: Shawn.

"Hey, Shawn!" We shook hands and he introduced the rest of the Klein family.

Then he looked at me, wide-eyed, "Gardener, you were awesome out there! I told my family—" While he rattled on, I checked the expressions on their faces. Mom was wary with a touch of hostility. Same vibe from his mate. Dad, on the other hand, was beaming.

When Shawn stopped for a breath, I slapped him on the shoulder; that was my Max mimic move. "You guys were pretty good yourselves." From the flicker in his eyes I knew he didn't feel that way.

I changed the subject. "So, what the hell are you doing here?"

Everyone got excited. They were starting a leather shop. Shawn went on to tell me about how they would have to do the tanning elsewhere because of the smell.

"Yep, we think leather is going to be huge. We plan on doing a lot of work in deerskin. The guy next to us is going to be making shoes, so we can go in together on leather buys. Mary, show Mr. Gardener our samples."

They had some cardboard boxes filled with their work. It was pretty good work. Knife sheathes, small- and medium-size pouches. Belts—with and without tooling. "We plan to do jackets and pants also." Everyone was nodding and smiling, and underneath it I could sense their fear. Fear that I might laugh. Fear that they might not sell anything. Fear that this, another step in their lives, would be stomped on by forces too big for them to understand.

"So what did you do before?"—meaning, we all knew, before everything went to hell.

His face changed slightly, just a quick cloud. "I was a program analyst for a company that no longer exists. Mary was an English teacher at Oakton High School. We did this on the side as a hobby. We were at the point where we had a booth at the Maryland Renaissance Festival and a web site when—" He stopped.

Mary quickly filled in for him, "When we went from pretending to be living in the sixteenth century to actually doing it." She was angry. You would have had to be completely oblivious not to hear it.

"I like these pouches. I tell you what. I'll take a big one for me and a smaller one for Night. What do you want for them?"

They didn't want me to pay. At one time I would have taken them for free.

"No," I insisted. "I pay fair-market rate. Maybe later, once you get going, I'll take a law enforcement discount." I grinned at them. "These might make good issue gear for the squad. How are you at making holsters and slings?"

We went on about that for a bit, and I left him with a silver dollar and some Zone scrip. When I left, I noticed the women had warmed up a little bit.

I stopped at the next shop and said hello to the owner. He was moving stuff around and seemed distracted. I let him be after a few minutes.

When I walked out the shop door, Freya was there.

"Hey, kid. What's up?"

"Nothing. I thought I would walk with you."

We walked in silence for a bit. I said hello to anyone we passed on the street. Plus, I stuck my head in a few more shops. It was the same: positive feedback from the men, reserved politeness from the women, and inquiries about Night.

Freya asked me, as we resumed walking, "Do you know why the women act the way they do?"

I thought, *So it wasn't my imagination.* I stopped walking. "No, kid. Tell me why."

"Because when they see you, they see the deaths of their men."

# CHAPTER FORTY-FIVE

Freya and I walked over to the tollbooth. I noticed a marked improvement in the guards' readiness and politeness. I wondered how long it would last.

"How we doing?" I asked one of the two women.

"Slow but steady. City is making payroll today," she said, grinning.

I smiled back. "That's good. It's why we work, isn't it?"

"Well, it isn't because I love the company."

Her partner, who had moved close enough to hear, replied, "Bite one, Auntie." They thought that was pretty funny.

I asked her, "So, what kind of folks are on the road today?"

"I try to find out, if we have time. That little woman of yours drilled that into me. How is she, by the way? Forgive me for not asking first off. Just got kind of rattled seeing you and that kid show up."

I filed away her *that kid* and told her that Night was sore but doing better. That was followed by a couple minutes of her praising Night, which I cut off as soon as I could get a word in edgewise.

"So you were going to tell me about the traffic?"

She laughed. I didn't.

"Well, some is our locals. Hey! Had a guy on horseback come through. Never seen him before. Mostly it's people who are coming out of the Zone to see family. We ought to shake them down. They usually got food they are bringing—" She must have seen my face change. "Oh, lordy, no. I don't mean it that way." Her face turned pale.

I didn't cut her any slack. "Go on."

"They always want to know about the roads. Are they safe? I tell them they should go up to the campground and caravan out."

"Any of them do that, you think?"

"Naw, the wives would, but the men—they just want to keep going. Afraid it would make them look like chickens, I guess."

"Interesting. Anything else?"

"Well, Jamie, you know him—Sheila's stepson?" I must have looked blank. "Oh, never mind. He said we had a UPS truck come through. Said the driver was not real happy about coming out here."

"No kidding."

"Yep. I haven't seen one of them in forever." She looked and sounded wistful now.

We said our goodbyes, and I headed back to the station.

That afternoon our truck came in from Big Daddy. To say it was lacking in goodies would be an understatement. We got some expired vitamins and MREs, plus a pallet of ammo that was probably Vietnam-era manufacture. We also got a hundred new U.S. flags and an equal number of DVDs that were highlights of the current administration's speeches. They would make good targets, I thought.

A few days later, Max stopped me after I'd read the daily log and was getting ready to walk the town. I had a couple of meetings scheduled and I was really hoping someone would stir up some moderate trouble to get me out of them.

I had one of the Motorola two-way radios now for my very own. I can't say I liked it a lot. It ruined the aesthetic of my gun belt. That was not something I'd say out loud, but it was true. Night liked it, probably more for the idea that now she could reach out and contact me wherever I was.

She was feeling a little better. She still suffered the occasional blue spell that she tried to hide from everyone. I hung out with her as much as I could until it was obvious I was getting on her nerves—obvious because she told me so.

Max said, "Let's go for a walk." I knew what that meant. It was time for a triple top-secret conversation. We walked into an open area, and he abruptly switched from talking about the squads to his real topic.

"The Burners are sending a couple of people to talk to us."

"Who is *us*?"

He smiled. "Well, that's what I've been thinking about. Right now it looks like me, you, Shelli, and Freya. Night, too, if she's up to it."

"She will be up to it. What's up with having Shorty there?"

"Let's talk about her," Max said. "I want to know more about what you saw when she was in your head."

I told him what I had seen and experienced, how I'd seen black and white aerial visions of what was happening on the ground. I knew it was from Freya, I just couldn't explain it.

He listened, nodded, and looked away for a bit when I finished.

"You ever notice that you always see at least one hawk in the air when she's around?"

I thought about that. *Damn*, he was right. "Yeah. So?"

"You know why the aerial feeds we get are in black and white?" He didn't wait for my answer. "I think it's because hawks don't see in color."

I waited for more. There wasn't any. "So are you going to share, Max? It's obvious she was busy ice-skating inside your brain, too. What did you see?"

I didn't think he was going to answer. I was okay with that; hell, it was his head.

He hesitated, but then he said, "It was the strangest thing, G. I guess the closest thing I can come up with is that it was like running down a hallway lined with huge flat panels, each one with a different image. They showed me what I needed to know, where I should go next."

I knew it! His was different, like he had the next version of the software. For a second I felt jealous and angry. Then I realized that he was welcome to it. Hell, once I got rolling I wanted to turn the damn thing off anyway.

Max must have seen the change flash across my face.

"It creeps me out a little too, G. I don't know what to make of her. We could always unplug her…permanently," he said. He knew he was taking a risk saying that to me, since he knew I had a soft spot for kids. And even if Freya wasn't a kid, she sure as hell looked like one to me. But I also understood what he really meant: If she turns into trouble, we have the option of turning her out.

"Max, you forgot to mention that she says she's a goddess."

"Yeah. Shelli thinks she is Freya incarnate. That's why the Burners are interested. You do know that Shelli is a Burner?"

"Yeah. She also makes a great apple pie."

He laughed. "Yeah, there is that. You think she's a goddess?"

I was tempted to say, "Shelli?" Instead I answered as honestly as I could. "Max, I don't know. If she is, then she is not a major one. I mean, come on, where's the cape? I looked up 'Freya' a couple of days ago. The Valhalla thing sounds cool. To answer your question, Max, I don't know and I don't really care. I do think the kid from that old movie *Firestarter* would be a lot more fun."

The biggest problem about the Burner meeting was deciding where to have it. All of us rallying into the conference room at the station would be guaranteed to draw attention and generate gossip. The town hall would have made it an official meeting and expanded the guest list. The pastor seemed to be a fairly tolerant man, but heading a discussion about the powers of kid goddesses might be asking too much. There were other pastors in town who, if they heard about it, would be racing each other to burn Freya at the stake. I wasn't sure she would burn, but by the time everyone figured that out, I would have shot a couple of pastors and a handful of zealots.

So, Shelli decided to have a dinner party. As Night and I were getting ready for it, I asked her, "Do you think Shelli will burn everything she cooks?"

"No. It will be fine. Wear the clean shirt I washed. Not that one."

*This is getting pretty formal*, I thought. I decided to skip wearing body armor but I brought it with me. I remembered the last time we had met with the Burners. It had been tense, but there had been serious money on the table then. Now it was just a goddess.

We were supposed to be there at 1900. We didn't make it on time. We were late due to Night's inability to find the right shoes. This was her first ever dinner party, and she wanted to look right.

Freya and I sat on the steps outside waiting for her.

"Anyone tell you what this is about, kid?"

"No, but I know."

"Okay. What kind of shoes are you wearing?"

She stuck out her feet.

It was the same pair of moccasins she had on when we found her.

We sat there silently until Night came out.

We were driving Tommy's car because ours was low on gas.

I had tried to fill it up two days before, but the pumps were down because there was no power. The guy running the place said he would fill my car and set aside a five-gallon container for me when the power came back on. He even told me "no extra fee" for doing it. If he was gouging locals, we were going to need to have a talk.

We got to Shelli's house late and had to park on the street. I'd recently given Night my opinion of the places she wanted me to look at. The house I liked was three doors down from Shelli. When I told Night, she wanted to know why that one. Then we—well, she—had spent two hours discussing the relative merits of each one. Damn, that had been boring. I wanted to scream, "Just pick a fucking house!" but that probably would not have been cool.

We knocked on the front door, and Shelli let us in. The house was nice. Red brick, old, fireplace, wood floors. Anybody who had been an adult during the real-estate boom saw houses as resalable objects first, homes second. Even I, who had been priced out of the market since I was born, had not been immune to the mindset Shelli had decorated the place very New Age. Not a surprise. I just knew there had to be an Indian dream catcher hanging somewhere. One of my coworkers had one in her cube when I worked at the mortgage company. I had hung a plastic spider in its web. She was not amused.

The Burners were sitting in the living room talking. As we came in, I noticed there was a shotgun hanging on the wall of the entryway. Max's work probably. We took off our coats, and it was time to meet the Burners.

It was the same team as before. The woman still looked good, too. We did our greetings and settled down in the living room. It was civilized—almost pre-Crash normal, except for the kerosene lamp that was throwing more shadows on the walls than any electric light ever did.

I was almost getting used to their smell. It was going to be interesting to see if we could keep enough K-1 on hand this winter, let alone come up with enough safe lamps to burn it.

Night and Shelli hugged like it had been a year since they had last seen each other. I nodded at Max, who was sitting in a leather chair next to the fire.

The Burners had gone completely silent. It was total focus-on-Freya time. They walked over to her, since she had made no move to come to them.

The woman looked over at Shelli. "You're right. My God, I can see it!"

The man with her began squinting. I guess he wasn't seeing it.

The woman asked, "Are you the . . . Freya?"

"Yes."

The woman put her hand to her throat, where a charm of some sort dangled. "Oh my. Well, my name is Electra and this"—she indicated the man next to her—" is Burning Sun." She stuck out her hand tentatively.

Freya ignored it. Instead she replied, "No, you are Denise from New Jersey, and this is Brad from Oklahoma." Then she laughed. So did I. Denise gave me the evil eye and dropped her hand.

Brad looked stunned. "How did you know that?"

Freya didn't answer. Denise did. "Because she is a goddess." Even I could hear the unspoken, *you idiot.*

I thought that was funny, too. Oh well, I was never good at this kind of thing.

Freya walked off toward the kitchen.

I told Shelli, who seemed a bit perturbed about how things were going, "If you have apple pie in there, you better go rescue it before she eats all of it." Shelli muttered something and disappeared after Freya.

We all stared at each for a while and then Denise asked, "So . . . how is the power situation out here?"

I groaned inwardly and sat down at the end of the sofa closest to the fire. *Maybe dinner will be served soon,* I thought. I sat and listened while Night and Max—it was his woman's house, so he had to—engaged the Burners in idle chitchat. I watched the flames dance until Shelli called us to the table.

The table looked nice with a white tablecloth and candles. We even had two forks. Freya joined us and ignored the Burners' attempts to draw her into the conversation. I was okay with that, anything to make the evening shorter.

After a bite of venison, Denise tried another tack. "I suppose you all are starving for news out here." I wasn't the only one who noted a hint of patronization in her tone.

I spoke up. "Yeah, how's the war going out West?"

Years ago, the Burners had been very successful in taking control of large parts of the West, so successful that a previous administration had declared them terrorists. Following that, the government committed serious resources to shutting down the Burners, including targeted assassinations. The government was very good at that sort of thing. It had had years of practice in various countries by then.

The Burners had regrouped, moved part of the organization underground, renamed its legitimate wing, and gone after political control. They called it the "Irish option." But it hadn't worked out. They weren't the only ones struggling for a piece of the federal carcass, and they had overestimated how dead the body was. A leg or two might have been gnawed off, but it wasn't going to give up the tax revenue from outlying regions that easily.

Brad turned to me. "We are making significant gains in Southern California, especially now with our new alliance with the Mexican Peoples Front. The clash in Oregon with the Fed storm troopers is entering a new phase, and we fully expect to regain control of the Portland area sometime in the next month."

Denise continued where he left off. "There have been some setbacks. The Fed's hunter-killer teams are quite good. That's why we need you, Freya." Here she went into sincere projection overdrive.

"We need your blessing. We need you to help inspire those who believe in you. You are the embodiment of so much of what we believe and are working for. Help us, Freya."

We all looked at the kid. She looked back at Denise.

"You do not understand, do you?"

"What, Freya? Tell us. What do we not understand?" Denise whispered this, leaning forward, eyes glittering. I felt like kicking her in the shins under the table just for the hell of it.

"That you have already lost. For what is coming, you have neither the fire nor the steel. You do not grasp that when the world turns, it is people like you who will be ground beneath the wheel. Now go. Fate awaits you."

To say that put a damper on things would be an understatement. After they got over their shock, Denise tried to put a better spin on it. The man listened to her try to salvage things for a moment or two and then tossed his napkin on the table. "Enough! We go."

Night and I sat at the table with Freya while Max and Shelli walked them to the door.

I looked at Freya. "Way to go. They probably would have fed you cookies every day."

"Those two? They will be dead in an hour. Do you think Shelli will serve the pie now?"

# CHAPTER FORTY-SIX

The next day I rolled into work. The weather had turned chilly and the clouds were thick, dark, and low. It smelled like snow. There was a Virginia State Police car in front of the station. That was unusual, but not abnormal.

They had come by twice a week for a while. Lately it dropped off a bit. Gas shortage was what one trooper had said. They also were patrolling two to a car now. The backup came in handy, and it kept the troopers busy when they could only fuel half the cars.

Everyone fell silent when I walked in. I did the greeting thing. The two troopers recognized me and gave me a nod and then went back to what they were talking about. Whatever it was, it had Diesel, Max, and one of the locals listening raptly.

"So you have no idea who those two were or what they were doing around here?"

Max answered, "No idea. I can check around if you want."

One of the troopers, a tall, older guy, waved his hand. "Don't waste a lot of energy on it. That was a Fed hit. I wouldn't give the Feds the sweat off my balls if they were dying of thirst." We all chuckled at that, as lame and old as it was.

"Yeah," he continued, "while they're running around roasting people from the skies, I don't see them doing squat about the grid being down. Y'all know about that, right?"

"We heard some rumors. Then again, power is mostly down nowadays up here."

The local—what was his name? Frank, I think—chimed in following Max's comment, "Them stupid son-sabitches ain't good for shit."

We all nodded at that little pearl of wisdom.

The trooper continued, "The whole damn thing is down now. The Feds are saying it was the Burners' fault. Them Burners were always going on about how we need a 'new power paradigm' or some such bullshit."

The other trooper added, "The Zones in D.C. lost it two days ago. Things are already getting weird down there. Word is, it might be weeks before it comes up again. If it's more than a week, y'all can expect company up here. Them people ain't gonna stay put if they start getting hungry."

Max asked them, "What's the state planning to do? You have a containment policy?"

Both troopers laughed. The older one answered, "Shit. There are almost two million people in them Zones. Maybe more."

His partner nodded. "They start moving, ain't nothing going to stop them. If they really start moving, well, me and Jim here, we're headed to a cabin we got with our families. I am not firing on hungry American citizens and their kids. Nope. No way."

They chatted a bit more and then headed over to the diner for the free lunch that Shelli gave them. As the door closed on the departing two troopers, Max swore, "Well . . . damn." That pretty much summed it up, I thought.

"We got some planning to do," he said. "Frank, see if you can get ahold of Night at the farm. Tell her to come in and bring the maps of the area she has on the wall with her. Diesel, find Ninja if you can. He's probably running one of the new squads over at the school gym. While you're at it, see if you can round up Miss Edna and the pastor. Then bring 'em all back here."

That left me and Max, with Frank on his headset. "Let's go walk some streets, G," Max said. "Frank, we'll be back in thirty minutes."

"You bet, Boss," Frank answered.

I mimicked him once we were out the door.

"Yeah, I know," Max said. "He is great at kissing ass and only so-so at doing the work." A few snowflakes floated past. I remembered chasing them as a kid, trying to catch them on my tongue. I'd always expected them to taste like sugar.

We walked across the road and past the diner. From there we walked half a block, cut across a parking lot, and were able to see the tollbooth on this end of town. Three cars were waiting to clear the booth. As we watched, it became five cars. That was about three more than we usually had, and that was unusual. We looked at each other.

"Yeah," was all I said. It was enough.

The snow picked up a little. We walked over to the booth and greeted the woman working it. She was listening to the driver who was saying "—yeah, they tell us everything is going to be alright, but we've been hearing that line since that idiot Bush." He saw us and decided to stop talking and drive.

"Hey, guys!" The tollbooth guard was chipper. "I just love snow!" She was a young, not bad-looking black girl, someone I hadn't seen except at a distance.

Max said, "So tell us what you're hearing, Shayla."

"Sure, Max. Hi, Officer Gardener. Some weird stuff happening in D.C. Got some peeps freaking out. Most of them—" She had to stop to collect the toll from the next car.

I took a look into the car through the windows. A white family, two kids in their early teens, and a packed car, including a small, yappy dog.

"Dang, I hate yappy dogs," Shayla said as they rolled away.

"Sorry, guys, I'm a little busy. But, yeah, folks are bailing because they think the Feds aren't going to be able to feed them. A whole lot of people out there are going to find family at their doors that they haven't seen in years." She turned back to take the next toll.

The driver yelled out the window. "Hey, fellas. You got anyplace to get gas around here?"

Max answered him. "We haven't had a delivery in a week."

The driver thanked him with a curse and drove off. I laughed.

"Come on, G. Walk with me while I think."

We walked down Main Street. The snow was starting to stick. Four more cars passed us. "Max, this is the busiest I have ever seen Main Street except when I was back here healing up."

Max stopped. He looked at the tollbooth we had just left and at the tollbooth ahead of us. Then he looked up and down Main Street. "Tell me what you think of this scenario, G. We get a couple hundred cars at the toll-booth, maybe more, all filled with hungry, scared people. How would you handle them?"

I surveyed the road, thought for a bit, and said, "Let them flow through. No toll. We would need to block every side street. Run them through a chute. Make sure no one turns back. We'd probably have to organize street patrols for a while. Perimeter patrols also. We are going to need to add some people at the farm." I looked at him. "Yeah, that might work."

"Why the 'might work,' G?"

"You know as well as I do, Max, what *can* go wrong, will."

The snow trailed off and the sun came out around noon. I watched it because I managed to evade the big "How can the town avoid being overrun by hungry tourists and riffraff" meeting. Someone had to muster the militia and set up security; I volunteered—something I generally avoided doing at all costs. The problem, as always, was a lack of qualified people that I could trust not to do something stupid. Then again, I found that my idea of stupid was vastly different from how others defined it.

I assigned the militia the job of pushing cars into the side streets. They would know far better than I would who was local and who wasn't. I told them to set up some fire barrels to keep warm around, and I would try to get them relief and something hot to eat.

I also spent a lot of time—for me at least—delivering words of inspiration and hope. The average conversation went something like this:

"Hey, Gardener, what the hell is going on?"

"There is no electrical power in America. The grid has gone down, and it may stay down, maybe for weeks."

"So that means no one has power?"

"Yep."

Then the self-appointed expert in the group would tell them all what that meant. They were not stupid; it was just too big for them to wrap their brains around. Hell, it was too big for me, even though I thought I had. I was still going into rooms and flipping light switches on and then going, "Oh yeah."

The conversation continued with my telling them, "People are going to be looking for food and a place to stay. Our job is to move them on." It spoke well for the folks in town that the idea of "moving people on" bothered them. But then I explained the potential numbers involved—numbers I had made up, of course, but hey, who really knew what was coming? I told them that too, just not in those words.

"It's like this. We will probably run out of food or be on reduced rations by March or April. That's our best-case scenario. We may have fifty . . . seventy thousand people or more come through here in the next month. If we feed them all just one meal and send them on their way, what happens to us?"

They would start seeing the light about then. Some had already gotten it. They just didn't want to say anything. But I would see their heads start nodding.

"Yeah, exactly."

For the really dense I had to make it clear. "We will all starve to death or we will end up on the road right behind the others. Nobody is going to make you do anything you don't want to do, but the odds are pretty good that it is going to get ugly. Really ugly." I left them with that and went to the next group.

Ninja found me, and I told him to split the two squads. I asked him for a pen—he was always prepared—and used a wall that had been painted white for paper. I drew a rough diagram of the town and divided it in half.

"Draw the same map for your people," I told him. "I want everyone clear on what and where they are supposed to be. I want the first squad here. I don't care how you do it, but I want a three-man patrol working this area. I want reports on who they find and what they see. They can eat at the diner before or after they go out. I want them using those damn night-vision goggles after dark. Everyone gets turned away."

"G, what if they don't want to turn away? What do we do then?"

I remembered how during the farm raid Ninja had let one deputy get past him because he didn't want to shoot the guy in the back. "Ninj, we don't have food for them. Tell them if they don't move along, you will cuff them and drop them outside of town limits without their shoes. Damn, tell them whatever you think will work."

"But what if they have little kids?" He would have to ask that.

"Same thing. Tell them somebody will take care of them further down the line." We both knew that was a lie, but if it made him feel better, so be it. "Figure out the duty roster with Diesel. I'm pulling Hawk and sending him to the farm." Those berms were going to pay off now. "Damn, I almost forgot. I need a three-person team at each tollbooth starting now."

"You forgot something else, G."

"What's that?"

"When are we going to sleep?"

I grinned. "Whenever you get a minute. Drive or push a car down to each tollbooth. Let one person sleep in the backseat while the others watch." I sent him on his way.

My radio had been amazingly quiet so far. Someone didn't want to pay for a meal at the diner. The patrol officers had handled that. I was going to use them as street patrol and a mobile reserve.

We were going to need some kind of logistics support and medic teams if this got too weird. And I'd have to get some ammo to each of the militia points and tollbooths for reserves.

Logistics made my head hurt. What I didn't like was how thin we were at the farm. I understood why we couldn't pull people from the town to guard our home. I didn't like it, though.

I also wondered where the hell Freya was. Probably mooching apple pie from Shelli.

I went back to the station the long way. I walked Main Street by zigzagging from side street to side street. Two-thirds of them were already blocked, and the rest were in the process of being blocked.

One of the militia suffered a minor heart attack, which slowed things down. I often forgot that most of these guys were old and not in the best of shape. He'd been taken home to rest and I made a note of his name. Max or I would need to find time to check on him.

The rest were in pretty good spirits. Some of the wives had shown up and were transforming the empty houses and storefronts into homey break rooms for their men. In the background I could hear a steady increase in the traffic.

While I talked to a group of militia, Max got me on the radio. "You got that road sealed up yet?"

"No." I looked over at Lenny, the de facto militia leader. "Probably in about an hour, Max." Lenny nodded to let me know that would work.

"Okay. As soon as you do, close both tollbooths. We are already getting a traffic jam here. Out."

"Got it. Out." I looked at Lenny. "We can do this?"

"Yeah." We both looked at the passing cars. He spit some Copenhagen in the street. "A freaking shame is what it is." I nodded in agreement, and I hoped I would never have to do CPR on Lenny.

A little later, I went back to the station. Shelli had sent some sandwiches over, and Night had saved two for me. I told her about getting food to the people, and I updated Max on what I'd done so far. After eating and talking a bit I went outside, carrying boxes of ammo and extra magazines for the M-16s.

When I dropped them at the tollbooth, I grabbed a militia member to help. We found some grocery carts to use for running ammo to the checkpoints. We passed Shelli and a couple of kids bringing food to the checkpoints. The next time we saw her, she had a cart, too. Carts got tougher to find after that, especially ones with wheels that all moved in the same direction.

Max had left word that he wanted to see me, so I returned to the station. He was still out with the patrols that were going to cover open areas. In theory, those patrols could monitor vehicles, but they'd more likely encounter people who had abandoned overheated or out-of-gas cars. Ninja and Diesel were working opposite sides of the streets. They stopped and talked to the group at each checkpoint.

Night had gone to sleep in a corner; she still wasn't 100 percent back. Freya was sitting in a corner sorting BDUs. I could hear the occasional horn honking, and decided to go outside to watch.

"Hey, kid. Want to take a walk?"

"Sure."

We headed out. "So what have you been up to?"

"Nothing."

"Yeah. Okay, this here is good." There was a pickup parked where it gave us a good sight line. I climbed into the bed and gave Freya a hand up. Then we got onto the roof of the cab.

The headlights of cars came and went. It wasn't a steady stream but it was unusually heavy for the town. A week ago you could have slept in the same street.

"What do you think, kid?" I was genuinely curious.

She looked at me, her face calm. "It is going to be uglier than you ever imagined."

"Yeah, kid? Well, I have seen ugly. I have lived ugly. Ugly isn't nothing to me but just another day."

"I know."

"Let's head back. It's getting cold." My radio, which I had turned down, still carried Max's voice to my ear. It wasn't music either.

"G, come on back. Over."

I squelched twice to let him know I was on my way.

# CHAPTER FORTY-SEVEN

Everyone who mattered to me was inside the station. There were no townspeople. I said, "Hi, sleepyhead," to Night and greeted the rest of the crew.

"You might as well pull up a chair," Max said. "This might take a bit."

I had been set up. It had to be a meeting.

Max addressed all of us: "Night is going to give us her estimate of what we can expect soon. I am not going to ask you for any decisions tonight. I have a good idea what she's going to say, and I want you all to think it over." He paused. "Okay, it's all yours."

Night stood up and faced us. The table behind her was covered with maps. We were arranged in a semicircle in front of her, draped in chairs in various positions of fatigue. Freya sat in the back, her hands folded in her lap.

"Think of it like this," she began. "Imagine a rock thrown into a pond, the ripples spreading out. Now picture those ripples being followed by more ripples. Do you all see that?"

We all nodded our heads or replied with some variation of yes.

"The Baltimore–Washington, D.C., megalopolis had around eight million people in 2009. Subtract Zone movement and all the other crap we have lived through, and my guess is we have six million people within a tank of gas of here. Go north to the Philadelphia area, and there are at least another three million people. Keep going north and we hit metropolitan New York. That area still has at least ten million people now.

"My guess is there are well over twenty-five million people in our region. We are close to Interstates 81, 66, and 95. These are going to be prime migration routes. That is, until they aren't, which should be any day now. We are on the edge of the largest tribal migration in human history. Only post–World War II Europe comes close." She paused.

"It's going to come in waves. This is all based on the assumption that the grid stays down for at least two weeks. What I see happening now is the early wave. People 'in the know' have started to bail. We are seeing that currently. If they are in a position to know, then they probably have a place to go and the resources to get there. The next wave will be bigger. The people will be desperate, hungry, but still semicivilized. The third wave, and anything thereafter, will be ugly. Very ugly.

"Our first waves of migrants will be from the Baltimore–Washington megalopolis. Their route will be either south or in our direction. Our direction takes them into the Midwest. They will try the interstates, but the sheer volume of traffic, roadblocks from the state, plus car wrecks, and what have you will cause people to take to the side roads. Any questions or comments so far?"

"Other than we are fucked?" This was from Diesel.

"Oh, you have no clue," replied Night. "Because right behind that will be the waves from the Philadelphia and New York City areas. Maybe even Boston. You see, it's winter and these people will all try to go south. Sure, some will head toward the Midwest. They'll run into the Chicago migration. About the time they hit Richmond, I think they will run into determined resistance. Like a wave, they will bounce off and flow backward. Oh, this is going to be fun."

I didn't like how her voice was becoming shrill. "Night, what happens if the power comes on in a couple weeks?"

"G, think about it. By then the situation will have spun out of control. How would the Feds be able to start up the distribution system? Would you want to drive a truck filled with food anywhere without an armored escort?"

"Actually, it might be fun." I looked around. No one seemed to agree with my assessment. That included Night.

"The power won't go off everywhere," she continued. "What was that old sci-fi book? *Hammer's Fall*? Some places will stay up. Some nukes will be waiting and ready to flow power. I don't know enough. My guess is it won't be so bad in some places. I just don't know. I do know that we may see a million people or more head this way. Do you have enough bullets for all of them, G?"

She was angry. Why at me I had no idea. Nor did I have a reply that would make her less angry.

I shrugged. "I'll do what I always do, Night. Fight until I kill them all or they kill me."

From the back of the room came the sound of Freya's laughter.

I spent the night at the station. I woke after a couple hours' sleep on a pile of BDUs, feeling less than refreshed. I headed for the bathroom, but seeing Frank slip in before me changed my mind. He may have been an okay person, but he could peel the paint off a wall. The man must have had a steady diet of toxic waste. I went outside instead. Max was walking toward the station, coming from the direction of Shelli's, and I decided to catch him before he went in. He did not look happy. For the first time I could see faint lines on his face—barely discernible, but there.

He saw me, so I stopped and waited for him and smelled the moisture in the air. I also felt how the flow had changed.

I have a talent for being able to feel the currents of emotion in an area. For me, it's the ability to recognize changes in what people are feeling versus what they are displaying, usually before they know it themselves. I don't think it is all that unusual. Being receptive to it and trusting it is where most people stop.

Today felt different. Very different. What was usually flowing was now coiling. What I normally saw as transparent wisps of color were now darker, uglier, opaque shapes. I summarized it for Max when reached me: "There is some weird shit in the air today."

"Yeah, I think the outflow has picked up a notch."

Nothing else was said. We started walking toward the tollbooth. We climbed up into the bed of the same truck I had sat on with Freya.

As people approached the tollbooth, they rolled down their windows and shouted questions at the guards. Our guys just yelled back, "Move on. Just keep going. There is help further along."

I looked down Main Street. The guys in the militia were standing by and sitting on their cars, weapons prominently displayed, grim looks on their faces. I saw one of them flip a driver off in answer to his shouted remark. It was kind of ironic. Not all that long ago, we would have greeted this much traffic with smiles and grandiose cash flow projections on the part of the business owners.

Without looking away from the traffic Max asked, "What do you think?"

I knew what he was asking and I was tempted to answer him the way the world expected me to. I didn't.

"It's time to go. This is going to go bad soon. When it does—well, everything here is going to get washed away. If we move now and we move fast, we can surf the front of the first wave and maybe come out untouched."

Max nodded. "Yeah. It's not like I haven't thought of that. Shelli isn't going anywhere. It's 'Do or Die' right here for her. I drove over to the farm late last night and talked to Tommy. Same thing. Plus, do you feel like we owe these people something?"

"The only people I owe are Night, you, and Ninja. I don't really give a shit about this town or its people. It's just a stop on the way to somewhere else for me."

"You ask Night what she wants to do?"

"I don't have to. I know."

"Yeah, that's what I thought. Well, we might as well gear up and get breakfast while we can. This is going to get messy."

We held the line for three days and nights with only minor problems. I told everyone working the main line—what had been Main Street—to paint their faces. I wanted them looking *Mad Max* crazy.

Some of them really got into it. But did they just stick with black and green? No, they had to be individuals. We had skull faces, a clown face on one guy that was downright creepy, and a whole group that looked like American Indian meets KISS. I think there were even a couple of Celts or Blue Face people. I didn't ask.

We had minor problems with the migration: cars overheating, running out of gas, or just breaking down. If the owners did not have gold or goodies, then they were moved on. I didn't care if they claimed to be congressmen, neurosurgeons, or the second coming of Alexander the Great. They walked out of town and kept going. I didn't have time to vet anyone, and I figured that there would always be time later to sort out the surgeons from the sturgeons. If there was a later.

People were slapping themselves on the backs and talking shit about how good we were doing. They weren't feeling what I was feeling. I am not a coward, but I felt the steadily increasing pressure of badness building. I wanted to take Night and get the hell out of town.

The farm had already reported incidents in which three people had been shot. Granted, Hawk was fast on the trigger. I told him to leave the bodies there for now. Let them be a warning. If they got too rancid, we could throw some lime on them.

Yet flood of migrants kept coming, and the crowd mix was changing. For the first few days, people had plans and preparations. They had somewhere to go. They were interested in one thing generally, and that was getting where they planned to go as quickly as possible. The current wave seemed to be people who were running only because they felt that somewhere else had to be better than where they had left.

I would go down the line when it wasn't moving. Nobody wanted to go far from their cars in those first days because they had all they owned inside. But after the third day, that began to change. In fact, I started noticing cars that didn't match the drivers: the Volvo with Juan, Rico, Marta, and Tito inside and a Harvard sticker in the back window. When I walked the line, I would talk to people. Actually, people would complain to me, and then I would ask questions. I had hoped that the cars would move smoothly and steadily past us. It didn't work that way. Someone always had to stop and talk, or break down, or both.

Most of these cars were overdue for servicing, because the owners hadn't been able to afford the upkeep. When they broke down, getting parts was a problem. There were not a lot of parts available, at least not new ones. So we had to make repairs with used parts. Then there was the gas situation. People had been joking for a while that the quality of the gas in Mexico was better than in America now. Some folks converted their cars to run on other fuels. That worked in an urban area, but out here in the sticks it was harder to find alternative fuels.

Food was its own problem, and what people told me was not good. The Zones never had a lot of food stockpiled, but there had always been food available. Even outside of the Zones, food had still moved, just not as much and often at a higher price. But that began to change. The rich and well-connected could still shop at stores that accepted the currency backed by the International Monetary Fund. The rest of us, though, began to experience chronic shortages, with only certain items available. One month everyone had potatoes—but only potatoes—because they miraculously appeared everywhere in quantity. I like potatoes, so I was happy. People who didn't like potatoes were not, especially since their trade value was low.

Skipping a meal was one thing; everyone was used to that. Eating food that could best be described as marginal was okay because it filled your belly. People starved, but not that many of them. The ones who did starve were usually old, sick, or unable to hustle their daily bread for some reason. Now things were worse.

By Day Three, there was nothing left on the shelves to buy or steal. The trucks didn't deliver because the warehouses were not getting shipments. Warehouse weren't getting shipments because no one was guaranteed of getting paid. We were long past accepting checks or "Net 30." Who was going to sell a truckload of anything on credit when you couldn't count on the buyer still being in business the next day, let alone thirty days from now—or be certain the truck would even arrive at the warehouse with a load at all?

What I was hearing was fear morphing into panic. People living in the Zones had relied on government help for so long that when it stopped, they reacted as if Christmas had been canceled. When the full realization hit that the government was no longer able to provide any help, the Zones were going to go nuts.

Hell, they were already starting to. Airdrops of expired MREs did not inspire confidence. People told me the big camps were getting restless.

That's what had flushed these citizens out ahead of everyone else. Watching "those people" going on a rampage was not what they had signed up for. The problem was the Feds had concentrated too many of *those people* into small areas and then made them totally dependent on the government's largesse.

They had gone along, sucked it up, skipped getting high, and taken the shit, but now where was the payback? Where was the food?

# CHAPTER FORTY-EIGHT

On Day Six the line broke. It failed because the community failed. It may have been due to maliciousness or it may have stemmed from sheer stupidity. When it comes to my fellow man, I never rule out either one. After five solid days, everyone was getting burned out. It was cold. The hours were long, and the people were increasingly obnoxious. You could see the attitude of the locals change from "Oh, those poor people; I am so glad I am not one of them" to "What a bunch of assholes." I had already been there on Day One, but that was my default mode.

What broke the line was a couple of dumb shits doing exactly what we told them not to do. We had told both the militia and the patrols, "No food or drink in front of civilians." We explained why. Everyone nodded their heads. Everyone understood. So what motivated two dipshits to have a picnic on the hood of a car in front of the migrating hordes, I will never know.

Not only did they have a picnic, they also invited a local woman to join them. My guess is that these dickheads thought she'd be so impressed by their manly, carefree behavior and wealth, that it would lead to them getting their knobs polished.

It didn't work out that way. The sea of humanity saw the steam coming off that food. Even more, they rolled down their windows and caught a fragrant noseful. They slapped those cars into Park and bailed right there.

It was immediate chaos. Even inside the station, I felt the change like a bolt of lightning. I grabbed my old BAR and a belt filled with magazines and hit the door. About the time I cleared the threshold my radio was talking to me about a "problem."

I made it to the tollbooth in record time. But the word that we had food and were giving it out had already spread at the speed of sound.

Meanwhile, the two idiot patrolmen had started arguing with the crowd. It was their food and they did not have to share. Less than a minute after it reached the yelling stage, somebody fired the first shot.

All this brought the migration to a halt. People got out of their cars and heard that it was a disturbance about "Food!" Since we had a line of cars that stretched for miles at this point, who knows what people were telling each other by the time it traveled a few hundred cars back.

The situation deteriorated rapidly. Bursts from M-16s and small arms echoed along the main line. I found out later that the militia had gotten spooked, thinking they were going to get overrun, and had just cut loose. That triggered a chain reaction among our people. They slaughtered civilians like so many cattle in a chute.

Not all of them went down without a fight. But the chaos just poured blood in the water for the predators. We had more than a few of them that we barely held in check as it was. They heard "Food" and gunshots and smelled opportunity.

Three cars that seemed to be a pack suddenly pulled off the road and gunned across the field, heading for a side street into town. With them moving, the dam broke. Everyone spooked and the herd stampeded.

I saw the cars hit the field and I laughed. I felt good. No more dicking around with containment and gently moving people along.

It was time to dance, and the BAR led off with a backbeat that was as steady as anything that came out of Muscle Shoals back in the day. These guys may have been predators back in the city, but they didn't have a clue about driving in wet Virginia clay, especially in front-wheel drive Hondas with low clearance.

I saw the lead driver's face contort as he fought the wheel. I saw his face change as he realized that perhaps this was not such a good idea after all. I confirmed that for him by splattering his head all over his buddy, who was riding shotgun. Then I walked the next three rounds across the passenger windows.

The second car, a Honda with a double-deck spoiler on the back, came screaming off a small rise and bottomed hard. I punched a couple of shots into the engine compartment, and the engine screamed at me in rage. I shot out the back window and refocused my attention; the third vehicle, an SUV, had decided to change course and was heading toward me.

I wasn't alone; it just felt that way. The patrol screamed at people to get back in their cars. It didn't do any good.

I started punching rounds into the grill and windshield of the oncoming SUV. Finally, one of the squad members detailed to the tollbooth realized that he could be more helpful by shooting the shit out of it instead of screaming at people who were not going to listen anyways. He hit the SUV with at least three bursts in the side.

Like a rhino it just kept coming. It took out the tollbooth and the female guard and caved in the side of an old Dodge van that was in the way. I heard screaming from inside the Dodge a few seconds after it hit. It sounded like kids.

That's when a man standing behind the passenger door of a BMW about seven cars down the line decided he wanted to kill me. I shot him through the door as I swung the BAR around; then I shot the driver through the windshield.

I looked across the field; the three-person team assigned to patrol about a mile back must have shown up. I didn't see them, but I heard them. I don't think anyone in the cars had figured out even approximately where they were firing from. That was a good thing. As Tom Clancy would have said, "They were operating in a target-rich environment." Not that they cared right then what he would have said.

About then I had my *Oh, shit* moment. At least seventy-five cars peeled out of formation and began an awesome demolition derby straight for town, using the field as an off ramp. Night was right: I didn't have enough bullets to kill all these people. In the meantime, people in parked cars were still shooting at us.

I ducked, rolled, and came up on the other side of the SUV. That's when Max got into the game with the Barrett. He was killing cars with single shots to the engine blocks. I realized immediately what he was trying to do: Let the cars come and he'd build himself a wall of dead iron.

Meanwhile I knew what I needed to do. I had to clear out the shooters who were too close to the booth. Eventually someone would move the militia down to the dead car wall. My job was to help hold the new line until then.

I undid the BAR magazine belt and slapped the squaddie who was raining fire on the assembled multitude on the road.

"Use this!" I handed him the BAR. He nodded. Then I was gone.

I could see in my head what needed to happen. Max would stop the headlong approach and fill the field with dead cars. The reserves would push into it to clear it. The three-man team firing from the field would nail anyone on their side. The tollbooth people would have to plug the road gap from hostiles moving in on foot. I had to clear the parked cars of hostiles far enough back that we could create a dead zone.

Then we'd torch the cars. Max would love that, the crazy little firebug that he was. I actually thought that, too. It was funny.

I ran around the white van, jumped onto the hood of the first car behind it and laughed. *Crazy little firebug! Crazy little firebug!* played on a loop in my head as I drew the Ruger and the Colt and shot the two people inside the car. They died staring at me goggle-eyed.

I hopped from car to car shooting anyone who was out of his vehicle. I leaped off one hood, hit the ground, rolled, and came up face-to-face with a mother and her kid. I screamed at them, "Run, you stupid bitch!" and shot the guy who was searching for me with a scoped deer rifle four cars down. Iron sights would have worked better.

I remember getting hit in the chest once. God bless armor. The force of the slug pushed me backward, and I let my momentum take me down. I rolled under a car, scrambled out the other side, and tried to spot whoever had nailed me. I didn't see anyone so I kept moving.

I made it back to the tollbooth. I was limping a bit. I had leaped onto a car hood that was slick with blood and had slipped off, landing awkwardly. I was also running low on ammo. There was a lull in the storm, at least where I was. I needed it.

We were holding the new line for the moment. But it wasn't going to last. The people on the other side of the cars were not stupid. And they were motivated by one of the strongest drives a human can experience: hunger.

When they did decide to advance, they would easily move around us and any barrier we could throw up. We didn't have enough bodies to set a wall around the town.

We might be able to hold part of the business section for a day or so. But then we would run out of ammo, and they'd be on us like the weevils of death.

*Where was Freya?* We could use her magic aerial display right about now.

I told the people manning the tollbooth area at our new wall that I was going for ammo and water and that I would be back. An occasional shot zipped past me as I ran.

Max was about three hundred yards down. I found him trying to organize the handful of militia that had made it over from the massacre. He was yelling, "Set some of those cars on fire! Come on, we can do this!"

I could tell it wasn't going to happen. One of the guys was crying, and not quiet tears. His were gut sobs with snot running from his nose. I knew he wouldn't be moving from where he sat.

Then the lull ended. I didn't know if the car people had seized the moment and organized or it was just a spontaneous charge.

What I did know was that a horde at least four times the town population was moving toward us. One little group rallied behind an American flag on a pole that some unlucky guy had gotten stuck carrying. Another group raised a Washington Redskins flag. *Really?* I thought. The crappiest team in the NFL was going to inspire them? They probably couldn't have given you a coherent answer if you asked them—and I had no intention of doing so.

I looked out at the approaching mass and I felt drained. There was no killing rage. No desire. No focus.

I knew it was over for me, at least for the time being. No way did I have it in me at that moment to shoot down all the children in front of me. Because that's what it would have taken to stop them. Hose them all and bury them in a pit.

I looked at Max. More hung in the balance than just the lives of the people marching toward us. I think, just for a second, he was considering the pit. And then he stepped back from the brink.

"Safe your weapons!" he roared at the militia that were scattered around us.

"It's over." This was not roared. It was spoken, yet it carried to every ear.

Almost every one of them looked relieved—almost, because there's always an asshole.

He heard Max, looked at the people, and yelled, "No!" Then he swung his M-16 up to his shoulder.

That was as far as I let him go. I had the Ruger holstered again before he hit the ground. I started walking back to the station. I made it about six paces when I stopped to look back at Max, "You coming?" He nodded.

I waited for him, and we walked together, headed toward the station. Usually I could read him. I wasn't seeing anything now. His face was stone. My radio was going nuts. I turned it off.

"So, Max. What's our Plan B?"

He didn't answer immediately, and I didn't press him. He stopped and we stood there. I saw smoke, from a house probably, since that was the only thing over that way.

Max spat on the asphalt and said, finally, "Well, I am going to get weaponed up, go over to Shelli's, eat some apple pie, and kill people until I am down to two rounds."

"Yeah. If Night doesn't want to try our luck elsewhere, then I guess I'll be doing the same."

We stared at each other. I held out my hand and we shook goodbye. "It's been real, Max."

"Yeah. Real fun." We both laughed and started walking to our fates.

I had gone about twenty paces when two assholes came racing around the corner, headed for the station. I dropped both of them and picked up my pace.

# CHAPTER FORTY-NINE

Radio Freya began broadcasting in my head. Digital quality, too. "Do you really think it is over?"

"Yep. Unless you got a Plan B?"

"Of course I do. It has only just begun for me."

Then she went aerial on me. It was like looking at a high-resolution gray-scale Google map taken from a low-flying helicopter.

"Shelli and Night await you in the station. Ninja is on the way. You have three minutes. This is the current status."

The helicopter or hawk pulled up a little higher. The view was ugly. We were being overrun. The hawk—if that's what it was—suddenly switched to a view from perhaps ten thousand feet.

I laughed. I could sense her amusement also. Whoever thought they were gaining themselves a town were in for a rude surprise before they finished their first stolen meal. Behind them was another wave, and another, and another. The town was just a tiny sand castle on a North Carolina beach, and the tide was coming in fast. Maybe a New

Jersey beach—someplace where the water came rolling in with all kinds of nasty shit in it. Beach-closing nasty.

"Hey, Freya."

"Yes?"

"Can you do a conference call?"

"What do you mean?"

"You know, can you have Max, Night, Ninja, and Diesel all hear me at the same time?"

"Yes."

Max had changed direction and was heading toward the station in long loping strides.

"Night. You there?"

I got a hesitant, "Yes . . . ?"

"You ready to go? Are you getting the aerial feed?"

"Yes. Please hurry."

"Oh, my God, Max! They're in the diner!" This was Shelli wailing into my ear "Shit! They're going to ruin it!"

Maybe this conference call thing wasn't such a good idea.

"What's going on, G? Why is this girl in my head?"

"No time, Night. We need to pack." Instead of talking I sent images. "Did you get that?"

"Yes."

I knew she was packing. Night may not have wanted to leave, but she never had a problem adjusting to new realities.

"This is cool. I can fax images. Hey, Max!" I sent an image of him with a horse's head in place of his. In response I got three variations on the theme of "Grow up and focus" and one with my head instead of his on it.

Freya sent an image of bottled water to Shelli and Night. A half minute later I went through the station door right behind Max. Shelli was throwing water bottles to Night, who was stuffing them into an old ALICE pack.

"Time to go!" There was no mistaking the urgency in Freya's voice or what the aerial view was showing.

Max thought, *Back door!*

I grabbed the pack and swung it over my shoulder and almost fell over. "Jesus, Night!" No wonder. It was filled with water bottles and .45 ammo.

Night threw me a box of .357 ammo and I jammed it into one of my pants pockets.

"Do not worry. I have food! Go!" Freya sent an image of five packs sitting in a line in the woods under a camo tarp.

"Where are we going?" I was surprised no one else had asked.

"Bruxton. Safety." She sent an image of a small camouflaged opening on the side of a mountain.

"Where are Ninja and Diesel?"

"We're here." Ninja sent a picture of them kneeling in the woods watching the town from just outside of it. Behind him stood Freya.

"Go this way!" Freya outlined a path through the back of the business district, through Trailer Town, and into the woods about a mile off the road to Bruxton. There were only about a thousand people between us and where we were going, I estimated. I heard Freya say, "1,134. No, make that 1,130."

"Thanks for the update."

I heard Max think, *Back door.* We had company. I grabbed a shotgun and made sure it was loaded. Then I poured two boxes of double-aught buckshot into my pants' pockets. I was a walking ammo dispensary now. Max had the Barrett.

"Now?" I sent.

"Now," Max replied.

I went out fast and hard. The lassitude and lack of focus I had felt before were gone. I had seen through Freya that there were four of them. Two looked to be wearing armor of unknown quality. The male reaching for the door wasn't.

I hit him as he opened it. I was moving at half speed, but I weighed over three hundred pounds with all the crap I was wearing or carrying. He went backward, and I went over the top of him and veered right. Max paused, and shot through the wall into the guy who was pressed against it, covering the lead intruder.

The remaining two stood where I expected them to be: one, wearing armor, in front of me; the other, to my left. The one to my left fired a three-round burst about a step behind me. I shortened the guy in front of me with a shotgun blast to the knees. The one on my left was turning to shoot me when Max came through the door and greeted him with a round from Mr. Barrett's can opener.

Shelli came out next and stumbled over the man I had knocked down. She landed hard on the asphalt.

Night shot the guy in the head, stepped daintily over him, and delivered a head shot to the one I had knee-capped.

I heard her think, *Die, asshole*, followed by a guttural, *My town*. I felt a wave of ice emanate from her. *God, she is hot*, I thought.

*Yep*, came back her reply.

Shelli was back on her feet because Max, who was covering our backs, yanked her up by her drag handle. She looked pissed. We were out and moving.

"I cannot hold this connection to all of you for much longer. I am not accustomed to this many." The image we got showed that *many* meant the mass of people. "I will give Max the aerial. See you." *Blink*, she was gone.

I tested it to make sure. "Night, have you ever noticed Shelli's waitress has a great ass?" No reply. She was gone.

At a trot, we moved in an arc away from the diner, which was packed with people. As soon as we swung away from the back of the station we formed a rough diamond with Shelli in the center. I had no idea what her level of competency with a weapon was. Since the revolver Max gave her was still in its holster, it was probably minimal.

We ran into people right away. They moved for us, especially after Max didn't stop and we went right over the top of a middle-aged man who thought we would go around him.

The air smelled of smoke and insanity. I don't know about the rest, but I had made the decision that anyone who pointed anything resembling a weapon in my direction was dead. We cut through that mass of people like a knife through yogurt.

I remember glimpses. A white woman—my mind automatically tagged her "Zone, upper class"—crying and yelling, "Mike! Mike!" A family of five running past us, their hands filled with bags from the food bank; one of the bags ripping and spewing green beans all over the street. They stopped to try and gather them—a stupid mistake. I didn't look back to see what happened, but I heard someone growl as he changed course to focus on the family.

Most of the people were minimally armed. Not all were. I caught a glimpse of a father-son team clearing a path through the food bank crowd by hosing the people in front of them with AK look-alike rifles. Hopefully they would both run out of ammo at the same time.

We encountered two groups of people who actually looked competent and were armored up. We moved past them with Max slowing down to let Night ahead of him. That put all four of us, with Shelli on my other side, in a row, with clear lines of sight. We didn't drop our weapons, but we didn't point directly at them. They did the same.

As we moved I imagined us as warships from the age of sailing. We were escorting a merchant vessel, one that was having problems keeping up with us. Shelli was starting to suck wind. We would change formation into a line of battle, then drop back into coverage and cruise.

As we cleared the last few houses, we surprised a young girl on her knees. In one hand she clutched a can of baked beans; in the other, the cock of a guy in armor who was standing over her. He smiled at us, giving us a thumbs-up as we pounded past him.

Night shot him in the head. I was going to have to start calling her "My little headhunter."

We made it where we supposed to be. Shelli had to stop along the way to throw up, but she had stuck with it. I think Max would have left her if it had come down to it, and I think at some level she knew that, too.

Freya was waiting exactly where she said she would be. We stopped. Shelli collapsed. Without even thinking, the rest of us took the same alert positions that Max had taught us on the hike here so long ago.

# CHAPTER FIFTY

The woods were relatively free of people, probably for a number of reasons. First of all, Zone people were not woods people. The woods were scary to them—a place to get lost, a place where bears, snakes, and maybe even worse monsters dwelt.

These people also were just not equipped for the woods. They were urban dwellers looking for a civilized place to retreat to: a place where you could take a crap and flush afterward, a place where you had walls, kitchens, and restaurants. If they went camping, it had to be on a level site they could park next to.

They were me back when I first became homeless, and I knew firsthand what an adjustment that was. Not even living as one of the Car People prepared you for what was coming.

From where we sat on the side of the hill we could see the town below. It looked like a big outdoor concert combined with a riot—or maybe a small civil war.

It was like peering down one of Dante's circles of Hell, the only difference being that some of the people down there seemed to be enjoying themselves. My guess was they would soon devolve into demons, or maybe really irritating and deadly imps.

Shelli was crying softly. Max was scanning the town with field glasses.

"Max, why are you using glasses?" I asked. "Is the bird down?"

"Yep."

I looked over at Freya. She looked pale. "You okay, kid?"

"I am fine. I just need to rest a bit."

Ninja was looking at her puzzled. He asked softly, even a bit hesitantly, "How do you do that? Is it magic?"

She sighed. "I do it because I am a goddess. It would help me greatly if all of you started believing that. I need the energy your belief creates. Magic? You ask if that was magic? Your grandfathers walked on the moon! Start believing in me, get me some followers, and I will show you some magic."

"Oh . . . okay," he replied. Then he started checking his weapons. Max had taught us well.

"Nice shooting," I told Night and gave her leg a squeeze. Then I stood up and walked over to the packs. I pulled off the camo cover and stepped back. "How do we know which one is which? Oh, by the way, next time get Ninja a Hello Kitty backpack. He loves them."

"There will be no next time," Max said. "Next time we train warriors, not cops. Next time we will be the ones burning the towns."

I shrugged. "Sounds good to me." I was distracted. My nose had caught a faint but familiar smell coming from the packs. I walked next to them, sniffing, and stopped at the last one.

"That one is mine!" Freya yelled.

"Gee, Freya. What did you pack?" I bent over and opened the pack as she yelled, "Stop."

"Damn, Freya. You have at least six apple pies in here." Shelli's mouth dropped open.

"I was going to share," she said sullenly.

"Sure you were. If you're a goddess, then you're as American as apple pie."

No one laughed and Night threw an acorn at me.

The leaves were gone from most of the trees. A few shallow traces of snow remained in the shadows. I passed out water to everyone. There was more than we needed as Freya had packed water also. The rest I left behind with the pack I had used to bring it here.

Maybe the girl with the can of baked beans clutched in her hand would make it this way and find it. Probably not.

We walked in silence and headed cross-country, a diamond with Shelli and Freya in the middle. I watched Max stuff Shelli's water in his pack. That, the Barrett, and the rest of his stuff meant that he was packing a heavy load.

It didn't seem to bother him. I watched Night. It had been a while since she had shouldered a load, but she was doing alright.

It was a cold night for everyone. Freya had packed a blanket in each pack, but we didn't have anything waterproof to put underneath ourselves, and we were not going to build a fire. Freya politely refused a blanket. She told us the cold never bothered her.

Off in the distance we heard gunshots. My guess was they were coming from the road, which we were paralleling at a distance. A lot of pain was happening out there.

I hoped Freya knew what she was doing. Otherwise we were going to be joining the ranks of the brigands and brigand wannabes in a matter of days.

I was surprised that I had no desire to become a highwayman. I saw nothing honorable or even enjoyable about it. That didn't mean I wouldn't do it if I had to—not a good mindset when everything depended on that extra edge that the right attitude helped generate.

Max had said earlier that from now on we were to be warriors instead of cops. I didn't know how I felt about that. I had saved my badge. No real reason, I just had.

We were a glum bunch, Night especially. She had lost our baby, her home, and all the work she had done. Shelli was pretty quiet, too. So was I.

I was never comfortable living without some kind of goal or reason, and I was having trouble thinking of one for the current situation. Survival was an obvious goal, but I needed more. Without Night it would have been a lot worse.


Two days later we were there. We waited until nightfall to cover the last mile, so there would be less chance of being seen. We had the night-vision goggles. We tried moving in the dark with them, but Shelli and Night both had trouble adjusting to them. It was not worth the very real possibility that one of them would fall and get hurt. Freya did not seem to need them. I didn't wear them either.

The Bruxton where Max and I had found Freya no longer existed. What remained looked like a war zone. Where the train tracks had run into the mine, nothing was left. Now there was only rubble where the side of the mountain had collapsed from the air strike. There were a few skeletons of buildings, mostly just a wall or two from the houses closest to the road. The rest was craters and debris.

We weren't going in the main shaft entrance. We headed to a spot partly shielded by a rock outcropping, at least a mile from the main entrance. Our way in was a plain steel door painted to match the rock set back in a shallow cave. Freya walked up to it and casually pushed it open.

The wind had blown leaves into the cave and piled them up against the door. She absentmindedly kicked them out of the way and said, "I set a ward." I don't know what the others thought, but I thought that certainly explained everything.

"Wait." This was from Max. "Why here? What is here?"

Freya seemed surprised. I guess a goddess isn't used to explaining herself. "I was kept here. This is how I left. None of them knew of it."

"Why were you kept here, Freya?"

"Because this is where the Burners were going to stage their coup against the king in D.C. They had soldier people helping them."

"Yes. But why were *you* here?" Max's voice had gone soft and gentle. She was going to literally lose her head if she didn't come up with an answer soon.

"Because my mother was a Burner."

She turned and walked through the door. Over her shoulder she said, "All the soldiers are dead from what they shot in the tunnel before the death eggs fell. They left much good stuff. Come. You will be happy."

She walked into the dark. I looked at the rest of them, shrugged, and followed. Ninja was the last one through.

The door shut itself.

# AUTHOR'S NOTE

The introduction of Freya, a supernatural being, may have confused or even bothered some readers. I feel she is an important element to the ongoing story because she represents the beginning of a new world. This isn't and was never intended to be a survival book. Rather, I am writing about the end of one civilization and the birth of another. I believe if we were really to encounter a complete breakdown of society, it is entirely possible that something brand new and unforeseen would develop.

# OTHER ULYSSES PRESS BOOKS

**American Apocalypse:**
**The Collapse Begins**
*Nova, $14.95*

*American Apocalypse* is a riveting com-
ing-of-age story. With the economy in
free fall, America's fragile democracy
collapses. Police and military forces
disband, and a once-proud America de-
scends into lawless anarchy. Forced to
adapt by the constant threat of starva-
tion and violence, one teenager finds
himself developing survival skills he
never imagined needing and a moral
sense that gives meaning to his struggle.

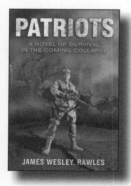

**Patriots: A Novel of Survival in the**
**Coming Collapse**
*James Wesley, Rawles, $14.95*

A thrilling narrative depicting fictional
characters using authentic survivalist
techniques to endure the collapse of
the American civilization. Reading this
compelling, fast-paced novel could one
day mean the difference between survival and perish.

*To order these books call 800-377-2542 or 510-601-8301, fax 510-601-8307,
e-mail ulysses@ulyssespress.com, or write to Ulysses Press, P.O. Box 3440,
Berkeley, CA 94703. All retail orders are shipped free of charge. California
residents must include sales tax. Allow two to three weeks for delivery.*